PRAISE FOR *IN THE NAME OF A KILLER*
AND THE NOVELS OF BRIAN FREEMANTLE

"An expert and thought-provoking work."
—*New York Times Book Review* on *O'Farrell's Law*

"Classy, atmospheric, and pleasantly cynical . . . every scene and conversation is a fencing match or chess game; every turn of events threatens to topple the dense edifice of politics, lust, subterfuge, and insanity. A real winner."
—*Booklist*

"Highly recommended."
—*Library Journal*

"Like most Freemantle novels, the plot moves swiftly, the dialogue crackles with life, and there is a real kick of an ending. In fact, the only predictable thing about a Brian Freemantle book—besides a quality story—is an unpredictable ending."
—*Flint Journal*

"Richly textured characters, the unusual premise, and the hypnotically cruel seduction—all make this one of Freemantle's finest."
—*Kirkus Reviews* on *Little Grey Mice*

St. Martin's Paperbacks titles
by Brian Freemantle

NO TIME FOR HEROES
IN THE NAME OF A KILLER

IN THE NAME OF A KILLER

Published in hardcover as
The Button Man

BRIAN FREEMANTLE

St. Martin's Paperbacks

First published in Great Britain by Random Century Group.

In the Name of a Killer was published in hardcover as *The Button Man*.

IN THE NAME OF A KILLER

Copyright © 1992 by Brian Freemantle.

Library of Congress Catalog Card Number: 93-17421

ISBN: 0-312-96048-4

Printed in the United States of America

St. Martin's Press hardcover edition/August 1993
St. Martin's Paperbacks edition/December 1997

St. Martin's Paperbacks are published by St. Martin's Press, 175 Fifth Avenue, New York, NY 10010.

10 9 8 7 6 5 4 3 2 1

For Ray and Vera, with great affection.

Author's note

For a number of years, after writing a non-fiction book upon the KGB, I was unwelcome in the Soviet Union. In late 1990, under the influence of *glasnost* and *perestroika*, that ban was relaxed. This book is the result of the first of my return visits. During that visit I was shown great help, guidance and friendship from Marina Sukhareva and her husband, Harry Edgington. And also from a man earlier expelled from Britain as a KGB agent. He insists the accusation was untrue.

I travelled to Moscow via the United States. In Washington, DC, I learned of the scientific expertise of the Federal Bureau of Investigation's training academy at Quantico, Virginia, from the courteous and delightful Bob ('Monk') Monroe, who also tried to help me avoid mistakes about the FBI in general.

I thank everyone in Russia and America for their help, which I hope is reflected in this book. If there are any factual errors, it is to them I must apologize first.

Cruelty has a human heart,
And Jealousy a human face;
Terror the human form divine,
And Secrecy the human dress.
         William Blake, Appendix to
Songs of Innocence and of Experience

Chapter One

Moscow sucked. Was that still the way you said you were pissed off, back home? She didn't know. Ann Harris didn't think she knew anything about America any more. Which was an obvious exaggeration, but one she allowed herself, more black depression to wrap around herself. She didn't care whether it was the right word or not. Moscow definitely sucked. Everything sucked: the job and her career and her future and the embassy and this affair. This affair most of all.

She walked without direction, uncaring, woollen hat pulled low, hands buried deep in the pockets of her inadequate coat, the only idea to get away from the claustrophobia of her apartment and maybe, too, what had just happened there. Or rather, hadn't happened.

He'd been in so much of a goddamned hurry there'd hardly been any point in their getting undressed: she hadn't been anywhere near her climax when he'd withdrawn and from the way he'd held himself over her she was sure he'd checked his watch with the same gesture. Bastard. But that was hardly the discovery of the century. There'd been the usual bullshit about love when it had first started but that was all part of the familiar, well practised ritual. Now they'd stopped bothering with any pretence. It was a fuck, pure and simple: at least it was for him. For her, like tonight, it usually ended up as pure and simple frustration. At least he rarely tried the worst of the funny stuff now: tonight he scarcely hurt at all. Which meant, she supposed, he was doing it to somebody else, somebody new. It had to be somebody in the embassy. She wondered who. The bastard.

Ann looked around her, with sudden concentration. She had to be somewhere close to Ulitza Gercena: somewhere in the embassy district, certainly. The next left should bring her on to a better-lit street: so near midnight this road, whatever its name, was dark and deserted, no one moving apart from her.

Ann continued on, deep in reflection again. What was she going

1

to do? Break it off, she supposed. She was impatient with this part of an affair, the let's-call-it-a-day part. It invariably dragged on, one waiting for the other to make the moves, each trying to give the other an easy escape, which usually made the whole business messier and anything but easy.

Maybe she wouldn't do anything positive. Maybe she'd just carry on until her tour ended in six months. Her return to Washington would make a logical end. A farewell dinner, a farewell fuck, the unmeant promises: *Look after yourself now. Write, so I'll know where you are. It really has been great.* There were others, of course. The one before this who knew he was reserve, still trying to get the pecker up to compete. It was amusing, sometimes, seeing him try. Fun. At least he tried to make her come. Sometimes she even did.

But would she be recalled in six months? She should be, according to the usual tour of duty. But by now she had expected to hear from the State Department whether she would be offered another overseas position right away or have to wait in Washington for reassignment. She'd give it another month. If there hadn't been anything in the diplomatic pouch by then she'd ask openly and get things moving from this end. Two years might be the usual posting to the Commonwealth that had once been the Soviet Union but she'd heard too many stories of oversights and misplaced personnel files and lofty, unconsulted State Department decisions to keep a person in place because of their proven value.

And she'd definitely proved herself a better-than-average economist in the embassy's financial division. She snorted an empty laugh on the lonely Moscow street: how come she was so efficient and so professional at work, never screwing up, while her personal life here had been such a fuck-up?

Moscow, she answered herself: it was the insular, unnatural existence of Moscow, everyone knowing everyone else, affairs begun, affairs ended, dinners accepted and dinners returned by rote, the same anecdotes today as the anecdotes of yesterday, never gaining in the telling. She hoped to Christ Uncle Walter proved right, about the career importance of Russia. If he was — if the promotion was as automatic as he'd guaranteed — then in hindsight it might have been worthwhile. Just. But if it didn't

2

happen like that, it would have been two years of imprisonment, without any time off for good behaviour or parole.

Ann saw the break in the buildings up ahead, the opening of the link-road she was seeking, and just slightly increased her step. It had been an impulsive, unthought-out decision to get away from the flat: the coat wasn't warm enough and she only had a thin cotton shirt and skirt on underneath, because there had been the Russian warmth in the apartment: even warmer in bed.

Ann's mind stayed on her uncle. He'd used his political clout to get her to Moscow. So he could use it to get her out. That would be the way to do it! Write to him before directly approaching the State Department, say how much she'd enjoyed the opportunity to work here and ask if he had any indication where she might be assigned next. Do it tomorrow, in fact: get the letter in that night's diplomatic bag to Washington. For the first time for several hours her depression lifted, although not by much.

Ann turned into the smaller side road, little more than an alley, disappointed at not seeing the brightness of Ulitza Gercena: maybe this road curved, obscuring the junction.

It was only in the last few seconds that she was aware of anybody else and then she did not hear anything. It was an impression of someone very close and she began to turn but the knife went in smoothly, not touching any bone. There was a moment of excruciating agony and the scream tore from her but the hand was over her mouth, clamping her nose, suppressing any sound.

Ann Harris was dead before her body collapsed fully on to the pavement.

The hair was clipped first, as close to the skull as possible. Enough was kept but most was sprinkled over her face. The buttons, on the coat and shirt and skirt, had to be cut off by feel and the clothes properly rearranged. All the buttons were kept. One shoe had dropped off, as she fell. The other was removed, to be placed neatly, side by side, close to her head.

It was 2 a.m. when the telephone roused Dimitri Ivanovich Danilov, the senior Colonel of the People's Militia for the Moscow region. He listened for several moments. Then he said: 'Shit!'

Olga stirred when he got out of bed but did not wake up. Over

3

the years, as the wife of a policeman, she'd learned how to sleep through such disturbances: she'd come to ignore quite a lot of things, in fact.

Chapter Two

There was not much blood and most of what there was had been absorbed into the coat. Ann Harris did not lie as she had fallen, because the body had been moved slightly while she was shorn and the buttons removed. Now she was slightly over the outline chalked on the pavement, disturbed a second time by the initial examination of the pathologist and the forensic experts. The narrow street, which did bend before leading out on to Ulitza Gercena, had been sealed at both ends by Militia vehicles drawn across it. Shielding canvas screens were around the corpse, which was unnecessary, because the only people there at 3 a.m. on a sub-zero February morning were police. The floodlights unnaturally whitened everything and everyone: the men grouped and moving around looked as bloodless as the victim at their feet.

Danilov edged into the group, which parted and began to break up when he was recognized. The movement caught the attention of the man bent over the body. Yuri Mikhailovich Pavin looked up and then nodded, when he saw his superior. Pavin rose, stiffly, as Danilov stooped to take his place. She'd been attractive, beautiful even, but now she was ugly. The eyes bulged, staring either in terminal terror or pain, and the lips were drawn back from her teeth in what looked like a snarl. The ugliness was made worse by what had happened to her hair: it had been chopped, in patches and close to the scalp, which was scratched and in places cut. Missed tufts stood upright. Her clothes did not seem unduly disturbed.

'How long?' asked Danilov. The woman's body already appeared stiff, with rigor.

Pavin shrugged. 'Maybe eight hours, maybe shorter. The doctor says the cold could have brought the temperature down quickly so he can't really say.'

As if on cue a blast of wind drove up the narrow street, making them hunch against it. Danilov had taken to having his own hair

5

cropped very short. This early in the year he should have worn his hat.

'Who found her?'

'Militia van, making the rounds. Timed at one twenty.'

'She hasn't been dead eight hours. Eight hours ago this street would have had people on it.'

'I know,' agreed Pavin.

Danilov was glad Pavin was going to be the evidence and exhibit officer again. And not just because of continuity. Pavin was the sort of back-up every investigator needed, a meticulous collector of isolated facts which, once assimilated, were never forgotten. He was a heavy, slow-moving man who looked more like a patrol officer than a Petrovka headquarters Major. Danilov privately doubted Pavin would rise any further in rank but didn't believe Pavin wanted to: he guessed the man accepted that he had reached his operating level and was content. Pavin knew every guideline in the investigation manual and observed each one: it would have been Pavin who ordered the unnecessary canvas screens. 'Any identification?'

'None. This is all there was.'

Danilov accepted the key, preserved for later fingerprint tests inside a glassine envelope. 'What makes you so sure she's American?'

'Clothes labels,' said Pavin. 'Every one American, inside the coat and the skirt and the shirt. The shoes, too.'

'Is that how they were?' asked Danilov, nodding towards the low-heeled pumps. At the moment they were only covered with protective, see-through plastic, not yet inside an exhibit bag.

'I checked specifically: the observer in the Militia van thinks he might have kicked into them when they first found the body, when it was dark apart from their headlights. They were certainly by the head but he doesn't know how neat.'

'He didn't touch them?'

'He says not.'

'Fingerprint the entire crew, for elimination.'

'I've already arranged that,' said Pavin. It was one of the basic, scene-of-the-crime rules.

'Who's the pathologist?'

'Novikov,' said the Major. Apologetically, as if he were in

6

some way responsible for the medical rosters, he added: 'I'm sorry.'

Danilov shrugged, resigned. In a court trial a year earlier he'd shown to be unsound a medical assessment reached by Viktor Novikov: the man had been forced to admit surmising rather than conducting a necessary test. The hatred was absolute. 'What's he say?'

'Single stab wound. He'll need the autopsy, of course, but it looks like a clean entry. Could be a sharp-pointed knife with a single edge. The head wounds are just superficial, caused when the hair was cut off. Some post-death bruising, to the left thigh and buttock, where she fell. No sign of her fighting: nothing beneath her fingernails where she might have scratched. Or hair, which she might have pulled.'

'Sex?'

'Her underclothes were intact: she wore tights over her knickers. Her outer clothes weren't pulled up or torn.'

Danilov handed the glassine envelope back to his assistant and said: 'That isn't a hotel key.'

'No.'

'She could have been robbed of her handbag, I suppose?'

'She's wearing a cross on a gold necklace. And a gold Rolex. And there's a signet ring, on her left hand. No wedding ring, though.'

'How far away is the American diplomatic compound?'

'Four, maybe five hundred metres. Behind the embassy on Ulitza Chaykovskaya. She needn't necessarily be a diplomat, of course.'

Danilov sighed. The wind scurried up the street again, although not as strongly as before. It would have been past midnight when Danilov had got to bed, because he'd stopped off to see Larissa on her shift change-over and then made sure Olga was asleep before he followed her to bed: he felt gritty-eyed with tiredness and knew he wouldn't sleep again for a long time now. 'You alerted anyone else?'

'That's your decision,' reminded the man who knew the rules.

'This is going to be hell if she is connected with the US embassy,' predicted Danilov. 'The fact that she's possibly American is bad enough.'

7

'You think the Cheka will want to be involved?' asked Pavin, using the original revolutionary name of the Soviet intelligence service, which was how the former KGB, now the Agency for Federal Security always internally referred to itself, with muscle-flexing bravado.

'Probably,' said Danilov. 'And I can't begin to imagine what the Americans will want.' At that moment he didn't even *want* to imagine.

'It would have been easier in the old days,' said Pavin, with a stab of nostalgia. 'When we didn't have to cooperate.'

'There aren't any old days, not any longer.' He paused and then added: 'Supposedly, that is.' Danilov had once been enthusiastic about *glasnost* and *perestroika* – still would have liked to be – but after all the unmet promises and expectations he was resigned like everyone else to their failure through obstructive bureaucracy and latent Russian inefficiency. Even in the old, uncooperative days this would have been a bastard, if she was American. 'Does Novikov know I'm the investigator?'

'He guessed, because of the other one. He said you'd have to take your turn: there are other autopsies ahead of you.'

'What about forensic?'

'Finished just before you arrived.'

'Anything?' Pavin would have told him already if there had been: he still had to ask the hopeful question. Pavin would expect it.

'Nothing immediate.'

Danilov gestured to the dark, glowering buildings all around. 'No one hear anything?' That was an even more hopeful question: Pavin would have produced any witness by now.

'It's mostly office buildings. I thought we'd start the house-to-house when it's light.'

Danilov nodded agreement. 'Photographs?'

'All done. The ambulance is ready, when you close the scene of the crime.'

For several moments Danilov remained silent, gazing down at the now frozen and mistreated body of the young woman. *Who are you, once-pretty girl? What hidden things am I going to find out about you that no one else knows? If they don't matter, I'll try to keep your secret. But how – dear, much doubted God* how! – am I going to find whoever did this to you? Who made you so ugly? Not for the first time since joining the murder section of the serious crime squad Danilov was glad he and Olga could not have children, for him to live in deeply wrapped apprehension that one day another policeman might stare down at the battered and maimed remains of his own son or daughter. He was never able to think of a dead body just as a dead body: to remain utterly detached. Always he thought, as he was thinking at this moment, that this ugly, brutalized thing at his feet had once been a living person with feelings and fears and sadnesses and joys. Professionally wrong, he supposed. Or was it? Didn't the fact that he *did* care make him more determined than most others at the Militia headquarters at Petrovka who he knew sneered and even laughed at him, on their way with open pockets to get favours returned for favours granted, Militia officers for the money-making opportunities the job presented, not because they were dedicated policemen? Danilov halted his own sneer, refusing the hypocrisy. Different now, since he'd joined the murder division. But what about before? What about Eduard Agayans and all the other grateful operators? He'd rationalized his own excuses, but he had no grounds, no *right*, to criticize other policemen. To criticize anybody. Allowing Pavin his scene-of-the-crime expertise, Danilov said: 'Is there anything else?'

'Not here I don't think.'

'Let's clear up then.'

Pavin gave the summons, which was answered within seconds by the strained-gear sound of the reversing ambulance. Danilov wished they'd shown more care, loading the body on to the stretcher. He said: 'I want all the occupied accommodation in the street checked, before anyone leaves for work. There's no doubt what we're looking for: I don't suppose there was before. I want every psychiatric institution in Moscow checked for discharged patients who might have indicated any of these tendencies.'

'*Every* one?' frowned Pavin.

Danilov nodded after the departing ambulance. 'If she's American, I'll get all the manpower I want.'

'Do you want me to push Novikov?'

'I'll do that.' The problem between himself and the pathologist

9

was an irritating, unnecessary hindrance in any investigation: certainly not an added complication he needed this time. Danilov normally confronted major difficulties himself, rarely delegating, but maybe this was an occasion to seek superior authority.

'Where are you going, if I need to get in touch?'

It was a discreet, friend-to-friend question. There were some times during the month when Larissa slept all night at the Druzhba Hotel and was happy to be awakened. Tonight, because of the shift change, she would have been home hours ago: she would be asleep now, turned away from the booze-soaked breath of Yevgennie Kosov, the Colonel-in-charge of Moscow Militia district 19, Danilov's old command. And now Kosov's personal fiefdom, which he ruled like a Tsar accepting tribute. Danilov guessed the man had gone far beyond the introductions he had provided, in the last days of the hand-over.

Danilov looked at his watch in the harshly white, deadening light. It was four thirty. 'Home. I'll call Lapinsk from there.' Leonid Lapinsk was the General commanding the murder investigation division at Petrovka: he was only two years from retirement with an undisguised ambition to see that time out as quietly as possible: tonight was going to set his ulcers on fire.

'He'll kill again,' predicted Pavin, gazing down at the chalked outline of where the body had been. It was a distant remark, the man practically talking to himself.

'Of course he will,' said Danilov.

The apartment, off Kirovskaya and conveniently close to the metro at Kazan for someone who did not currently have a car, was in the twilight of approaching dawn when Danilov got back. He considered vodka but dismissed it at once. He couldn't be bothered with coffee, which – in contrast with his now spurned gift-receiving days – was Russian, not imported: powdered grains that floated on top of the cup, like dust, no matter how hot the water. And tea was too much trouble.

Danilov settled, head forward on his chest, in his personal but now lumpy-seated chair, just slightly to the left of the ancient and constantly failing TV that had been a grateful present from Eduard Agayans when he had commanded his own Militia district with such personal discrimination, before the transfer to Petrovka.

The investigation had been difficult enough already. But this morning – this gritty-eyed, cold, gradually forming morning – the murder of an unknown American girl was going to compound his problems in ways he couldn't even guess. There was one easy surmise, though: Pavin was probably right about the Cheka or the KGB or whatever they wanted to call themselves. They wouldn't consider an investigator from the People's Militia – even the senior investigator with the rank of Colonel – qualified to head an inquiry like this. Domestic homicides or quarrel killings, maybe: they were ordinary, unimportant. But the murder of an American was different: that became political, exterior: something possibly to focus international attention upon Moscow and the disintegrated Soviet Union. What if they took over? Danilov confronted the possibility. If it was an official decision, there was nothing he could do to oppose it. But if it stayed just below that authoritative level he *would* resist any attempt to shunt him aside. In Russian law, the law that almost miraculously was increasingly *being* the law, despite the failures of the other reforms, the stabbing and the defilement of a dark-haired, brown-eyed girl of about thirty was the indisputable responsibility of the homicide division of the duly appointed Criminal Investigation Department of the Moscow Division of the People's Militia. *His* responsibility. The most difficult case of his life, Danilov thought again. Did he want such a responsibility? Wouldn't the safest way, professionally, be to surrender, after a token protest, to pressure from the Federal Security Agency, just as he'd always taken the easy way in other directions when he'd been a uniformed, more persuadable officer? Undoubtedly. So why didn't he just back off? He didn't *want* to, he decided. The old, look-the-other-way days had gone and the benefits with them. And he didn't mourn or regret their passing. Rather, he enjoyed the self-respect, a self-respect he knew no one else would understand, with which he felt he ran his life at Petrovka.

It was barely five fifteen. Still too early to disturb his commanding General. Larissa would be stirring soon: this week she was on early shift. It would be difficult for them to meet as regularly as they normally did if he was allowed to remain in charge of the investigation. He'd be under too much scrutiny for unexplained, two- or three-hour disappearances. What about the hypocrisy of sleeping with another man's wife? And the deceit of cheating his own? Where was the integrity and honesty in that? Not the same as work: quite a different equation. One he didn't want to examine.

He wished he wasn't so tired. He needed to be alert for all the unknowns there would be before the day was out. Instead, before anything had really started, he felt exhausted. It would be better when those unknowns became known: the adrenalin would flow then, to keep him going. He hoped. Wise, upon reflection, not to have taken any vodka. Alcohol would have dulled him even more.

Olga's voice startled him and Danilov straightened almost guiltily in the chair, realizing he'd dozed. 'What?'

'I said what are you doing in the chair?' She was standing at the bedroom door, her brown hair dishevelled and her face still puffed from sleep. She hadn't tied the robe around her and the nightdress beneath had a dark grey stain over her left breast. The slippers were partially split at both heels: she had to scuff to keep them on when she walked.

'I was called out.'

'I didn't feel you get up.'

'I didn't want to disturb you.' It was seven fifteen: almost time to call the Director.

Olga shuffled towards the kitchen area. 'I'll make tea.'

'That would be good.' He still felt tired, despite the doze.

'Who was it?' She had her back to him in the kitchen annex, filling the kettle to brew the tea and prepare the Thermos, the modern Russian equivalent of the samovar, to keep the water hot.

'A girl.'

'Bad?'

Could a murder ever be good? 'We think she's American.'

Olga looked across from the stove. 'That's going to be complicated, isn't it?'

'Yes.'

'Where?'

'In the street: near Gercena.'

'How?'

12

'Stabbed.' He wouldn't tell her of the connection. Or the details. He didn't think she would be interested anyway.

'Sexual?'

'It doesn't seem so.'

'That's something at least.'

But not much, Danilov thought. He watched his wife filling the teapot, wondering what the stain was on her nightdress.

'Do you want your tea there?'

'I'll speak to Lapinsk first.'

The commanding General picked up his receiver on the second ring. 'Something difficult?'

Danilov recounted the similarity before disclosing the possibility of the girl's nationality.

When he was stressed Lapinsk would punctuate his conversation with short, throat-clearing coughs. There was a burst now. He said: 'That couldn't be worse.' There was another rattle of coughing. 'There's no question of it fitting the pattern?'

'The buttons are something new.'

'It's the same man,' the General accepted.

'I want to approach the American embassy: I need it arranged, through you. Do we have to clear it with anyone? A ministry?'

There was another series of short coughs. 'I'll advise the Foreign Ministry. And call the embassy at nine.'

'What about the Cheka?'

'They'll probably try to take over,' agreed Lapinsk.

'It's our jurisdiction.'

'Rules can be changed.' Lapinsk sounded hopeful.

Danilov felt some pity for the Director. Lapinsk despised and habitually derided the former KGB for its arrogance and imagined superiority. But with so little time before retirement it was easy to understand the man's anxiety to avoid a murder inquiry like this. Everyone searching for the easy life, thought Danilov: the Russian way. He said: 'It's already an established, ongoing investigation.'

'Tell me the moment you have an identity,' Lapinsk parried.

'Novikov is the pathologist.'

'Bugger!' Lapinsk knew of the antipathy.

'I want the autopsy today: he told Pavin there are others ahead of me.' Danilov didn't enjoy asking for further intercession.

'I'll fix it. Be careful at the embassy. I don't want any problems beyond what we've already got.'

'If she's not a diplomat, it might be difficult getting an identity. She could be officially registered at the embassy, but it's not a requirement.'

'What if she's not?'

'We'll check the Intourist guides and the foreign visitor hotels first. Then the visa records, for a photograph. The death pictures will be unpleasant.'

'Too bad to publish in newspapers to get an identity?'

'Probably,' warned Danilov. That death snarl would be a further denial of dignity for whoever she had been: they could wait, he supposed, until the rigor relaxed.

'I'll clear my diary, after talking to the embassy. And be in the office all the time. If there is any difficulty, call me.'

Olga had poured the tea, despite being asked not to: it was cold by the time he sat down opposite her at the kitchen table. She hadn't cleaned off the previous day's make-up, heavy blue around her eyes. He added more water from the prepared Thermos, to warm the tea.

'Lapinsk will be shitting himself,' Olga said.

'Your nightdress is stained.'

Olga looked down curiously, seemingly aware of it for the first time. She rubbed at it, half-heartedly. The stain remained. 'It's an old nightdress. I used to be able to get them from the importer, remember?'

Without payment of course, Danilov recalled. Like the television set that had now developed picture slip that couldn't be corrected. He'd personally liked Eduard Agayans, the moustachioed, fiercely nationalistic Armenian who'd always insisted on toasts in his republic's best brandy before any favour-for-favour conversation. The document-switching entrepreneur had maintained his largest warehouse in Danilov's old Militia district and was always generously grateful for Danilov's guarantee of unimpeded delivery of double the quota registered on the import manifest it was the Militia's duty to check. 'Why not buy more?'

Olga laughed derisively. 'Which of the hundred well stocked designer shops in Moscow would you suggest I try first?'

'Why not just look around,' suggested Danilov, indifferently.

14

Olga continued to examine the stain. 'It looks like oil. But it can't be.'

Danilov saw she'd spilled tea – or something – on another part of the nightgown, near her waist. 'Why not wash it?'

'The communal machine isn't working. And our own is broken: you know that.'

Their personal machine had been another gift from Agayans, who had been his chief source of unobtainable luxuries. 'You could handwash it.'

'Do you want anything to eat? Breakfast?'

He never ate at the beginning of the day, but this day had begun a long time ago. He still wasn't hungry. 'I don't think so.'

'Elena wants me to go to the cinema tonight. It's a war movie: I don't know which one. She's asked Larissa, as well.'

Larissa had already warned him: told him she was going because the hotel shifts were convenient. Elena was the supervisor in the Agriculture Ministry post-room where Olga was a typist. 'Why don't you do that? I'm involved now, day and night.'

'We might eat afterwards. Elena says she knows somewhere you don't have to wait: one of those trade-run cafés, a writers' place.'

Danilov had heard of such restaurants, set up by craft unions whose members no longer accepted the delays of ordinary Moscow eating houses. 'Get a taxi home.'

'Why?'

'It's safer.'

'I'll need some money.'

Danilov handed twenty roubles across the table. Olga smiled acceptance and put it into the pocket of the loose dressing-gown. There were no thanks. 'Definitely get a taxi home,' insisted Danilov. A long time ago he'd discovered Olga hoarded money he gave her: he pretended not to know about the leather satchel in which she kept it, in the box that contained all her family memorabilia.

'All right,' she said, too easily.

Danilov pushed aside the tepid tea, half drunk. He looked down at himself as he stood from the table. Slumping in the chair – and then dozing – had concertinaed his suit: he guessed the back of the jacket would be worse than the trousers. Be careful at the embassy, he remembered: it would be careful to dress smartly. 'I have to change.'

'Why?'

'It's necessary.'

His other suit, the grey one with the faint stripe, was jammed at the far end of their shared closet, crumpled where one lapel had been bent backwards by a dress of Olga's being thrust in too closely against it. Danilov tried to smooth and then flatten it out: it was better but the crease mark was still visible. His black shoes needed cleaning and he wasn't sure if there was polish back in the kitchen: he hadn't noticed before the actual tear in the paper-thin leather on the left toe. Black polish would cover it. Danilov unsuccessfully searched the top level of the chest of drawers where his shirts were kept and then checked, equally unsuccessfully, the drawer below. The second drawer held Olga's blouses, crisply folded: there was one, patterned in red check, which reminded him of the shirt the dead girl had been wearing. When he returned to the main room, Olga was still sitting at the kitchen table, both hands around the tea which now had to be completely cold.

'I can't find a clean shirt. I need a clean shirt.'

'There should be one.'

'There isn't.'

'I told you the communal machine isn't working: they promised it would be fixed by tomorrow. People stuff too much in.'

Although the apartment was theirs alone, they had to share certain facilities. A basement washing machine was one. 'So I haven't got a clean shirt?'

'Not if there isn't one in the drawer.'

Each shirt in the laundry bag was as badly creased as the other. He took a blue patterned one with the cleanest cuffs and collar and said: 'Could you press this for me?'

'It's not washed.'

'I know. I've just got it from the dirty bag.'

'I'll be late for work.'

'Fuck your being late for work!'

Olga looked at him in astonishment. 'What the hell's wrong with you!'

'Please! I just want a shirt ironed.' He wouldn't bother about the shoes: it was only a tiny tear.

Begrudgingly Olga got up from the table and noisily took the ironing board from its crevice between the cooker and the store cupboard. Searching for an attack point, she said: 'The cuffs are frayed: the left one, at least. You need more shirts: shall I look while I'm choosing nightdresses?'

Danilov didn't want to fight. 'The fray won't show.'

Abruptly, confusingly at first, she said: 'Would it have hurt: what happened to the girl last night? Would it have hurt?'

'Horribly.'

'I'll definitely get a taxi.'

Danilov supposed he should have warned Larissa, as well. He'd have to remember to do so.

The hum was discordant, high and low, high and low, without a tune: it was good to hum. He liked it. It was noise: noise was safe. Not always, of course. Not just before it happened. Noise was dangerous then. Had to be quiet, like a shadow. Only safe to hum afterwards. Like now. They said it was an indication to hum, all those experts, but they were wrong. About humming anyway. He wasn't mad. The opposite. Clever: always clever. Clever enough to know all the signs but stop them showing.

The hair had this time been more difficult to tie neatly in its tiny, preserved bunch, like a wheat sheaf: kept slipping out, before the cord was properly secured. All right now. A neat, tidy bunch – always important, to be neat and tidy – with the top cleanly trimmed completely flat. Perfect match with the other one. It had been right to take the buttons. She'd been a woman: got it all right last night. Especially the buttons. A neat and tidy pattern, red ones and green ones and a brown one, all assembled in their perfect arrangement on the special souvenir table, together with the hair-clipping scissors. Always had to have buttons, from now on. And always a woman then. Important to plan for the future, always to stay ahead. The knife had to be sharpened, stropped like a razor, to slide in like silk. That was the good part, the way the knife slid in. Just like silk. That and buttons. Felt happy, to have got the buttons. There'd be the challenge, soon: a hunt. There had to be a hunt. That was going to be the best part: what he was looking forward to. Look, fools, look! But they never would. Not properly. Just a little longer, touching the

17

souvenirs. Holding them. Exciting, to hold them. Then put them away. Safely, for later. Another one soon. Always women, from now on. And buttons.

Chapter Three

Pavin drove the car, drawn from the Militia pool. He did so meticulously, as in everything else, observing all the signals and keeping strictly within the speed restrictions. He did not, however, attempt to use the central reserved lane, which they could probably have done as an official car on official business, automatically waved through every possible junction obstruction by the GAI police in their elevated glass control boxes, like goldfish out of water. Not that there had been obstruction: it had been nearly ten o'clock before Lapinsk returned the authorizing call to go to the American embassy, so the morning traffic had cleared. As they made their way towards Ulitza Chaykovskaya, Pavin said the house-to-house inquiries hadn't found a single witness. He was still trying to work out how many extra officers it would need to carry out the search of psychiatric hospital records: it would be a lot.

'Novikov is being ordered to do the autopsy immediately,' said Danilov.

'That'll annoy him.'

'Everything annoys him,' dismissed Danilov.

They turned into Chaykovskaya, towards the embassy. Pavin nodded ahead and said: 'It'll be difficult for me to keep a proper record, without the language.'

'We'll stay in Russian,' Danilov decided. 'If the man we're going to see doesn't speak it there'll be an interpreter.' Lapinsk had arranged the meeting with someone named Ralph Baxter, a Second Secretary. From the diplomatic lists he'd already studied, Danilov knew nearly everyone was described as a Second Secretary.

'You're not going to tell them?' Pavin smirked, appreciatively.

Danilov had read English, with French as a second subject, at Moscow University: just prior to graduation he had considered a career utilizing linguistics but the Militia had a better pay structure, more privileges and inestimably more practical benefits

19

for an easy life, so he hadn't pursued the idea. Occasionally, watching on television interpreters at the shoulder of Russian leaders on overseas summits, Danilov regretted the decision. Interpreters didn't get woken in the middle of the night to look at dead bodies, for one thing. He said: 'Not at the beginning: it might be useful, being able to understand what they say among themselves.' *Be careful at the embassy.* He thought the potential advantage outweighed any later recrimination.

The uniformed Moscow militiamen on duty outside the American embassy had clearly been alerted to their coming by Militia Post 122. They were deferentially admitted through the main entrance and directed by a secondary guard of American marines from an inner courtyard to the right of the mansion. The door they approached was mostly glass. The reflection was distorted, but Danilov decided he'd been right about the haircut: the greyness wasn't obvious at all now. The mirrored image made him seem smaller, too, dwarfed by the ponderous Pavin behind. The only advantage was that he also looked slimmer, with no hint of the developing paunch about which both Olga and Larissa mocked him, one more gently than the other. The suit looked smart but it was only just a year old, one of the few genuinely bought articles after the halcyon period heading a Militia district.

There was a reception desk where Danilov identified them both and asked for Ralph Baxter by name. The American appeared at once, a slight, quick-moving man with rimless spectacles and a moustache that seemed too big in proportion to the rest of his features. His shirt collar was secured behind the knot of his tie with a pin: Danilov had seen Americans wearing that style on television and wished such shirts were available in Moscow. He would have been happy with any sort of clean shirt that morning.

Baxter said: '*Dobrah'eh ootrah*' in badly accented Russian and offered a weak handshake. He turned at once to a man who had followed along the corridor and said in English: 'Will you ask them to come into the office?' To the receptionist Baxter said: 'Warn Barry we're on our way.'

The translator was intense and young, leaning forward when he spoke and carefully picking the grammar and the intonation. Danilov guessed it was the man's first posting, after language school.

The corridor was buffed to a highly polished sheen and the walls hung with prints of American pastoral scenes. Halfway along there was a large plant in a tub, the wide green leaves almost as glossy as the floor all around. Baxter halted at the far end and stood back, gesturing the two Russians ahead of him. Danilov concluded it was not a working office at all but an interview or conference room. Another man rose at their entry. His hair was thinner than Danilov's. He wore a double-breasted sports jacket, a hard-collared shirt with a club tie and sharply creased trousers: the impeccable appearance was completed by highly polished brogues. Barry, guessed Danilov, from what he had overheard in the foyer.

'My colleague,' said Baxter, offering no further introduction.

There was another nod but no handshakes.

Baxter indicated chairs set against the table: the Americans placed themselves in a facing half-circle and Baxter said: 'We have been told this is a police matter. Serious. Possibly involving an American national.'

The intense young man's translation was completely accurate. Pavin took out a notebook and prepared to write. The American in the sports jacket did the same.

Danilov outlined the finding of a young woman wearing American-labelled clothes earlier that morning, saying nothing about the shorn head, the buttons or the shoes. 'Has any American employed here failed to turn up for work this morning?'

Baxter shrugged. 'Maybe. Personnel aren't all rostered at the same time. There are usually people sick.'

Danilov accepted he was going to have to produce the pictures Pavin had collected before they'd left Petrovka. They were good reproductions but the harsh whiteness of the spotlights had made the snarling face even more grotesque. He took the file from his briefcase. There were six facial photographs, each from different angles. He separated them so that all were displayed before sliding them across the table.

The American in the sports jacket said: 'Holy shit!'

Baxter said: 'Oh dear God!' and repeated it, three times.

The young translator blanched and swallowed several times. It seemed difficult for him to do so. When Danilov asked: 'Is she

21

attached to the embassy?' it seemed a long time before anyone responded.

'Ann Harris,' identified Baxter, dully. 'Her name is Ann Harris. She is a . . .' He stopped, to correct himself. '. . . *was* a member of our economic section.' He paused again, then said: 'Oh my God!'

So the identification had not proved the protracted difficulty it might have been, Danilov acknowledged. A minimal breakthrough: he was not encouraged.

The American named Barry said: 'What else, apart from the hair? Was she violated in any other way?'

'There was no physical indication at the scene,' replied Danilov, able to remain strictly truthful. 'There is an autopsy being performed today.' I hope, he thought.

'You any idea the heat this is going to bring down?' demanded the man, talking sideways to Baxter. 'Her uncle is Walter Burden, for Christ's sake: chairman of the Ways and Means Committee . . . ! He's got more power than God. *And* he doesn't like Moscow . . . ! Oh holy shit!'

An American Congressman! Politically it couldn't be worse, Danilov recognized instantly. He went expectantly to the interpreter. Baxter intercepted the look and said quickly: 'Don't translate that!'

'Say something!' demanded Barry. 'He's staring at you: they both are!'

'Say we're shocked,' instructed Baxter. 'Horrified.'

Danilov waited, forever patient. 'Ann Harris was unmarried?'

'Why?' The question came from Barry.

'I need all the information possible.'

Again Barry spoke only to the other American. 'I'm going to have to take this over, of course. Washington will insist. No investigation could be left to these guys! They're amateur night, win a balloon and a lollipop if you get past the first clue.'

'Shut up!' Baxter's recovery was difficult. 'We'll have this sort of discussion later.'

Danilov decided he'd let it run long enough. 'Was Ann Harris a single girl?' he repeated.

'Yes.' It was Baxter.

'Any relationships?'

'What does that mean?' Barry intervened.

'Did she have a boyfriend?'

'Why?' he persisted.

'I'm investigating the murder of a young girl. I have to know as much as I can about her.'

The words came from Baxter like heavy footsteps. 'She was single. An extremely popular girl: highly competent and highly respected, from the ambassador down. She did not have a regular boyfriend: any romantic involvement at all of which I am aware.'

On this occasion the other American's statement was direct, intended for translation. 'This is a maniac: a perverted maniac.'

'It would appear so.'

'I tell you, it's amateur night!' came the repeated aside.

Baxter turned to the man, irritably. 'And I told you to shut up! You'll get your chance, soon enough.'

The contemptuous man sneered at the rebuke. Maintaining the expression, he said to the Russian: 'So what are you doing?'

Danilov was abruptly impatient: it had to be the tiredness. He said: 'Starting at the beginning. Hoping to get to the proper end.'

'I saw the movie!' The sneer remained.

Now a wash of definite fatigue engulfed Danilov, like a wave. How would they have reacted, if he'd spoken next in perfect English? They'd been extremely careless. There might be some excuse, because they would have been shocked, but he found it difficult to allow them very much. He said: 'There was a key, in her pocket: to her apartment, obviously. I need the address.'

'Hold on here now, Ralph!' said the perpetual critic to the one identified man. 'We can't have Russia's answer to Dick Tracy going through her things. We've got to insist on diplomatic protection.'

Danilov wondered who Dick Tracy was.

Baxter said: 'I need proper guidance on this. Why the hell was she like she was; you know what I'm saying.'

'I'll get a handle on it, as soon as Washington puts the pressure on for me to take control,' Barry assured him.

'We've got behind with the translation,' protested Danilov, mildly. 'I asked for the lady's address.'

'I don't have it, to hand,' avoided Baxter, weakly.

'It wouldn't take more than a few moments to obtain, would it?'

'There's a great deal for us to consider. To discuss,' said the diplomat, still avoiding.

'Of course there is,' agreed Danilov. 'That doesn't affect my getting her address, does it?'

'Stall the bastard, Ralph!' ordered his companion. 'I don't give a fuck how you do it, but stall him. If Washington hear we've let them stumble around we're each of us going to be swinging in the wind with piano wire round our balls. Jesus, what a fucking mess!'

FBI, guessed Danilov: and just as presumptuous and conceitedly believing himself above all censure as every KGB investigator Danilov had ever encountered, which fortunately had not been too many. Danilov supposed the discussion would have already begun about poor, brutally shorn Ann Harris at Security Agency headquarters in Lubyanka Square.

Baxter made a conscious effort to compose himself. The American said: 'This has been an appalling shock. She was a girl we all knew. Respected.'

'I understand that,' said the Russian detective.

'We need the opportunity to discuss it: there are family to be advised, in America.'

'I understand that, too.'

'I would ask you to give us an hour or two.'

'I don't follow the reasoning.'

'To discuss things, here in the embassy.'

'I still don't follow,' persisted Danilov. 'Any discussion here – the way you advise the family – is entirely a matter for you. All I want is an address, so I can continue my inquiries.'

'We'd like to have that discussion, before we go any further,' refused the desperate Baxter.

Danilov intentionally let the silence build across the table between them. Finally he said, accusingly: 'You are obstructing a criminal investigation into the murder of an American citizen.'

'No!' protested Baxter.

'Don't let him pressure you, Ralph,' warned the other man.

The good old days that Pavin yearned for weren't completely gone, Danilov reflected: there might still be an inquiry avenue open to him. But first this had to be concluded. He said: 'I regret you have refused greater cooperation.'

'Fuck him!' said the contemptuous one, after the dutiful translation. 'This jerk won't be around much after today.'

'I regret that this is your opinion,' Baxter said to the Russian, with diplomatic stiffness.

Danilov looked too obviously at his watch, surprised nevertheless at the lateness. 'We will leave you the location of the mortuary. I will need a member of this embassy there at exactly three o'clock tomorrow, for formal identification . . .' The pause was as theatrical as the time-check. '. . . You will appreciate, of course, that there can be no question of releasing the body until all our inquiries are completed . . .'

'Now wait a goddamned minute . . .' said the critic. 'Burden will go apeshit at the thought of his niece preserved here, on ice.'

'I cannot accept that,' protested Baxter, to Danilov, with increased professional formality. 'I will personally make that identification and at the same time present both to you and to your Foreign Ministry the positive request for the return of the body of Ann Harris.'

'Until all our inquiries are completed,' echoed Danilov.

'We'll burn his ass,' said the sneering American, looking directly and venomously at Danilov. 'I'll *personally* burn his ass.'

'I think I have to talk to your superiors,' said Baxter.

'There is probably the need for higher authority on both sides,' said Danilov. *Be careful at the embassy*, he remembered again. Beside him Pavin tore the mortuary address from his notebook. 'Three o'clock,' Danilov reminded, passing it across to Baxter. At the same time he began to pick up the photographs still displayed.

'I want those,' insisted the American who had done most of the talking. 'They're evidence I shall need.'

Baxter said, through the interpreter: 'We would like to keep the photographs.'

Danilov completed the collection, tapping them tidily into their folder. 'They are official police exhibits, the property of the Moscow Militia.'

'Son of a bitch!' exploded the predictable American.

Danilov rose, before anyone else. Pavin followed, very quickly.

Danilov said: 'Thank you again, for this meeting,' and stood waiting for Baxter to escort them from the building.

The journey back to the exit was made in complete silence. At the door Baxter did not appear to know what to do. Finally he said: 'I have the mortuary address.'

'I'll be expecting you,' said Danilov.

Pavin waited until he had negotiated the embassy forecourt and they were back on Ulitza Chaykovskaya before he spoke. He said: 'I didn't need a translation to know it was bad.'

'She's related to an American Congressman.'

'Mother of Christ!'

Danilov wondered if the Major genuinely had any religious beliefs: they'd never discussed it. Neither had they ever discussed special arrangements possible in this new Militia district from which Danilov might have benefited, as he'd benefited before. He was sure Pavin would have a source: probably several. Everybody had their special sources. 'They don't think we're competent enough. They expect to take over. They refused to tell me where she lived.'

'Do we go back to Petrovka?'

'No. Drive slowly towards the scene. She wasn't dressed to go out walking, in that temperature. She probably lived close.'

'The embassy compound, surely?' Pavin frowned.

'Some embassy staff live outside,' said Danilov. 'It's worth checking.' His first call from the car telephone was to the Foreign Ministry. He quoted his official ID, explained in great detail to the Records division what he wanted and promised to call back. The clerk, a man, said the checks might be difficult. Danilov said he'd try anyway. Danilov's second call took longer, because he had to be transferred through several departments to put the forensic team on standby. They were back in the side road off Gercena before he tried to reach Lapinsk. As he dialled he looked out to where Ann Harris had lain, spread-eagled, only a few hours before. The small amount of bloodstaining had congealed like black oil, not red, and the chalked outline was practically trodden away beneath the morning dampness of slightly thawed frost and fog. Unnoticing, unconcerned people were scuffing over the blood and chalk with the toe-to-heel care of Russians expert in walking over slippery, frozen surfaces.

'Why haven't you come back here?' demanded the Director.

'I need to seal the flat.'

'There's been an official complaint, through the Foreign Ministry! What the hell happened?' There were several barking coughs.

After a detailed explanation Danilov said: 'They expect to take control. I don't know the man's name but I think he's FBI.'

'It's preposterous – arrogant – for them to imagine that!'

'I hoped that's how you'd feel.'

There was a momentary silence, from the other man. Then Lapinsk said: 'I've been called to the Foreign Ministry. The Agency for Federal Security have been summoned too.'

'Do you want me to be there?' suggested Danilov. It hadn't taken long for the pressure to begin.

'Novikov is doing the autopsy this morning: I told him to expect you. Stay on the investigation. Did you tell the Americans about the other business?'

'No. Or everything that happened to the girl.'

'I accept you were badly treated. I'll see that a protest is made, to counter theirs.'

The Records clerk at the Foreign Ministry said they *had* been lucky: it was the benefit of the new Western-style computerization. The official registration details of Ann Harris, an American national, for whom a diplomatic visa had been issued in May the year before last, listed her address as Ulitza Pushkinskaya 397. The man, who was obviously a gossip, asked what she'd done wrong. Danilov told him it was nothing, a technical matter.

'Outside the compound!' Danilov announced triumphantly, to Pavin, keeping the telephone in his hand to summon the waiting forensic scientists.

'The Americans are going to be furious.'

'I'm not exceeding any authority,' Danilov insisted. 'The address is not within the official diplomatic residencies.'

'It's probably still considered diplomatic territory, beyond our jurisdiction.'

'We'll worry about that later,' decided Danilov. He paused. Then he demanded, suddenly: 'Who's Dick Tracy?'

Pavin frowned quickly across the car. 'I don't know. Why?'

'I'm curious.'

Over the next three hours the repercussions of Ann Harris's murder rippled quickly throughout widely differing parts of the world.

The American Secretary of State was halted by an aide just before taking off for Hyannisport for a sea fishing trip. He decided to cancel.

On Capitol Hill, in Washington, DC, a polite State Department officer hesitantly entered the Dirksen Building suite of Senator Walter Burden and said: 'I am afraid, sir, there's some unpleasant news. The Secretary of State asks you to call. He wishes to tell you personally.'

At the FBI headquarters on Pennsylvania Avenue, at the bottom of Capitol Hill, a priority cable arrived from Moscow and because of Ann Harris's family connections was hurried immediately to the Director. Although the Director was a judge himself, he convened a conference of the Bureau's legal department.

Simultaneously, a matching priority cable was received at the CIA headquarters at Langley, Virginia. The Director called his own legal conference before telephoning his counterpart on Pennsylvania Avenue. Both Directors agreed to get separate legal opinion and talk later.

In Moscow Lieutenant-Colonel Kir Gugin hurried officiously into the Foreign Ministry, irritated there had been no reason for the summons, but curious to see if there could be any benefit for the newly created Agency for Federal Security.

And senior Militia Colonel Dimitri Danilov, with assistant Major Yuri Pavin, arrived at a third-floor flat on Ulitza Pushkinskaya ahead of any American presence.

Petr Yakovlevich Yezhov had carried out two known assaults on women. During the second he had completely bitten off the left nipple of a prostitute who in unintended retribution had given him gonorrhoea minutes before the bite.

For both attacks, mental evidence having been called at each trial, Yezhov served periods of detention in Moscow psychiatric institutions. As a result he had developed an obsessional hatred of incarceration and was determined never to be locked up again.

Yezhov's was one of fifty names to emerge during the case history search of the city's psychiatric clinics and hospitals.

Chapter Four

Danilov disliked entering the homes of murder victims. He'd had to do it too many times and always had a sense of awkwardness, feeling he was intruding into the privacy of someone whose privacy had already been too much violated. In the minute entrance hall he said: 'This isn't a normal situation. I want everything – and I mean *everything* – completed *now*. There won't be another chance. There must be no damage . . .' Nodding towards Pavin, who carried the specimen case, Danilov said: 'The Major will compile a complete and detailed inventory of anything removed. List it *at* the moment of collection. I want nothing overlooked, to be complained about later. Understood?'

There were grunts and nods from the assembled men: as if investing him with the responsibility for what might go wrong, they remained slightly behind as Danilov went further into the apartment.

The curtains were drawn, but all the lights still burned, showing an apartment luxurious by Russian standards, comfortable by Western. The wallpaper was heavily patterned, unlike any Danilov had seen in Russia, and the furniture was obviously also imported. There was an extensive stereo system along one wall, with records stacked on a shelf above. All the books in a cabinet against a far wall were English-language. Cushions on a couch and an easy chair fronting a small table were crumpled from the pressure of being sat upon. There were two glasses – one still containing some clear liquid – on the table. Delicately he sniffed and then carefully dipped his finger into the liquid. It was vodka.

Ann Harris's handbag was on a small occasional table that supported a sidelamp, which was on. The bag was the sort that secured by a snap clasp. The clasp was undone.

With a wooden medical spatula Danilov opened the handbag fully, so that it gaped, and used long-armed tweezers to lift out the contents, one by one. As he did so, he listed the items for Pavin to record. There was a compact, with a fixture at the side,

29

empty, for a lipstick canister. The billfold was Vuitton: it held American Express and Visa cards, American and Russian driving licences, a plasticized embassy ID card, seventy-five roubles and eighty US dollars. There was one photograph, a studio portrait without any background, of a smiling couple, both grey-haired. Danilov estimated their age at about sixty. The address book was very small, clearly designed for a handbag or a pocket. Danilov flicked through, quickly, seeing both American and Moscow numbers. He offered it sideways to Pavin, who held out a waiting plastic envelope. The diary was a slender one, pocket-sized again, with a line-a-day entry. Danilov looked more intently than he had at the address book, realizing at once it was very much an appointments record, with no personal entries. The line for the previous day was blank. That, too, went into a plastic exhibit envelope. Danilov gestured to the fingerprint man for the handbag to be tested.

The kitchen was clean, with no indication of a cleared-away evening meal the previous night. The dishwasher – a dinosaur rarity in a Russian home – was empty. Everything in the store cupboards carried American labels, bought from the embassy commissary. The tins were regimented on the shelves, sectioned by their contents, so that selection would only take moments. Even the perishable goods in the refrigerator, like milk and butter and bread, carried American brand names.

There was an extensive range of alcohol in a cupboard beneath sink level, bourbon and scotch whisky, brandy and gin. The vodka bottle was at the front, half empty. All the labels – even the vodka – showed them to be imported. There were fifteen bottles of wine, a selection of white and red, laid in a rack where the kitchen cabinets ended. All came from California.

The bedroom was at the end of a corridor. The door was half open: Danilov used the spatula to push it further, so they could enter. The bed was in chaos, most of the covers on the floor, the sheets crumpled into kicked-aside rolls.

Pavin indicated the pillows and said, needlessly: 'Both indented.'

Danilov called back into the lounge for the evidence experts. When they reached him he said: 'I want this room checked everywhere for prints . . .' He nodded to the bed. 'Search it, now, for fibres or hair. Then take it all to the laboratory. I want any stains checked, for blood, semen, anything.'

Perfume, skin-care creams and cleansers were ordered along the glass top of the dressing-table. In addition there were three framed photographs. One was of Ann Harris taken in Moscow, against the background of the onion domes of St Basil's Cathedral. The second was of the couple whose picture had been in her handbag. The third was of a man standing in such a way that the Capitol in Washington was in the background: the photograph had been taken low, but even without that trick for elevation the man appeared large. The dressing-table drawers held carefully folded underwear, sweaters and scarves, each in allocated places. Danilov sifted through, with the spatula: nothing was concealed between the folds of the clothes. The closets were just as carefully arranged, first suits and then dresses and finally separate skirts. There were twelve pairs of shoes, in a rack at the bottom of the closet. Danilov guessed there were more clothes than Larissa or Olga owned between them. Reminded, he thought he would have to contact Larissa sometime: she'd have to be told how difficult it was going to be for a while. How long, he wondered.

There was another framed photograph of the large man, this time with Ann Harris beside him on Capitol Hill, on top of a cabinet to the left of the bed. The upper drawer held a blank pad of paper and a pencil, a jar of contraceptive cream, a packet of contraceptive pessaries and Ann Harris's American passport. The larger cupboard beneath held only a padded silk make-up bag. With some difficulty Danilov eased the zip open with the tweezers. It contained a battery-driven vibrator and a small jar of lubricant jelly. Danilov's fresh discomfort was neither from surprise nor criticism but once again at the intrusion: this had been her business, her intimate pleasure, something to which she'd had the right of privacy. Invariably there were secrets, he reflected, recalling his mental promise to the dead girl in the alleyway. I'll go on trying, he promised again.

He found her correspondence in the cabinet on the other side of the bed. She had kept her letters in their envelopes and held packs together, about ten at a time, with elastic bands. At the back – he couldn't decide whether they were intentionally hidden

31

or not – was a thicker bundle, different-sized sheets of paper without envelopes.

'Everything,' decided Danilov. Pavin offered one of the largest exhibit bags.

The adjoining, American-style bathroom was as well kept as the rest of the apartment. There was an abundance of chrome and glass with more cleaning creams in tight lines. The cabinets contained analgesics and shampoos and hair conditioners, a proprietary brand of American cough linctus and, surprisingly, a small phial of mosquito repellent.

Back in the bedroom Danilov said to the fingerprint expert: 'There are a lot of good surfaces in the bathroom. And in the kitchen cabinet there's a vodka bottle I want checked. Anything so far?'

'Two different sets on the glasses back in the lounge. On the door here and the dressing-table, too.'

'I'll get her elimination prints from the pathologist later today,' undertook Danilov. To Pavin he said: 'We'll take the glasses.'

'There are a lot of shoes,' the Major pointed out.

'Some women like lots of shoes.'

'They seem important to the killer, too.'

'Anything we might have missed?' Danilov asked the man of routine.

Pavin considered the question, looking around the apartment. 'Not obviously.'

'That's the problem,' said Danilov. 'Nothing's obvious.' He became uncomfortable at the banality. He looked reflectively at the dishevelled bed, then gestured towards it. 'Apart from that, which looks as if she got up in a hurry, it's an extremely well kept apartment. There's virtually no dust, anywhere: everything in the bathroom is highly polished.'

'Yes?' agreed Pavin, questioning.

Danilov didn't respond at once to the curiosity. Instead he said to the technicians: 'Let's see what's on the plastic of the telephone receiver. I particularly want to know if the prints are new.' Coming back to his assistant, Danilov said: 'She got up and left urgently: not even covering the bed, which someone as neat as she was would almost automatically have done. Maybe she was called out, in a hurry.'

'Knowing her killer?'

'It's possible.'

Pavin remained frowning. 'Why call her out?'

'To make it seem as if she *didn't* know who it was.'

Pavin's doubtful look remained. 'There would be no way to trace a call, if it was incoming. Some outgoing calls might possibly be registered.'

'Check the exchange to see what's available,' ordered Danilov.

'*Just* the exchange?' queried Pavin, heavily.

Danilov smiled in understanding. 'I'll do it,' he decided at once. 'Or try to persuade Lapinsk to make the inquiry. Certainly the Cheka monitored diplomats' telephones in the past. I'd guess they're still doing it.'

'It would mean the Cheka officially admitting they're continuing to eavesdrop,' warned Pavin.

'That could be easily hidden,' dismissed Danilov.

'It could be the excuse for the KGB to involve themselves.'

Danilov wondered why the other man used the old, official title for the first time. 'We still don't know yet whether they'll be ordered to take over. They might not even need an excuse.'

'I would have expected the Americans here by now.'

Danilov looked at the forensic team: the fingerprint expert was already in the bathroom and the other man was delicately folding the sheets and pillows, edges inwards to hold anything trapped inside. As Pavin held the exhibit bags open, Danilov said: 'Anything?'

'No blood that's obvious. Some staining that could be semen. Or might not. What looks like make-up traces, on both pillows. Head hair and some pubic.'

The fingerprint specialist emerged from the bathroom at the end of the conversation. 'The two sets of fingerprints are in there, too.'

'How much longer?' asked Danilov.

The men exchanged looks. The technician with the bed linen said: 'I think we're pretty well finished.'

Pavin said suddenly, 'Knives! We didn't check kitchen knives.'

'Go on back with what you've got,' Danilov ordered the technicians, anxious to get them and the exhibits away.

Pavin was standing beside a knife rack attached to the wall

above the cooker when Danilov reached the kitchen. He pointed, saying nothing. The rack had hollowed-out, grooved positions for seven knives, graduating small to large from left to right. The middle, fourth position was empty.

'Everywhere you can think of!' Danilov was annoyed with himself at the oversight: Pavin was invaluable. It took fifteen minutes to search all drawers and possible put-aside places where the knife might have been carelessly discarded by a girl who didn't, from the condition of the flat, do anything carelessly. They didn't find it. Danilov said: 'I'll go through the rest of the apartment. I want the most precise measurements: length, width, thickness. Don't try to do it here: take the whole thing as an exhibit.'

Danilov didn't find the knife anywhere else in the flat. By the time he returned to the kitchen, Pavin had released all the wall screws and was putting the knife rack into the specimen case. It fitted snugly without the apartment-sealing equipment which Pavin removed. Pavin said: 'The make of the knives printed on the rack isn't Russian.'

'It wouldn't be,' anticipated Danilov. 'It says "Kuikut".'

It took a long time for Pavin to bolt to the outside of the apartment door the fixings for the cross chain for which there was only a Militia key, to criss-cross the further barrier of adhesive tape and to insert the blocks into the existing keyholes, to render them inoperable. Pavin held a cigarette lighter sideways to melt the wax which Danilov positioned to drip on to the ties of the official notice, declaring the apartment secured against unauthorized entry. Danilov was impressing the official seal into the wax when the Americans arrived.

'What the fuck . . . !'

Danilov turned to the sports-jacketed man he'd encountered earlier at the embassy and guessed to be FBI. Baxter was slightly behind in the corridor.

The leading American said: 'Oh Jesus! Oh dear Jesus now the shit's *really* going to hit the fan in every which way! Just wait until Washington hears about this!' He was shaking, either from suppressed rage or nervous energy: maybe a combination of both.

'What right do you think you've got, intruding on to diplomatic property?' demanded Baxter. 'I want that seal taken . . .'

'. . . They don't understand English,' interrupted the other American. 'We've got to get back to the embassy and bring down some heavy pressure about this. I'm going to have his ass for this! Christ am I going to have his ass!'

'We can't just walk away like this!' Baxter protested. 'I want to know what they've been doing in there!'

'Don't you think I want to know the same thing?' demanded the second American.

'We're trying to catch a murderer,' said Danilov, quietly.

'I don't care what you're trying . . .' began Barry before the realization registered.

'You bastard!' he said, although quietly as well, someone unable to believe what had just happened. The shaking worsened.

' "Amateur night",' quoted Danilov, verbatim. ' "Win a balloon and a lollipop if you get past the first clue." Who's Dick Tracy? I don't know who Dick Tracy is.'

Both Americans became momentarily speechless. Stiffly again, Baxter said: 'I know there has already been a formal protest, about your attitude at the embassy. This time the protest is going to be much stronger: possibly from the ambassador himself. I demand, with the authority of the government of the United States of America, that you unseal these premises and return into the custody of the United States embassy anything you might have removed from Ann Harris's apartment.' The heavy moustache quivered.

'You smart-assed son of a bitch!' said sports jacket, through tight lips. 'You just don't know the league you're getting into, do you?'

It was quite true, conceded Danilov. He said: 'As I tried to explain this morning, I am investigating the murder of an American national. This apartment remains sealed. Mr Baxter knows my office number.' He moved, to walk down the corridor. The first man squared up, blocking the way. He was about the same size as Danilov: there was the aroma of sweet cologne, clashing with tainted breath. Danilov wondered which of them was the most apprehensive of what might develop: he was very nervous but he was glad he wasn't shaking like the other man. He felt Pavin's bulky presence close behind and was glad about that, too. Danilov stared directly at the American and said: 'Don't be ridiculous,' grateful that his voice remained even.

'Back off, Barry!' warned Baxter.

'Why don't you do that, Barry?' demanded Danilov, and wished he hadn't attempted the tough-guy mockery.

Barry stood reluctantly aside, face aflame. He was having difficulty in controlling his hands. 'Wait!' he hissed, lips tighter than ever. 'Just wait!'

Danilov walked easily by, emboldened by Pavin's presence behind: relieved, too, that his assistant did not speak until they got down to street level.

'What happened back there?' said Pavin.

'They were upset,' said Danilov. He knew the American had wanted to hit him: he felt lucky the whole stupid episode hadn't ended in a brawl.

Danilov expected a protest gesture, but not what Novikov staged at the pathology division. From Novikov's office he was directed downstairs where an attendant further guided him to the examination theatre. The smell when he got there – a collision of formaldehyde and disinfectant and stale human body waste – clogged in his throat; it was even worse when he pushed through the door, to enter. Novikov wore a stained gown and a cotton protective hat which made him look hairless. He stood at the sink, washing his hands, a mask pushed down around his throat. A sheet, also stained, covered the body of Ann Harris.

'I was sure you wouldn't mind coming here,' said the pathologist, without any tone of apology. 'I realized from your having Lapinsk intercede that it was incredibly urgent so I knew you wouldn't want to wait upstairs. You could have asked me yourself, of course.'

Novikov was a large, fleshy man, bulbous-nosed and thick-lipped. His hands were large, the fingers sausage-like. He didn't even look like a surgeon, Danilov thought: surgeons should have delicate, tender hands. He supposed it wasn't necessary to be tender with a dead body. He said: 'I don't mind at all,' which wasn't true.

'Some people haven't got the stomach for dissecting rooms.'

Fuck you, decided Danilov. 'I said I don't mind.' Coming

through the door he'd had to swallow against the smell: he wanted to do so again but didn't.

'Tough policeman, eh?'

'I need the preliminary report.' He didn't want to spar and score debating points. He wanted to learn things that might help him trap a madman. And get out as quickly as he could, away from the smell and away from this man who had hands like a butcher.

'I suppose senior colonels get all the most important cases.'

Danilov waited. His stomach felt loose. He made himself go further into the room, closer to the covered body. One foot protruded from beneath the sheet: she'd painted her toe-nails a pale pink. Danilov liked the colour. Larissa painted her nails sometimes: Olga never did. Olga even forgot to cut them.

Novikov spent a long time drying his hands and took off the protective hat, releasing a fall of lank hair, before he spoke. 'White female Caucasian, aged between twenty-five and thirty. Weight, 54 kilos. Brown eyes. Black hair. Cause of death a puncture wound, from the rear, between the eighth and ninth ribs, under the scapula. Clean entry, with no bone contact. The weapon entered from the right side, through the intercostal muscle and lung, severing the aorta before penetrating the heart. There were superficial wounds to the head, which did not contribute to the cause of death . . .' He paused. 'I'm not going too fast: you're managing to assimilate all this?'

'I'm managing.' Danilov almost retched after just two words.

The pathologist smiled, as if he realized. 'No organic disease. Appendicectomy scar, lower right abdomen. As I told your man at the scene, it's difficult to establish a precise time of death: I'd estimate between eleven and one o'clock. How's that?' He smiled again.

It was inadequate to the point of being absurd: the bastard was forcing him to stay in the room and ask questions. 'Depth of the wound?'

'Nineteen and a half centimetres.'

'Blunt or sharp instrument?'

'I said a clean entry.'

'Pointed then?'

'What else could it be?' Novikov smiled, a magician arriving at his best trick. 'Why not see for yourself?'

The sheet came back with a flourish. Ann Harris lay on her back. The rigor had left the body, which had a wax-like sheen and like wax appeared to be melting, bubbled and flaccid. Only the snarl remained, more horrifying than before. Novikov *had* examined like a butcher. The body incision, from neck to crotch, was carelessly jagged, the subsequent stitching uneven. Nothing had been swabbed clean, after being sealed.

'You'll have to help me turn her over.'

'Cover her,' said Danilov, tightly, not looking. When was the mutilation of Ann Harris going to stop?

'I thought you wanted to see?'

'Cover her.' Strangely, Danilov's stomach was settling, despite Novikov's charade. When the pathologist didn't move, Danilov himself pulled the sheet back over the disfigured corpse. Even-voiced he said: 'So it was a tapered wound?'

Novikov's disappointment was visibly obvious, a vein pumping in the man's right temple. 'It was a tapered wound,' he agreed.

'Width, at the point of entry?'

'Five centimetres.'

'Thickness?'

'Five millimetres, at its thickest: the back of the knife.'

The other man shifted, with apparent impatience, and Danilov thought, your game, you bastard: now you stay and play it. 'Any surface tearing of the skin at the point of entry?'

'Why didn't you look for yourself?'

'Any surface tearing of the skin?'

'I said it was clean!'

'A sharp knife then?'

'Yes.'

'*Especially* sharp?'

'How can I answer that?'

'By telling me if there was any fractional indentation of the skin immediately around the wound.'

'There wasn't.'

'Which would indicate the knife being especially sharp?'

'It's a reasonable assumption.'

'Any indication that the knife blade was serrated?'

38

'Smooth-bladed. No serration.'

'It could have been a kitchen knife?'

'It could have been.'

'Anything to show a struggle?'

'I told your man last night.'

'Tell me!'

'There was bruising to the left thigh and buttock. It was post-mortem lividity: that means it occurred after death.'

'I know what it means. What about fingernail scrapings?'

'Nothing. Death was practically instantaneous.'

'Sexual assault?'

'None.' Novikov hesitated, then said: 'But there had been recent sexual intercourse.'

Danilov sighed, exasperated. 'Which you haven't thought important enough to tell me until now?'

'It would have been in my complete, written report.'

'I don't want to wait until your complete, written report!' The obstructiveness was back-firing, making the man himself appear incompetent: Danilov wished there had been others to witness it, like before.

'There was semen, in the vagina.'

'Sufficient for blood grouping?'

Novikov nodded. 'B. Rhesus Negative.'

The most common, Danilov reflected, bitterly. 'What was her group?'

'B again. But Rhesus Positive.'

'Why are you sure it couldn't have been rape?'

'Rapists don't replace tights and knickers. She was properly dressed. There was no vaginal bruising.'

'Was there bruising around the wound?'

'Very slight.'

'Was it a stab? Or was the knife driven in?'

'Driven in.'

Abruptly, again, Danilov realized a further important omission. He gestured to the covered body. 'You didn't say how tall she was.'

'One point six five metres.'

'And you didn't tell me the *direction* of the wound. Was it

39

upwards? Downwards? What?' The pathologist swallowed and Danilov doubted the man had properly checked.

'Across, from right to left: slightly upwards, perhaps.'

'So the killer could be approximately the same height? Or slightly smaller. If he were taller it would have a downward direction, wouldn't it?'

'Yes.'

'It didn't come into any contact with bone?'

'I already told you that.'

'How difficult is it to thrust a knife into someone and get cleanly between the ribs?'

Novikov considered the question. 'Someone did it: she's dead.'

'Help me!' demanded Danilov, exasperated. 'You know the problem! You did the first autopsy!'

Novikov smiled, pleased at the other man's outburst. 'There's usually some bone contact.'

'There wasn't last time: there hasn't been now. So could it be someone who has medical knowledge?'

The pathologist shook his head. 'I *can't* help you. On a darkened street, presumably walking, it would be incredibly difficult for anyone even with medical knowledge to avoid any bone contact.'

'Meaning?'

'That missing any bone was a fluke: that you shouldn't attach undue significance to it.'

Danilov decided he couldn't ignore it, either. A wash of fatigue, a recurrence of that morning's tiredness, swept over him. He began to put out his hand, to support himself against the dissecting table upon which the sheeted body lay, but stopped when he realized what he was about to do. 'When can I have your written report?'

'A day or two,' the pathologist dismissed.

Danilov was suddenly furious at the other man's posturing. 'What reason did Lapinsk give for wanting the autopsy today?'

'Just that it was urgent.'

'She's an American,' Danilov disclosed. 'The niece of an important politician in the United States. People in the White House here *and* in America are going to be watching this.'

'Oh,' said the other man, the obstructive arrogance fading.

'I want the report by tomorrow,' demanded Danilov. 'Two. The Americans will want their own copy.' He looked at the covered body, then back to Novikov. 'They'll see the way you carried out the autopsy when the body is released.'

The pathologist made as if to speak, to argue, but didn't. Instead, after a pause, he said, dry-throated: 'I'll make two copies.'

'Is there anything you haven't told me? Something that's going to be in your written report that I should know now?'

'I don't think so.'

Danilov held out his hand. 'I need her fingerprints.'

Novikov's throat moved. 'They'll come with the report.'

So he hadn't taken them yet. 'Don't forget anything else, will you?'

'But it's been almost a fortnight,' Larissa protested. He'd reached her from a street kiosk.

'This is different: unusual.' He hadn't given her any details, just that it was a murder.

'Tomorrow?'

'I'll try.' He thought she might have asked about an unusual murder.

'You don't sound very interested.'

'You know that's not true! And I don't want to argue.'

'I want to *see* you!'

'I really will try tomorrow.'

'Don't let me down.'

'I won't,' said Danilov. I hope, he thought. Or did he?

There are four psychiatric clinics in Moscow. The best known is the Serbsky Institute for Forensic Psychiatry, in Kropotkinskii Street: during the oppressive, population-controlling era before the second Russian revolution, it was the place in which the KGB detained political dissidents, claiming they suffered paranoid schizophrenia.

Major Yuri Pavin personally led the record-searching team on its first visit, to explain their needs to the white-coated principal. The man was shaking his head before Pavin finished talking.

'It would need a computer to do a thorough search,' the psychiatrist protested.

'Your records aren't computerized?'

'No.'

'How long could a physical search take?'

'Months, to be completed properly.'

Pavin looked to the other two detectives with him: both were already frowning at the potential task ahead of them. The search wouldn't be conducted properly, Pavin knew: here or anywhere else.

Chapter Five

Power in Washington is layered, and those layers are divided again, between publicly known influence and private, behind-the-scenes importance. Senator Walter Burden, who did not welcome the political cartoonists' impression of him as a living version of Kentucky Fried Chicken's Colonel Sanders, although the physical similarity was remarkable, enjoyed both. And expertly used both, to the public and private promotion of Senator Walter Burden. One day – a day of his choosing – he intended to occupy the White House. Which some pundits considered inevitable. And which was why, within twenty-four hours of the alert from Moscow, a conference was convened by Secretary of State Henry Hartz with the Directors of both the Central Intelligence Agency and the Federal Bureau of Investigation in Hartz's seventh-floor office at the State Department, in that incongruously named part of the city called Foggy Bottom.

Hartz, who but for his German birth, which constitutionally precluded his seeking the office, considered himself a Presidential candidate, stood at the window overlooking the unseen, sunken memorial to the Vietnam war dead, his mind completely occupied by the news from Russia. Even before a moment's examination of all the implications, it was obviously going to be hell: sheer and utter hell. Which worried him. Denied his presidential aspirations by the mischance of his birthplace, Hartz believed he had achieved the next best thing. His periods as Secretary of State had been times of unmarred diplomatic success, properly acknowledged by the incoming President who had asked him to remain in office, after succeeding the previous White House incumbent. Hartz had seen the request continuing under Burden. Ahead of any discussion of additional information from Moscow, he knew that expectation could be jeopardized if Burden were not handled like the prima donna he was. Hell, Hartz decided again.

The intercom warned him of the arrival of the two Directors

and Hartz was at the door when they entered. Richard Holmes, head of the CIA, was a tall, dark-haired man with a sun-bed tan and the attitude of think-twice caution of a Washington survivor. He neither smoked nor drank and had been an intelligence professional all his life. There were outstanding offers, all in excess of $1,000,000, from three New York publishing houses for his memoirs. Holmes was a happy, contented man.

He entered ahead of the FBI chief. Leonard Ross had believed his political ambitions fulfilled the previous year with his appointment to head of the Bureau. But no longer. In just one year he had become first disillusioned and then sickened by the shadow-watching political intrigue of the capital until now he yearned to return to the New York State bench where he had served with distinction as its senior judge.

There were handshakes and greetings and Hartz led the group towards the couches and easy chairs in that corner of the office furthest from the windows and their hotchpotch view. Hartz said: 'I thought we might benefit from some conversation ahead of Burden getting here.'

'How's he taking it?' asked Holmes. He was pleased with the Agency's legal advice that there was no way the CIA could become involved. He'd already wired the Moscow station to stay clear.

'Predictably,' said Hartz. 'He's already phoned our ambassador in Moscow direct. Asked me what the President was doing about it. He's demanding investigation, from both of you. Actually told me he wants the bastard – his word – who did it brought back for trial in this country.'

The FBI Director shook his head in cynical bemusement. Washington at its best – or worst – he thought. 'He can forget it.'

Apprehension settled heavily on Hartz. 'What, precisely, is the legal guidance?'

'The CIA doesn't have any jurisdiction or authority,' said Holmes, quickly. He wished the relief hadn't sounded so obvious.

'The Bureau has a criminal investigation capacity but again no jurisdiction or authority in the Russian Commonwealth,' said Ross.

'Burden expects there to be both.'

'I don't give a damn what Burden *expects*,' said Ross, who in

44

addition to his disillusionment also had the financial independence to speak his mind. 'I'm stating the legal reality.'

'The Russians are behaving arrogantly,' said Hartz. 'I don't think they should have entered her apartment as they did.'

'What are you doing about that?' asked Holmes.

'There's been a complaint, from the embassy. I'm calling the Russian ambassador here, to emphasize it.'

'I don't know the diplomatic protocol, but the Russians *are* investigating a murder,' Ross pointed out, mildly.

'You approve what they did?' asked Hartz.

'If the situation were reversed and it had happened here in Washington I wouldn't have censored any of my people for doing the same. And there's not a lot of practical purpose in complaining after the event, is there?'

The desk buzzer gave another warning, but Senator Walter Burden was already through the door before the Secretary of State reached it for a personal welcome. Burden nodded in recognition to both Directors and said in advance of sitting down: 'I want to know everything that's happened! All the developments!' The man was immaculate in a broad-striped suit and pink shirt: the tie and pocket handkerchief formed a matching combination. He sat on the edge of his seat, leaning towards them intently: for no obvious reason he put on heavy reading glasses. He nodded, as if giving everyone in the room permission to speak.

'I'm afraid the information is limited,' Hartz apologized. He recounted what had been relayed from Moscow, aware for the first time of an odd mobility of Burden's face: the man frequently widened his eyes, as if he were constantly astonished at what he was being told, an unnerving, intimidating mannerism.

'Mutilated her?' demanded Burden, when Hartz talked of the hair.

'She was shorn,' confirmed Hartz pedantically.

'What about sex?'

'There's been no report of any sexual assault,' said Holmes, entering the conversation. The Senator really *did* look like the Colonel Sanders logo.

'They got the bastard?'

'Not as far as we know.'

Burden looked to each of the three men. Then he said: 'So,

45

what are you doing about it?' The word-biting New England accent was very pronounced.

Both Directors looked to Hartz for a reply. The Secretary of State said: 'At the moment, waiting for more information from Moscow.'

Burden's eyes widened. 'I meant doing *practically*. How many investigators have you assigned? What's the command structure? Has the President been informed?'

Ross gestured towards the CIA chief and said, with impatient bluntness: 'Dick and I have both taken legal advice. Neither agency has any right of investigation whatsoever.'

Burden shook his head, seemingly incredulous. 'I don't believe what you're telling me! You telling me that a sweet, innocent American girl – my niece – has been slaughtered in Moscow and that you're not going to do a damned thing about it? Because if you are, think again, every one of you. I want that killer found and I want him tried and executed and I want it all done by Americans. You hearing me?'

The FBI Director reddened, the restraint clearly difficult. 'I can understand your feelings. You have my sympathy. But as it stands at the moment there is nothing we *can* do. There's no way of our getting involved.'

'*Find* a way!' demanded Burden, loud-voiced. 'I'm not having the murder of my niece investigated by a bunch of Russians using Stone Age techniques and methods! And I know the American public won't have it, either.'

Hartz recognized that Burden could get as much media attention as he wanted. Hartz said: 'I am calling in the Russian ambassador later to demand an assurance that everything possible is being done by the Russian authorities.'

Burden gave another head shake of disbelief, his eyes widening and contracting. 'I asked if the President has been informed.'

'I had a message sent to Camp David,' replied Hartz. 'He's deeply shocked and asked me to pass on his condolences.'

'That all! He didn't talk about what we were going to do?'

'He knows of this meeting. He's asked to be kept informed.'

'*I'll* inform him,' said Burden, threateningly. 'He'll take my call.'

'I'm sure he will,' agreed Hartz. He decided to make his own contact, as well, to correct whatever slant Burden imposed in his account: it would be a very personal interpretation.

'I would expect our investigative technology *is* more advanced than the Russians,' offered Ross, reflectively. It was a professional remark, not offered as a defence against the Senator's pop-eyed outrage.

'I'm damned sure it is!' said Burden, aggressively.

'So?' queried the CIA chief.

'Maybe that would be the way to get in,' suggested the Bureau Director. 'Offer all and every access to our scientific facilities.'

'Offer!' echoed Burden, sneering. 'Ask, you mean? Cap-in-hand?'

Ross sighed loudly. 'I thought the point was to become involved.'

'I think it's a good idea,' said Hartz. 'I'll raise it with the ambassador.'

'We sure this is a genuine murder?' demanded Burden, with sudden suspicion. 'Has anyone thought that this might be an official assassination?'

Now it was the two Directors who looked incredulous: it was the unintimidated Ross who spoke for both, although still restrained. 'What possible reason could there be for assassinating Ann Harris?'

'I'm no admirer of Russia,' admitted Burden, openly.

Hartz was well enough aware of Burden's conceit, but decided this verged on megalomania. 'Everything that has come from Moscow indicates a street mugging.'

'Put it to your people in Moscow,' ordered Burden, talking to the CIA Director. 'I want that checked out.'

Now it was Holmes who reddened slightly. He nodded, saying nothing. Son-of-a-bitch, he thought.

'Be direct with the ambassador, too,' said Burden, continuing the instructions.

'I'll do what I consider best,' said Hartz, finally resisting, although very weakly.

Pinpricks of colour now registered on Burden's face and his mouth formed into an angry line. 'This isn't an ordinary murder: this isn't the killing of someone who didn't matter. Don't forget that.'

'The Bureau doesn't consider anyone who gets murdered to be unimportant,' said Ross, increasingly impatient.

'I want a daily briefing,' Burden insisted to the Secretary of State. 'I want to know the outcome of the meeting with the ambassador and I want to hear everything that comes out of Moscow . . .' He hesitated, looking to the CIA Director. 'And don't forget, either, to check the assassination theory.'

No one spoke in the first few moments after Burden's departure. Then Holmes said: 'What fucking assassination theory? Jesus Christ!'

'I believe he thinks he's Him,' said Ross. 'Can either of you begin to imagine what it will be like if he *does* become President? Thank God I'm not a Washington careerist.'

'Power and influence,' warned Hartz. 'When he says jump, Congress jumps. All together. And Burden controls the budget like a miser worried about cash flow.' A diplomatic negotiator on every level, Hartz added: 'If we were allowed in, it would be the Bureau responsibility, right?'

'Yes,' said Ross.

'Would you use your man already at the Moscow embassy?'

The Bureau Director shook his head, at once. 'From the Bureau here.'

'Why not run a feasibility, just in case?'

Throughout the day Walter Burden made himself available to all three major television networks and every newspaper or magazine which approached him, which was a lot, not just American but foreign publications as well. He declared himself devastated by the crime. Ann Harris was a niece whom he'd loved dearly, whose life had been only just beginning. He had spoken personally with the President and had been assured that all necessary steps were being taken by the Russian authorities to arrest the killer: the full resources of American criminal investigation agencies were being offered to Moscow. In response to several questions, Burden said he might consider going to the Russian capital himself. Every television appearance was accompanied by still photographs of Ann Harris, some taken with Burden. They were all good reproductions, showing a smiling, typically American girl with brace-sculpted teeth and flowing black hair. Which was how Burden wanted people to think of her, so he said nothing about the shorn hair.

The Ann Harris murder and Walter Burden's interview remained the lead item through the day on Cable News Network, so William Cowley saw it several times on his office set in the FBI headquarters building. The anger at not already having been informed, which he considered he should have been as a courtesy at least, began and was just as quickly curbed. To have been informed *would* have been a courtesy, because his responsibility for Russian affairs was officially restricted to counter-espionage within the United States. And it was certainly not a courtesy he could have expected from the FBI agent stationed in Moscow, for altogether personal reasons.

The old memories were inevitable, of course. He wished they hadn't been. As he wished so much else, too late.

William Cowley accepted that he was probably at the pinnacle of his professional career. Promotion beyond his existing position, as director of the Russian internal desk, was invariably political: he was, in fact, lucky to have achieved this much, after the carelessness. He certainly wasn't careless any more: didn't really concede he had been dangerously negligent in the past. He'd never put the job at risk. And now he was unquestionably the copy-book careerist in every way: utterly dedicated, first to arrive, last to leave, FBI personified. Which, he assured himself again, was how he'd always been, professionally. Maybe that was how the personal carelessness had arisen, from the confidence of a natural-born policeman who'd been additionally lucky with the breaks: achieving G–15 grade at the age of forty, eight highest-category commendations on his personal sheet, the most exemplary for jointly controlling with an Italian prosecutor the destruction of a Mafia-backed heroin operation when he had been attached to the embassy in Rome.

Beneficial professionally but disastrous personally, Cowley decided, coming to the bitterest reflection of all. The posting to London had been a direct result of the Rome success: London where the FBI maintained a four-man office and where one of the agents had been Barry Andrews, finger-snapping, smart-as-a-tack, good old Barry, everybody's buddy. Cowley had regarded the man as his *best* friend, never suspecting he was more particularly Pauline's friend. The bitterness was brief, because after so long he'd become objective, the most sensible acceptance of all that none of it had been Pauline's fault. Not really Barry Andrews's, either. If the break-up hadn't happened in London it would have occurred elsewhere: he was neglecting her completely by then, the drinking at its worst, the womanizing open and blatant. Everything had been his fault.

So now he had his career and his title on the door and was as lonely as hell and by the Sod's Law of fate had the permanent mockery of Barry Andrews in the same department although not in the same division.

Cowley made a conscious effort to slough off the reminiscence and was reaching forward for the stop button to shut off a repeat of the Burden television interview when the telephone rang.

'The Director wants you,' said Ross's personal assistant. 'Now.'

Petr Yezhov walked almost every night, a regular route and late, when there weren't many people about. There'd always been people crowded around, in the hospitals. To walk, without people, meant he was free. No walls or locked doors, keeping him in. He'd walk tonight. But not near the Intourist Hotel. There were prostitutes hanging around the Intourist Hotel. Didn't want to meet any prostitutes.

Chapter Six

Danilov was later than he expected getting back to Militia head-quarters. He'd let Pavin take the pool car, to get everything back to headquarters for forensic examination, and he'd delayed himself further telephoning Larissa. There was another man with Lapinsk when Danilov entered the Director's office. Danilov instantly identified the uniform and the shoulder-boards of rank.

'Lieutenant-Colonel Kir Gugin,' introduced Lapinsk.

'Formerly KGB, now of the Agency for Federal Security,' added the man, as if his authority needed emphasis. He was fat and swarthy with the mottled red face of some physical condition, blood pressure perhaps. 'We've been waiting a long time,' he added, complaining.

The curbs and disbandments throughout the organization after the failed coup of 1991 had done nothing to diminish the arrogance, reflected Danilov. 'I'm involved in an investigation.' Had Gugin waited to announce his takeover?

'Anything I should know?' demanded Lapinsk, anxiously. The General was a grey man — grey faced, grey hair, grey suited — and had the slightly tired attitude of someone gratefully declining into retirement. Danilov thought Lapinsk looked very much the grandfather he was: there were two framed photographs on the desk of Lapinsk's daughter, with her two sons. On the wall behind the man there were larger photographs of the devastation of Stalingrad and a separate picture of a very young Lapinsk, in army uniform. The man had survived the entire siege of 1942 as a corporal in Chuikov's 62nd Army and was justifiably proud.

'She'd had sex. But she hadn't been raped: Novikov is adamant about that. We've taken from her apartment a rack of kitchen knives. One that could have caused the wound that killed her is missing.'

'There's been a second, more forceful protest from the Americans claiming that you broke into the apartment,' said Gugin. He didn't know how, not yet, but there were very definitely some benefits to be manipulated here.

'I did not break in,' retorted Danilov. He was determined against being intimidated by the KGB officer: certainly one of lesser rank. 'We've managed to conduct a reasonably thorough forensic examination, which we would not have been able to do otherwise.'

Lapinsk sighed at the squabbling. His ulcer began to nag. 'What's the significance of the sex and the knife? That she knew her killer?'

'I'm not attaching any special significance: merely telling you what might be important. I'm getting Novikov's written report tomorrow. I need to compare that with the verbal account.'

'Have you considered the political aspects of this?' demanded Gugin. 'It could mean that this woman knew a mass murderer: that he could even *be* American!'

Danilov looked for guidance towards Lapinsk, who said: 'I had to explain everything at the Ministry.'

Danilov's tiredness was worsening: his concentration kept ebbing and flowing so that sometimes he heard quite clearly what the other two men were saying and at other times could hardly hear them at all. 'What else is there from the Foreign Ministry?'

'The relation, the Congressman, has been in direct contact with the American ambassador, who's sought a meeting,' said Lapinsk. 'The man is apparently important. We're being inundated with demands for information from the Western media. There's an offer from Washington of technological and scientific help . . .'

'Which means they despise our investigatory capacity!' Gugin broke in. After the organization's most recent problems, it was going to be important to distance the KGB from any dangerous criticism.

It was difficult for Danilov to hold a thought but again he wondered why the KGB officer had not by now announced KGB control. 'What's the official response going to be?'

'Mainly political,' Lapinsk disclosed. 'The Minister is waiting for the meeting with the ambassador.'

Danilov looked pointedly at Gugin. 'There is some technical help I would appreciate from here.'

Gugin returned the attention in apparent surprise, in reality wondering if this was going to show him the way. 'What?'

Danilov leaned forward, offering a slip of paper upon which he'd copied Ann Harris's telephone number. 'Would there have been any monitor?'

Gugin stared steadily back at the detective for several moments. 'I won't know, until I check. We could never admit it.'

'I don't want to admit it. I want access to numbers she might have called. If the man she slept with isn't her killer at least he might know why she got out of bed to walk around Moscow in the middle of the night.'

'It would be extremely useful,' encouraged Lapinsk.

'I'll inquire,' promised Gugin. But think and plan first, he decided: there probably would have been a monitor, upon somebody so well connected politically. This really could be the way.

The reply confused Danilov. Now they were openly inviting KGB involvement and still the man wasn't making the control demands there should have been. 'I'd like something else.'

'What?'

'File photographs of Ann Harris. I'd like to see who she circulated with, socially.'

'She might not have been targeted. If anything came up, during, say, a normal embassy event it might have been retained.'

'She was related to a prominent American politician!' Danilov pointed out. By now he was totally confused by Gugin's practically acquiescent attitude: it wasn't right.

'I'll check that, too.' Gugin was sure of an advantage now. It could be very good.

'That would be extremely helpful.'

'I'm sure it will be,' said Gugin, amusing himself. He amused himself further with the obvious surprise of the other two men when he terminated his presence by abruptly announcing he had other meetings for which he was already late. He was anxious, in fact, to consult with others back in Lubyanka.

When they were alone Lapinsk said: 'How are you going to take this forward?'

'Routinely. Pavin's setting up the checks on the mental institutions. It's going to tie up a lot of personnel: possibly mean other cases will have to be put aside.'

'That's unimportant!' declared the Director at once, anxious again. 'There is only one priority. This case. Everyone's frightened. The Foreign Ministry – and the Interior – are terrified of overseas newspaper and magazine stories of monsters and madmen roaming Moscow's streets.'

'There is one,' said Danilov, unhelpfully. He jerked his head in the direction of the door through which Gugin had left. 'I don't understand what the Cheka are doing. Or rather, not doing!'

'Neither did I, at first,' Lapinsk confessed. 'Then I sat through a half-hour lecture from the Foreign Minister and his advisers about the pitfalls and the Cheka attitude became entirely clear. They'll cooperate in what we've asked: it makes them look willing participants. But they're always going to be on the outside, free from any responsibility. They can't afford or risk any more censure, can they?'

The explanation was still hardly an expression of confidence in either him or the Militia, Danilov recognized. 'So it begins and ends with us? With me?' Wasn't that what he'd wanted? Already determined to fight for?

'The KGB have far more expertise at political and diplomatic manoeuvre than we have. They've always needed it more.'

'Are there any special instructions?' And was he going to regret his own ambition, he asked himself. He hoped not.

'Find who did it, as soon as possible,' said Lapinsk.

'I hardly need to be told that.' The Director's fatuous reply showed the strain under which the man believed himself to be.

'You *do* need to be told to be careful in diplomatic situations. You went too far, entering the apartment. Think more, before you move. Otherwise there'll be mistakes. And we can't afford mistakes, any more than what used to be the KGB.'

'I won't have gone too far, if it helps me find who did it.'

'Don't argue with me about this, Dimitri Ivanovich! There isn't going to be any glory in this investigation. Just problems.'

'I'll try not to offend.' Danilov could see through the window that it was already dark outside. He tried to remember what Olga had told him she was doing tonight but couldn't, only that she was going out. So there wouldn't be any food in the apartment. And he hadn't eaten at midday.

'You can call upon whatever facilities you want,' offered the

Director. 'Everything's got *top* priority. I want morning and after-noon briefing: I'm going to be getting queries constantly.' The man paused. 'I'm frightened there's going to be another one.'

'There obviously will be, unless we're lucky. And I don't really know what I mean by being lucky,' admitted Danilov, with aching resignation. It wasn't until he was struggling against the crowd at the metro station that he realized one of the facilities he could probably demand was a permanent police vehicle. He'd have to remember, tomorrow.

Olga had not left him anything to eat. Danilov poured the Stolichnaya he had denied himself in the long ago early hours of that morning and carried it to the bedroom. He only drank half before falling asleep. His last conscious thought was to hope that Lapinsk was wrong and that there would be a lot of personal glory if he carried out an impeccable investigation and made an arrest.

The world's press had a story of a predicted American Presidential candidate – already a well-known politician – connected with a murder in Russia.

The coverage was staggering.

The demand for press conferences and interviews and infor-mation was overwhelming, bewildering Russian ministries which believed they already understood the needs of the Western news media, but in fact knew them not at all. The sideways shuffle was as automatic as it was instinctive.

The responding discussion was held at the Foreign Ministry. It was attended by a deputy official of the Interior Ministry and the Federal Prosecutor. General Leonid Lapinsk obviously rep-resented the Militia. The Foreign Ministry delegate lectured on the political importance. The Interior Ministry deputy insisted upon the need for a quick resolution. With weight of authority, both ministries argued that the statement should come from the Federal Prosecutor, a thin, skin-sagged lawyer named Nikolai Smolin. The Prosecutor tried to spread responsibility, summoning Lapinsk the following morning to judge – and for the man to be enmeshed in – the communiqué. It said the Russian authorities deeply regretted a foul crime. Every effort and every available officer had been assigned to the investigation, for which there was every expectation of a quick conclusion. All information and developments would be made available to the media, as they arose.

'Well?' demanded Smolin. He had a croaking, dry-throated way of talking.

'It seems to cover what they have been asking,' said the media-raw Lapinsk.

'I'm sure it will satisfy them,' smiled Smolin.

It didn't, of course.

Another one soon. More buttons. More hair. Leave a trail: like a paper-chase. Had to taunt: to dare. Different coloured buttons than the reds and the green and the brown. Had to get this pattern right. Maybe try for red again, after all. Just a different shade. Difficult, of course: dangerous, trying to choose. Always the risk of attracting attention. Never sure what the colours truly were, in the dark, unless you were dangerously close. Had to be very close – risk the danger – to ensure it was a woman. Do it soon: quite soon. Important not to begin to like it, though. It would be madness, to like it. Wasn't mad. That was the most brilliant part of it all: that he wasn't mad. Only he knew that, though. Brilliant.

Chapter Seven

William Cowley attracted attention – which for a law officer was sometimes a disadvantage – because he returned it, intently. He was a large man, both tall and heavy-shouldered, the build of the college football player he had once been, long ago. But unlike many men of such size he did not try to come down to the stature of smaller people but walked purposefully and upright and invariably concentrated absolutely upon the person to whom he was talking. It was a natural confidence, often mistaken for conceit, which *was* a mistake, because William Cowley was not a conceited man. He was a very realistic, pragmatic man. A sad one, too.

Both secretaries started to rise eagerly when he entered the Director's suite: the younger, a corn-and-milk-fed blonde, won the race. Cowley answered the smile but politely, without any come-on flirtation: another reform, to go with all the rest. Cowley identified himself and the girl said Mr Fletcher was waiting. Fletcher was the Director's personal assistant. The man emerged unsmiling from an inner office and said: 'Thank you for coming,' as if there had been a choice. Then he added: 'The Director's waiting.'

Ross's fifth-floor office was at the corner of Pennsylvania Avenue looking up towards the Capitol. The walls were hung solely with large, official photographs of the present and past Presidents and past FBI Directors. Cowley wondered where Ross's photograph would hang, when the man left office; there didn't appear to be any space left. There was a predictable furled American flag in one corner, behind the desk at which Ross sat. The carelessly fat man in the crumpled suit didn't rise or move his face in any greeting. He nodded thanks to Fletcher, for the escort duty, and nodded again to Cowley, to be seated.

'Senator Burden's niece has been murdered in Moscow,' announced the FBI Director, without any preamble. 'For all the reasons that don't need me to explain, we're trying to get into the situation.'

Imagining his guidance was being sought, as an acknowledged before-and-after-the-changes Russian expert, he said: 'I could probably come up with something in a day or two.' Andrews was going to be as busy as hell: something with a fall-out like this would be a bastard.

'Already decided,' said the Director, briskly. 'We're offering technical expertise. The sophistication of Russian criminal investigation will be light years behind ours.'

'Will they go for that?'

'Depends how it's argued. It isn't going to be easy, from what's happened so far.'

'What *has* happened?'

So this was the forthright directness referred to in Cowley's last personnel assessment, a trait which seemed to upset some people here on Pennsylvania Avenue. Ross, who rarely for a legal man preferred one word to a wrapped-up sentence, didn't find it offensive. 'The investigation is under the jurisdiction of the People's Militia: that's controlled by the Interior Ministry. There've been official complaints of arrogance and undiplomatic behaviour.'

'Providing them laboratory room here isn't going to give us much of an in.'

'Which is why we've got to maximize it, if we get the chance,' the Director insisted. There was a pause. 'And which is why I want you to go.'

'Me!'

'You've got Russian,' said the Director, itemizing the qualifications. 'You've got overseas embassy experience. You're up to date with every investigatory technique, from the courses at Quantico. And before your promotion to the Russian desk, you were the senior inspector here . . .'

'But . . .' broke in Cowley, intending to point out the gap of three years since his last in-field investigation experience.

'I'm aware of the personal complication,' Ross broke in, misunderstanding the interruption. 'That's why I'm seeing you personally. I want your complete assurance.'

'Why not Andrews himself? It's his field office.'

Ross nodded. 'And he's more than competent enough to handle it: we accept that. But if we admit to an in-field agent it will be official confirmation of an FBI station at the Moscow embassy, which we don't want. Presidential ban, in fact. He's already accredited as a cultural secretary, so the Russians would know the scientific offer was just our way of getting in. And he's due for relocation, although that, of course, can be postponed for as long as you decide. His function will be to assist, within the embassy.'

How could the Director talk glibly of being aware of personal complications and make a suggestion like this? Cowley didn't consider there were any remaining personal difficulties about the break-up: there were still cards at Christmas and birthdays and once a year a digest of events in their lives, over the preceding twelve months. But this was professional: an intrusion into the job to which Andrews had always been committed to the exclusion of every other consideration. He'd obviously see the murder of Ann Harris as his investigation, even unofficially at this stage. It *was* his investigation, by right if not by political and diplomatic choice. Now – if they got in as the Director was hoping to get in – it was about to be peremptorily taken away. And by the man who had been Pauline's first husband, thus completing the confused circle where it was going to be hard, for Andrews at least, to separate what was personal and what was professional. Maybe for himself, too. He said: 'If we do get involved, I'd like you to brief Andrews fully by cable why it's being done this way. And why I'm the person being sent in.'

'So there *are* going to be difficulties!'

'I'm considering the investigation, nothing else. Resentment is inevitable, isn't it? It would be unnatural if there wasn't.'

'Not if he's properly professional, which he should be. And reads the instructions I'll send.'

'Let's hope he does,' said Cowley, doubtfully.

'You can back off, if you want,' offered the Director.

Cowley realized, abruptly, that he didn't want to back off. He wanted to return to the field and prove how good he was: how good he had always been, as an investigator. Was that all? Didn't he like the idea of taking over from the man who now had his wife, being in charge of the man, personally telling him what to do? Of course not, Cowley told himself. That was absurd: worse than absurd, it was totally unprofessional. 'I'll go in, of course,' he said, shortly.

The Director smiled. 'You'll need velvet gloves, diplomatically. I want you to clear your desk. The preliminary request – offer – has already been conveyed by our ambassador in Moscow. It's being reinforced, by the Secretary of State . . .' He patted a dossier on the desk in front of him. 'There's not much but you can read what Andrews has sent from Moscow. Let the Duty Officer know where you'll be, at all times.'

'I'm usually at home,' said Cowley. It was a dismally honest admission of his loneliness. He'd need velvet gloves *all* the time, not just diplomatically, he decided.

'Sure you don't want to think more about it?' suggested Ross.

Knowing the Bureau's adhesive attention to detail, he supposed it was obvious there would be a full history in Personnel records about the collapse of his relationship with Pauline and of her subsequent marriage to Andrews, but Cowley was still vaguely unsettled by it. 'Quite sure.' Another sweeping commitment, he realized. Despite the assurances he was giving today, it hadn't been particularly easy, during the last meeting three years earlier. *Couldn't be better, how about you? Couldn't be better. Glad to hear it. You look terrific. You too.* Like Muzak played in supermarkets.

'There's a hell of a lot riding on this,' said the Director in further warning.

'I can imagine,' said Cowley. Could he, he wondered.

Eduard Ustenko was one of the new breed of Russian ambassadors, a professional product of *perestroika* reforms and the supposed Russian adoption of Western market philosophies: his university degree was actually in economics. He was always immaculately suited – usually in greys and blues – and always a sought-after guest on the Washington cocktail circuit, with a vivacious wife who managed to look as if she were dressed by a Paris couturier house, even if she wasn't. The Style section of the *Washington Post* judged them the most popular diplomatic couple in the city.

Today, dressed for the occasion, Ustenko wore dark, almost

60

funereal, grey. Henry Hartz met him at the door of his office suite, as he had the CIA and FBI Directors earlier. As with the Directors he led the man to the easy chairs.

'It's a terrible tragedy,' said Ustenko. 'On behalf of my government I offer our deepest and most sincere regret. I intend extending that personally to Senator Burden and the unfortunate girl's family.'

'There should have been consultations before the girl's apartment was entered,' Hartz complained. He wondered how long it would take. And how difficult it would prove to be.

'We would have also hoped for more cooperation towards our investigators when they visited your embassy. The entry and examination of the apartment was entirely consistent with a murder investigation. Every item removed for forensic examination has been listed.'

'The apartment was sealed before the arrival of any of our officials,' persisted Hartz. 'We would expect an immediate copy of that list.'

'I will pass that request on at once,' promised Ustenko. 'I can foresee no problems arising there.'

Russia ten, America nil, scored Hartz. 'You must understand our extreme concern at such a savage killing of an American citizen: an American diplomat?'

'Particularly in the circumstances,' said the politically aware ambassador.

Hartz felt the perspiration start: he was glad it was only slight. He had intended immediately raising the offer of American technological assistance but quickly changed direction, to use Ustenko's opening. 'Senator Burden is an extremely influential politician here in Washington.'

'I recognize that,' Ustenko accepted. 'He – and his views – are well known to me. Although not personally, of course.'

'A man very aware and adept at domestic politics.'

'That's my belief.'

'But sometimes, unfortunately, with stubbornly held and preconceived ideas which do not reflect the reality of current situations elsewhere in the world.'

Ustenko nodded but said nothing this time.

Hartz realized, uncomfortably, that he was teetering on the very edge of a diplomatic abyss. 'Senator Burden's particular influence is upon allocation of overseas aid.'

The ambassador nodded again but still remained silent.

'On the subject of aid, we are very sincere in our offer of any technological assistance that might be useful in tracking down the killer of Senator Burden's niece.'

'We appreciate that,' said Ustenko, speaking at last. 'I understand the Russian gratitude has already been officially expressed.'

'Not having suffered the economic difficulties unfortunately experienced by your country in the last few years – difficulties you know we are anxious to alleviate – it's conceivable that our law enforcement agencies have developed some quite unique techniques.'

'Quite conceivable,' agreed Ustenko.

'I would like you to reiterate our offer to your government.'

'I understand,' said the ambassador, who did, completely.

He was doing his best to disguise it but the anger was obvious as he thrust into the compound apartment and from experience Pauline said nothing, waiting for him to speak. It was important always for him to lead a conversation when he was angry.

'The investigation has been taken away from me!' Andrews announced, hands tight against his sides. 'They're sending somebody from Washington.'

'You're due for recall anyway,' said Pauline, quickly, wanting to help.

'I hadn't finished talking,' Andrews complained. 'The somebody is your ex-husband.'

'Oh,' said Pauline, lost for anything else.

'I've been told to help, with anything within the embassy. That's all.' Fucking messenger boy, he thought.

'How . . . ?' Pauline stumbled. 'I mean, it's got to be . . .'

'It's going to be fine,' Andrews interrupted, subduing his fury, not wanting Pauline to know how he felt. 'We've worked together in the past. No reason why we shouldn't again.'

'If you're sure,' said the woman, uncertainly.

'It'll be good, being back together again, like the old days!' insisted Andrews, his face clearing. 'You'd like that, wouldn't you?'

'Not if he hasn't changed,' said the woman, finding her own answer and believing it was what her new husband would want to hear.

Chapter Eight

The first victim had been a man.

His name was Vladimir Suzlev. At the time of his death he had been fifty-two years and three months old, a married man with two teenage children, an off-duty taxi driver. And quite drunk: Novikov's autopsy suggested, from the alcohol level in his Group O blood and stomach contents, that Suzlev has consumed more than one flask of spirit, perhaps almost two. Danilov wondered if that much alcohol had numbed the pain of the knife going in: he hoped so. Certainly the death scene photographs at which he was looking, laid out on his overflowing desk in his overflowing office at Ulitza Petrovka, didn't show the terrorized agony frozen on Ann Harris's face. Absurdly Suzlev appeared almost to be smiling, a happy man in sudden death. No more than asleep. Dreaming. The head shearing hadn't been so horrific here because absurdly Suzlev has been almost bald. According to the bewildered and grief-racked wife who worked as a telex operator for a joint-venture Russian-Swedish company, Suzlev compensated for a completely hairless pate by allowing the peripheral hedge to grow long, almost collar-length. In death, the man had simply had a haircut, a short-back-and-sides tidying. A lot of the hair cut off was scattered over his face, as much of Ann Harris's had been strewn over hers. Suzlev's shoes were placed neatly beside the right side of his head.

Danilov stretched back from his desk, slightly pushing the Suzlev file away, mentally examining what he was doing. Or trying to do. Routinely checking, as he'd told Lapinsk: the bedrock of all police investigation. Looking for what, here? A thread, he answered himself; a common denominator, linking both crimes. So what were the links? Unquestionably the cutting of the hair, to be sprinkled over the face. And the shoes, positioned as they were to the right side of the head. But what about buttons? None had been taken, from any article of Suzlev's clothes. And there'd been enough, on the man's jacket and topcoat: even securing the flaps on the hat he'd worn. Why from the girl but not from the man? Danilov leaned forward, logging the first inconsistency on the blank sheet in his evidence book. He stared again at the photographs of the man, then at those of the girl. Pictured as found, he remembered, from both sets of discovery evidence. But not as they'd fallen. Novikov's written report on the taxi driver stressed the after-death bruising to the side and front of the man's thigh, supporting the supposition that having been stabbed from behind he'd fallen forward. The identical bruising suffered by Ann Harris. Yet both had been found as they'd been photographed, splayed on their backs. So the killer had turned his victims, after they'd fallen. But not immediately, Danilov guessed: it would have been easier to cut the hair when they were face down. He made another notation, in his book. What else? The wound, he recalled at once. Vladimir Suzlev had been killed from a thrust to the right-hand side of his body with a single-edged knife. The depth of the wound had been slightly less than nineteen centimetres. The entry width was five centimetres and the thickness, on the unhoned edge, had been five millimetres. Apart from the depth variation, the same as Ann Harris. Between the eighth and ninth rib, like Ann Harris. And like Ann Harris, with minimal bruising around the wound. Again a sharp knife. Which hadn't encountered any bone obstruction. Danilov made another similarity note and then hesitated. There was more to record, from the wound: obvious, to a trained investigator, but still needing to be stated as evidence. Both wounds showed entry from the right, crossing to the left of the body to penetrate the heart. So the killer was right-handed. Had he been left-handed, attacking from behind, the wound would have been *from* the left. Was there anything else this early in the inquiry? Novikov's voice echoed in his mind: *access from right to left: slightly upwards, perhaps*. Ann Harris had been one point six five metres tall: Vladimir Suzlev had been four millimetres short of two metres, and with the man the pathologist had definitely recorded the entry path as upwards. So the killer was quite short. How many right-handed, middle-height people lived in Moscow?

Danilov forced himself on, through the dead man's file. Suzlev has been a gregarious, well-liked man with no enemies. He'd drunk with three other drivers the night of his death, having found a liquor store with supplies near the Belorussian railway station. It had been a pleasantly drunken evening – they'd sung, according to the other drinkers – with no arguments or disagreements. He had not been robbed: when he'd been found he still had ten roubles in his pocket and his watch was on his wrist. He had no criminal record. His wife was sure he'd loved her and she claimed to have loved him: there was no extramarital involvement. He'd been a doting, if strict, father, although there was no complaint that he'd ever actually beaten either of his children, both boys, one fourteen, the other sixteen. The autopsy had discovered he was suffering a hernia his wife hadn't known about: there was the beginning of cholesterol build-up in the arteries but it would not have become a health factor for possibly another ten years.

Danilov straightened again, still looking at his file but not focusing on the details. An ordinary man leading an ordinary life until one night, a month ago, he stopped being ordinary and became a murder victim. So why Vladimir Vasilevich Suzlev, a Moscow taxi driver? And why Ann Harris, a pretty, successful, presumably high-earning American whose life was so different they might have come from separate planets? Virtually *did* come from separate planets. Where was the connection, the link he could logically follow to make the arrest and prevent it happening again? There wasn't one, he conceded, hopelessly. And it *was* hopeless: depressingly, emptily hopeless. Murders were committed by people – men and women – who knew their victims. They were husbands and wives or lovers or acquaintances: investigations *were* routine, plodding back through the lies and deceits and evasions until eventually it became obvious, usually accompanied by a tearful, apologetic confession. This case – these murders – weren't going to be solved that way. Danilov wished he knew how they were going to be solved.

Found. The one word suddenly seemed to come into focus from the rest of the unseen blur and Danilov concentrated forward, trying for a connecting factor. Ann Harris had been killed just off Ulitza Gercena. The body of Vladimir Suzlev had been found in another badly lit alley, running off the Ulitza Stolesnikov. Close, Danilov decided. Possibly the first positive common denominator, the comparatively compact area in which the killer was operating. Danilov wrote down the two street locations, drew a circle around each and joined them, with a single line. Above the line he put a question mark.

Danilov spent another fifteen minutes with both files, moving from one to the other and back again, but could not find anything else to join with a connecting line. He reassembled and closed the file on Vladimir Suzlev, intending to remove it completely from his desk, but stopped, uncertainly, with the hard-topped folder in his hand, unable to find anywhere to put it. Danilov's office was a filled up box of a place, enclosed in the very middle of the Militia building and therefore without even an outside window. One of the three bulbs which had to burn permanently, for illumination, had failed a week before and maintenance insisted there wasn't any more in store to replace it: they'd been expecting a delivery for a month. Danilov was uneasy because the bulb in the desk lamp had started to flicker. Every drawer in the two filing cabinets – some half open as if in proof – was jammed with past case files and documents that Danilov retained for reference, along with the books in the three crammed shelves, and the tops of both cabinets supported more precariously lodged files threatening an avalanche at the slightest vibration. There was more paperwork on the only visitor's chair and a growing wall stacked to the left of Danilov's desk.

The appearance, of completely disorganized chaos, was however entirely misleading. Danilov knew the location of every record, file and book and usually found his research facilities better – and certainly swifter – than the official basement archives staffed by uninterested clerks resentful of any inquiry.

Remaining uncertain, Danilov stood, the Suzlev case record still in hand, seeking space that didn't exist. Finally he heightened the wall of folders beside his desk: it was, after all, something he was going to need as close to hand as possible.

Ann Harris, the neat and tidy economist, had kept her correspondence meticulously: Danilov realized, the moment he unfastened the first bundle, that she had packaged them in their elastic bands strictly according to the date of receipt, creating a consecutive record of every letter she had received since her arrival in Moscow, eighteen months earlier. He sorted through, placing the packs in their proper chronological order, reading from the beginning. There seemed to be four main correspondents, her parents, who lived in Hartford, Connecticut, being the most regular. There was a man, John, who wrote from a New York address and whom it took Danilov some time to identify as a brother. Judy Billington, who lived in Washington, DC, emerged to be a fellow economist and former college friend. Senator Burden's letters were always typed – Danilov guessed by a secretary, because there were none of the mistakes of an amateur, two-fingered effort – and signed with a flourish of curlicues, a signature intended for posterity.

Although the correspondence was necessarily one-sided, nearly all a response or reaction to something the girl had written from Moscow, it soon became clear to Danilov that Ann Harris presented a different persona to different audiences. To her parents in Connecticut she was a polite and caring daughter, solicitous about their well-being, an eager reporter of the unusual experiences and pleasures possible in Moscow. *It's good to know how much you like it,* her parents had enthused, in a letter six months earlier. There seemed to have been plans for the elderly couple to visit. The girl had assured her father, who suffered from angina, that there was an excellent embassy doctor: she had proposed trips to the Bolshoi and the State Circus. Everyone was going to have a great time.

The letters from Senator Burden continued to reflect an unqualified enjoyment and a grateful awareness of the career benefits of the Russian posting, although more stiffly expressed, just as the politician's letters were stiffly typed. Although, from the way some of the letters were phrased, it was obvious Ann Harris was giving the necessary guarantees, there was frequent urging from Burden for her always to be conscious of the political influence being exerted on her behalf. Those urgings were invariably accompanied by assurances that back in Washington the man was monitoring and guarding her career. *I am proud,* Burden recorded in one letter. *You're rightfully earning the chance to the highest promotion, which I am going to see you get* insisted another. A third said, pompously: *It gratifies me to hear you have positively decided to subjugate all personal feelings and thoughts to repay with success the efforts I have made on your behalf.*

With the brother and the college friend, the tone changed dramatically.

In repeated promises from New York, John Harris undertook never to tell their parents or their uncle of her unhappiness in Moscow and its insular diplomatic environment. *It can't be the virtual prison that you describe*, the brother had protested, within two months of her arrival. It seemed to be a consistent complaint, because prison was a word that appeared in several letters. There were also inquiries about her social life. In a June letter the man had written *Sorry about the man shortage*. In July the reference was *A girl's got to do what a girl's got to do, but I would have thought there were enough eligible bachelor diplomats to go around*.

The most revealing and intimate correspondence was from Judy Billington.

The very first recorded letter contained the phrase *I know it's not the same, but if you're that frustrated there's always your bedside friend*. Near the conclusion of the next letter, six weeks after Ann Harris's arrival, the Washington-based friend had written: *I know fucking isn't everything but agree it helps a lot*. Judy Billington had been quite explicit about her own sex life – Danilov wondered what the phrase *giving head* meant – listing her bed partners and awarding them performance scores, out of ten.

The interesting, intriguing reference surfaced in a letter dated ten months earlier. At first he missed the beginning of the sequence, because the words were so innocuous. It was only an odd sentence that followed that made Danilov re-read the entire page to pick out what he thought was important. *At least it's better than nothing*, Judy Billington had written. Then, after the separation of two unconnected sentences, there was: *I don't like pain, either. Why not go back to one of the others?* There was an entire further unconnected paragraph and then, cynically, *They always say they love you: that's part of the necessary bullshit: I thought you'd know that by now. But be careful with this one*.

Danilov broke away from that particular letter, leaning back in his creaking chair to gaze up at the unlit, unreplaced bulb in the overhead socket. He was not shocked by open references to sex and sexuality, any more than he'd been shocked by what he'd found in Ann Harris's bedroom cabinet. The correspondence with the other American girl was merely a confirmation of what the bedroom contents indicated, a liberated woman behaving and talking as she had every right to do. But with whom? He'd already known, from the verbal report from the pathologist, that Ann Harris had been engaged in a sexual relationship. Now he knew it had existed for ten months. And there seemed to have been others before. But this one included pain. He was sure the word, in the context in which it was used, meant physical discomfort. So how much was he further forward? Maybe a few millimetres. Ann Harris had eased her sexual frustration for ten months, right up until the night of her death, with a man who enjoyed either inflicting or receiving pain. He partially re-read the letter before him. *I don't like pain, either . . .* More likely receiving what the man inflicted, he decided.

There were ten more letters from Judy Billington and Danilov went through each more slowly than any of the rest, examining the contents word by word, desperate for a clue – the merest hint – to whom Ann Harris's partner might have been. From one passage Danilov guessed the woman had confessed to some sort of sexual activity in the open, in Moscow's botanical gardens after a river cruise. *Tell him you don't like it* was a repeated piece of Washington advice in another. The second-to-last sheet in the batch said: *You were wise about the bondage. Jim was into it; it was pretty damned scary to be trussed up like a chicken, not able to move, not knowing what the hell the kinky bastard was going to do next. I only ever did it once.*

Danilov made a note on the pad before him and sectioned off with a paper-clip the letters he considered might have some relevance. The remainder he rebound in their elastic bands, in the order in which the girl had retained them, and stacked them neatly in the stiff-sided evidence container that Pavin had already titled with the girl's name and accorded an index number.

Sighing, his shoulders cramped from concentration, Danilov pulled the slender, line-a-day-diary towards him. His immediate impression in the apartment appeared correct: it was very much an appointments record. Predictably Ann Harris wrote in precise, complete legible handwriting. Thursdays seemed to be the day for conferences, the participants unlisted. Someone called Paul featured frequently, sometimes on conference days. Most of the

American national holidays were noted with embassy receptions. The birthdays of her parents, Burden and Judy Billington were also entered.

And the dates of Tuesdays were often circled, although apart from an occasional embassy notation it seemed to be a day in Ann Harris's schedule that was usually free. A sharp awareness came to Danilov and he concentrated more intently: it had been Tuesday – or to be strictly accurate the night of Tuesday, running over into Wednesday morning – that she had been murdered. He went back to the beginning of the year and counted, lips moving. Every Tuesday – except for three consecutive Tuesdays, all in January – was picked out with a circle. Another awareness registered and although he was sure, confident of his retentive memory, Danilov went sideways to the Suzlev file. It only took him minutes to confirm that the taxi driver had died on a Tuesday. The Russian wrote the two names, separated by the word Tuesday, and made another of his looped chains. The diary followed the letters into the evidence container.

It was a crowded address book, obviously a continuation of a contact register begun in the United States: it was frequently easy with a naked eye to see the different ink colours – the American faded, the Moscow heavier, more recent – between entries on the same page. Danilov's immediate concerns were the obvious Moscow numbers. Under E, the main embassy exchange (252–00–11) headed the listing, beneath which was a lengthy series of separate direct-dial numbers, according to the Moscow telephone system. The British and French embassies were also noted. There were reminders of the Bolshoi, Kirov and Pushkin theatres, the numbers of Sheremet'yevo airport and the in-town air terminals. The National and the Ukraina Hotels were also included. Having found the obvious, the diligent Danilov went back to the beginning of the book, searching not the written-down names of the addressees but to the right of each name, for the three-by-two-by-two sequence that would tell him they were Moscow numbers. He found a listing for someone called Hughes, whose initial was P. There was a Janet (Edwards) and a Pam (Donnelly).

A functional, efficient aid, judged Danilov: but then what had he expected? The address book went into the evidence box, leav-

71

ing him with the notes bundled together, without envelopes. Further aids, he recognized, as he unpeeled the elastic band: scribbled reminders and telephone message slips, some already printed with lines set out to show who the call had come from, the date, the time, their number and whether it was required to call back. Often the spaces had not been completed.

The majority of the slips served as an addition to the already studied diary, appointment reminders or conference queries: he even retrieved the diary for a date-by-date comparison and confirmed the connection for five entries.

And then he came upon the discovery.

It was in handwriting he knew was not Ann Harris's, on a piece of white paper completely blank apart from the written words, which were in English. The one he came upon first said *I didn't mean to hurt.* There was no date but the paper was dogeared where it had been enclosed in the elastic band and was discoloured, as if it had been retained for some time. The second note, again on unmarked paper, apart from the message, contained just three words: *Please like it.* The third was the last in the pile. Only one word: *Call.* On this one there was a date, three days before Ann Harris's murder. Prompted by the date, Danilov went back to the beginning of the pile. A lot of the messages and reminders were undated but those that had been were in chronological order and Danilov thought it safe to presume she had preserved them in the sequence in which they had come. He fixed the three pieces of paper in a clip, separate from the other notes, as he had the correspondence he believed might help. He was putting the notes back into the evidence folder when Pavin came into the room. He was carrying a large envelope and a notebook.

'We really do have influence and special privileges,' announced the burly Major. He was smiling, self-satisfied.

'Just *how* much?' queried Danilov.

'I put in a request for additional men: I wasn't happy with what we had for the amount of checks that have to be made at the psychiatric places. We've been allocated another squad of ten. I got a car, a Volga, without the slightest obstruction. And it's new: only six months old. No police markings, although there's a telephone. I was even asked if we wanted a driver. I said no.'

Danilov guessed the newness was for any further visit to the American embassy to be in a presentable vehicle: most police cars – certainly the unofficial ones – were battered by careless use. 'No time limit?'

'None. And we've been allowed a place of our own for evidence: the old interview room at the end of the corridor!'

'I want it posted off-bounds, throughout the building: I don't want people wandering in and out. Try if you can to get all the keys. I don't want any cleaning staff in there, either.'

Instinctively Pavin began making reminder notes to himself. 'What are we going to need in there?'

'Display facilities. Blackboards, pinboards, benches. And I want as good a street map as possible of Moscow . . .'

'Street map!' interrupted Pavin. Street maps, like Moscow telephone directories, were practically unobtainable, even officially.

'We definitely need a map,' insisted Danilov, aware of the difficulty. 'What about forensic?'

'The empty slot in the knife rack is twenty-four centimetres deep, straight-sided, no tapering at the bottom. It is six centimetres across and five and a half millimetres thick.'

'So the knife that killed Vladimir Suzlev *and* Ann Harris would have fitted?'

'Four of the other slots – those that held knives of different lengths and thicknesses – were exactly the same size as the empty one,' Pavin pointed out. 'Forensic say these things are mass produced by machine in America.'

Danilov retrieved the three handwritten notes he had just read. 'Get forensic to check the manufacture of the paper and the ink.'

'What does the writing say?'

'It's about pain,' said Danilov, shortly.

Pavin offered the manila envelope and declared: 'A gift from the Cheka.'

There were two photographs of Ann Harris. Both were sharply in focus and had obviously been officially taken at diplomatic functions. She *had* been pretty, Danilov acknowledged: beautiful even. In one shot the dark hair that had been so savagely shorn from her hung almost to her shoulders: in the other it was swept up into a sophisticated chignon. She was smiling in both – openly laughing in the loose-haired portrait – and her teeth were flawless.

The chignon photograph was fuller than the other. The dress hugged her figure, outlining her breasts: Danilov wondered if she was holding herself to accentuate their heaviness. At once he checked himself, for allowing the impression. He shouldn't be influenced by the revealing correspondence he had just read into making surmises like that. In the second photograph the camera had caught her with her hand resting on the arm of a snow-haired, patrician-featured man. He had not been looking at Ann Harris, however, but at an older, less attractive woman on his other side. Danilov reversed both. There were no names, to identify anyone.

Danilov looked back up to his assistant. 'What about phone calls?'

'Nothing.'

'Have you tried direct, using Militia authority?'

Pavin nodded. 'The supervisor said dialled calls weren't recorded, by specific numbers. Only those connected by an operator. Or if someone asks for operator assistance, because of dialling problems.'

'Get back to . . .' began Danilov but stopped. With the inflated ego of a Lieutenant-Colonel, Gugin probably wouldn't even take a telephone call from as lowly a figure as Yuri Mikhailovich Pavin, a mere Major. He'd have to do it himself: maybe Gugin would refuse to talk to him, too.

'Yes?' queried the assistant.

'Nothing. Have you got the evidence list?'

'With a copy for the Americans,' Pavin confirmed. 'And Novikov called. He wanted to know if you needed his written report sent or whether we would collect it. I said we'd collect it.'

Reminded of the appointment, Danilov stood, shrugging into his coat. Today he remembered to bring a hat: he carefully smoothed his crewcut, which was showing a tendency to regrow spikily, before putting it on as they walked down the corridor. He said: 'It's only five days until another Tuesday.'

Pavin frowned sideways. 'What's that mean?'

'Nothing, I hope.'

There was nothing that could not have been discussed in minutes by telephone but Burden insisted on a personal meeting, so the

74

politically conscious Secretary of State agreed. He announced at once that the FBI had a man on standby.

'What's his name? Is he good? I want the best. I'll need to speak to him before he goes, of course.'

Hartz smothered the sigh. 'I didn't get a name. Obviously the Director thinks he's the best. He'd hardly send a second-team player, would he?'

Burden frowned, as if suspecting impatience. 'I'm going to call the ambassador in Moscow again. The child's got to be brought back from there, for a Christian burial . . .' He paused and then, fervently, said: 'The bastards!'

'I've already cabled the embassy, asking for an early release and return here,' said the Secretary of State, glad he had done so in advance of the demand.

'When the hell are you going to stop asking and start telling?'

'When I think it will achieve some worthwhile purpose,' said Hartz, curtly. He knew he would never be Secretary of State under this man.

There were round-the-clock demands on every possible Russian ministry from every possible media outlet with staff representation in Moscow. That was multiplied by some organizations, European as well as American, assigning correspondents to Moscow specifically to cover the murder of Ann Harris. Russian embassies throughout the West, not just in Washington, DC, were inundated. There was another responsibility-avoiding conference at the Foreign Ministry. There it was reaffirmed that the Federal Prosecutor, the man who would present an eventual charge against the murderer, should be the news source. This time, however, Nikolai Smolin successfully argued that the Militia chief, whose office would provide the convicting evidence, should share the burden.

'There will have to be a press conference,' said Smolin.

'Not yet,' cautioned the coughing Lapinsk. 'There's nothing to tell anyone.' He took a pill to subdue the turmoil in his stomach.

Chapter Nine

The pathologist's office, two-windowed and spacious compared to Danilov's hutch, was neater than Danilov could recall from any previous, hostile visit and he recognized at once the obvious preparation. We're all anxious to impress America, he thought: or avoid offence, at least. Was he personally anxious? It would be important, however this unfolded, not to let that dismissive nonsense at the American embassy bother him: he'd won the exchange, after all, belatedly revealing his understanding of the language.

Viktor Novikov wore a subdued check suit and an attempted air of neither an inferior awe nor patronizing superiority at the prospect of an American presence. The effort was too much either way and the man's demeanour see-sawed awkwardly from one attitude to the other, like the uncertain light on Danilov's desk.

Danilov was courteously a few minutes ahead of the scheduled appointment. Novikov hovered around the half-circle of chairs, further obvious preparation, so he was ready when the Americans arrived, opening the door for them expansively.

The man accompanying Ralph Baxter was the patrician-featured diplomat in the second photograph Danilov had seen that morning, the person upon whose arm Ann Harris's hand had been lightly resting. The hair *was* pure white, combed forward Roman statesman fashion, to hide the fact that it was receding, the face beak-nosed and close to being unnaturally grey, putty-coloured. The man wore a black suit and a completely black tie: a dead man mourning the dead.

Danilov waited, expectantly. It was not until Novikov said: '*Pazhalsta*' – which in the circumstances was a clumsy welcome – that the pathologist realized a difficulty for which he had not prepared.

'I'll translate,' Danilov offered, first in Russian, then in English. At least, he thought, I'm achieving that long ago ambition.

Baxter nodded acceptance, without speaking. Novikov's face

darkened. Danilov wondered why he had to bother with all this: it was practically a hindrance in trying to catch a mentally deranged killer. Determined on names this time, Danilov thrust out a hand, forcing the unknown American to accept the gesture and by so doing to identify himself. The reluctant hand was soft and moist. The man said: 'Paul Hughes, senior economist at the embassy.' He paused before adding: 'Ann worked in my department.'

An address-book name to which to put a face, thought Danilov. He politely completed the introduction to Novikov and took over the pathologist's role, offering them seats.

'We don't expect this to take long,' said Baxter, as if he were already late for something else.

'A necessary formality,' insisted Danilov.

As Danilov translated the exchange for Novikov's benefit, the diplomat said, in Russian: 'I understand the language.'

In English Danilov said: 'I know. But there won't be the unfortunate misunderstanding there was yesterday.'

Baxter's face blazed and the economist looked curiously between the two of them. The ill-feeling came down like a lowered curtain.

'What is this?' queried Hughes. He had a clipped way of speaking, shortening the end of his words.

'Nothing important,' Baxter dismissed. Returning the other American's look he said, expectantly: 'Shouldn't we get on?'

Hughes took the cue. From his briefcase he extracted a batch of legally bundled documents, secured with pink tape, and extended them towards Danilov. The Russian made no attempt to accept them. Hughes said: 'These are legal demands for the return to American custody of the body of Ann Harris, the opening and return to American jurisdiction of Ann Harris's apartment at Ulitza Pushkinskaya 397, and a return to American custody of each and every article taken by the Russian authorities from that apartment.'

Danilov remained with his hands beside him, taking his time to repeat to Novikov what the American had said: towards the end, imagining trouble for Danilov, the pathologist's face relaxed just short of a smile. To the white-haired man Danilov said: 'Legal demands under whose law? American or Russian? I am unfamiliar with any Russian legislation that would be open to you.' This was another hindering distraction. He wouldn't let himself become involved.

Now it was Hughes who coloured, although not so fully as Baxter. So whey-faced was the man, however, that the effect was more marked, two patches of bright red on either cheek like rouge badly applied. The man said: 'I would suggest you accept these writs. My authority is as Ann Harris's superior: head of the section.'

'And I would suggest you present them to the appropriate legal department of the appropriate Russian ministry,' replied Danilov. 'This isn't a matter for me.' He thought men with flamboyant face whiskers that wobbled as Baxter's did shouldn't get angry.

Baxter swung sideways to his embassy colleague and said: 'I told you . . .' before jerking to a stop.

'Identical demands have today been served upon both your Foreign and Interior Ministries,' said Hughes. The man's anger made the threat sound slightly too artificial.

'Then there is no need whatsoever for me to have copies, is there?' said Danilov, in further rejection. He hesitated, then said: 'Although I appreciate your courtesy, in making it available to me . . .' There was another pause, while he went to his briefcase. '. . . In return for which I need to give you this. It is the complete list of every article and possible piece of evidence removed from Ulitza Pushkinskaya . . .' He thrust it towards Baxter, who regarded the list uncertainly, then took it. More rapidly than before, Danilov relayed the complete exchange to the pathologist. 'You prepared a duplicate of your examination, I hope?'

Novikov was aware of the tension in the room, but despite the complete explanation did not fully understand what it was about. He said: 'Yes . . . I . . . of course. It's here . . . fingerprints I promised, too . . .' and took several sheets of paper from a folder on his desk.

Danilov reached forward and the pathologist dutifully handed it over. It was not until Danilov was passing it on to the Americans that Novikov realized the policeman had taken from him the opportunity he considered rightfully his. He'd even rehearsed a brief explanation.

Baxter took the offered document. Unthinkingly he began to open it, as if it had to be studied and questioned. Beside him

Hughes pulled back the hand holding the legal demands. Baxter said: 'I will report this obstruction, to the ambassador.'

'Then please report it accurately,' said Danilov. 'In no way and at no time are you being obstructed.'

'Are you going to release the apartment and the items taken from it?' demanded Hughes. Without seeking approval from the man whose office it was, he fumbled to light a cigarette, a strong-smelling French Gitane.

'When I am ordered to do so by my superiors,' said Danilov.

'You will be,' said Baxter, positively.

'We're here for a purpose,' said Danilov, briskly, not wanting another trouble-making argument. 'Let's get it over.'

Novikov led along the corridor but stood back, herding them into the elevator ahead of him. They descended unspeaking. The muscles stood out on Baxter's cheeks, where he was clenching his jaws in determination. Hughes's grey face had a sheen of perspiration.

Danilov detected the smell before they reached the examination room. When Novikov paused at the door, Hughes said: 'I don't have to make the actual identification. I'll wait out here.'

Baxter frowned at his colleague, denied support, but said nothing. He nodded his readiness to the two Russians. Novikov led again; Danilov was the last to go into the room. The formaldehyde and disinfectant stench was as strong as before, but Danilov was not as upset this time. At their entry an assistant withdrew the coffin-sized drawer from the refrigerated bank in a wall to the left: there were puffs of whiteness from the freezing air inside colliding with the warmer, outside atmosphere. Novikov was careful to pull back the covering only to expose Ann Harris's face and shorn scalp. The face was grey, like the American economist's in the corridor outside: the death snarl had almost completely melted away.

'Oh dear God!' said Baxter, his familiar phrase. He swayed and then retched, so badly that Danilov thought the man was going to vomit. He put a handkerchief to his mouth, coughed, and then wiped his eyes. He said: 'I'm sorry.'

'Is this the body of Ann Harris?' demanded Danilov, formally.

'Of course it is,' said Baxter. 'Oh my God! Poor Ann.' Wet-eyed he looked to Danilov for guidance. 'What must I do now?'

'Nothing. That's all,' said Danilov. He stopped just short of taking the man's arm, gesturing him instead towards the door. Immediately outside Baxter leaned back against the wall, ignoring Hughes for several minutes. Once he almost retched again, at the last minute turning the distress into a cough, behind his bunched-up handkerchief. Hughes was smoking a fresh cigarette.

'Awful,' said Baxter, talking to no one. 'It was awful.'

Denied translation for a long time, Novikov said: 'What's the matter?'

'He's not accustomed to dead bodies of people he knows,' said Danilov. 'Few are.'

Baxter remained indifferent to an exchange in Russian, still slumped against the wall.

'Are there any other formalities?' demanded the economist.

'No,' said Danilov.

'Let's go,' said Hughes, taking control of the other American. Baxter obediently fell into step as the Russians saw them to the elevator. The exit was just one floor up. There was uncertainty at the door: Hughes made as if to offer his hand but then quickly withdrew it. Baxter, making a conscious effort to recover, said in a strained voice: 'We expect to be hearing from you, very shortly.'

'Thank you for coming,' said Danilov, refusing to rekindle the dispute.

The two Russians watched the other men go towards their embassy car, parked at the kerb with the driver holding the door open. Novikov said: 'I didn't need to speak the language to understand. You've upset them, haven't you? They're annoyed!'

'Let's hope your post-mortem report is comprehensive enough not to upset them further,' said Danilov, irritated by the other man.

The permanently assigned police car was outside, about twenty yards behind where the American vehicle had been. Pavin had remained at the wheel. Danilov opened the passenger door but didn't get in, leaning through instead. 'Go back without me,' he said. 'I'll be there in a couple of hours.' He could get to the Druzhba Hotel just about the time Larissa finished her shift.

'You'd better come with me,' said Pavin, nodding towards the car phone. 'Lapinsk called. He wants to see you at once. Says it's urgent.'

Just short of the Militia building Danilov pointed to a street kiosk and said: 'Stop there. I need to phone.'

Pavin halted, not needing to ask why Danilov didn't use the car telephone. Calls from the car were recorded and logged.

The Director was taking a stomach pill as Danilov entered. There was a staccato of nervous coughing as Danilov went further into the room. 'There've been more complaints. Official demands for the release of the body and what you took from the flat.'

'I know. They wanted to serve papers on me at the mortuary: I refused to accept.'

Lapinsk got up from his desk, going to the window to keep his back to the other man. 'People are beginning to question if you should be allowed to remain on the case.'

'I don't think there has been any mistake so far in the investigation.' At the very moment of speaking Danilov was abruptly seized by the impression that he *had* missed something that was very important. It was an unsettling, unnerving thought.

'I think you've made enough personal protest, for whatever happened at the embassy. Your independence now is becoming idiotic.' Lapinsk turned back into the room, to look directly at Danilov.

'I don't want to continue any antagonism,' insisted Danilov. Nor bow to it, from the Americans, he thought.

'Is there any good reason for not releasing the body?'

'I only got Novikov's full report an hour ago. I haven't had time to study it.'

'The body could be released, once you're satisfied with the report?'

Danilov decided that the man who had always supported him was anxious for concessions. 'I suppose so.'

Lapinsk returned to his desk, with the slow walk of a tired man. 'What about the stuff you took from the flat?'

'I've provided a full list. It's too early yet for me to know what I may or may not want.'

'Why does the apartment have to remain sealed?'

81

'I might want to examine it again. Something might come up from what I've already got. Or from the forensic report.'

Lapinsk released a breath, loudly. 'Why the hell did you go barging in there in the first place?'

'I wouldn't have got in at all, any other way.'

'I almost wish you hadn't. It hasn't achieved anything, has it?'

'I don't know, not yet.' Or did he? He'd learned a lot about Ann Harris and was intrigued by a situation which apparently involved pain. And there was the coincidence – which was as high as he was putting it, enticing though it was to invest it with more importance – of a missing kitchen knife. But realistically he had to acknowledge he had found nothing to help him discover a killer. The only surmise he would allow at the moment was that the killer of Ann Harris and Vladimir Suzlev was the same person.

Lapinsk sighed again. 'The Americans are insisting upon a progress report. There's no progress *to* report, is there?'

'It's fatuous to expect it so soon,' said Danilov, defensively.

'What leads?'

'None.' It sounded pitifully inadequate: there was every reason for irritation and impatience, from everyone.

'What's the possibility of something emerging soon?' demanded Lapinsk, the anxiety becoming desperation.

'None,' conceded the investigator again.

'It's not very good, is it? Or encouraging?'

'No.'

Lapinsk sat examining him over a scrupulously clean desk for several moments, as if making a decision. Finally he uttered his bark-bark cough and said: 'There are to be some changes.'

So he *was* being removed. Danilov supposed it was inevitable after the American animosity and the absolute failure of any development, however unreal that expectation might have been. He still felt resentment. It was taking away the support for his fragile integrity, and the inner pride which that integrity had in turn provided. Not once since his untarnished, totally uncompromised transfer to Petrovka headquarters had he been taken off an inquiry. Some – although not many – had never been concluded. Others couldn't ever be solved, because the criminal proved cleverer than he had been: blows to his pride, although rarely admitted. Whatever, he'd adjusted. So why was this bizarre, inexplicable case, file number M-for-Moscow 175, any different?

Danilov, near to personal embarrassment, confronted the fact that this time it was more than integrity or pride. Maybe the reverse side of both. He'd *wanted* this case: *ached* for the chance thrust upon him. From those very first initial minutes in the wind-swept alley off Ulitza Gercena, Danilov had realized the opportunity. This could have been *it*. This could have been his unchallenged pathway to succeed Lapinsk: to earn the promotion and salary (with the official car!) and the interrupted privileges. But he'd pushed too hard: offended too many people in his anxiety, because he'd *wanted* too much. But still in proportion: material benefits, maybe, but the ambition had overwhelmingly been professional.

Who would take over? Kanayev was the most likely successor, next in seniority: three failed fraud cases in the previous two years and Kanayev drove a gleaming new Volga. Petrukhin was another possibility, although two recent prosecutions had failed through casual evidence assembly, which was suspicious, although it probably wouldn't affect any selection. Zabotin was an outsider: too eagerly impetuous but he'd won his cases and he didn't even own a car. It didn't really matter whoever it was: he'd help as much as he could whichever man was selected. Not that there was a lot to contribute: hardly anything, as he'd already admitted. At least he could spare them the routine of initial evidence assembly. He'd spend a day – perhaps two – handing over what he'd got, careful to avoid passing on his own possibly misleading impressions or guesses or even preconceptions. He smiled, trying to keep the obvious regret from the expression, and said: 'Who?'

Lapinsk's face went beyond a frown, into a grimace. 'Who?'

'Is being assigned to take over?'

The coughs came, like an engine reluctant to start. 'There is to be no reassignment. You are to remain the investigator. But we have had to make political concessions. The decision has been taken, beyond the Foreign Ministry, to accept the American offer of technical and scientific assistance.'

Danilov sat absolutely unmoving, trying to understand. There had to be more. 'What else, beyond technical and scientific help?'

'The American FBI have suggested a liaison officer.'

'It becomes a joint Russian and American investigation?' He hadn't lost it! But what fresh dangers were being imposed upon him?

'It's judged necessary, politically,' Lapinsk insisted. 'And it's to our advantage.'

'The entire responsibility is no longer ours?' anticipated Danilov.

'Exactly!'

Neither would a successful conviction be entirely his, either. Another balance was quick to settle. Nor would a dismal failure. There was very definitely an advantage, political or otherwise. 'How is this liaison going to work?'

Once again Lapinsk stared intently across the intervening desk, using the silence to make a point. '*Absolutely*,' the Director insisted. 'I want the attitudes of the past, whatever the causes, forgotten. I am *ordering* you – because I have been ordered myself to see that it happens – to cooperate completely. Everything shared: nothing withheld.'

'Which includes Suzlev?'

'Of course it includes Suzlev.'

'Nothing like this has ever happened before,' said Danilov, more to himself than the other man.

'Never,' agreed Lapinsk. 'A successful investigation will be the most visible example yet of the bond between ourselves and the United States of America.'

Danilov was momentarily silenced by the brutal cynicism. Ann Harris was no longer a pretty girl made ugly, the victim of a maniac. She'd become a political pawn, to be shifted around an international chessboard: roll up, roll up, here's Ann Harris, snarling-in-death example of Russian/American cooperation. He said: 'Yes.' It was all he could manage for the moment.

'It's our protection,' insisted the nervously coughing man. 'I never thought we'd be this lucky.'

'Yes,' repeated Danilov. Stirring himself, he said: 'Do we have a name: know who the liaison is going to be?'

'Not yet. Just that he's coming from Washington.'

Danilov fully recognized, belatedly, that he has survived. And still had the opportunity to gain all the professional benefits and advantages he'd hoped to achieve. *If* the investigation trapped a killer. 'I'll do nothing to create problems,' he assured his superior. He probably wouldn't get a further chance.

'One more problem,' warned Lapinsk, in immediate confirmation of the unspoken thought. 'That's all it will take. One more mistake and it will be taken away from you. Everything. You might be allowed to remain in the department but effectively your career will be over. I won't protect you any more: couldn't risk protecting you any more.'

Danilov decided he was a prepared and trussed sacrifice for any future difficulty or disaster. His mind stayed with one word – *trussed* – momentarily unable to recall where he had encountered it recently. And then he remembered. It had been the word used by Ann Harris's economist friend in Washington, to describe what it was like to be the victim of bondage. Danilov decided he didn't feel quite that helpless, not yet. Close, though.

Larissa was annoyed and determined to show it, irritably shrugging off his first attempt to kiss her, slumping in the narrow hotel room chair that enclosed her like a protective cast so that the only way he could make any effective contact was to kneel at her feet, which he guessed was what she wanted. When he stretched up to kiss her from the ungainly kneeling position she again turned her head away from him.

'I got here as soon as I could.' He should really have gone back to his office to study the pathologist's report. He hoped it would not be incomplete, forcing further contact with the childishly obstructive man.

'I felt like a whore, hanging around the lobby!'

She would have been in competition with a few other genuine professionals: Danilov had positively isolated three in the reception area, fifteen minutes earlier. 'I've said I'm sorry. I warned you it was going to be a problem for me, these next few weeks.'

She smiled down at him, with feigned reluctance, the beginning of forgiveness. 'It's cut down the time we've got together: they want the room back in an hour.'

Two other hotel receptionists as well as Larissa were involved in affairs and had evolved the system for assignations in a city where there was no such thing as casual accommodation. One used a room awaiting occupation while the others ensured there was no interruption or premature registration by a genuine guest. With Novikov's material to digest Danilov was glad there was a short time limit. He wondered, idly, who the *bona fide* occupants would be in an hour's time. And what their reaction would have been to knowing what the room had been used for, immediately prior. Larissa allowed herself to be kissed properly at last, twisting in the chair to put her arms around his neck to pull him to her. His knees were beginning to hurt.

'I've missed you,' she said.

'I've missed you, too.'

'How's Olga?'

He shrugged. 'Like she always is.' Larissa wasn't neglected and untidy, like his wife. The receptionist's suit was still crisp, with no stains anywhere, and the white shirt didn't look as if it had been worn all day. She smelt fresh and perfumed and Danilov guessed she had prepared herself for him: her soft red lipstick was fresh and the eye-line was newly applied. On impulse he took one of her hands. The varnish matched the lipstick. He took off one of her shoes. Her toe-nails were painted, too, a slightly harsher colour than Ann Harris had used.

'What are you doing?' she frowned, artificially.

'Nothing.' He stayed with her foot cupped in his hand. What reason – what fetish – made the killer put the shoes neatly beside the shorn head?

'I hate Yevgennie!' she announced, with sudden vehemence. 'I can't bear him touching me any more.'

'Does he touch you?' Danilov felt a vague stir of jealousy, which was ridiculously hypocritical. Yevgennie was her husband: he had the right.

'Sometimes. He wanted to last night but he was too drunk.' She came forward on the chair, parting her legs around him as much as the tight skirt would allow. 'He was boasting about knowing the Dolgoprudnaya, trying to impress me.'

Organized crime was an unadmitted development of *perestroika*: the Dolgoprudnaya was the most powerful group, openly referred to as the Mafia family controlling northwest Moscow. There had been nothing like it in Danilov's Militia days. 'Your husband's a greedy fool.'

'You could officially report him, if you wanted to.'

'I don't want to.' Danilov had introduced Kosov to all his grateful black economy contacts before passing over control of the Militia district: it was the way the system worked. Eduard Agayans, the ebullient Armenian, had been the first. They'd drunk the brandy, as they always did. Agayans had winked and told everyone not to worry: he'd look after the newcomer. Kosov had smiled back, telling Agayans not to worry, either: that he'd continue the care he knew Danilov had shown in the past.

'Why not?'

'Don't be silly, Larissa. You know why not.'

'You could never be incriminated, not after all this time.'

Danilov couldn't remember telling her of his activities: he guessed her husband had. He said: 'Nothing would happen: he'd pay off the investigation.' It was a valid objection; there were probably more corrupt than honest policemen in Moscow.

Larissa eased fully off the chair but stood very close to where he knelt, undressing for his enjoyment. 'It would be so much better for us, if Yevgennie weren't around.'

'I don't want to talk about Yevgennie,' said Danilov, thickly. Larissa was naked, her black wedge only inches from his face. She'd oiled herself there, planning what she wanted him to do.

'So much better,' she repeated, thrusting the scented feast for him to eat, which he did. It was good, which sex always was with Larissa. She made love with complete abandon and in every way, with no inhibitions, anxious to exchange every pleasure, arching beneath him when she finally climaxed in time with him. Danilov grimaced at the pain of her nails driving into his back, fearing she had marked him. He'd have to be careful, later. Danilov moved off her, propping himself on his side. Her look-at-me breasts sprouted proudly upright, demanding approval. Seeing him look Larissa said: 'They're yours.'

Danilov kissed both nipples. 'We have to go, soon.'

'Your fault for being late that we can't do it again.'

Danilov wasn't sure he could have done it again. Her hair, long and richly brown, was disordered on the pillow, framing her face. Abruptly remembering where she lived, he said: 'How will you get home?'

Larissa frowned. 'Walk, of course. I always do.'

It would mean her passing completely through the area where Vladimir Suzlev and Ann Harris had been murdered. 'Don't,' he urged. 'Take the bus. Or the metro. A taxi, even.'

The woman brought herself up on her arm, to face him. 'The buses and the metro will be crowded.'

'The murder I'm working on. It's bad. Quite near your area.'

She became serious. 'You mean I should be especially careful?'

'That's exactly what I'm telling you.'

'Shouldn't there be a warning, in the newspapers or something?'

Maybe he should discuss the matter of a public alert with Lapinsk. 'Just be careful.'

'You are going to catch him soon, aren't you?' demanded Larissa, smiling uncertainly. 'He's not going to get away? Roam the streets?'

At the moment that was probably what he was doing, thought Danilov: roaming the streets, seeking another victim. 'I'm going to catch him.' It was a personal promise.

'I'll take a bus,' she decided. Quickly, her mind butterflying, she said: 'When we were at the cinema Olga suggested we all get together soon. Said we hadn't done it for a long time.'

This was how the affair with Larissa had grown: two Militia colleagues introducing their wives, dinners reciprocated in each other's apartment, bribery-equipped flat compared to bribery-equipped flat, bored Larissa flirting, he first surprised, then flattered. 'What did you say?'

'That it would be nice. It would, wouldn't it?'

'Yes,' said Danilov. He wasn't sure that it would be.

'I should clean your room.' Valentina Yezhov was a big-bodied, domineering woman who had convinced herself her husband had deserted them through his shame at fathering a mentally disturbed son, which was not true. The man had come to detest her, during the marriage.

'I've cleaned it myself. It's all right.'

'What have you got in there?' she asked suspiciously.

'Nothing,' insisted Yezhov.

'Why can't I go in?'

'I don't want you to.' In the hospitals nothing had been private, the nurses and the guards opening everything, poking into everything, as the fancy took them.

'What do you *do*, when you go walking at night?'

'Just walk.'

'I don't want any more trouble.'

'I'm better.'

She'd been foolish, not getting a duplicate of his bedroom key before giving it to him. 'I'd just clean. I wouldn't pry.'

'It's all right.'

'Please don't do anything silly again.' The little-girl plea sounded odd, from such a big person.

'I said I'm better!'

Chapter Ten

Danilov recognized this as continuing the familiar part of an investigation: the part where there was still so much to read and so much to assimilate but from which, hopefully, an inconsistency would suddenly flare up to illuminate a pathway, a brief light in the dark tunnel. At the moment he still felt enclosed in blackness.

Already waiting for him when he got back to his office were the promised forensic findings and a sealed envelope upon which Pavin had written Telephone Log. There were additional notes from his assistant, reporting that the evidence room had been equipped as requested, all the evidence containers deposited there and every known room key in the building surrendered, to prevent unauthorized entry. The cleaners had also been warned off.

To the line of documents already set out on the desk Danilov added the pathology report and sat for several moments staring down at it all, unsure where to begin. And then didn't begin at all, not immediately. Olga responded on the third ring. He said he still had a lot to do and would be late. There was some bortsch she would leave on the stove, for him to heat if she was already in bed. He said he wasn't hungry but agreed he might be, later. There had been a letter from the supplier, confirming their order for the Jiguli was still on record but there was not yet any date for the car's delivery. The washing machine in the basement was repaired but two other women in the block were ahead of her: she wasn't sure if she'd get the shirts done that night, but she was going to try. The film she had seen the previous night with Elena and Larissa had been good. Danilov said he was glad. The union restaurant afterwards had been good, too: she'd have to take him there sometime. Danilov said he'd like that.

'Got the murderer yet?' The interest in Olga's voice was about the same as her intonation when she'd discussed the soup she'd leave on the stove for when he got home.

'Not yet.'

'The taxi was expensive last night: nearly six roubles.'

'I'm still glad you took it.'

'If you used some influence like you did in the district we'd have our own car. Look how easy things seem to be for Yevgennie and Larissa. I've arranged an evening with them, by the way.'

'I . . .' started Danilov, unthinking. 'Fine,' he concluded.

'At their flat. Not here.'

'If you don't want to do it, say so!'

'I want to do it.'

'I probably *will* be asleep when you get home.'

The pathology account first, he decided: the Americans held a copy, so it was the likeliest source of immediate discussion. He had to be prepared. Danilov's instant impression was that Novikov had rewritten and redrawn the entire report, after the warning the previous day of the victim's identity. The presentation was faultless, with none of the written-over mistypings with which Novikov was normally prepared to let his documents be distributed. There were margin sub-headings, too, another innovation.

Danilov was particularly careful to check the details of the wound against Novikov's verbal account, convinced the man would have checked every note and supposition after learning of the American involvement. The depth of the wound was now given as nineteen and a quarter centimetres and the thickness wad qualified as just under five millimetres at the back of the knife but with minimal evidence of sideways cutting at the other edge, indicating extreme, easily entering sharpness. So as well as being sharply pointed the blade had been honed, as well. There was an abrupt change of opinion, needing another reminder pad notation, about the direction of the entry wound. During their conversation, Novikov had said the knife had entered in a *slightly* upwards trajectory. Now he stated categorically that having entered between the eighth and ninth rib, the wound graduated upwards to be a whole centimetre higher at the point of contact with the heart from the place of entry into the body. Danilov broke away, scribbling on his pad, noting beside it that Ann Harris had been one point six five metres tall and writing 'killer height?' and encircling it.

Danilov felt a jump of irritation, reading on, at something Novikov had not told him the previous day. Then just as quickly refused the annoyance: without the intriguing references in the correspondence that only he had read, the significance would not have been obvious to the pathologist. Novikov had found contusions to both breasts, the more severe to the right, near the nipple, where the skin had been broken. The man judged the bruise to the right breast consistent with a bite. There was further contusion, to the right hip, again with evidence of teeth marks. None of the marks showed post-mortem lividity but were recent, within hours. What were bite marks to the breast if not sexual assault? thought Danilov. As quickly as before he stopped the criticism. His question to the man, the previous day, had concerned sexual assault at the scene. If the bruising had occurred before death, then it probably happened in the apartment on Ulitza Pushkinskaya, during the lovemaking which had left the woman with a semen deposit in the vagina. Novikov had found additional contusions to both nostrils and to the central nose cartilage, extending for six millimetres on to the upper lip. There was also a small laceration inside the upper lip. Danilov added the new information to his pad, with the reminder to check the autopsy report on the first victim, wondering how much of the injury would have been visible if he had brought himself properly to look at Ann Harris's body.

Shortly before her death, Novikov estimated not more than four hours, Ann Harris had eaten a meal. The stomach contents disclosed undigested pork and some apple and grape skin. There was also the presence of acetic acid, consistent with the consumption of wine, in addition to the traces of stronger alcohol, which Danilov took to be the vodka which he knew the girl and her companion had drunk in her flat.

The kitchen at Ulitza Pushkinskaya had been clean, with no indication of any food preparation or cleaning. So where had Ann Harris eaten? And drunk wine? And with whom?

There was another apparent omission when Danilov turned the page, and this time he allowed the anger. He distinctly remembered Novikov saying there was no sign of Ann Harris having fought her killer. *Death was practically instantaneous*, the man had said. Yet here he had recorded that two nails – on the index and middle finger of her left hand – had been broken. Danilov searched hurriedly but unsuccessfully through the next five or six lines, seeking a measure of how long the woman's nails had been, and then sat back reflectively. Had she fought after all, despite Novikov's insistence to the contrary? If she had, sufficiently strongly to break two nails, the possibility was that the killer would be marked, scratched on the face or hands or possibly both. The inconsistency registered immediately. If she had scratched her killer there would have been scrapings of skin or blood or hair from beneath her nails. And he'd specifically asked about that. *Nothing*, Novikov had said.

Danilov scribbled another reminder to himself before thrusting the report to one side, turning to the forensic account.

There had been two obviously different sets of fingerprints and a small number of indeterminate smudges which were older, from the evidence of surface particle cover. The ridges of Harris's fingerprints had been whorled. The second set had registered lateral pocket loops. Danilov at once isolated a peculiarity about the second, unidentified prints. Around the empty vodka glass in the living-room there had been a complete set of a right hand and two further full markings of both left and right, one on top of the dressing-table in the bedroom and the third on the sink surround in the bathroom, as if the person had leaned forward on outstretched, supporting hands. Yet they were *not* complete. Recorded against each was the fact that the index finger on the right only half registered. On what would have been the little finger of the same hand the print was marred by a tiny triangular patch, clean of any loops, which was labelled as scar tissue. Nowhere else in the apartment, where single prints had been located, had the index finger been found complete. The only prints on the vodka bottle belonged to Ann Harris.

Comparative analysis had matched some head and pubic hair recovered from the bedsheet as that of the girl herself but there were also samples from someone else. There had been minimal semen staining, from which a B Rhesus Negative blood grouping had been identified. There was separate staining by spermicidal chemicals forming part of the formula of the contraceptive pessaries recovered from the bedside drawer. Microscopic examination of the bottom sheet, near where a pillow would have been, had revealed a small patch of blood. It was B Positive, the same group as the dead woman. The pillow on the left of the bed was marked, again so minimally that it only showed under a microscope, with traces of anhydrous lanolin and white paraffin. Both were common in skin-care cream or skin cleansers.

Samples of wool, rayon, polyester and silk fibres had been collected throughout the apartment. All the dyes were American. No fibres identifiably Russian had been recovered at all.

Initially disappointed, Danilov put the forensic report alongside that of the pathologist. He'd hoped for something more, without knowing precisely what it might or could have been. So what *did* he have? Largely confirmation of things he already knew, apart from the oddness of the unidentified fingerprint. It was the only item from the report he'd singled out for separate notation.

He sat quite alone in the empty, mostly darkened building, immersed in thought for several moments. And then, suddenly, he isolated what was possibly the most important disclosure in what he'd read: important for what it did *not* say.

Sometime during the evening of her death Ann Harris had entertained a lover at Ulitza Pushkinskaya. They had sat together in the living-room, drinking. He had moved about the flat, into the bathroom and the bedroom. In the bedroom he had undressed, taken her to bed and made love to her. From past experience, Danilov knew it would have been practically impossible for something – a thread or a fibre – *not* to have come from the man's clothing during that degree of activity. Yet the conclusion of the report was quite emphatic: nowhere in the apartment was there anything forensically identifiable as Russian. Danilov smiled, no longer disappointed. He had a pathway to follow. He wondered where it would lead and thought at once that the last document he had to read might show him.

The telephone monitoring covered the immediately preceding month. The list of outgoing calls was comparatively short and from his earlier study of Ann Harris's address book Danilov was able to identify most of them. There was one number she had called more than any other.

Definitely a pathway, Danilov decided. There was possibly a very practical benefit from the impending arrival of an FBI officer. Were they referred to as officers or agents? He wasn't sure.

It was difficult, to control the shaking, the fear vibrating through him, almost causing a physical ache. So close: so incredibly, near-

94

disastrously close. It was a miracle they hadn't seen the knife, the knife that had actually been moving towards her back, almost touching the thick brown material. It would have slid in so easily: just like silk. That's how it had to go in, just like silk. Her hair had been wonderful, long and blonde. It would have been good, to have collected blonde hair. And the buttons, of course. There would have been a lot of buttons. So close: close enough to hear her say how sorry she was to be late and see the smile of forgiveness as the man came forward from the shadowed alley off Ulitza Kislovskii to kiss her. Shouldn't have hurried, wanting too much to do it again. Should have taken more care, to be sure she was alone, not meeting anyone. Not a bad failure: no cause to shake like this. Hadn't been caught. Do it right next time. Just like silk. More hair. More buttons.

He'd taken her before she was properly awake, hugely aroused, and it had been difficult in her surprise for Pauline to respond fully to his excitement. She hadn't matched him at the end but she didn't think he had realized: she knew he was pleased, at how it had been. Afterwards Pauline made breakfast in her housecoat. Andrews was fully and immaculately dressed when he emerged from their bedroom.

'I'm going out to Sheremet'yevo to meet him tonight,' Andrews announced.

Pauline poured the coffee as her husband sat down. 'That's considerate.'

'Want me to pass on any message?'

She frowned down at him. 'Hello, I guess. What else?'

'How do you feel about seeing him again?'

Pauline replaced the coffee-pot, aware she had to be careful with the answer. 'I don't think I feel anything.'

'We'll have him here for dinner. You'd like that, wouldn't you? Having him to dinner?'

'If you want to.'

'Do *you* want to?'

'It's your decision, Barry. You know that.'

'Yes,' he said. 'My decision.'

Chapter Eleven

Andrews positioned himself close to the doors beyond the Customs area and hurried forward the moment Cowley emerged, but then didn't seem to know what to do with his hands, holding both before him initially and then clasping them behind his back. The smile was hesitant. 'Hi! . . . Hi Bill . . . Good to see you.'

'I hardly expected you to meet me in.' Could it ever be good to see the man who had taken his wife? Not taken, Cowley corrected at once: he'd lost Pauline's love long before Andrews had appeared on the scene.

'How you doing?' The smile lasted slightly longer this time.

'OK.'

There was an uneasy silence between them in an airport full of noise. Then Andrews said: 'Thought it best to get it out of the way. You and me.'

'You get a briefing, from the Director?'

'A long one.'

'It was a headquarters decision. Political.'

'That's what the briefing said.'

'I hope we can work together.'

'Why shouldn't we?' The smile came on again.

There was a jostle of people around them and Cowley felt two men very close, whispering in English the offer of taxis.

'Let's get the hell out of here!' said Andrews. He half reached for Cowley's bag but then drew back. The embassy car was directly in front of the terminal. The road surface of the main highway into the city was pockmarked with holes, jarring the vehicle. 'Just like New York!' said Andrews.

'How's Pauline?' It would have been ridiculous for Cowley not to have asked.

'Good . . . very well . . . says to say hello.'

'Say hello back.' It was going far better between them than he had expected.

'Ambassador wants to see you first thing tomorrow,' announced Andrews. 'Political lecture, I guess.'

'I already had one in Washington.' Cowley didn't remember the man speaking like this, firing rather than saying the words. Cowley detected a cigar odour in the car: he couldn't remember Andrews being a smoker, either. Cowley stared out, not able to see very much in the darkness apart from faraway lights, to the right. 'There doesn't seem much information available.'

'Being *made* available,' qualified Andrews. 'The investigator is an asshole. Name's Danilov, Dimitri Danilov. Sneaky son-of-a-bitch.'

'I understood there was to be cooperation?'

'We should have taken complete charge, not shared it. That's what I expected. There'll need to be a lot of arm twisting, to get what we want. There's an autopsy report you won't have seen.' Andrews patted a dossier beside him. 'Got it here.'

Buildings began to form ahead, high-rise apartment blocks, and the darkness began to lift, with street light. 'Tell me about Danilov.'

'Typical jerk, small-time policeman, out of his depth and trying to hide it. Got into her apartment before we could get to it: sealed it. We're burning ass over that. They've given us a list of what they say they took, but we've no way of knowing if it's accurate. We're demanding a return of the body, too.'

'Anything special in the autopsy?'

Andrews smiled across the car. 'She'd been screwed. How about that! Senator Walter Burden's virgin niece had been screwed.'

'I thought there was no evidence of rape.'

'Screwed before she went out into the street.'

'Boyfriend?'

'She didn't have one, as far as I know. The original Frigid Bridget.'

'You know her?'

'In her company a few times, at dinners, stuff like that.'

'What sort of a girl was she?'

'Attractive. Good body: nice tits. Sure of herself: knew she had uncle's pull, back home. Didn't bother much with the hired help, like me. Saw herself at ambassador and First Secretary level.'

The car turned on to Ulitza Chaykovskaya and Cowley saw the embassy ahead. 'So you didn't like her?'

The other man shrugged. 'Didn't like or dislike. As I said, I didn't know her that well.' He turned down the sideroad by the old embassy towards the new legation and accommodation compound at the rear. 'We're using the living quarters but the bastards insisted on local labour and bugged every fucking thing in the new embassy. We've got to pull it down and rebuild.'

The suite allocated to Cowley consisted of a sitting-room, with an alcove kitchen to one side, a bedroom and a separate bathroom equipped with a shower. The living-room had American furnishings, a couch and two easy chairs covered in rough-weave, oatmeal-coloured material on a white shag carpet, and a dark wood dining set of table and four chairs. The bookcase held mostly National Geographic publications. The majority of the books displayed were guides or explanations of the new Russian confederation and Russian life. There was a video player beneath the television set.

Andrews nodded towards it and said: 'Television here is crap, apart from CNN, by satellite. There's a video library, though. And the marine sergeant can get stag movies.'

'I don't anticipate much time for television,' said Cowley. 'Your cable said the investigator . . .' He paused, for the name. '. . . Danilov . . . it said he speaks English?'

'Motherfucker tricked us with that,' admitted Andrews. 'Sat there gabbling Russian and listening to everything we said, among ourselves. Asshole! Mind if I smoke?'

Yes, thought Cowley. 'Go ahead,' he said. Cowley wondered just how much he would need the language he'd begun to learn in military intelligence, which had been his original career choice before joining the FBI, where he'd brought it up to near fluency at the Bureau language centre at Monterey. For the Russian to have feigned ignorance of English to hear everything that was said seemed hardly typical jerk, small-time policeman. 'I guess I'm going to have to work out how to operate as I go along.'

Andrews crossed towards the kitchen to go unerringly to a cupboard containing a selection of bottles, kindling a cigar as he went. 'Stocked up for you!' It was an anticipation rather than an announcement. 'What do you want?'

'I don't drink, not any more.'

Andrews regarded him with a look verging on disbelief. 'You've got to be joking!'

'No.'

'Jesus! Who would have thought it?' Andrews poured himself scotch, over ice.

Cowley refused any annoyance at the open condescension. He *had* been a drunk, so someone who'd known him as well as Andrews was entitled to disbelief. And if he showed any reaction, Andrews might imagine the reason deeper than simple annoyance, at being patronized. He said: 'What sort of steer can you give me?'

'Don't take any of Danilov's shit. Keep the asshole jumping. Let him know who's going to be calling the shots from now on.'

'Thanks for the advice,' said Cowley. The other man appeared to miss the reservation.

'I've been pretty uncertain about this, ever since I heard it was you who were coming,' admitted Andrews. 'Haven't you?'

'Naturally.'

'I don't see any reason why there should be difficulties. There won't be, as far as I am concerned.'

Cowley was surprised that the other man had accepted the secondary role so readily, despite Washington's orders. 'Or from me.'

'Pauline said . . . suggested . . . that if it all went well tonight . . . you and I, I mean . . . I was to say how about coming for dinner one night? It's miserable here, all by yourself. Would that be a good idea? I mean Pauline and I feel OK about it, if you do.'

Cowley was finding everything different about Andrews from what he had expected. Or remembered. 'Sounds good to me. Why don't we think on it?'

'Good! She'll be pleased.' Andrews gestured around the apartment. 'Meanwhile, any food you want you can get from the commissary. If you don't feel like cooking for yourself there's the embassy mess. Funny telephone system here: everything is direct dial, straight into anyone's office: would you believe there are photographs of the entire fucking government, in the front of the

99

telephone directory . . . !' He offered a card. 'That's my home number. Anything you want, you call, you hear?'

And Pauline's home number, Cowley thought. 'Got it.'

Andrews finished his drink in a head-tilted gulp and said: 'While you're with the ambassador I'll fix a meeting with Danilov.'

Cowley nodded. 'You mentioned the autopsy report?'

Andrews handed over the dossier. 'You're going to crack this one and come out covered in glory!'

But not if he failed to solve it, thought Cowley. 'I'm glad we're going to get along,' he said.

'He said to say hello back,' declared Andrews. He went straight to the cocktail cabinet, but more for effect than for the drink he poured himself.

'How does he look?'

Andrews held up his glass, smiling. 'You're not going to believe this! He's given it up.'

She didn't believe it, Pauline decided: William couldn't have changed that much.

'It's going to be interesting, working together again.'

'I hope it is,' said Pauline. She hoped he wasn't too upset by what had happened: despite being married to him for more than three years she still often found it difficult to guess what Andrews was really thinking.

Chapter Twelve

Jetlag brought Cowley awake when it was still dark, just after five in the morning. He had expected to rouse earlier and decided, pleased, that it would only take a couple of days for him fully to adjust. He remained for a while where he was, trying to anticipate the day. The meeting with the ambassador probably *would* be a warning political lecture. So the uncertainty was Dimitri Danilov. Sneaky son-of-a-bitch? Jerk? Motherfucker? Asshole? Or one very upset Moscow-based FBI officer suffering a grievance, real or imagined? Despite the good beginning – the surprising beginning – Cowley decided he would have to guard constantly against any personal assessments influencing his professional judgement of whatever Andrews did or said. More than just be careful: determinedly objective. Unfair, after the airport greeting and the later conversation here, last night? Yes, Cowley decided. He was prejudging, on experience from the past: more revolving circles.

The autopsy report was on the bedside table where he had put it aside the previous night, together with copies of everything else Andrews had so far assembled. Cowley was sure he knew it all but pulled everything towards him to read completely through again. He concentrated particularly on the pathology examination, memorizing the details. It had been translated, of course. Cowley wished there had been a copy of the Russian original, for him to make a comparison to agree the English version. The medical account appeared comprehensive but there would need to be another post-mortem in America. Would it be automatic, without his suggesting it? A mistake to presume anything: he'd recommend it, as soon as the body was released. The list of articles removed from Ann Harris's apartment was frustrating, because that's *all* it was, a list with no indication of the significance of any single item. The knife rack was intriguing. And he wondered what had emerged from what was simply recorded as 'correspondence'. He hoped Dimitri Danilov fitted none of the descriptions offered by Andrews: it would be impossible to proceed unless he and the Russian worked with at least some element of cooperation.

It was after six, but still quite dark when Cowley got out of bed. He put coffee on to percolate, and saw as he did so that the door to the liquor cupboard was ajar. He stood before it briefly, looking in at the selection: there was not the slightest desire, not any more. He closed the door, positively, collected his coffee and took it with him into the main room: close to the window he saw the whiteness of frost outside, despite the darkness; he was comfortably warm even though he was only wearing a thin robe. He supposed efficient central heating was essential in a country with such a climate. He hadn't made any special preparation and hoped the clothes he'd brought would be sufficient. There were two views from the window, one directly towards the embassy still in blackness, the other sideways down a street of sleeping, lightless buildings. He was abruptly held by the absolute contrast to any American city he had ever known: there was no movement, of people or cars, anywhere. Nor the slightest sound, either. Cowley shivered, suddenly, although he still wasn't cold.

He remained at the window for a long time, as what was to become the day gradually formed before him, and quickly realized it was never going to be a proper day at all: a thick, orange-grey fog smothered streets and houses and proper sight of anything, shrouding out any full light. He was able, though, to see his immediate surroundings: here his reaction wasn't exactly shock but something close.

From the freshly built, red-brick residential compound and the never-to-be-occupied new legation he was looking directly at the rear of the old, pre-revolutionary embassy building. In between — actually built on to the back of the mansion like some inoperable growth — was the original accommodation compound, a crumbling warren of green-painted, small-balconied apartments as lifeless as everything else all around. But it was not the living quarters which caused the surprise. Accustomed to the baroque splendour of the US mission in Rome and the enormous, eagle-surmounted block forming one entire side of Grosvenor Square, in London, Cowley was amazed at the embassy itself. The mansion might once have been impressive but now it was completely neglected. It was dirt-grimed, the walls streaked with soot smears, the majority of the grit-coated windows sealed on the inside with either cardboard screens or wooden sheets. And again there was no sign of life anywhere. Cowley thought that rather than the diplomatic centre of the richest nation on earth, it looked like the abandoned home of the increasingly desperate poverty-stricken who'd finally boarded it against squatters or vandals until the arrival of the overdue demolition squad. He supposed the lack of maintenance or upkeep would have been understandable, if the transfer to the contemporary embassy had happened. But as it had been decreed uninhabitable he would have expected a greater effort to keep the existing building presentable.

Cowley took his time showering and dressing, choosing the thickest of the three suits he'd brought with him, debating whether to wear a sweater beneath and finally deciding against it. He was still ready early, waiting for the time to pass, when Andrews arrived, attempting some sort of rhythm in the way he knocked at the door. The man was wearing a three-quarter-length quilted coat, with a fur-trimmed hood. His trouser bottoms were tucked into fur-lined boots.

'I'll need to sign you in, the first time,' announced the local FBI man. 'I've got accreditation ready for you in the office. I'll show you where that is in the embassy, too, so you can find your way there after you're through with the ambassador. Name's Richards, by the way: in full, Hubert J. Richards III. Family money from oil. Not a political appointment, to repay election contributions though. He's a career professional. Not a bad guy. Anything you want?'

Cowley wondered how the other man managed to say so much without apparently taking breath. Careful, he warned himself at once: never critical, always objective. 'You seem to have covered it all.'

Cowley followed the other American out of the complex, instantly conscious of the chill through his wool overcoat. His breath clouded whitely in front of him, a personal contribution to the fog. They had to go by the green-painted compound. Closer Cowley saw barbed wire coiled protectively along the enclosing walls. There was a Russian Militia guard in a sentry box at a minor entrance who looked at them without expression and made no challenge as they entered. The side entrance was in fact a

103

long corridor: halfway along there was an American checkpoint, guarded by a marine who nodded and smiled familiarly at the resident FBI man. Andrews insisted on a formal introduction, assuring the marine Cowley would have his own ID after today. The marine said Hi: a new face, the highlight of his day.

The interior of the embassy was better than the exterior – cleaner at least – but there were cracks in some places in the high-ceilinged corridor and the wall covering was faded with age. Their footsteps echoed. Andrews's office was on the first floor, with a window unobstructed by either cardboard or wooden screens. It overlooked an inner courtyard in which, inexplicably, there were a number of metal posts, some connected by wire. Cowley hung his own coat on a rack while Andrews shucked off his quilted anorak and changed his boots for gleaming loafers. Beneath the shapeless protective coat he was crisply dressed, as always: sharp-as-a-tack, Cowley remembered.

'You've got to sign for this,' said Andrews, officiously, presenting the accreditation tag.

It was exactly the same as those issued at Pennsylvania Avenue, where they fitted security key slots to gain and record admission to the different departments in the building. It was already equipped with a chain, to wear around the neck as everyone did in Washington, and a file photograph which had been among the personal material sent ahead. Cowley put the ID in his pocket. He lowered himself into the only other chair in the room, curious about the poles in the courtyard. It looked something like a volley-ball court but he didn't think it could be.

'No problem, overnight?'

'None that I can think of.'

Andrews sat at the window, with its strange view. Without looking back, he said: 'This job could make a career, couldn't it?'

'What?' frowned Cowley, momentarily confused.

Andrews turned. 'I mean Burden. All the power and influence the guy's got. Find the nut who killed his niece and Burden is going to be eternally grateful, isn't he? A friend for life!'

Cowley regarded the other man steadily, remembering the previous night's conversation about glory. 'If we make a case, your participation will be recognized. I promise you that.'

'Privately?'

'It'll count, where it matters.'

Andrews didn't respond at once. Then he said: 'Sure.' There was a further pause. 'What time do you want me to tell Danilov to get here?'

Cowley's frown deepened. 'Why don't we ask what time I could go see him?'

Andrews's face tightened perceptibly at the unspoken correction. 'You forgotten what I told you last night, about how to handle him?'

'I said I'd work the patch my way.' He didn't like the reversal, from the first day: didn't at all like the tension he could feel between them.

'It's a mistake.'

'My way, OK?' He didn't have to give in: he was in charge.

The resident FBI man nodded, slowly. 'Whoops, mustn't get out of line, must I?'

'Let's not build an issue out of it.'

There was another slow nod. 'You'll need transport.'

'There'll be cabs.'

'Moscow's not like anywhere else. Maybe I should go with you?'

Cowley shook his head, positively. 'Nothing to identify your true position here. You had the Director's briefing: you know that.'

There was further head movement of begrudging acceptance. 'Easy to forget.'

'Let's keep it easy,' placated Cowley, hopefully.

'Sure.'

'This is a two-man operation.'

'Whatever.'

Silence came briefly between them. Cowley said: 'I'll accept whatever time Danilov suggests.'

An internal telephone shrilled on Andrews's desk, surprisingly loud. 'The ambassador's ready for you.'

'Good,' said Cowley, gratefully.

Hubert J. Richards III *looked* a professional career diplomat, impeccably dark-suited, pink-cheeked and quiet-voiced: at the

105

end of every sentence there was a suggestion of a smile tempting agreement with the offered opinion, but not too fulsome against a contrary opinion having to be courteously considered. He stood to shake Cowley's hand and waited until Cowley was seated before sitting himself. He hoped Cowley had had a good journey and found his accommodation – 'always difficult, here in Moscow' – adequate. It was a horrible business, most upsetting. Coffee was served by a bulky, broad-hipped woman with iron-grey hair and a slight limp.

'It is not normal for me to become involved in things that are not . . .' Richards slowed to a halt, unusually finding it difficult to finish. '. . . strictly diplomatic,' he managed clumsily. 'But of course this is. Diplomatic, I mean.' The smile was more obvious, apologetic. 'I don't wish any disrespect: I appreciate fully the valuable job you and your colleagues in other agencies perform . . .'

'I understand what you're saying,' said Cowley. He guessed the enormous office had originally been a reception room. An ornate chandelier hung from the ceiling and there were fireplaces at either end of the room, both big enough for a man to have stood upright in either. Neither was lighted. The room was still very warm, almost too hot. The three floor-to-ceiling balcony windows looked out over Ulitza Chaykovskaya: layered glazing defeated any noise from the cars finally flowing along Moscow's inner ring road. There was some wood barricading along the windows' lower half, which would have been concealed from the outside by the balcony rails.

'And political, as well as being diplomatic.'

'I was briefed by the Director, before I left Washington.'

'Senator Burden has called direct, several times.'

'He talked of coming personally, in a television newscast.'

'He's said the same to me on the telephone.'

'What did you advise?' Cowley judged the coffee better than he had made himself that morning.

'He didn't ask my advice.'

'The Russians have been obstructive? Autocratic?'

'That's what I have been told, by my Second Secretary. And others.'

'So you didn't personally experience it?'

'No. I've protested, on their behalf. And upon instructions from Washington. With some effect, it would seem. I've been informed this morning they are going to release the body. I've ordered all the arrangements, of course.'

We're going to burn ass, Cowley remembered: he mustn't forget the request for a second autopsy. 'According to what I've read so far, she lived on Ulitza Pushkinskaya.'

'Yes.'

'I understood all diplomatic staff lived in the compound.'

The smile flickered. 'Insufficient accommodation. About half the personnel are outside. Many prefer it.'

Cowley was scarcely surprised, from what he'd seen from his guest quarters that morning. He was curious, at what he thought to be an odd tone in the ambassador's voice. 'Did Ann Harris prefer it?'

'She insisted upon it.'

'*Insisted?*'

'She was an extremely strong-willed girl: most definite, once she made her mind up.'

For strong-willed read sure of uncle's muscle, thought Cowley. 'And she made her mind up about living on Pushkinskaya?'

'I believe she was shown the available accommodation and chose to live in an outside hotel until she located an apartment.'

In diplomatic surroundings Cowley supposed he should be diplomatic. 'What sort of girl was she? Part of the American community here? Gregarious? Or apart from it, a loner? Any special friends, here at the embassy? Any problems with her? Was she happy? Lonely?' There were surely enough openings there.

Richards sat head bowed for several moments, considering his answer. 'She was highly popular, but properly so. I have never received any complaint about her behaviour. She was certainly an asset at every function she attended in my presence. I am not aware of any particular friend. In my company she always appeared quite happy.' The ambassador smiled, hopefully.

'What about *outside* the embassy? Any particular Russian friends?'

'None of whom I am aware.'

'The autopsy found evidence of sexual activity: intercourse,

107

not rape,' said Cowley, abandoning diplomacy. 'That indicates a special friend.'

The smile became a wince, of distaste. 'I said I did not know of anyone.'

'You are the authority here at the embassy,' Cowley reminded him. 'You are more likely to be told the truth than I might be, as a complete stranger.'

'About what?' There was no longer any smile. Or wince, even.

Cowley swallowed the sigh. 'Ambassador,' he said, patiently, 'I'm trying to pick up a murder investigation without knowing whether I am going to get the slightest cooperation from people so far described, at best, as obstructive and autocratic. We both accept it's a diplomatic and political swamp. The sooner the inquiry is resolved, the better for everyone at every level. So I need all the assistance I can get. Which is what I am asking, from you. I'm not concerned with morals or embarrassment, although if I can avoid the latter then I will. I am asking you, with your full authority as ambassador, to inquire of people who would be the most likely to know if Ann Harris had any special friend in this embassy.'

The pink face grew pinker. Richards said: 'To what purpose?'

It was becoming difficult for Cowley to cover his irritation. 'Whoever made love to her was probably the last person to see her alive: he might be the murderer! If he isn't he might know where she had come from or was going to!'

'Are you suggesting that somebody attached to this embassy might be involved?'

'Sir, I am not suggesting anything. I don't *know* anything, not yet. But why not? Somebody stabbed and disfigured her. I have to find out who.' Not officially, Cowley corrected himself at once: officially his function was liaison. He'd have to keep that in mind later, with the Russian investigator.

Richards shook his head, as if he were refusing. But he said: 'I'm sorry. I'll make the inquiries, of course. In return I want to be fully informed. About everything.'

'You will be,' promised Cowley. To the limited extent I consider necessary, he added, mentally.

Barry Andrews was expectantly behind his desk when Cowley returned to the lower-level office. 'How did it go?' the man demanded at once. He gestured, encouragingly, with the hand that held an already lighted cigar.

Cowley shrugged. 'Politely, I suppose.'

'Just a political lecture?' pressed the man.

'I asked him to help me about any particular friend or friends she might have had, here at the embassy. He said he'd ask around.'

Andrews nodded, unspeaking for several moments. Then he said: 'Danilov suggested noon. I said OK.'

To say anything about the earlier, pointless discussion would seem like mockery. 'The Russians are releasing the body, according to the ambassador. I'd like to send a cable, on your wire, asking for a second autopsy.'

'I'll do it in your name,' undertook Andrews.

'Where do I find Danilov?'

'Moscow Militia headquarters: Ulitza Petrovka 38. You taken up smoking since we last met?'

Cowley frowned, confused. 'No.'

Andrews took a packet of Marlboro cigarettes from a drawer and offered them. 'Moscow survival pack. Cab drivers will probably recognize you as a foreigner anyway: the Marlboro packet confirms it, guaranteed to make them stop. You'll probably get a gypsy – a private car – stopping as well. They'll either want the cigarettes or hard currency: dollars. Fix the price before you set out. They'll start high, naturally. Three bucks is more than enough, for around the city. I know it sounds ridiculous, but it's the system.'

Cowley accepted the cigarettes and the new patronizing lecture, allowing Andrews whatever small victory he needed.

'I told Pauline you were going to eat with us,' said Andrews. 'She's looking forward to it. Wants to see you.'

'We'll fix it, when I'm settled in.' Was she really looking forward to it? Or was that casual politeness?

'She'll be pleased,' assured Andrews. 'And remember when you meet Danilov, don't take any . . .' He stopped, quickly. 'I already told you, didn't I?' he finished.

'Yes,' said Cowley, wearily. 'You already told me.'

The FBI Director considered refusing the call but decided it was a pointless evasion. He depressed the telephone console button.

Without any greeting, apart from identifying himself, Burden said: 'I told Hartz I wanted to see the man you were sending, before he went to Moscow! Didn't he tell you?'

'He told me.'

'So what happened?'

'About what?' said Ross, intentionally resistant.

'Hartz told me this morning an agent has already gone. Without my speaking to him!'

'That's right.'

There was silence, from the other end of the line. Then Burden said: 'Director, have we got a communication difficulty here?'

'I don't think so,' said Ross. 'I saw no point in your talking to my agent.'

'*You* saw no point!'

'Mine was the responsibility, for briefing the man. No one else's.'

There was a further, although shorter silence. 'I consider your attitude impertinent!'

'I don't see any purpose in this sort of conversation, Senator. I will, of course, contact you with whatever I consider relevant, from Moscow.'

'I'm not accustomed to being spoken to in this manner,' threatened Burden.

'Neither am I,' said the unafraid Ross, pushing the boredom into his voice. 'So why don't you stop it? It isn't achieving anything.' Now the difficulties at the budget agreement sessions would be enormous: but it would be worth it.

Petr Yezhov had been committed to the Serbsky Institute after being found guilty of both attacks. His name was isolated on the third day of the checks by the apathetic men who had been with Pavin for the meeting with the principal. Yezhov became the sixth on their list.

'No one's said how far back we should go,' the first man pointed out.

'A year?' suggested his companion.

'The doctor was right. It could take forever.'

'Why don't we stop, when we've got another two or three names on the list? It's nonsense anyway.'

Chapter Thirteen

Dimitri Danilov considered being in the reception area for the American's arrival at Petrovka but decided against it. The FBI presence had been described to him that morning as supportive, a scientific assistance. To have been waiting in the foyer might have conveyed the impression of deference. Which would have been wrong. So after the required but brief encounter with the Director – a worried diatribe from Lapinsk about the press conference running over into Lapinsk's now familiar injunction to avoid worsening the already existing ill-feeling – Danilov remained in his jumbled office, waiting. He did, however, warn the reception desk of Cowley's appointment, to avoid the American being kept waiting, as visitors to any Russian government building or organization were invariably kept waiting.

A professionally trained investigator would quickly realize the cul-de-sac into which they were blocked, Danilov accepted. And William Cowley would most definitely be a professionally trained investigator as well as – if not more so – someone with scientific expertise: it would be a matter of pride, apart from anything else, for the Americans to assign the best-qualified man available. Danilov felt a stir of unease, which bothered him. There was no reason for him to feel uneasy about the forthcoming meeting. Every recognized police procedure had been correctly followed, nothing overlooked, nothing forgotten. The reassurance didn't come. He would be under new and different scrutiny from now on, a Russian detective being critically judged by an American. Wouldn't he be making the same examination of the American? Of course he would. And if he did it properly, looking for the additional benefit, not the possible criticism, then the presence of another expert mind was something to welcome, not to balk at. It was going to be important, always to keep that balance in mind.

Danilov was at the office door when Cowley approached along the corridor – a polite ten minutes before noon – so the American had a chance before any physical contact to examine the Russian with whom he would be working. About forty, assessed the American: forty-five tops. Yesterday's suit – maybe yesteryear's – and definitely yesterday's shirt, looking more like it had been rolled on than properly laundered. A hint of a belly bulge, so he didn't exercise: conscious of it, too, from the way he was holding himself. Typically square, Slavic face, which was pale-skinned, another indication of an indoor, non-exercising man. Fading brown hair, close-cropped to be more than a crew cut but growing again, needing attention. Good personal control. Here was a Russian policeman heading an investigation into the murder of an American girl with heavy-duty US clout. And knowing it. Yet he was giving no facial reaction of either too little or too much uncertainty, calmly standing there, waiting.

As Cowley, accompanied by an escorting officer, reached him the Russian thrust his hand forward and said: 'Dimitri Ivanovich Danilov.'

The American answered the handshake and in English said: 'William Cowley, although of course it's Bill, not William . . .' The smile grew, just slightly. In passably accented Russian he went on: 'How we going to do this? In Russian? Or in English? Guess there'd better be some ground rules.'

Danilov nodded to the withdrawal of the escort, backing further into his office, gesturing Cowley in with him. In English he said: 'Whatever you feel most comfortable with.' Surely a friendly offer, from the start? Although maybe it showed a conceit about his English.

Confident of himself and his language ability, gauged Cowley: stroke with velvet gloves, he remembered. 'Why don't we just work our way along with a combination of both? Anything I don't get, I'll ask: anything you don't get, you ask.'

Condescension? Or further politeness, like arriving ahead of time? Danilov said: 'That sounds OK.' He indicated the only visitor's chair, which he'd cleared of file papers that morning. 'Sit. Is there anything I can get you? Tea?' He hoped Cowley didn't accept: everything from the canteen was abysmal. The tea was like sewer water.

'Not at the moment.' The finger-touching courtesy was almost overdone. Cowley prevented himself making any examination of the cluttered office. Someone with little social contact since the break-up with Pauline, Cowley had spent a lot of the past three years watching television: this room reminded him of a natural history series he'd enjoyed, particularly the cut-away shots of underground nests of animals who'd dragged all sorts of crap into their holes and settled right in the middle of it.

Danilov's strongest impression was of the American's size. The man filled the already overfilled room, the chair inadequate and lost beneath him. The suit, which wasn't travel-creased, would have had to be specially made for him. Possibly the shirt, as well. Cowley's hair was dark and tightly crinkled, beyond being wavy, combed straight back from a heavily lined forehead. The man had a direct, almost unblinking manner of looking at another person through eyes quite a light, almost unnatural, blue. As Cowley casually crossed one hand over the other, Danilov saw the heavy ring, with a large red stone, that Cowley wore on the little finger of his left hand: Danilov believed it had something to do with American college societies but wasn't sure. The other American who had confronted him first at the embassy and then outside the girl's apartment had worn a similar decoration. Cowley appeared quite at ease and relaxed in unfamiliar surroundings, showing no outward disquiet. In English Danilov said: 'I suppose it *is* important for us to establish ground rules.'

'Your choice,' insisted Cowley. 'I know all the exchanges between our two governments: my function is advisory . . .' Cowley stopped, unhappy with the choice of words. 'Help, where possible . . . to suggest technical or scientific ideas, maybe,' he finished, badly. He hadn't thought sufficiently before he spoke. And he really *had* been trying to appear friendly, conciliatory even to someone who would naturally regard his being in Moscow as an invasion of territory.

People advised and offered help from superior positions or ability. Danilov guessed the American hadn't meant to say that, not quite so bluntly. So what could have appeared the acceptance of a secondary role could equally be a patronizing one. Danilov moved consciously to stop the drifting analysis. Wasn't there a danger, in constantly seeking several meanings from every word and phrase? He'd already decided, so many times that he'd lost count, that he was confronting an investigation more difficult

114

than any he'd encountered before. And accepted he was getting nowhere. So he needed all the help he could find. He looked intently at the other man and thought once more, *a professionally trained investigator*. And then called to mind another previous reflection: *the best-qualified man available*. Wasn't there more sense, more practical personal benefit, in putting to one side the suspicion and resentment, none of which had been caused by this man, to take advantage of the fresh mind and the fresh approach? 'I don't imagine it's going to be easy, for us to adjust to working together. But if it *is* to work, we've got to be totally open with each other. Which I'm prepared to be.' Danilov was sure the offer had sounded completely right, without any of the cynical opportunism that was there.

Where was the sneaky, smart-assed son-of-a-bitch mother-fucker? wondered Cowley. Respond in kind, he concluded, this time thinking ahead of what he was about to say. He smiled again, taking any criticism from the remark, and said: 'It didn't get off to a very good start at the embassy, did it?'

Danilov smiled back, briefly. 'Misunderstandings on both sides.'

Cowley nodded, accepting the inference of a new start. So why not let it run that way, completely to ease his way in? All he had to do was to remain alert; careful against any advantage being taken from him. 'Those ground rules suit me fine. Which means I'm missing the forensic examination of her apartment. Whatever the importance might have been from what you took from it. And if there was anything of importance in what's simply listed as "correspondence" which you also removed.'

Cowley had itemized everything a trained detective would need to see, in addition to whatever had already been made available. Testingly, Danilov said: 'My assessment? Or the material?'

He would probably have posed the same question himself, Cowley acknowledged. 'Both. But the material first: I don't want to assume any preconceptions you might express, in advance of my seeing what evidence is available.'

Danilov again recognized the correct professional reaction. 'Everything's along the corridor.'

There was certainly no room for it in this nest, thought Cowley:

he hoped he hadn't let his attention wander. 'I'd better start getting up to date.'

Cowley thought the Russian exhibit room pitiful: three baize-topped, collapsible tables (one containing a map, the other completely barren), two obviously new filing cabinets (presumably unfilled), two long-corded telephones, brown Formica everywhere (Formica wall strips and Formica panelling and Formica wall platforms), and heightening the whole scene into farce a new, multi-horned pedestal coat-rack upon which no coats hung. And with no office personnel whatsoever. In America, had the murder victim been a Russian diplomat with the sort of political connections of Ann Harris, there would have additionally been a computer bank, staffed by operators, possibly a mini-telephone exchange, an exhibit and evidence controller in charge of an assembly group and at least three more display boards, one clearly indicating hour-by-hour and day-by-day progress. Cowley said: 'Seems pretty well organized to me.'

Danilov looked at the American curiously, pointing towards the one occupied exhibit table. 'That's what you want. I'll be back in my office. Take your time.'

Cowley lowered himself to the table as the Russian left the room but did not move at once to the document files, trying instead to assess the encounter. It barely qualified as preliminary. But was useful nevertheless. Certainly very different from what he might have expected from the warnings from Barry Andrews. So Barry had mishandled it, at the beginning. He wouldn't completely ignore the warnings, though. He would simply wait, as he'd always intended to wait, to reach his own judgement on the Russian investigator. What was that judgement so far? Ill-dressed and uncomfortable with it, from the frequent shrugging together of his jacket and the fingering of his tie, against his crumpled shirt. But reasonably sure of himself, which was an advantage. In Cowley's operational past, personal uncertainty of any sort in a partner – and he had to think of the Russian as a partner – had always been a hindrance as well as sometimes a danger in the field. He thought Danilov was clever, too. If there was one conclusion – premature maybe, wrong possibly – that Cowley had reached about Dimitri Danilov it was that the man was definitely not a fool. Which was another advantage. Enough, so

116

early in the acquaintanceship: perhaps more than enough. He leaned forward for the first of the correspondence bundles.

Back along the corridor, Danilov reached the Director at the first attempt on the internal telephone, anxious to cancel the pointless afternoon briefing. The meeting with the American had seemed to go reasonably well, he assured Lapinsk. Cowley was now studying the outstanding documentation. After which they were to talk again. Beyond that, there was nothing to report apart from forensic proof that the notes referring to pain which had been retained by Ann Harris had been written on American paper in American-manufactured ink: the report had been waiting when he'd returned from the morning briefing, which was why he hadn't mentioned it then.

'It's amicable, then?' demanded the Director, an elderly man needing to be reassured more than once.

'It seems to be, so far,' said Danilov.

'How much does he know?'

'We've only talked about the woman at the moment.'

There was a burst of coughing. 'Call me at once if any problems arise later. I want to be warned in advance.'

Pavin entered the office as Danilov replaced the receiver. The Major said: 'How's it gone?'

'We've agreed on complete openness. He's looking at the correspondence and the forensic report on the flat. It's really too early to decide what sort of man he is.'

'Do you think he'll keep his word about sharing everything?'

'I don't know,' Danilov admitted. 'We'll have to see.' Did he intend sharing everything? And how could he check on the other man's honesty? He was going to have to remain very alert.

'He's certainly big enough,' said Pavin, another big man. 'I was downstairs when he arrived. He came by ordinary taxi. I thought there would have been an embassy car but there wasn't. Just an ordinary street taxi.' Pavin appeared surprised.

'We're talking again, when he's completely filled himself in. You'd better be here, to meet him.'

'How good is his Russian?'

'Seems all right.' The two men looked at each other, nothing left to say and with nothing positive left to do. An absolute cul-de-sac, Danilov thought again. He was genuinely anxious now

117

to expand the conversation with the American, to see if a fresh mind would come up with anything new. Only four more days before the next Tuesday, he remembered. 'What about the case history search of psychiatric clinics?'

'We're still assembling lists. It isn't easy,' Pavin apologized. 'I'm having the house-to-house done again, around both scenes. And I've got a street map, from the bookstall at the Intourist Hotel: I've already pinned it up. It's not as detailed as I would have liked – misses out a lot of the alleys and sideroads, although the street where she was killed is there – but it's the best I could do: at least we can section off the area where they both happened. Stationery here say they've had maps on order for six months. If they get some they've promised to let me know.'

'How many Militia posts cover that area?' demanded Danilov, suddenly.

'I'm not sure,' admitted the Major, doubtfully. 'Eleven and 122, certainly. Depends how wide you really want to extend the area.'

'Mark out a radius maybe two or three kilometres beyond where both bodies were found and see if that takes in any other Militia districts,' ordered Danilov. 'And have the street patrols from all of them checked. I want every report of prowlers, stalkers, Peeping Toms, any violence that can't be explained as an ordinary street brawl, where everyone involved has been identified. Go back . . .' He paused, seeking a manageable period. '. . . a month before Vladimir Suzlev was killed.' Guessing the cause of the scepticism on Pavin's face, Danilov said: 'We can demand any facility we want. I know it'll take time but assign extra men.'

Pavin shrugged acceptance. 'The criticism has already started at the amount of resources we're utilizing. This will make it worse.'

'What sort of criticism?'

Pavin shifted, uncomfortably: the smile was apologetic. 'That the power . . . the possibility of becoming known internationally . . . has gone to your head. Affected you.'

Danilov laughed, genuinely amused. 'What about the risk of failure? Where will the glory be then?' Lapinsk had warned there would be no glory, he remembered.

'A lot are expecting you to fail. Making bets.'

'Any complaints about resources can go direct to General Lapinsk,' dismissed Danilov, confidently.

'I don't imagine any are going to be made officially. Our demands provide a good excuse for failed investigations elsewhere, don't they? Can actually be useful.'

To add to all the other excuses to shield those receptively open hands, thought Danilov. He said: 'Keep me in touch, about what's being said. And by whom.' It was always useful to know one's enemies. Was that overly paranoid? No. Just properly self-protective. He'd need a lot of protection, if he did fail.

Pavin turned first, at the sound at the doorway, ahead of Danilov realizing the presence of William Cowley. The American *was* big, conceded Danilov, at once: standing as the man was, at the very threshold, he virtually blocked the entrance. Cowley remained where he was, as if waiting for an invitation to re-enter. Danilov provided it by introducing Pavin and identifying the Major as the exhibit officer. Cowley offered his hand first and went through the meeting ritual in Russian, thinking as he did so that if the Major was the exhibit officer he hadn't really been over-extended assembling what had been set out in the room he'd just left. To Danilov, the American said briskly: 'Now we can talk.' He perched himself delicately upon the inadequate chair. 'How do you want to run it? My impressions to you? Or yours to me?'

Deferring here, too, acknowledged Danilov: providing a way to build bridges between them. 'No point in lectures, one to the other. Let's just talk it through, compare points that stick in my mind to those that might have come into yours.'

The Russian had not taken the offer of command. Intentional avoidance, to put them level? Or hadn't he realized the offer was there in the first place? 'I'll follow you.'

'Why was she out on the street at all?' began Danilov, rhetorically. 'You'll have seen it's difficult to establish a reliable time of death, precisely *because* of the cold. Between eleven and one o'clock on the night Ann Harris was killed, the Moscow temperature fluctuated between four and six degrees below zero. She wasn't dressed for that degree of cold – her topcoat was comparatively thin – so why did she leave a warm bed in a warm apartment to get where she was found?'

'Assignation?' suggested Cowley.

'She'd just had one *in* her apartment.'

'Called out, from one lover to another? I don't know what guidance I'm going to get from the embassy, but from the correspondence and from the paraphernalia you found in the bedside cabinet she was a pretty busy girl, sexually. Possibly experimental, too.'

'Which could throw up a number of possibilities,' Danilov chimed in. 'There could have been jealousy, from the lover she left at Pushkinskaya. Or from the one she was going to.'

'Or neither,' Cowley completed. 'The on-the-scene forensic report made a point of the minimal blood leakage. Could she have been killed elsewhere and then dumped, where she was found?'

'I think the blood loss was absorbed by the coat. She definitely wasn't killed in her apartment.'

'I've read the forensic findings at Pushkinskaya,' agreed Cowley. 'I just think the possibility of another murder scene should not be overlooked.'

Which up until now it had been, Danilov accepted. 'The pathologist says the knife was very sharp: minimal bruising around the entry wound. So the wound could have sealed itself, upon withdrawal.'

'There's no medical evidence of that, in the report.'

With no intention of further criticism of the inefficient pathologist, Danilov said: 'He claims no evidence of nail scrapings, where she might have fought. But the written account lists broken fingernails. We have to go back on that.'

Cowley nodded. 'I was told by our ambassador this morning that the body is being returned to us. I've asked for another autopsy in Washington.' He was possibly coming to the first moment of positive difficulty: it had been inevitable, although he hadn't wanted it to arise quite so soon. Consciously trying to soften the statement – certainly not to appear condescending – the American said: 'There's an analysis procedure we use in America, to confirm death-at-the-scene: blood volume calculated by a victim's height, weight and body size.'

'I'll keep that in mind.' It would be wrong to let the chill growing between them develop. With a briskness matching that of the other man, earlier, Danilov hurried on: 'Like you said, sexually she appears to have been a busy woman. But from the correspondence she puts herself in different lights to different people.'

'Yes?' said Cowley, curiously.

'She was particularly confessional to the college friend, Judy Billington. If there'd been any personal contact between them – telephone calls or vacation visits – she might have said even more than she did in the letters: hinted the identity of the lover.'

'The Billington girl certainly needs to be interviewed.' He was enjoying himself, Cowley abruptly realized. He was back where he felt he belonged, in the middle of a complicated and at the moment insoluble investigation, the sort of environment he didn't know any more from an administrative desk in Pennsylvania Avenue. And he wasn't finding any personal difficulty, with Andrews. The self-criticism was immediate. He'd barely spent two hours in the other FBI agent's company, so how could he decide there wasn't any personal difficulty? And there was still the meeting with Pauline. Three years, he thought again. How much would she have changed, in three years? How much had he changed in three years? Virtually completely, he supposed. He wondered how she'd like the transition. Cowley recalled the Director's remark about distraction, determinedly stopping the way his mind was drifting. He smiled across at the Russian. 'Anything else?'

It was right to have come this far discussing only the girl, whose murder was the sole interest of the other man, but they couldn't go any further. Danilov said: 'Possibly quite a lot, but I don't think we should consider it by itself.'

Cowley frowned. 'I don't understand.'

'Ann Harris wasn't the first murder victim,' said Danilov, simply. 'She was the second.'

Senator Burden had demanded the meeting but it took place at Henry Hartz's urging, insisting upon the FBI Director's attendance and further insisting it was not possible so obviously to disdain the politician, which had been an irritated Leonard Ross's initial intention. Richard Holmes also regarded it as a nuisance having to come into the city from the CIA headquarters at

Langley, but not with the same obvious ill-will as his Bureau counterpart. They assembled in the Secretary of State's suite at Foggy Bottom, again ahead of Burden's arrival.

'The more we tolerate his nonsense, the worse it's going to get,' complained Ross.

'We don't have a choice,' said Hartz, flatly.

'Why not?' demanded Holmes.

'Burden is playing with a marked deck,' said Hartz. 'The President needs Burden's constant support, up on the Hill. And he's going to need it through the term. The damned man – and his party – controls Congress. The moment Burden pulls the plug, we get a lame-duck President whom Burden can defeat for a second term, which every incumbent President starts campaigning for from the moment of his inauguration. All of which makes Burden as powerful as hell. And he knows it: every little bit and particle of it.'

'He's made open threats?' anticipated Ross, with weary resignation.

'Last night. During a fifteen-minute private meeting at the White House,' confirmed the Secretary of State, just as wearily. 'What Walter Burden wants Walter Burden gets. And that's the word of God. It might not be officially recorded as such, but you'd better believe that it is.'

'Shit!' said Ross, viciously.

'Shit's the stuff that fuels politics,' reminded Hartz, with unaccustomed cynicism.

'The President might need the arrogant bastard's influence,' said Ross. 'I'm not at all sure I do. Or that I'm officially supposed to.'

'The feed from the White House is that he's got to be handled with care,' insisted Hartz. 'Let's keep our personal feelings to ourselves, OK?'

The Secretary of State didn't try to greet Burden at the door on this occasion and probably wouldn't have reached it in time anyway, so quickly did the politician enter from the outer office.

'I'm not satisfied,' announced Burden, once again before he was properly seated. 'I'm getting a run-around and I don't get treated that way.' The clipped-voice warning was delivered quietly, ominously without any outward emotion.

'What exactly is it that you *want*?' said Hartz, accepting his role as convenor.

'To be told everything that's happened. What progress has the FBI agent . . .' Burden paused, directly addressing Ross. '. . . The FBI agent I was specifically prevented from speaking with, before his departure . . . made in the investigation? Are there any definite leads? The likelihood of an arrest . . . ?'

'. . . Our agent has only just arrived,' interrupted Ross, impatiently, immediately disregarding the earlier instruction because he was damned if he was going to be threatened by this man. 'I've already told you I will pass on anything you should know. These meetings achieve nothing.'

Colour flooded Burden's face and momentarily he appeared unable to speak. Before he did so, Hartz hurriedly intervened. 'We have been officially informed that the body is being returned. Will you inform the parents? Or would you have us do it? There's a procedure for this sort of unfortunate affair, where there's been a sudden death.'

Burden initially seemed unwilling to withdraw from the dispute with the FBI Director, his open-and-close eyes moving in anger. But then he said, tightly: 'I'll do it.' He turned quickly to the CIA Director. 'Well?' he demanded.

Holmes stared back, nonplussed. 'I'm sorry?'

'What about the idea of assassination?'

'None whatsoever,' said Holmes, smoothly. He hadn't made any inquiry of the Moscow station, just reiterated his hands-off-at-all-costs order.

'No doubt whatsoever?' persisted Burden.

'None. It was a street crime.'

'Keep your people on it: I still think it's sinister.'

Holmes nodded, not deigning to reply.

Burden looked to each of the three other men, addressing them all. 'What about when the bastard's caught? We got the extradition warrants under way? I want him back here, a proper trial for everyone to see. And a proper sentence . . .'

'Execution, you mean?' Ross, the former judge, cut in.

'That's exactly what I mean!'

'You know something we don't, Senator?'

Burden concentrated again upon the overweight FBI Director. 'What's that mean?'

'You know who did it?' demanded Ross. 'That he's an American? That's the only chance in hell I could ever see of us being able to demand jurisdiction and extradition, and even then I'm doubtful of the legality. But let's carry the hypothesis on, to see where it gets us. How do you want him executed? You favour the electric chair? Or lethal injection? Gas chamber, maybe? How do you imagine it's going to work: some sort of lottery in reverse, getting all the States that still have the death penalty to put in bids for the right to try and pronounce judgement on him? We going to afford this guy a lawyer or have we decided to dispense with that: might slow the process up and I'm not sure you want that, do you?'

Burden was utterly exposed and he knew it, like everyone else in the room. His face was an even deeper red now, the prominent vein that had reacted before to anger jumping again in his forehead, eyes bulging, his hands twitching in frustration. When he spoke it was with difficulty, the words jerky and uneven. 'I had a very important meeting last night ... a meeting at which I received certain undertakings. I don't believe those undertakings are being fulfilled by people here this morning.'

'I'm sorry you should feel that way,' said Hartz, anxiously. 'I'm not sure what more any of us could have done, at this early stage.'

Burden made an obvious effort at recovery. 'It seems to me the only way I am going to find out what I want is to go to Moscow myself.'

Pauline Andrews decided that despite there having been nothing in the Christmas cards or the yearly digests Cowley must have remarried. To somebody whom he clearly loved much more deeply than he'd ever cared for her: it still hurt that he hadn't loved her as much as she'd loved him, which had been absolutely, able for so long to forgive all his mistakes and all his thoughtless disregard. Having remarried was the only explanation she could find for Barry's insistence that Cowley had stopped drinking. He'd certainly not been able – or not wanted – to stop during all the years when she'd begged and pleaded. She hoped he was happy, with whoever it was. It was going to be strange, seeing him again. She felt ambivalent about it. Sometimes, since learning of his coming to Moscow, she'd wanted to meet him, meaning it when she'd told Barry she was looking forward to the encounter. But other times not, frightened it would all be too hard. But why should it be? The other times hadn't been difficult, not really. Frosty, maybe: very much arm's-length. But what else could she expect? She'd once loved him so much. Always felt so secure, so protected. Which was before she'd discovered he was screwing around, practically boring his way through every female in every embassy to which they'd ever been assigned. And before the drinking. Which had come first? She couldn't decide. Her recollection was that it had seemed to happen at the same time. It would have been good, to feel secure and protected again. Too late, like so much else.

Pauline determined to try particularly hard with the dinner. Boeuf-en-Croûte. That had always been his favourite.

She wondered if he would bring a photograph of the new wife. She'd like to see a picture: find out what his new wife looked like. Or would she?

Chapter Fourteen

The American remained absolutely motionless but in an attitude of wariness after Danilov's announcement, head curiously to one side, as if he imagined he had misheard. 'When?' he demanded, finally.

'A month ago.'

'Exactly the same?'

'The head shearing and the shoes. And the hair sprinkled over the face. But buttons weren't taken off . . .' Danilov paused. 'And the victim was a man.'

'Jesus.' It was Cowley's only lapse from complete control and even then it was muted, a thought spoken aloud to himself. He shifted on the inadequate chair, blinking out of the momentary reverie, jerking his head vaguely towards the outside corridor and the exhibit room beyond. 'That the Russian-language paper-work, back there?'

'We'll get a translation.'

'I'd like to hear it all from you, in the meantime.'

Danilov didn't need anything from the dossiers, so well did he know the facts. He recounted the first murder in strict police narrative, date, time, circumstance, family history, medical findings and finally the forensic opinion.

Throughout the account the American remained motionless again and looked away from Danilov in absorbed concentration, making no interruption. When Danilov stopped there were a few moments of silence before Cowley stirred. 'Check me out on the similarities,' he demanded. 'Both killings at night, stab wounds from the rear, running right to left across the body. Hair shorn, shoes placed neatly to the right side of the head. But in the case of Suzlev no buttons taken. Hair scattered over the victim's face, both times. No obvious robbery, in either case. Anything I've left out?'

Danilov thought, briefly. 'The area. Pavin's marking it out on the map: both were reasonably close together, so the proximity could be a factor. There's nasal bruising, in each case. Both killings were on the night of a Tuesday, maybe going over into the early morning of a Wednesday. And the measurements of the knife wounds are the same.'

'Matching the knife missing from the apartment?'

'Possibly.'

'What about forensic at the Suzlev scene? Any separate hair or blood samples, other than Suzlev? Fingernail scrapings?'

'None.'

There was a silence. Cowley broke it. 'So we've got ourselves a one hundred per cent nut!'

'Nut?' It was the first verbal misunderstanding.

'Maniac,' corrected Cowley.

'Unquestionably.'

'What about records; cases of attacks like this in the past?'

'We're running checks. And on psychiatric hospitals, obviously. Nothing, so far. Because the area of both killings is fairly contained, I'm having all the police stations in the district asked about prowlers, suspicious characters, street violence that might connect.'

'You think Tuesdays are important?' asked Cowley.

'It's a possible connection, that's all.'

'We've got too much,' said Cowley, distantly, again in private reflection: any thoughts about operational complications between himself and the Russian detective didn't seem a factor any more. An already difficult case had been compounded a hundredfold and his only consideration was upon the information with which he had just been presented. Still reflective he went on: 'Too much and at the same time nothing at all. Just confusion.'

A fresh mind with the same conclusion as himself, thought Danilov, disappointed.

Think! Cowley reasoned: he needed to think, to assemble evidence lists of his own, to put things in what he considered the proper order of importance. 'Why haven't you connected the Suzlev case until now with what you've given us?' The demand was openly critical – an unspoken accusation that the Russians were holding back – but Cowley was unconcerned at that moment.

Danilov regarded the other man quizzically. 'I had one personal meeting at the embassy at which I was treated like a fool: denied any cooperation by anyone. The opportunity didn't even arise to set the situation out. I regard this as the first chance there's been.'

'Sorry,' Cowley apologized at once and sincerely. 'That was out of order.' The FBI agent hesitated. 'You get a lot of serial killing in Russia?'

'Serial killing?' queried Danilov, meeting the second misunderstanding.

'Multiple homicides committed by someone who kills for no other reason other than personal gratification.'

'No,' said Danilov. He'd resolved multiple killings where a mother or a father or some other relation had destroyed a family, but nothing within the terms the American had described. He had a vague feeling of inadequacy at not recognizing the phrase ahead of the explanation. He couldn't believe these were the beginnings of Russia's first experience of such a crime, but recognized it gave a further cause for all the panic and confusion that Lapinsk and the Federal Prosecutor and the Ministries were showing.

'Serial murders are the worst, detection-wise,' offered Cowley. 'Routine rarely works. You can only hope for some scientific break, to lead you in the right direction. Or a mistake by the guy himself, so you catch him red-handed.'

'I've already accepted another one is inevitable.'

'What about publicity?' asked Cowley, following routine that did apply.

The Russian's misapprehension was slightly different this time, because of his recollection of General Lapinsk's preoccupation that morning with a press conference. Danilov said: 'I understand it has been very extensive, in the West. There's been quite widespread coverage here, too . . .'

'That wasn't what I meant,' Cowley broke in. 'Suzlev's killing was obviously maniacal: the girl's killing is confirmation, if any were needed. So what about public warnings, through the media?' Again the American conceded the possibility of offence and again was unconcerned.

Danilov looked down upon his desk for several moments, thinking before he spoke. 'It was a conscious decision, to withhold the Suzlev killing, because it *was* obviously the act of someone

128

deranged . . .' The Russian smiled, apologetically. '. . . Our press is much freer now but it is still possible to control if there's sufficient reason. And in this case there was judged to be sufficient reason, to avoid unnecessary alarm . . .'

'. . . Unnecessary . . . !' Cowley tried to break in, incredulous, but Danilov raised his hand, stopping the interruption.

'. . . I obviously believed there was a stronger consideration when Ann Harris was killed, clearly by the same person . . .'

'. . . Then why not . . .' Cowley came in again, determined upon the definite criticism.

'From the moment of identifying Ann Harris I have been constantly reminded of the political delicacy of the case,' Danilov pointed out, and this time stopped without Cowley's interruption.

'So?' demanded the FBI agent.

'Ann Harris was killed after leaving her apartment, where she'd entertained a lover. You've read the forensic report on that apartment. There's no trace – literally not a single fibre of evidence – of any Russian presence whatsoever . . .' Danilov halted again, for further emphasis. 'But missing from it is a knife which conceivably could have been the weapon which killed her. And also killed Vladimir Suzlev.'

'I don't see . . .' began Cowley but then hesitated, because he did. 'An American! Someone attached to the embassy!'

'I'm not suggesting anything, at this stage. I just want the doubt eliminated. And until it is – if it is – then it might be better, certainly from the political aspect, not to put out sensational stories about maniac murderers on the streets of Moscow.'

'Politically, perhaps,' Cowley accepted reluctantly. 'As a law officer, no. There *is* a maniac out there somewhere, killing people. In America, there would be a public warning.'

'This isn't America,' Danilov pointed out. 'And are you absolutely sure about there being a public warning in America if there were sufficient political reasons for it being temporarily withheld?'

Cowley weighed the question. '*Almost* every time,' he qualified.

'My Director is preparing a press conference, particularly for the Western media but obviously Russian journalists will attend as well,' disclosed Danilov. 'I'm prepared to recommend a warning announcement if you're prepared to go along with it as well. You can decide.'

Cowley gave another shift of discomfort on the tiny chair, aware, without rancour, how the responsibility had been manoeuvred. 'Maybe I'd better consult. Set out all the circumstances.'

'I think that might be wise.'

Cowley was thinking of that morning's discussion with the ambassador and of the man's reaction to the slightest suggestion that someone at the embassy might be involved. 'I feel I should thank you, for the forethought.'

'There's a lot to come from your embassy, about the sort of girl Ann Harris really was,' Danilov reminded.

The American regarded him curiously. 'You making a special point?'

'At the embassy, when your people didn't think I could understand what was being said, there was a peculiar remark from Baxter. They were upset, of course. But Baxter said: "Why the hell was she like she was; you know what I'm saying." *I* don't know what he was saying: I'd like to.'

'So would I,' Cowley agreed. Could it be only the sort of independence that led her to refuse to live in the embassy compound? Or was there something more? The jetlag tiredness was pulling at him now but he was glad it had stayed at bay so long.

'And particular names,' continued Danilov. 'In the month prior to her death, Ann Harris made sixteen telephone calls from her flat to Paul Hughes, her department head.'

'Maybe I should clear the embassy inquiries out of the way tomorrow?' suggested Cowley. If I can, he thought.

'It might produce something,' Danilov agreed.

'We could always speak by telephone, if there's the need.'

Danilov nodded. 'There's something else.'

'What's that?'

'Who's Dick Tracy?'

'What?' Cowley was utterly bewildered.

'Dick Tracy? Is he a person?'

'A comic book detective. Always mixed up with a lot of dumb characters.'

'Successful?'

Cowley shook his head, still bewildered. 'I guess.'

'Dumb characters,' reflected Danilov. 'Quite accurate, really.'

The FBI Director was considering a cable to Cowley, warning the agent of the possible arrival in Moscow of Senator Burden, when Cowley's message arrived for him. Cowley had prepared the report with a digest of the important points superseding the fuller account, so Ross very quickly came to the Russian reasoning for not issuing a public media warning connecting the murder of Ann Harris with that of Vladimir Suzlev.

Without bothering to read on, Ross got into immediate telephone contact with the Secretary of State. 'We need to meet, as soon as possible. There could be a problem we didn't ever imagine.'

'Serious?' asked Hartz, instantly worried.

'If it turns out to be right, about twenty on the Richter scale,' said the FBI chief. 'And the Richter scale only goes up to ten.'

'So you *are* involved?' queried Pauline, hopefully.

'Handling communications,' qualified Andrews.

'I'm sorry,' said Pauline. 'If it bothers you, I mean.'

Andrews smiled across the meal table. 'I'm not going to let it. I'll do whatever Washington wants: they're the people who have got to be impressed with the final outcome. Them and Senator Burden, our future President. This way I'm off the hook, if it stays unsolved. The responsibility will be entirely Bill's, won't it?'

'I suppose so,' said Pauline, unsurely.

'Bill's really out on a limb here: I never properly realized it until last night, at the airport. If it goes down the tube, he goes with it.'

'Perhaps it won't stay unsolved,' said Pauline, hopeful again.

'Perhaps,' said Andrews.

Chapter Fifteen

Cowley's meeting with the ambassador mirrored that of the previous day: the same considerate welcome, the same inquiry after his comfort, the same excellent coffee served by the same broad-hipped woman.

Cowley sat in the oasis of calm diplomatic equanimity, speculating how it would all fall apart if he revealed to the complacent man the unarguable connection between a murder of a drunken Moscow taxi driver and the killing of Ann Harris. Maybe the State Department would inform Hubert Richards, despite his specific overnight mesages to FBI headquarters that he be allowed to work on the embassy leads before any disclosure or alarm. Cowley supposed there would eventually be a complaint from the ambassador, for not being told. He was satisfied there were good professional reasons for withholding the link at the moment.

Gently encouraging, Cowley said: 'I'm curious, sir, if you've come up with anything: particularly about any male friend she might have had here at the embassy. That becomes even more important now: forensic examination of the apartment rules out it being a Russian she went to bed with on the night of her murder.' Was it right, even to approach the ambassador first? It would be, if Richards gave him something positive. The man moved an ornate silver paperweight around the blotter on his desk and Cowley thought the ambassador's colour was starting to grow.

'Didn't expect a girl like Ann to sleep with a Russian, did you?' said Richards, pompously.

'I don't know what to expect at the moment,' said Cowley. 'I'm extremely anxious to find out who the man was.'

'Don't know,' said the ambassador, close to childlike shortness.

'No one could give you any indication at all?'

'None,' insisted the diplomat. 'Ann was a gregarious girl, well liked socially. But properly so, if you know what I mean. Postings here to Moscow are invariably accompanied, wives stationed with husbands.'

'I *do* know what you mean,' assured Cowley. 'And I told you yesterday I'm not interested in morals or embarrassments.'

'I have asked,' Richards insisted. 'I have been told of no one, married or otherwise.'

The silly old fool was lying, guessed Cowley, angrily. But probably not lying directly. From his previous embassy postings Cowley had learned that diplomats avoided accusations of evasion or deceit by *failing* to discover unpalatable things: what they didn't know they couldn't impart. It was Cowley's definition of diplomacy. It *had* been wrong, to bother with the ambassador first. 'If a relationship within the embassy were to be discovered by the Russians – and if their investigation ended in what we would regard as the worst possible conclusion – any embarrassment would be compounded, don't you think?'

'I do not need that pointed out to me. Neither do I consider it worthy of a response.'

'An American involvement would be better contained – better handled – *by* an American,' Cowley persisted.

'You are repeating yourself! And impertinently!' said the other American.

A very definite waste of time, Cowley accepted. It would even be pointless getting annoyed about it. 'We *are* discussing a murder. The murder of someone with rather important connections.'

'I will not have impertinence in my embassy, sir!'

'Let's hope, Mr Ambassador, that you don't have a murderer, either.'

Richards's face was blazing. Through tight lips he said: 'I have an extremely busy schedule. Is there anything else you feel it's necessary for us to discuss?'

'Not at the moment,' said Cowley. 'But if you do hear something you will tell me, won't you?'

'Of course,' said Richards.

Success of some sort, thought Cowley: he'd trapped a diplomat into telling a direct lie.

Barry Andrews was at his window with the scrap-yard view when

Cowley walked into the FBI office. Cowley's overnight messages were lying on the man's desk.

'What the hell have we got here?' Andrews demanded loudly. 'You saying she's the victim of a serial killer?'

'That's what I'm saying.'

'Jesus! The waves this is going to make!'

'I haven't told the ambassador. I don't intend to, yet.'

'Sure that's wise?'

'The bastard is snowing me. I've got to talk to people here at the embassy today and I'm going in cold: they can bullshit me all they like and I wouldn't know it. So what about it, Barry? *You* tell me about Ann Harris. Someone's got to.'

Andrews shrugged, pouring them both coffee from the Cona machine by the window. 'I told you already. Attractive girl. Knew she had Uncle Walt back home in Washington, playing short stop. Aloof. Nice enough kid, though.'

'Barry, someone was fucking her! And it wasn't a Russian because there wasn't a trace of anything Russian in that apartment. So who was it?'

'I don't know. Maybe it was somebody from another embassy: there's fraternization with friendly allies, you know.'

Cowley sighed. 'In a letter the Russians took from her apartment, she calls life here a prison. I would have thought relationships would be pretty obvious to everyone.'

'It's not *that* enclosed.'

'Tell me about Ralph Baxter,' Cowley demanded.

'Ralph? What's he got to do with it?'

'I just want to talk to him. About something odd he said. So what about him?'

Andrews sat with his coffee-cup held before him. 'He's OK. Baseball fanatic. High flier: already served a lot in Asia. If he had more friends in Washington, I guess he'd have his ambassadorship by now.'

'He married?'

Andrews nodded. 'Nice girl. Jane. Great cook. She and Pauline swop recipes and techniques a lot.' He smiled. 'Pauline's still the Goddess of the kitchen.'

'Would Baxter have been screwing Ann Harris?'

'Ralph!' Andrews laughed, aloud. 'I doubt it. Jane keeps those kitchen knives close to hand: poor little Ralphie is a much oppressed spouse. If Jane suspected he was waving it around, she'd cut his pecker off and put it in the stew.'

'What about Paul Hughes?'

Andrews put down his coffee-cup, to hold up shielding hands. 'Let's ease up a little here, Billie boy. I want to know what's going on. I need to be filled in on a few things.'

Cowley didn't like being called Billie boy, but if he expected Andrews to help, he supposed he had to offer some explanation. 'There appears to have been a lot of telephone contact between him and the girl.'

'What's so surprising about that?' demanded Andrews. 'She worked for him. Paul Hughes heads the economic unit here. Actually seems to like the place, if you can believe that! Ballet buff. My regular racquet ball partner in the embassy gym; he's a hell of a player. Always needs to win, every time. Speaks pretty good Russian.'

'Married?'

'Angela. Their two kids are at school back home but Angela takes a kindergarten class for the young children who are with their folks here. She was a teacher originally, in Seattle.'

'What about Hughes? He a special friend of the dead girl?'

There was a gap, before Andrews replied. 'They'd obviously be closer than Baxter: you think he was the guy in her apartment the night she died?'

Cowley shook his head. 'I don't know. Did Ann Harris get involved with the social life of the embassy?'

'She attended some things . . . national holiday celebrations, stuff like that. But she wasn't at the club every night. Lived outside, of course: no way of knowing what she did away from the embassy.'

'She never talked about it?'

'Not to me. But then she wouldn't. I didn't know her that well.'

'Who *did*? What about one of the women here? She have a particular friend among them?'

'Not that I know of.'

'What about the scuttlebutt? Everyone must be talking about her, since the murder. What are they saying?'

135

Andrews shrugged. 'Nothing that helps, I don't think. Everyone liked her. Can't understand what she was doing out in the street, at that time of night; street muggings happen in Moscow, but not particularly in that area.'

'What about *Russian* male friends? You ever hear her linked with a Russian man?'

Andrews shook his head. 'It's not encouraged, for obvious reasons. Wasn't there any lead, from what the Russians took out of her apartment?'

'Nothing that amounts to a bag of beans,' dismissed Cowley. 'You know what I can't understand? Everyone keeps telling me that she was Mary Poppins's doppelganger. And I don't think Ann Harris was that at all. I think Ann Harris could have gone into business designing bedroom ceilings, from looking up at so many.'

Andrews shook his head again. 'I still find it difficult to believe she was like that.'

Chapter Sixteen

Ralph Baxter's office was on the same level as the ambassador's and Cowley guessed the room had originally been virtually as big, possibly a minor reception chamber or annex. But it was partitioned now by ill-matched plasterboard into a series of smaller working areas, practical-sized suites with no wasted space. Baxter's had a window, overlooking the ring road. The preventative glazing wasn't as effective as in Richards's office: the traffic noise intruded, as a low murmur. The sharply moving diplomat bounded across the room to greet Cowley. The man was in his shirt-sleeves but with the waistcoat of a charcoal-grey suit buttoned completely across a diet-hard body. He smiled openly, offered the predictable coffee, which Cowley declined, and asked what it was he could do to help, insisting if there was anything, anything at all, then he would do it. Cowley decided the man's moustache was peculiar: it moved up and down when Baxter spoke but seemed strangely out of time with his upper lip, as if it were false and tenuously stuck on. Cowley couldn't understand why the man wore it at all.

'At least we've got the body returned. It's already gone back,' announced Baxter, as if declaring a personal achievement.

'I heard it was being released,' said Cowley. 'I want to ask you about her. Did you know her well?'

'As well as anyone, I suppose. A wonderful girl. Beautiful. An asset to the embassy. It's a shocking, horrible thing to have happened.'

'She seems to have impressed everyone the same way.'

'There was only one way.'

Cowley felt the frustration rise and then dip, as he suppressed it. Staring directly at the diplomat, he said: 'Why the hell was she like she was? You know what I'm saying.'

For several moments Baxter gazed blankly across the desk. 'What in heaven's name are you saying? I don't understand.'

'Not that remark? Not "Why the hell was she like she was? You know what I'm saying." '

Baxter shook his head, bemused. 'No!'

'Wasn't that what you said, maybe the very words you used, when you learned Ann Harris had been murdered?'

'No!'

'You absolutely positive about that? That first day here at the embassy, when Danilov came with the photographs and you met him, with Barry Andrews?'

'That what Andrews says? He tell you that's what I said? It's not true.'

'Didn't you say it?' Cowley sidestepped.

'No!'

'That's what I hear.'

'It's not true, I tell you!'

'Why? About what?'

'Me. What I said.'

'What do you think you said?'

'I don't know. Doesn't matter.'

'It matters a great deal, Mr Baxter. It seems to indicate something about Ann Harris quite different from what I'm being told by everyone.'

'It's all a misunderstanding!'

'Clarify it for me!' demanded Cowley. 'She was arrogant, wasn't she? Thought she could do anything – behave however she liked – because of her uncle?'

'She was strong-willed, certainly.' Baxter fumbled his rimless glasses from his nose to polish them: it was an interrupting, delaying gesture, not a necessary one.

'Arrogant?' persisted Cowley, pushing the demands to a limit but believing he was guessing correctly. 'Upset a lot of people quite a lot of the time?'

'No!'

'Did she upset you?'

'No!'

'Never?'

'No.'

' "Why the hell was she like she was?" ' quoted Cowley, yet

again. 'That sounds like you were exasperated. Angry. Upset, certainly.'

'Exasperation isn't anger,' tried Baxter.

Cowley snatched at the doubt. 'But you did say it!'

'I don't remember, precisely,' said the diplomat, qualifying further. 'I resent this inquisition! Won't have it. You've no right.'

'An American embassy is American territory, irrespective of the country it's in,' Cowley reminded him. 'An FBI agent is empowered by federal statute of the United States of America to investigate murder within the territory and jurisdiction of America. That's the law.'

'I'm sorry . . . I didn't mean . . . you confused me . . .'

'Why are you confused, Mr Baxter?'

'I want to help, really. But this *is* harassment. An inquisition . . .'

The diplomat was rocky, Cowley judged: but enough to blurt out something without thought? ' "You know what I'm saying," ' he quoted, relentlessly, going on like a dog picking at the last scraps on a bone. 'What *were* you saying, Mr Baxter?'

'Just that,' said Baxter, desperately. 'That she was arrogant. Exasperating.'

'Sufficiently arrogant and exasperating to be murdered?'

'No! That's ridiculous! You're twisting words!'

'Were you her lover, Mr Baxter? Had you been with her that night?'

'No! This is intolerable! I won't be treated this way!'

'Who was then?' persisted Cowley. 'I know, from the scientific examination, that no Russian was in the Pushkinskaya apartment last Tuesday.'

'I don't *know*!' Baxter shouted so loudly that his voice cracked, causing the man more disorientation. 'I'm sorry,' he said, quieter now but still unsettled. 'You *are* harassing: not giving anyone time to think.'

'There's nothing to think about. All I want from this enclosed, insular embassy is to know the name of Ann Harris's lover, so that I can talk to him. Just a name. That's all.'

'I don't have a name,' said Baxter, stubbornly, face set more firmly. '*Why* has her lover necessarily got to be attached here?'

Cowley decided the man had pulled himself together;

withdrawn behind the barrier of a professional diplomat. Not so rocky after all: the annoyance now was at himself, for allowing the escape, not at the foot-shuffling evasion he believed he had been encountering. 'So you can't help me?'

'I'm afraid not: not on this line of inquiry.'

'Or won't?'

'That's a contemptible question I will not answer.'

'This isn't going to go away, Mr Baxter. If there are embarrassments, nothing can stop them coming out.'

Baxter's face flinched but became impassive again as he regained control. 'I don't choose to comment upon that remark, either.'

'Think upon it then,' urged Cowley. 'If you decide there *is* anything you can help me with, I'd like to hear from you.'

The economic section was on the most dispiriting side of the embassy, directly fronting a shabby Moscow apartment block over a tangle of barbed-wire security and almost completely obscuring the beautifully restored town-house of Fedor Chaliapin, the opera singer rehabilitated after years of being banned as a non-person during the reign of Stalin. So depressing was the outlook – and so little of the Chaliapin mansion visible – that the windows were boarded from ceiling to floor, so that lights had to burn permanently to enable the financial staff to work.

Again the department had been formed by partitioning a huge original room into smaller units. Paul Hughes occupied the largest part of the conversion, befitting his position as controller. The designation was actually spelled out on a door inscription and again on another name-plate on a large mahogany desk. The entire area to the left of the desk was occupied by two computer terminals, with connected printers, and tape storage facilities. Directly in front were telephones on short leads to attach to the computer modems. There were two large framed photographs on the desk, one of a smiling woman holding her hair from her eyes in an obvious breeze, the other of two children, a boy and a girl, in Sunday-best clothes, posing formally. The girl was smiling but awkwardly, trying to conceal rigidly braced teeth.

Hughes remained behind the desk. There was no smile of greeting, either. 'Barry Andrews told me you were coming, but I don't know what I can do to help you,' he announced at once.

There was a pervading smell of tobacco in the room. The man was smoking a cigarette and there were several butts already in an ashtray on the desk. Paul Hughes's features were striking, thin-faced but with a beaked nose and pure white hair combed forward. The striped blue suit was impeccable, clearly hand-made with a lapelled waistcoat across which a gold watch-chain linked two flapped pockets. Had Hughes chosen straight diplomacy and not economics, Cowley guessed the man would have already been short-listed for an ambassadorship. Cowley said: 'Ann Harris was a member of your staff: you must have known her well.'

'Reasonably.'

'Did you get on, personally?'

'This is a small department of an embassy in an unusual environment,' lectured Hughes. 'It's essential to be compatible: things would become unworkable otherwise.'

'I'm not completely sure I understand what you've just said.'

'It's necessary to make a conscious effort to get on well with everyone.'

'Did it need a conscious effort to get on with Ann Harris?'

'Not at all. She was a very pleasant girl.'

'How would you describe things between you? Division controller to employee? Or friends?'

Hughes gazed unspeaking across the desk for several moments, and Cowley was caught by the stillness with which the man held himself. Finally Hughes said: 'Neither. There was always the proper degree of respect between us but there was not a rigid distancing: as I said, that wouldn't work here. But I would not go as far as to say we were close friends.'

'I didn't actually ask if you were close.'

'It was amicable,' allowed Hughes.

'Did you mix socially?'

'Everyone mixes socially: it's an enclosed society.'

'Regularly?'

Hughes shrugged. 'As and when. There's usually something organized here at the embassy every week, but people don't go every time. There's a fairly active dinner circuit.'

'Ann Harris has dined with you?'

'My wife and I.'

'And you with her, at Pushkinskaya?'

'I think so: yes I'm sure we have.'

'But not recently? If you'd been there recently you would have remembered more easily?'

There was another unblinking stare. 'No, not recently.'

'Where do you live, Mr Hughes; you and your wife? In the compound or outside?'

'Outside.'

'Isn't it difficult to get outside accommodation? I thought it was at a premium.'

Hughes brought both hands up on the desk, leaning forward to light another cigarette from the butt of the old. They were French, Cowley saw, identifying the packet. Hughes said: 'Is a conversation about the accommodation problems of Moscow going to help find Ann's killer?'

Now it was Cowley who hesitated, looking at the man and the way he was craning forward. 'I don't know. At the moment we're a long way from finding the killer. Where is your apartment?'

Hughes sighed. 'Pecatnikov. We were lucky enough to take it over from my predecessor. I really can't see the point of this conversation.'

'Do you want to help find Ann Harris's killer?'

'Of course I do!' said Hughes, indignantly. 'That's an absurd question.'

'I'm sorry, if it's upsetting you.'

'It's not upsetting me! That's absurd also! Your questions simply seem obtuse.'

There was colour to Hughes's grey face, and Cowley thought that everything he was doing that day was making embassy staff go red. It didn't seem to be achieving much, though: so far no one had lost their temper sufficiently to make any unguarded remark. 'I'll try to be less obscure,' he promised. 'Who was Ann Harris's lover?'

'I've no idea. I didn't even know she had one.'

'Not in this narrow, enclosed society?'

'No.'

'You want to reflect on that, Mr Hughes?'

'What are you saying? Suggesting?'

'Just that you reflect on what you're saying.'

Hughes came further forward over his desk. 'I've agreed to help you – I want to help you – but I won't tolerate this sort of questioning. The inference is obvious and I reject it completely.' The man's voice was even, just occasionally snagging on words in his anger. The cigarette was stabbed out, forcefully.

'What inference is that, Mr Hughes?'

The other man's hands were clenched in front of him now, some of the knuckles even whitening. 'That I am being less than honest with you.'

'But you are, aren't you? Being honest with me?'

Hughes pushed himself back into his chair. 'I've helped you all I can. I'd appreciate it if you left, right now.'

'I'd appreciate something else,' said Cowley, settling further into his chair. 'I'd appreciate your telling me why, from her apartment in Pushkinskaya in the month prior to her death, Ann Harris made sixteen telephone calls to you.'

There was a twitching movement through the other man's body, as if he were wincing from a blow, but that was the only reaction, although the knuckles stayed white. 'How do you know about telephone calls made to me? *What*, about telephone calls?'

'You've said you want to help me. I'd hoped you'd help me about those, particularly.'

The movement that went through Hughes's body this time was more of a shudder. 'She was attached to this department. It is not at all unusual for members of my staff to talk to me on the telephone after normal working hours.'

'Staff that work for you throughout the day?'

'Yes. Why not?'

'Was Ann Harris efficient?'

'Of course she was. She wouldn't have been assigned here if she hadn't been efficient.'

'You never had cause for complaint about her work?'

'Never.'

'Yet during the month before she was killed she remembered sixteen things to talk to you about that she'd forgotten during the day when she was here with you and which couldn't wait until the next morning.'

'Is that a question?'

'If you like. I find it curious, don't you?'

'No.'

'Do other members of your staff consult you, after working hours?'

Instead of replying, Hughes depressed a button on a flat keyboard close to his computer complex. Cowley heard the door open behind him. Hughes smiled up and said: 'Pam. Come in, won't you?'

The girl who entered Cowley's view was slight and dark-haired, bobbed short. She wore black-framed glasses which she removed as she approached. The twin-set was fawn, with a knitted-in flower motif which was picked up in the skirt, completing the ensemble. She looked curiously between the two men and Hughes said: 'Pamela Donnelly, my other senior economist. William Cowley.'

From all the material he had read, Cowley knew Ann Harris had been twenty-eight years old: he guessed Pamela Donnelly to be the same, maybe a year or two older. Not knowing the reason for her summons, Cowley said nothing. Neither did the girl. Both looked at Hughes.

The finance controller said: 'Cowley's investigating Ann's murder. Seems to think there's something unusual about us talking together after we leave here at night. How often do you and I talk, out of hours?'

The girl gave a shoulder movement of uncertainty. 'I don't know. Once or twice a week maybe: sometimes more, if there's some particular thing going on.'

'Why?' Cowley asked the question of the girl but was conscious of the other man smiling, in expectation.

'The time difference,' explained the girl. 'Mr Hughes very often stays on for queries coming in from Washington: if it's important we speak to each other, if it's something we've been involved with during the day . . .' She hesitated, finally smiling back at the financial chief. 'Mr Hughes likes to keep things up to date: we work an action-this-day system . . .' There was another pause. 'I still can't believe what happened. Have you found who did it?'

'Not yet,' said Cowley.

'Satisfied about the telephone calls now?'

To the girl Cowley said: 'Thank you. That was very helpful,' and remained standing until she left the room. Seated again, Cowley said: 'What was that all about?'

'Another question I don't get.'

'Why bring her into the conversation?'

'Corroborative evidence. Isn't that what you detectives look for, in an inquiry? Corroborative evidence?' Another cigarette clouded into life.

'Do you think you need your word corroborated, Mr Hughes?'

'No, I don't think I need it at all, Mr Cowley. Do you?'

'I don't know: I don't know very much at all.' A lie, thought Cowley: he believed it was turning into a very productive day. This whole affair might be resolved very quickly. But with some severe embarrassment.

'What else can I help you with?' The man appeared more relaxed, not holding himself so rigidly.

'Ann Harris's office,' declared Cowley. 'Where was that . . .' He hesitated, looking about him. '. . . in relation to this room?'

'Next door,' said Hughes. 'Ann to the right, the secretary to the left. All made a neat, compact unit . . .'

'. . . what happened to it?' broke in Cowley, suddenly worried.

'Happened to it?'

'There are usually some personal things in a private office. Have they been gone through?'

'Of course,' said Hughes, impatiently.

'By whom? Who has it now?' This was an overdue inquiry: one he should have made the first day. He couldn't believe he hadn't done it then and almost at once answered his own doubt. A lapse of proper professionalism, he recognized, critically: he'd been away from active operational work too long and become sloppy. He was made uncomfortable – actually, briefly, disorientated – by the awareness.

'I'm not sure,' said Hughes, frowning. 'Maybe Barry Andrews. I know he was there when everything was boxed up by embassy security. I guess you should ask Barry.'

'Boxed up?'

'The personal bits and pieces. There wasn't much. Just one box. Small, too.'

'Do you have it here?' demanded Cowley, too hopefully.

Hughes gestured uncertainly, lighting another cigarette. 'I just took over the official embassy stuff she was working on. Which wasn't much, fortunately. She really was an efficient girl: job started, job finished. Action-this-day, like Pam said. Again, about the other things, you'd better ask Barry.'

Cowley was suddenly impatient to leave this man, to get back to the resident FBI officer, but held back, knowing it would be a mistake to make an abrupt departure. 'I'm very grateful, for all your help. And I really do hope I haven't caused any offence.'

'Why should you think that?'

'You seemed tense sometimes.'

'I've never before personally known somebody who was murdered. And in such an appalling way. Nor been questioned by a detective, ever before. Did you really expect me to behave as if I were enjoying it?' Despite the question there was an amiability about the finance director now, an impression of a man at ease in his surroundings.

'Perhaps not,' agreed Cowley. 'You've been very patient.'

'Poor Ann,' said Hughes. 'Poor, dear Ann. She really was a wonderful girl.'

'So everyone tells me,' said Cowley. He positively thrust out his hand, forcing the financial director to rise to take it. As they shook, Cowley thought: very productive indeed. He hesitated directly outside the room that Ann Harris had occupied, tempted to enter, but abandoned the idea. There would be nothing left now. Continuing on, he wondered where Pamela Donnelly worked. All the doors were closed, with none of the more lowly occupants designated by name-plates.

Barry Andrews was in the FBI office where Cowley had left him: the only difference from the earlier visit was that Andrews was now wearing his suit jacket. A cigar was smouldering in a bowl near the telephone. Seeing Cowley's look towards it Andrews said: 'First today: limit myself to three.'

'You got something to tell me?'

'How's that?'

'Ann Harris's office: you helped clear it yesterday, of her personal things. What's there to tell me? I'd like to see the stuff.'

Andrews picked up the cigar, considering its lighted end. 'I think we've got a slight problem here.'

Cowley experienced a stomach dip. 'What sort of problem?'

'There was nothing: hardly anything. Just odds and ends.'

'I'd still like to go through it myself.'

'The body was shipped back yesterday. You knew that.'

'What about the personal things that were in her office?' persisted Cowley, his temper slipping in anticipation.

'I asked the ambassador what he wanted me – or security – to do. He said her personal stuff should go back with the body.'

'You *asked* the ambassador! About what should be done to articles belonging to a murder victim! What in the name of Christ are you talking about?' This was work – professionalism – and Andrews had fucked up, so he had every reason for the anger: their personal situation had nothing whatsoever to do with it.

'I was trying to help!' protested the local man. 'There was nothing, I tell you!'

'You made an inventory?' Cowley felt cold with fury: at himself, for permitting the first mistake, and at the other FBI agent for perpetuating it. How could the man have been so unprofessional?

Andrews brightened, perceptibly. 'Sure I made an inventory!' He fumbled open a drawer to the left of his desk, took out a single sheet of paper and read from it. 'Three framed photographs. Some Bolshoi Theatre ticket stubs. A map of Moscow. One of those monthly season tickets you can get here for both the metro and the buses. And a set of Gorby dolls . . .' The man smiled up, eagerly helpful. 'Maybe you haven't seen them yet. They're tourist things: a set of the traditional *matryoshka* dolls, a whole family that fit one inside the other. But the Gorby set go back through the Soviet leadership, Gorbachov, Brezhnev, Krushchev, Stalin and Lenin. You can buy them on the Arbat . . .'

'. . . Barry! I don't want to buy any fucking dolls. I want to know why conceivable evidence has been shipped back, unchecked, without any scientific examination! Nothing!'

'There *was* no conceivable evidence!' insisted Andrews. 'But what are we talking about here? Settling old grudges, maybe? Saying things you've wanted to say for a long time?'

'Don't be fucking stupid! Possible evidence is *all* I mean. I don't confuse grudges with work: and I don't have a grudge, anyway.' What then? he asked himself. Was he trying to absolve himself from guilt for not personally checking the girl's office by heaping the responsibility on to the other man, perhaps? He snatched the list and said: 'Memorandum! This says there was a memo pad?'

'Blank!' insisted Andrews. 'It was one of those joke things you get for Christmas: some stupid crap written on the top of each page. But the pad itself was clean. I definitely checked.'

'I want a cable to Washington.' It would probably only be a minimal recovery – maybe not even that – but it was worth the effort: and he'd phrase the message not to carry the can for what Andrews had done. Or rather hadn't done. He'd have to cool off, before he wrote anything, though: wrong – unfair – to apportion all the blame.

'Saying what?' asked Andrews, cautiously.

'Everything's to be tested: which it should have been before it even left here.' Cowley found the cigar smell distasteful. 'There could be an item in what's gone back that'll connect with something that came out of her apartment.'

'Maybe I should have checked with you,' conceded Andrews. Humbled contrition wasn't easy.

'It's too late now,' dismissed Cowley, impatiently.

'So how'd it go, with Baxter and Hughes? Get anything to build up your picture?'

'Some.'

'Look,' said Andrews, placating. 'Personally, we're in a goddamned strange situation. Which we've accepted. So no problem. Now let's talk professionally. I *work* here, for Christ's sake! *Know* a lot of people, which means I might pick up something if they're snowing you, like you think the ambassador tried to do. Why not bounce it all off me? We're on the same side, aren't we?'

Cowley gazed past the other agent. Outside in the courtyard a man in overalls, the handyman Cowley guessed, was moving among the metal poles and their sagged connecting wires. Cowley watched the man individually lift and then drop three separate strands, achieving nothing: it was another foggy day, grey dampness sponging everything. He thought Moscow seemed to be a city with a blanket always pulled over its head. The handyman shrugged and walked out of sight. Cowley came back to Andrews, accepting the logical common sense of the suggestion. 'Why don't I do just that?'

Andrews smiled. 'No reason not to.'

'I'm going to need all the help I can get,' admitted Cowley.

'You got it,' assured Andrews.

'So it's working well?' said General Lapinsk.

'It was a satisfactory first meeting,' Danilov allowed, cautiously. He was disappointed that nothing more had emerged from the routine inquiries. The Records search had so far produced nothing. Neither had the assault or prowler checks throughout the Militia stations in the murder area. He reminded himself to ask Pavin about the psychiatric institutions.

'You didn't get any impression of them wanting to take over the investigation?'

'No.'

'That's good,' said Lapinsk. There was a spluttered cough.

'I'm letting the American have some of the clothes she was wearing when she was stabbed: there's a test for blood content of the body he wants to make, in Washington.'

The Militia General nodded. 'What did he say about the first one?'

'That there should be a public warning. Then he took our point about holding back in case there is embarrassment involving the American embassy. Realistically, we'll have to do something about an announcement soon.'

'The uncle wants to come,' Lapinsk disclosed. 'There's been a visa application in Washington. It's going to be granted, of course.'

'He'll create a lot of publicity.'

'Which is something we have to talk about. It's been decided who is going to take part in the press conference. It's going to be the Federal Prosecutor, myself . . .' The older man hesitated. '. . . And both yourself and the American.'

Danilov was stunned. 'Me!'

'It is apparently how major crimes with great public interest are handled in America.'

Copying to conform, thought Danilov. 'Have the Americans agreed?'

'It's been proposed. There's no reason for them to object.'

Possible difficulties shared were definitely difficulties spread sideways and backwards, Danilov supposed. Like manure. 'Will it be a big conference?'

'The main assembly hall at the Federal Prosecutor's building is to be used.'

He would have to ensure Olga got his shirts washed and pressed, Danilov decided. He'd have to talk to her about it that night. Olga always needed time, to get things done.

Chapter Seventeen

Larissa and her husband lived in one of the better apartment blocks just off the inner ring road, the newest-built high-rises for members of the Party. The unthinkable collapse of communism in 1991 had terrified Yevgennie Kosov, who had never conceived its possible demise. He'd graduated into the Party direct from the Komsomol youth organization for the privileges of membership – which included superior living accommodation – not from any political ideology. Kosov's personal ideology was the enjoyment of life as one of the Moscow élite and he had been initially frightened he might lose it all. He'd resigned and abandoned the Party, of course, like all sensible survivors. But still waited, in those early months, for official retribution. None had come. Now Kosov had completely recovered the shaken confidence, sure that things weren't really going to change, but ready, at a moment's notice, to adjust if the need became necessary.

Danilov retained the allocated but unmarked official car, knowing it would please Olga. She twisted back and forth in the front seat the moment he set off from Kirovskaya, swivelling fully after a few minutes to examine the rear seats and then announcing: 'This is *exactly* the sort of car I want!'

'This is a Volga. It's not the model we've ordered. If we try to change we'll go to the end of the queue.'

She tried to get the telephone off its rest but couldn't release the clip: Danilov didn't try to help her. She said: 'Does this work? Could I speak to someone now, while we're driving along?'

'It's official. All the calls are recorded.'

'I want to call Larissa! Let her know we're on our way! How do I pick it up?'

'There's no point in doing that.

'It could be explained as an official conversation. Yevgennie is a policeman, isn't he?'

'It won't impress anyone: they'll know it doesn't belong to us.'

'I want to!'

Danilov released the telephone and handed it across the car to his wife. She dialled incorrectly on the first attempt and he had to explain the transmission procedure as she dialled. Olga chattered her way through an inconsequential conversation about non-existent traffic delays, talking far more loudly than was necessary, and Danilov felt sorry for her. As she handed the telephone back to him, to be reclipped, she said: 'Larissa was laughing. Why would she laugh?'

'Maybe she thought it was funny.' Danilov was not looking forward to the evening. For a while during the afternoon he'd considered cancelling. Larissa had protested that he shouldn't, when they'd spoken: 'I promise to keep my hands off you, even though it won't be easy,' she'd said. Perhaps she'd been laughing at the memory of the conversation, not at Olga's showing off with a car telephone.

He managed to park immediately outside the apartment. Olga waited for him to walk around to let her out, as if she was reluctant to leave the car until the very last moment. He did so and began leading the way into the building, but she said: 'What about the windscreen wipers! You know they'll be stolen if you don't take them off.'

Danilov turned back, irritated at having forgotten a basic rule of Moscow motoring. He returned to the vehicle, unsure how to disconnect the wipers on a model he didn't know. The spring was too strong on the passenger side, briefly trapping his finger before he unhooked the blade. When he got into the better-lit vestibule he saw his hands were filthy with grease and that his shirt cuff was stained. His finger was bleeding slightly, where the spring had caught him.

'You're a mess,' complained Olga.

'I shouldn't have bothered.'

'It would have been awkward if it rained, on the way home.'

'They might not have been taken.'

'They would,' insisted Olga. She liked to conclude any dispute, no matter how trivial.

Danilov felt foolish entering Larissa's apartment carrying windscreen wipers. It didn't help that she giggled at him. He smiled back, not knowing where to put the blades. 'I need to wash.'

'You do, don't you? Why don't you leave them in the kitchen?'

Danilov did so, and managed to get most of the grease off his hands in the sink there. Larissa stood watching, but by the door, as far away from him as possible. He thought she was going to remain there as he tried to get into the main room, forcing him to squeeze by and bring them close together, but at the last minute she came further into the kitchen, unblocking the doorway. As he went by she said quietly: 'I might break my promise,' and laughed again.

Yevgennie Kosov was in the middle of the living-room, in the process of helping Olga out of her coat: having done so the man felt out, putting his hands around Olga's waist, and said: 'What a body: trim as a bird!' and kissed her. He kept his hands where they were. Olga smiled happily, unoffended at being groped.

Danilov had forgotten Kosov's tactile need to touch and feel: when they shook Kosov enclosed Danilov's hand in both of his and held on with one while he pummelled and patted Danilov's shoulder with the other.

'Too long, too long!' boomed Kosov, with shouted exuberance. 'Old friends like us shouldn't leave it so long!'

Danilov wondered how much the other man had drunk before their arrival. There was a glass and a whisky bottle on a small table: it was Chivas Regal, displayed like a spoil of war.

'Champagne for the ladies, a man's drink for us,' announced Kosov. He was a naturally large man made larger by constant excess, stomach sagging above his trouser belt and hardly disguised beneath a sweater which Danilov guessed he was supposed to admire: it was obviously cashmere. Kosov's face had an alcohol glow and there were some broken red veins along both sides of his fleshy nose. The champagne was French, not Russian.

Kosov grinned as he passed the drinks around and said: 'You didn't have to get all messed up like that. No point in having influence if you don't use it. I make damned sure the Militia patrols are around this block all the time and the villains know it. Anyone committing crime anywhere near my home knows I'll have their balls for a necklace!'

'I should have realized,' said Danilov, mildly. He wondered how many other innovations Kosov had made.

'Olga's had her welcoming kiss! Where's mine?' demanded Larissa, in mock protest.

Danilov leaned forward briefly to brush her cheek, not reaching out to hold her: with their bodies shielding the movement, Larissa felt out and quickly squeezed his hand, a taunting gesture. She didn't let go, however, bringing Danilov's hand up as he stepped away from her. 'You've cut yourself! It's bleeding. Come on, I've got dressings in the bathroom.'

'It's nothing. It's not necessary,' Danilov tried to escape.

'I don't want you bleeding all over the apartment!' complained Larissa. 'Come on! I insist.' She kept hold of the injured hand to lead him along the corridor to the bathroom, a dazzle of imported fittings. Inside she said: 'Now you can kiss me properly!'

'Stop it!' protested Danilov.

'Why?' She had her head to one side, knowing his awkwardness, enjoying being the coquette.

'It's dangerous.'

'Kiss me!' she ordered.

He did. Larissa immediately put her hands on his buttocks, grinding her crotch into his. Danilov positively parted from her and said: 'You'll get blood on your dress.' It was cashmere, like Kosov's sweater, a pale blue. Larissa smelled as perfumed and fresh as she always did. Her hair as perfectly brushed, loose for his benefit, and her make-up almost flawless. 'Your lipstick's smudged.'

'And you're wearing it,' Larissa agreed. She wiped it from his face and repaired her lipline while he wrapped the offered antiseptic covering around his finger. He saw ingrained into both hands some grease he'd missed in the kitchen and tried again in the bathroom sink. Not all of it came off and he guessed he'd need cleansing spirit to get rid of it completely. She said: 'It's good having you here.'

'How can it be?'

'I like looking at them and then at you. And thinking what we do, which they don't know anything about. I get all excited. Do you want to feel?'

'Stop it, Larissa!'

'Tomorrow afternoon?'

He'd arranged to go to the mortuary again, with the American this time. 'I'm not sure. I'll try. We should get back to the others.'

He wondered what Cowley had achieved at the embassy: there hadn't been any telephone contact.

'Sure you don't want to feel?'

Danilov didn't reply, walking out of the bathroom ahead of her. Olga and Kosov were sitting side by side on a couch that ran more than half the width of one wall of the apartment. Kosov was holding Olga's hand, resting on her thigh.

'Isn't this the most wonderful flat?' demanded Olga. 'I've never seen a television that big. And it's got a video player: they can watch movies, right here in their own home!'

'Wonderful,' agreed Danilov, dutifully. He didn't think he'd ever seen such a large television, either. It was enclosed in a cabinet, with louvred doors that could seal it off. The video equipment was on a lower shelf. There was an extensive stereo display right next to it, close to the chairs that made up the suite. Danilov wondered how much had come from the grateful importer whom he'd introduced to the other man. The wallpaper was hessian and the ceiling-to-floor curtains were a heavy green velvet, shaded to match the thick and slightly darker green wall-to-wall carpeting.

'Nothing to it if you've got the proper friends, is there, Dimitri?' Kosov gestured towards Danilov. 'Taught me all I know, on how to operate in a Militia district . . .' He leaned forward towards Danilov, solemn-faced, responsibly serious policeman to responsibly serious policeman. 'We're looking after that inquiry. Checking out every street incident that could be relevant. And a lot more. I've put the word out, among special friends I've made since you were here. If there's a whisper about, I'll hear it. Don't you worry.'

To judge from the other man's dialogue, Danilov thought a lot of the video movies Kosov watched on his cinema-sized television screen had to be American crime thrillers. He was about to question what Kosov had told him when Larissa perched on the arm of his chair. To her husband she said: 'How are you involved with Dimitri?'

Danilov supposed he should have realized from the geography of the city that his old Militia district would be included in the checks he'd asked Pavin to initiate, but until that moment he hadn't. He wished Larissa hadn't sat as she was, so close their legs touched. Before Danilov could find a dismissive reply, not wanting to talk about the murders, Kosov said: 'The city's detective force need uniformed officers to help them find a mass murderer.'

'Two is hardly mass murder, is it?' said Larissa.

Kosov got up from the couch to refill glasses. 'It'll be mass murder when he kills again,' insisted Kosov, belligerently. 'A maniac, killing and maiming.'

'They weren't maimed!' contradicted Danilov.

'Scalped!' insisted Kosov. 'Her and the man. That's the information we've been given.'

'Neither one was scalped!' rejected Danilov, exasperated. 'The hair was cut off.' How could any inquiries throughout the Militia districts be objective if they were going to be interpreted like this? He'd have to go through the phrasing of the check request with Pavin first thing tomorrow.

'Don't you think it's the work of a maniac?'

'Of course it is,' said Danilov, still wanting to terminate the conversation. 'But this is hardly the place or time to talk about it, is it?'

Larissa shuddered and said: 'Just think. He could be quite close to us now: just a street or two away.'

'Why hasn't there been any announcement about it yet?' said Olga. 'All I've read about is the girl. And it didn't say anything about cutting off her hair.'

'There might be, soon. We don't want to cause any panic,' said Danilov.

'I'm glad . . .' started Larissa, unthinking, then hurriedly stopped. '. . . that you've told us now,' she finished, badly.

Danilov felt a warmth and hoped he wasn't colouring at the nearness of Larissa blurting out his earlier hotel bedroom warning. Quickly he said to Kosov: 'What do you mean, about putting the word out among your special friends?'

'Just that,' said the Militia commander. 'People know who's in charge of Militia station 19: and when I say I want help they know I mean it. So the word's out. Any kinky bastard wandering around my streets I'm going to know about it, don't you worry.'

Danilov realized the other man was glorying in the situation, posturing to impress. Surely the fool hadn't inquired among the

Dolgoprudnaya crime syndicate Larissa had told him about? At once Danilov realized that was *precisely* what Kosov would have done. The Dolgoprudnaya would probably laugh at him. Danilov resolved to treat with extreme caution anything that came from Kosov's police station. Wearily Danilov said: 'I look forward to getting anything you find out.'

'Just like the old days,' Kosov enthused. 'The two of us working together again.'

Danilov couldn't recall an investigation they had jointly handled, when they were in the same district. Wanting to change the subject, he said: 'I sometimes miss uniform work.'

'Surely there are benefits at Petrovka?' sniggered Kosov.

'I'd like to know what they are!' Olga came in, ahead of her husband. 'We haven't even got a television that works properly.'

'You want a favour, all you've got to do is ask,' offered Kosov, generously. 'My friends are your friends: you even knew some before me.'

'I don't believe you *really* miss it.' Now Larissa was openly goading. 'I think it takes *very* special qualities, to be a detective. Not like ordinary policemen. Don't you think that, Yevgennie?'

Her husband squinted across the room, mind blurred by whisky. 'Control detectives,' he said. 'Part of my staff. I'm in charge.'

'Administratively. And your detectives don't investigate *murders*, do they? Not like Dimitri.' Larissa smiled ingenuously at the other woman. 'Aren't you proud of him, Olga? Knowing how clever he is? Hunting murderers? Maniac murderers?'

Danilov tried to press his leg warningly against hers: Larissa answered the pressure, smiling down. 'I think you're very clever. Brave, too.'

Olga seemed to have difficulty in finding an answer to the question she'd been asked. Eventually she said: 'Yes, I suppose. I don't really think about it. It's his job.'

'Which I didn't come here to discuss,' said Danilov, renewing the effort for another subject. 'I came to eat dinner.'

Larissa had to get up from the chair arm to serve it and Danilov was relieved. Olga went to help and Kosov insisted on more whisky, while they waited. With the caviare Kosov served chilled vodka. There was imported French white wine with the cold fish

157

and red, French again, with the duck, which Larissa served with marinated cabbage, both red and white. When Olga politely praised the meal Larissa said everything had come from the open, State-free market next to the Circus: every conceivable foodstuff was available providing you were prepared to pay the price. Kosov, who belatedly appeared to realize his wife had been mocking him about the degree of responsibility of a Militia post commander, told interminable police anecdotes whose point or denouement he frequently forgot, relapsing into shrugs and hopeful, join-me laughter and mumbled 'you know' and 'so that was that'. Everyone felt varying degrees of discomfort.

Kosov poured brandy for himself and Danilov while the women cleared away. Kosov said: 'Isn't there really any understanding operating at Petrovka?'

'I believe so, in the general serious crime section. Not in the homicide division though. There couldn't be, could there?'

'Of course there could,' argued the expert. 'Use the contacts of the serious crime squad *not* involved in murder.'

'I haven't got around to it yet,' Danilov hedged.

'Don't want to obligate yourself, with other colleagues?' guessed Kosov.

'Something like that,' said Danilov, taking the excuse.

'Then let me help. All you've got to do is ask.'

Which would mean he would be taking favours from both members of the family, Danilov thought, knowing a different sort of discomfort. 'I'll remember that.'

'Any time,' said Kosov. 'That's what friends are for.'

Danilov couldn't remember the other man being quite so openly condescending before. There was some desultory talk about films when the women returned and some quite animated conversation when Kosov announced that he was thinking of applying for exit visas so he and Larissa could take a vacation in Europe, probably both France and Italy. It was Danilov who brought the evening to a close, pleading pressure of work. Kosov kissed Olga goodbye and promised Danilov he would be hearing something from him in a few days. 'The word's out on the streets. Trust me.'

When Danilov kissed Larissa farewell she looked directly at him. 'Don't forget what Yevgennie said earlier: let's not leave it so long until we get together again.'

'Our turn next time,' insisted Olga as they left, Danilov carrying the wipers in a piece of paper towel.

Danilov trapped his finger again replacing them on the police car but this time didn't cut himself. He used the paper towel to wipe off as much fresh grease as possible.

'Isn't that going to be embarrassing?' demanded Olga, when he got in beside her.

'What?'

'Having them back to us next time. Can you imagine what they'll think of our apartment? I can remember the time when we had things every bit as good as theirs: better even.'

'Don't invite them then.' Danilov didn't want another evening like tonight. He'd swung between boredom and embarrassment with Kosov, and Larissa had made him constantly uncomfortable in other ways. And she'd known it: he guessed she hadn't just felt superior to her husband and Olga but to him as well.

'We *have* invited them.'

'Not a specific date. Just don't do anything more about it.'

'Do you like her?'

Danilov looked quickly across the car and wished he hadn't, from the guilt it might have conveyed. 'Larissa?'

'Who else do you think I mean?'

'Of course I like her. We've all of us been friends a long time. Why do you ask?'

'She was all over you tonight.'

'Rubbish!' said Danilov, almost too forcefully.

'What were you doing in the bathroom?'

'You know what we were doing. She was dressing my finger.' It sounded pitifully inadequate.

'It seemed to take a long time.'

'I tried to get more muck off my hands.'

'She had to stay and help you do that?'

'We were talking.'

'What about?'

'I don't know! Things at the hotel. How I enjoy working at Petrovka. Just talking.'

'She's very attractive, isn't she?'

'I haven't thought about it.' That had sounded wrong, too. Now Danilov was aware of Olga looking across the car at him.

159

'Her dress was French. She told me, in the kitchen.'

Danilov didn't reply. Despite the distraction of the conversation inside the car he found himself staring out into the quiet streets along which they were driving, looking. For what, he demanded angrily of himself. A figure wielding a knife? Or running with a handful of hair?

'It showed her figure. She hasn't got any fat, not like me, has she?'

'I didn't notice.'

'She was so close to you I wouldn't have thought you could have missed noticing.'

'If we're making comparisons, which we seem to be doing, I thought you and Yevgennie clung together pretty much tonight.' Now it was petulance.

'Yevgennie! Don't be ridiculous. He's always like that; always has been.'

Danilov edged off the inner ring road, to cut through minor streets in the hope of reaching Kirovskaya as quickly as possible. Wind-driven rain began misting the windscreen and Danilov had to start the wipers. There was a hard scraping noise as they cleared the screen and he guessed he had re-attached them wrongly.

'At least he was interested in some physical contact with me. I haven't been aware of you showing much recently.'

'Don't start an argument where one doesn't exist, Olga!' He was surprised at not being able to remember the last time they'd made love.

'I . . .' started the woman, loudly, but stopped. Controlling herself she went on: 'I don't recall you and I thinking of a vacation in Europe, when you were in charge of the district.'

'Travel was much more strictly controlled when I was in charge.' Danilov confronted a No Entry sign he hadn't expected. He turned left, to make his own detour, acknowledging it wasn't any longer a shortcut.

'We still didn't think about it,' insisted the woman, stubbornly.

'Yevgennie didn't say they *were* going. It's the sort of thing he'd do, talk about visas as if the trip is all fixed.'

'Are you going to do it?'

'Do what?' Danilov rerouted himself on to the road he wanted, hoping there would not be any further obstruction. He'd certainly been uncomfortable with Larissa but he hadn't expected the situation between them to be quite so obvious. Olga could only have a suspicion: he just had to deny any outright accusation and ridicule whatever innuendo she might make. Damn Larissa! She *had* been amusing herself and in doing so had created stupid, unnecessary difficulties.

'Take up Yevgennie's offer to put us into contact with people who can get things . . . like the old days.'

'I don't think so.' Danilov began to recognize his surroundings and was relieved they were almost home.

'Why the hell not?' erupted Olga, loudly again. 'I'm pissed off, going on like we are now! You told me Petrovka was promotion. Promotion means better things: more benefits. What benefits have we got, since the transfer? None! We've actually lost out! You expect me to go on like this?'

Danilov wondered what alternative she was threatening. 'The job's not the same any more.'

'What's the job got to do with it? Why did you have to give up all the connections you had? There was no reason.'

'I just wanted to do things differently.' She wouldn't understand if he tried to talk about honesty in an environment and in a country where if they had the chance people — even policemen — didn't regard it as dishonest to use unofficial markets with unofficial money. It scarcely was dishonest by Russian values. No one really got harmed apart, perhaps, from the State whose *perestroika* boasts had failed and whose fault it therefore was that a second entrepreneurial society was necessary. Danilov wasn't sure he could have properly expressed the way he felt, even if Olga had been interested, which he knew she wasn't.

'So we all have to suffer!'

Danilov supposed that from Olga's viewpoint there was no other way to describe it. He wanted very much to present an argument to put against her, to justify his attitude, but couldn't think of one. Lamely he said: 'Let's get this other business over. Then we'll see.'

'You will let Yevgennie introduce you to some of his friends?' seized Olga, eagerly.

The Dolgoprudnaya was a properly organized crime syndicate,

not a loose-knit group of black marketeers who'd wanted warehouses overlooked and delivery lorries unhindered. What blackmail potential would he be exposing himself to if he let the new-found integrity slip? It would . . . Danilov halted the reflection, surprised he had let it begin at all. Risk of blackmail from professional criminals was not the obstacle, real though that risk might be. The only consideration *was* his fragile integrity, the feeling he hadn't properly analysed until now but thought of as being clean. And he didn't want to surrender it. He didn't want to continue this snappy conversation with a suspicious Olga, either. 'We'll see,' he repeated.

'It'll be wonderful, having things like they were before,' said Olga, misunderstanding. She was quiet for several moments, as Danilov coasted the car to a stop outside their apartment block. Then she said: 'Rather than have them back to eat with us here we could take them out, of course. But we'd need dollars, so we could go to a hard-currency place.'

'Shit!' exploded Danilov, registering what she'd said.

Olga stared at him in bewilderment. 'What is it?'

'I've realized something I should have thought of before,' admitted Danilov, angrily. It was too late – and there would be no benefit anyway – to call Pavin now. It would have to wait until the morning. Shit, he thought again: shit! shit! shit!

During the enforced bachelorhood after the divorce from Pauline – whose hobby had been cooking – Cowley had become a gourmand of convenience food. That evening he'd stocked up from the embassy commissary and prepared a Lean-Cuisine veal for dinner in the guest apartment. He was undecided between chicken and braised beef, for the following night.

He watched CNN while the veal heated, curious if there would be a reference to Senator Burden's intended Moscow visit, after the warning cable he'd got that night from Washington. There wasn't. Cowley appreciated the Director's guidance, to refer any difficulties to him and not to become personally involved in any disagreements. He couldn't imagine what those difficulties might be: he saw the politician's visit being handled by the ambassador, with his participation entirely peripheral, a courtesy briefing session maybe.

Cowley's mind was more occupied by other things.

Uppermost was the embassy itself, and Cowley's belief that he saw a way forward there. The dilemma was how *to* go forward. He had a suspicion wholly unsupported at this early stage by one single incriminating fact. Yet if he was right, the killing of Ann Harris could possibly be an entirely American affair, with the suspect liable to arrest on technically American property, able to be returned to American jurisdiction and presumably tried before an American court. So was that how he should proceed, completely cutting out Dimitri Danilov and the Russian side of the investigation? It was his first inclination to do just that, until he rationalized it further and recognized that some at least of the incriminating facts necessary for a conviction would have to come from the Russians. Who – prior to the murder of Ann Harris – had another killing to solve. Which compounded the dilemma. Possibly under international law there was provision for an American national accused of the homicide of another American to be returned to United States jurisdiction. But what about any trial for the fatal stabbing of Validmir Suzlev, very much upon Russian soil and very much under the jurisdiction of Russian law? Although he could not conceive the connection, he didn't doubt the killer of both was one and the same person. And it was absurd to imagine the Russian authorities agreeing to the Suzlev trial taking place in America, any more than Cowley foresaw Washington agreement for a Moscow trial of a US citizen for the Ann Harris crime. Dilemma on top of dilemma on top of dilemma, he decided: a *matryoshka* doll of legality. Which needed a mind far better constitutionally trained than his to lift, separate and decided upon.

What did he need, to confirm his suspicion to the point of an open accusation? Certainly one piece of comparable forensic evidence he knew to be at Petrovka. And possibly to meet the widow of the taxi driver, to try to find the so far elusive link.

All possible tomorrow, Cowley decided. And with it reached another decision. He wouldn't give Danilov the slightest indication that he had a lead. It was still far too early – and the ruling on how legally to handle the matter after an arrest would have to come from Washington – and anyway he was not beholden to the Russian, owing an exchange on a *quid pro quo* basis. The priority always was a quick and diplomatically acceptable conclusion to the investigation, not how to win Russian friends and influence them.

Cowley stirred himself to turn off the unwatched television and retrieve the veal parmesan from the oven, moving automatically, still deep in reflection. It was always wrong – positively lectured *against* at the FBI academy at Quantico – to allow personal feelings to intrude into any investigation. But he was looking forward to the upheaval among those supercilious, arrogant sons-of-bitches at the embassy if he were proven right. Allowing himself the cliché, Cowley decided it would hit the place like a bombshell. More friends he ultimately wouldn't win and influence.

He wasn't sure about the joint American-Russian press conference he'd been told to attend: there'd be the need for further guidance from Washington about that, particularly about whether to link the taxi-driver murder, which at the moment they wanted kept separate.

Cowley, who had developed a living-alone neatness, had almost finished clearing away and tidying the kitchen when the telephone rang, momentarily startling him. He answered expectantly, hoping it might have been Danilov with some sort of news. Instead he immediately recognized Barry Andrews. The man sounded slightly drunk, his words slipping at the sibilants.

'Just got back from the social club,' announced Andrews.

'Yes?'

'Talking about you, Pauline and me. Wanna know when you're going to come to dinner, like old times.'

In those old times Pauline had been *his* wife, Cowley reflected. 'I'm still trying to sort out a work pattern,' he said, cautiously.

'You're not working day *and* night. You're not working now!'

Why was he avoiding the decision? Nervous of seeing her, now the opportunity was there? Of course not! Ridiculous! What conceivable reason was there for him to be nervous? Any date could possibly be disrupted if things moved as quickly as he hoped they would now. 'What is most convenient for you? I'll fit in.'

There was a brief mumble of conversation, as Andrews talked away from the telephone. 'Night after tomorrow?'

'Perfect,' agreed Cowley.

'Pauline's here!' announced Andrews. 'You wanna say hello?'

There was another mumble of conversation, the delay longer this time, before a faint voice came on to the telephone. 'Hello.'

'Hello.'

'It's a surprise, your being here.'

'For me, too. You OK?' Pauline sounded uncertain, but he supposed that was understandable. Three years was a long time.

'Yes. You?'

'Fine.' An inconsequential exchange of strangers, Cowley thought. He didn't consider himself a stranger. He hoped she didn't, either. It was good to hear her voice, frail though it sounded.

There was a silence, neither knowing how to go on.

'The day after tomorrow then?' said Pauline.

'Don't go to any real trouble,' urged Cowley, knowing she would. She'd enjoyed entertaining, in Rome and London.

'You want to speak to Barry again?'

'I don't think so.'

'I'll be seeing you.' Cowley remained by the telephone, staring down at it. He decided he was genuinely looking forward to seeing her again. Although looking forward didn't really seem to be the right phrase.

'Well?' demanded Andrews. He looked at her over the top of his brandy bowl.

'Well what?'

'How was it, speaking to him again?'

'Don't, Barry!'

'It's a simple enough question.'

Pauline wished it were. 'It was nothing. You know that.'

'Good,' said the man. 'Wear your red dress. I like your red dress.'

'All right,' agreed Pauline, at once. It would be a mistake to tell him Cowley hadn't liked her in red.

Chapter Eighteen

In his anxiety to correct the oversight, Danilov was at Petrovka before his assistant, which was unnecessary because it was still too early in the day for the man to begin the inquiry. Major Pavin listened without expression to the briefing, not showing in any way that he knew it to be overdue and clearly forgotten until now. Danilov said: 'It was obvious, knowing there hadn't been a Russian in the apartment. And that she'd eaten. It's my fault.' Only to Pavin would Danilov have made such an open admission.

With attempted helpfulness Pavin said: 'I didn't think of it, either. They just might have eaten in a Russian-currency restaurant.'

'Would you, with easy access to dollars?'

'No,' Pavin admitted.

'And neither would Ann Harris. Remember the apartment? *Everything* was American. And the letters? How much she disliked it here? She ate the night of her death in a hard-currency restaurant, with as little contact as possible with anything Russian. I'm sure of it.' He paused. 'And those restaurants can be checked!'

Pavin gave a resigned grimace. 'It'll occupy a lot of people again.'

'How about the Militia posts in the area of the murders?'

'Nothing so far.'

'Take men off that: this has priority. But not off the hospital inquiries: I don't like the time that's taking.' He was still personally angry at overlooking basic routine: it *had* been obvious. He'd even isolated the fact that she'd eaten from the pathologist's written account, marking it for significance! 'Work through from top to bottom, tourist hotels and hard-currency and credit-card places first. Leave until last those that also take roubles.'

Pavin nodded to the instructions, smiling to one side of Danilov's desk. 'So you finally got a new bulb!' he said, satisfied the pressure on maintenance had got results.

The bulb that had been dead in its socket for several weeks had been replaced before Danilov arrived that morning. Instead of thanking his assistant Danilov said, uncomfortably: 'There's a problem with the car.'

'It's almost new!'

'I parked overnight outside my flat,' said Danilov, in another admission he wished he didn't have to make. 'The wipers were stolen.' He'd already decided not to tell Olga.

'A lot of people take them off.'

'I should have done,' said Danilov, shortly. Hurrying to end his further embarrassment he said: 'Let's start the restaurant checks, OK?'

'I'm not sure what I'll be able to do about the car.'

Belatedly showing his thanks Danilov said: 'It's better in here, with the proper light.'

Danilov had warned the reception area again and Cowley was ushered into his office minutes after he replaced the telephone from his initial, nothing-to-report contact of the day with the Militia Director.

'You had some inquiries to make at the embassy?' prompted Danilov, at once. How much of the truth would he really hear?

Cowley had already determined that an edited account would be quite easy: all he had to do, almost literally, was stick to the truth. He repeated the explanation for the out-of-hours telephone calls given by Paul Hughes and declared that none of the diplomats to whom he had talked could suggest who the girl's lover had been: there'd been no indication whatsoever during the social rounds at the embassy.

So much for cooperation, thought Danilov, disappointed. Interested in the effect it would have upon the other man, he said: 'So they lied to you, too?'

The reaction tilted Cowley, putting him on the defensive. 'I'm sorry?'

'Can you honestly believe there would be *no* indication who Ann Harris's lover was, in that closed situation?'

Cowley smiled, humourlessly. 'It's difficult,' he conceded.

'Wasn't there anything, from anyone? Baxter and Hughes particularly?'

'Nothing positive from anyone.' His first direct lie.

'I didn't ask that. I asked if there was *anything*.'

Cowley guessed the Russian didn't completely believe him: he wondered at the black stains on the other man's shirt cuffs. 'Nothing,' he insisted.

Danilov was convinced the other man was holding back. 'How did they treat you, your people?'

Cowley smiled again, for better reason this time, toe-stretching for firmer ground. 'Badly,' he admitted, honest again. 'They resent the suggestion of dirty smells inside their own house.'

Clever, decided Danilov. He regarded that as a truthful answer – an invitation for empathy between the two of them – which made him unsure where the *un*truthfulness was. 'So it was completely unproductive?'

'At the moment.' Cowley would have preferred being open with the Russian: having another investigative opinion against which to put his own impression and get an impression back.

Danilov picked out the qualification immediately: *at the moment*. So what did the other man hope to discover later, after this moment? And where? And how? And about whom? The pathway had to be pointed by the American. 'So where do we go from here?'

Cowley retreated thankfully into his edited preparation. The inconceivable link between a drunken Moscow taxi driver and an American diplomat was one of the most glaring implausibilities: he thought there would be some advantage in his examining once more the Suzlev file and perhaps in their both re-interviewing the widow.

Throughout what became an uninterrupted dialogue Danilov sat not looking directly at the American, but down at his desk: towards the end he began impressing a dotted pattern into a blotting pad which was too difficult to replace to be treated that way. He shouldn't have taken risks with the pencil, either. Cowley had been provided with transcripts, and where available English-language copies of every documentary file, which he now had at the embassy. So there would be no need to refresh himself upon any of that. Which only left the forensic exhibits. But all those material exhibits had been explained in the written analysis. Was there something he had missed in the suggestion to interview again the widow of Vladimir Suzlev? 'I think we can fit that in,' he said, finally looking up from the punctured blotter. He *hated* not knowing: being kept in ignorance.

The response was too noncommittal for Cowley to get a guide to whether the Russian had accepted what he'd said at face value. Would he himself have accepted it in the same circumstances? Maybe. Then again, maybe not. 'How about things from your side of the fence?'

'Still routine,' said Danilov. Believing the other man was reneging on their understood arrangement, Danilov felt no reluctance about holding back himself.

'I have to appear at this joint press conference,' said Cowley, moving the exchange along. 'And I've been told Senator Burden is personally coming here.'

The reintroduction of beguiling honesty? Answering in kind, Danilov said: 'I have to appear at the conference as well. Why is Burden coming?'

'God knows,' said Cowley. 'Not our problem.' He smiled encouragingly. 'Could we get through those other things today?'

Professional dedication? Or impatience, to confirm a missed point? Danilov said: 'I'm sure we can.' Would he get the guide he wanted, while they were doing it?

It took Danilov a total of six minutes to arrange to visit Natalia Suzlev where she worked, at the offices of a Swedish-Russian joint-venture company selling Russian natural gas to the West. Cowley was back from the evidence room in precisely seven. Far too quick to have properly studied any of the closely typed pages, Danilov assessed. So the interest *had* to be among the material exhibits. 'Refreshed your memory?' he challenged.

'I think so,' said Cowley. He had the confirmation he wanted!

The offices of the joint-venture company were on the second floor of a modern, interlinked block of buildings on Leninskii Prospekt, opposite the huge cinema. Natalia Suzlev, who worked there as a telex operator, had obviously warned the rest of the staff that she was expecting an official visit: their arrival caused no surprise but a lot of interest. As she led them to an empty side-room Natalia's head moved from side to side, to encompass the watching people, and Danilov got the impression she was enjoying the attention.

The side-room contained just a table and four chairs, all of which looked as if they were about to collapse. There was one print upon the wall, of an anonymous dacha, snow-covered in winter. Natalia Suzlev was a slightly built but wiry woman. Her fading brown hair was close-cropped, almost mannish, and her figure was mannish, too: she was quite flat-chested and angular-bodied. She wore no make-up. The skirt was stained and the buttoned cardigan badly hand-knitted.

She sat down heavily, regarding Cowley curiously, clearly marking him out as a foreigner. 'What is it?' she said, looking from one policeman to the other. 'Have you got him, the man that killed Vladimir?'

She seemed to have no difficulty talking about the killing. From the murder dossier Danilov knew they had been married for almost thirty years. A marriage from which all had gone but companionship, he guessed. Like so many others: did he regard Olga as a companion? He said: 'No. We need some more help, so we can get him.'

'What?' This time she asked the question of Cowley.

'Did your husband have any regular clients? People he drove for on a regular basis?' asked Cowley.

Instead of answering, the woman said: 'You're American. I can hear the accent when you speak.'

Cowley nodded, agreeing: 'Did he?'

'What's Vladimir's death got to do with America?'

'We don't know that it has,' said Danilov. 'We're just making inquiries. Did he have any regular clients?'

Natalia thought for a few moments. 'Not that I can remember him saying. He just drove the streets. He was radio-controlled, of course: he could be directed, if anyone called in.'

'I'm sorry if it distresses you, but I want to talk about the day he died,' said Cowley, kindly. 'He was off duty that night. What about during the day? Had he worked that day?'

'Of course,' said the widow. 'Started early, about seven. Left before I got up. He was home, when I got back. He said Igor — that was one of his friends, Igor Morosov — had found a liquor store selling vodka that day and that he was going across, for a

170

drink. And that I wasn't to wait up. So I didn't. In the morning I thought he'd gone straight to work . . .' There was the briefest of pauses, still without any emotion. 'But he hadn't. He'd been killed.'

'He kept his taxi at home?' asked Cowley.

'Yes.'

'But he walked to Igor's place? Did he often do that, walk when he could have driven?'

'Sometimes. Igor doesn't live all that far away.'

'It was winter: freezing.' Danilov picked up the questioning. 'Doesn't that surprise you, that he didn't take his car?'

The woman shrugged. 'I don't know. He just didn't. He didn't say what he was going to do, apart from go to Igor's and that I wasn't to expect him back early.'

'Did you ever drive with him?' asked Danilov. 'I've seen people – wives or girlfriends – with taxi drivers sometimes.'

'Prostitutes!' declared Natalia, at once.

'Not always,' argued Danilov, patiently. 'Did you?'

'A long time ago,' said the woman, distantly, hinting at Danilov's earlier thoughts about the marriage. 'He used to like me going out with him at night sometimes. But not for a long time.'

Cowley put his hand to the outside of his jacket pocket, feeling the outline of the Marlboro cigarette packet: Andrews's advice had got him a cab within minutes every time he had used it. He took the packet from his pocket now, gesturing with it towards the woman. 'Did Vladimir stop for these?'

The woman sniggered, finding the question amusing. 'Of course.'

Cowley seized the chance. 'You said he just drove the streets, but he wouldn't have simply done that, would he? He would have driven along particular streets, where he knew people would have these . . . foreign tourists.'

Natalia looked warily between them. 'He didn't do anything wrong . . . and anyway, he's dead.'

'We're not saying he did anything wrong . . . not looking into anything like that,' said Danilov, in eager reassurance, sensing an opening. 'We're just trying to find who killed him. Don't hold anything back that might help us.'

'I don't know,' said the woman, stubbornly, looking away from them.

Guessing the reason, Danilov said: 'I know *why* drivers stop for anyone showing Marlboro cigarettes. I'm not interested how many dollars or how much foreign currency Vladimir saved. It's yours.'

The wary look was still there. 'Maybe he did,' she allowed. 'Drive in certain places, that is.'

'Tell me the places,' insisted Cowley.

'The hotels, mostly,' said Natalia. 'He preferred the ones close to the centre. Intourist, the Metropole, the Savoy. Didn't bother much with the Cosmos: said it wasn't worthwhile.'

'Hotels mostly,' echoed Cowley. 'What about particular streets? He *did* have favourite routes, didn't he?'

The reluctant shrug came again. 'Maybe.'

'Come on, Natalia!' pleaded Danilov.

'Chaykovskaya,' said the woman. She identified the street upon which the American embassy was situated quietly, as if she were imparting a secret between the three of them.

'There it is!' Cowley spoke quietly, too, but triumphantly and in English.

'It could still be coincidence,' warned Danilov, also in English.

The widow said: 'What was that? What's wrong?'

'Nothing's wrong,' said Danilov, smiling in the hope of further reassurance. 'You've told us something which might be important. Vladimir drove along Ulitza Chaykovskaya in the hope of picking up Americans, right?'

'Yes,' she agreed.

'And did he?' Cowley came in.

She hesitated. 'He said he was better than the other drivers: knew exactly the times to go up and down.'

Cowley came forward on his chair. 'So he must have been talking about people working in the embassy? There couldn't have been special times for casual visitors.'

'I suppose so.'

'The customers *were* people who worked at the embassy?' pressed the American.

Another shrug. 'I suppose so.'

172

'Don't suppose, Natalia! *Were* they?' urged Danilov, forward himself now. 'It's important; very important.'

'Yes. He said they liked him. He spoke quite good English: didn't try to charge too much, like a lot of the others.'

'What about regular customers?' demanded Cowley. 'If people at the embassy liked him – preferred him to other drivers – he must have had regular customers.'

'I suppose so,' said Natalia, falling back on her favourite phrase. Immediately realizing the negative repetition, she hurried on: 'I'm not trying to be evasive. Of course he did. But he never mentioned names. He never *knew* names. He'd just say things like "I had the quiet one today" or "the one who tries to talk Russian" or "the rude one, who thinks he knows Moscow better than I do". That's all he ever said.'

'Men?' asked Cowley. 'Did he always talk as if they were men? Or did you ever get the impression there might have been women who were regular customers?'

Natalia Suzlev frowned across the table. 'He never said anything about women.' There was a pause, the first indication of any difficulty. 'Vladimir wasn't interested in women ... other women, I mean.'

Danilov wasn't sure precisely what she meant. 'Customers could call central dispatch, to order a taxi?'

'Yes.'

'By name? Did Vladimir ever say if people from the American embassy asked for him by name?'

Again there was a delay, while Natalia apparently considered the question. Abruptly she said: 'No, never.' There was a hesitation, to gain courage. 'What is this all about? Please tell me. What did Vladimir do wrong at the American embassy?'

'Nothing,' said Cowley, urgently. 'There's not going to be any trouble. You've been very helpful.'

Back in the car on Leninskii Prospekt, Danilov said: 'It would be a mistake to attach absolute importance to what she said; it *could* still be a coincidence.'

'Or it could be something else,' countered the American.

Danilov realized for the first time that somehow Pavin had got the windscreen wipers replaced on the car. There was another far more important function he had for Pavin: one he didn't intend discussing with Cowley. The American should have thought of it himself, but he hadn't. Or perhaps it was something else he was keeping to himself.

Senator Walter Burden didn't like irritation, so he always travelled with an organizing entourage. Beth Humphries was an extremely efficient secretary. She was also a strikingly attractive, blue-eyed blonde who very obviously needed a 36 D-cup: Burden took a middle-aged man's pleasure in the close presence of beautiful women and the misconception of other men that he slept with them all, which he didn't and couldn't since the precautionary prostate operation for a malignancy that had proven benign. John Prescott, one year out of Harvard, was eager to put the political degree to practical use and believed the patronage inherent as Burden's personal assistant to be invaluable; his true ambition was actively to run for office in his native New Hampshire, but realistically he recognized the uncertainty of elected office against the better and longer-term career prospects as a Capitol Hill lobbyist. At the moment, he didn't know which way to jump.

Charles Easterhaus had been baptized Carlos and was included in the circus because Burden liked to convey to the influential Hispanic electorate in his constituency that he did not hold the racial prejudices that he actually did. Easterhaus's function was difficult to define. The job description was also that of personal assistant, but his graduation had been from the streets of New York's Little Italy, although no evidence of the background remained, either in his appearance, behaviour or accent. He was more basically a fixer than the Harvard graduate and usually better at it. Easterhaus got favoured tables at restaurants with month-long waiting lists, theatre tickets for blocked-out shows and presidential suites in hotels which had months before confirmed the reservations to other guests. He was a dark-haired, archetypal Latin who possessed an enviable address book to supplement necessary public events with girls who looked every bit as good as Beth Humphries and sometimes better. Some were professionals. Burden paid and Easterhaus slept with them: he was a man who enjoyed complete job satisfaction.

James McBride had been with Burden since his earliest days as a Congressman, which made him invaluable as a media organizer.

McBride knew every favour received or bestowed, every deal struck or broken, every trick practised and played and every shortcut Burden had ever taken to become the power he now was in Washington, DC. It meant McBride was always ahead when some ambitious journalist tried to rake the muck, which they sometimes did. He had a book, like Easterhaus, but McBride's tome recorded the indelicate embarrassment of those who tried to expose the embarrassments of the Senator. He called it his shield, which it was. He was the only man who, late at night when they were drinking, could openly call Burden an asshole to his face and get away with it because no matter how drunk Burden became, he knew McBride could never be replaced. Deep down Burden knew it was true, anyway.

Despite the individual expertise and the team's cohesive efficiency, their Moscow arrival was disorientating. Each and all of them were accustomed to special receptions and it didn't happen at Sheremet'yevo airport. They had to stand in the immigration line like everybody else and wait interminably in the Customs reclaim for their baggage. Ralph Baxter did succeed in getting to them there, but there were no porters, so they had to pay a foreign currency dollar each for a cart to wheel their own cases into the crowded, jostling concourse.

Easterhaus was left to guard the carts while the rest, led by the Senator, ascended to the VIP lounge on the first floor for the Burden-convened press conference.

It was exclusively for Western correspondents and television reporters and cameramen. Burden agreed to the print media conference first and television interviews afterwards. He had come personally to Moscow to find out what had happened to his niece; until now he felt he had been denied information by American officials and looked for more cooperation in Russia. He was determined the killer would be brought to justice. Meetings were scheduled with a number of Russian officials and ministries. Towards the end of every interview, he introduced his favourite speculation, wondered if it were coincidence that the victim had been his niece. The reference was sufficiently intriguing to guarantee headlines across America. Burden was extremely pleased with the coverage.

Chapter Nineteen

Danilov hadn't expected the Security Service's Colonel to agree to an immediate meeting, but Gugin had insisted he was free, so Danilov had obviously accepted. The monolithic, yellow-washed headquarters of the disgraced and much reduced State Security Service formed before him as Danilov drove up the hill from the direction of the Kremlin. Of all the changes to Moscow squares and streets and boulevards, supposedly to erase the discredited legacies of communism, Danilov found the renaming of Dzerzhinsky Square the most illogical. Although Lubyanka was the pre-revolutionary original, Danilov considered the word far more emotive and reminiscent of past horror: Lubyanka, the prison which the KGB had grown to absorb, was infamous as one of the centres of Stalin's slaughter, the title indelible in every Russian's mind.

He had to stop, for the circulating traffic flow, so he had a complete view of the building occupying one entire side of the square. Above ground, in his obvious view, the building at its highest reached eight storeys. But Danilov knew that below ground it was more than twice that size, a vast underground city of separate buildings and offices and streets and command and communication centres, complete with its own underground train system constructed deeper than the publicly known metro, linked directly to the Kremlin. So what he could see was the tip of the iceberg. Which was fittingly accurate. Apart from the reduction in control upon the ordinary people of the country the new security organisation hadn't changed dramatically, despite the supposed divisional and staff purges. It had adapted *to* the changes, like a chameleon adjusting quickly to changing surroundings, colouring itself to conform. For once, Danilov found himself hoping that even the internal surveillance had not diminished too profoundly.

Danilov edged into the traffic swirl and drove to the side of the building, as Gugin had directed. Danilov's name was listed at the checkpoint. An escort got into the car to guide him to a parking area and then took him through two separate admission procedures at which his credentials were checked and listed.

Gugin was sitting, waiting, when Danilov was finally ushered into his office, a small man behind a large desk. He was in uniform, the left of which was marked with more decoration ribbons than Danilov would have expected. The man was too young for any of the obvious wars, and Danilov wondered how the man had achieved the decorations. Perhaps in other wars, the sort that no one knew about. Despite the honours, Gugin's office was at the rear of the building, overlooking the original prison exercise yard. Not just the exercise yard, Danilov remembered. The conveyor belt executions had been carried out against those grey walls. Would the concrete slabs and blocks still be pitted by the bullets? It would probably be the sort of obscene monument the KGB would want, for their never *really* interrupted posterity: pockmarked macho. What Gugin's room lacked in outlook it compensated for in fitments. Danilov realized the huge desk comprised part of a furniture set, all heavy and ornately carved, a towering, close-fronted bureau, a ceiling-to-floor bookcase and a side-desk with a roll-top covering, which was pulled down. If it was opened, would Stalin emerge, moustached and glowering, wanting to stand at the window for the bullet-spattered display down in the courtyard?

'So?' demanded Gugin and smiled, because this meeting was precisely what he had wanted. He was sure the benefits would be considerable: the stupid policeman wouldn't realize the manipulation.

Danilov realized he should have been surprised by the quickness of the appointment. Gugin doubtless saw it as confirmation of the old KGB belief in Militia inefficiency, a cap-in-hand visit for help that could be laughed over later in some services' club. Danilov smiled back, hoping the grimace didn't appear as false as it was. 'Our investigation is progressing extremely well,' he lied.

Gugin's smile remained, a disbelieving expression. 'No problem with the American?'

Eager to show the security service's awareness of everything, gauged Danilov. His mind ran on, worryingly. He'd known from the beginning that the investigation had the self-protective interest of the former KGB. So how closely were they monitoring him, personally? There wasn't any real reason for him to be concerned at their discovering his affair with Larissa, but she was the wife of another Militia officer. It would give them an advantage over him if ever they needed one. 'None that has arisen so far. Everything seems to be going quite well.'

'Sure you can trust him?'

Was that an instinctive question? Or did Gugin have some private information? 'Can he trust me?' That was wrong, too: pretentious.

'You tell me,' demanded Gugin, enjoying himself. 'I have no idea what's going on.' The policeman *was* stupid: it was going to be easy.

'When it's convenient.' Pretentious again. But quite truthful.

'I would have thought trust was necessary,' said Gugin.

Was there a point in this discussion? 'Nothing has occurred so far to make me mistrust,' Danilov lied. It was why he was here at security headquarters.

'There is going to be an arrest, soon?' It was more of a smirk than a smile.

'As soon as possible,' said Danilov, regretting the emptiness.

Gugin picked up on it at once. 'I'm sorry it's not going better.'

There was nothing to be gained by creating an argument. 'I appreciated the assistance you gave, with the photographs. And the telephone log.'

'Now there is something else?'

'Not exactly something else,' said Danilov. 'Something to complete it.'

It was like operating puppet strings, thought Gugin. 'Complete what?'

'The telephone lists,' said Danilov. 'More than telephone numbers were recorded, weren't they?'

'You only asked for numbers.' He had to play for a while, to avoid the Militia Colonel guessing the manoeuvre which had already brought congratulations from the chairman himself.

'I am extending that request,' persisted Danilov. Continuing formally, in the way of Russian bureaucracy, he added: 'I repeat the same understanding as before — I will have it reinforced by

178

the Director if you wish – that at no time will there be any disclosure of the source of the information.'

'There wouldn't have to be a disclosure. The source would be obvious to a child of five!'

'I need to know.' Danilov supposed that first by the telephone call and then by agreeing so quickly to come to see the man he had shown his desperation. Contradicting the earlier assurance, he admitted: 'I think we are being lied to, by the American.'

'*We?*' queried Gugin.

'*I* am being lied to,' Danilov further conceded. 'I need the information to compete! To win!'

For several moments the small, bubble-fat man regarded Danilov over the expanse of table, like a mole emerging from the far side of a field to find the cause of heavy footsteps overhead. 'If I continue to refuse, would you try through your Director? Go as high as you could?'

Danilov was unsure what answer the man wanted, guessing the wrong reply would terminate the negotiation. 'Yes. And the argument would be that I didn't want the American FBI coming to Moscow and resolving right under our noses a murder inquiry that I could have probably solved ahead of them, had necessary information not been withheld from me.'

There was a further silence, of continued examination across the desk. Eventually Gugin smiled again, a vaguely admiring expression this time. 'That's good!' he congratulated. 'That really is very, very good.' It was almost time for the apparent concession.

'Wouldn't you say that in my place?' asked Danilov, anxious not to alienate the man a millimetre more than he believed necessary.

'That's exactly what I'd say,' Gugin admitted.

'So?' Danilov was echoing the greeting he had received when he first arrived. They'd virtually turned the complete circle.

'That's all you get,' Gugin insisted.

'You mean there's more?' snatched Danilov. The balance had shifted, putting him in control now.

'No more,' the officer repeated, worried he had been careless. He didn't want it all to go at once: the information had to drip slowly, like water eroding a rock.

One demand at a time, Danilov resolved. He sat, waiting. Gugin sat, appearing undecided. Finally, abruptly, the man felt sideways into a desk drawer, retrieved several sheets of paper and offered them across the desk. He couldn't reach fully and had to toss them the last part of the way, so they skidded on the shiny surface. Danilov collected them eagerly, scanning the listed exchanges.

'They liked sex, didn't they?' said Gugin. It was a thoroughly satisfactory meeting. How far and how fast would the ripples spread?

Danilov looked up from the intercepts. 'I can't be manipulated now.'

You just have been, thought Gugin.

Cowley was late for Burden's reception, delayed by the amount of material he had to send to Washington: he would have been later if Andrews had not helped with the actual transmission. Cowley hoped there was enough for work to start upon the psychological profile at Quantico's Behavioural Science Unit. It was something else he hadn't discussed with Danilov. He'd have to remember to do so, during their next meeting. As he finally made his way from the communications room to the ambassador's quarters Cowley's mind was occupied by what had come in from Washington. Results were promised in the overnight diplomatic pouch on the second autopsy upon Ann Harris and also on the forensic examination of the girl's personal possessions too hastily sent back from her office.

Cowley decided it would be better to postpone his planned confrontation. It was already late, and although in normal investigatory circumstances that would not have been a consideration, there might just be something extra in the scientific material arriving the following day from America. In addition to which he still couldn't make up his mind how much Dimitri Danilov was holding back. And the man about to be confronted couldn't go anywhere, anyway. So Cowley was confident he could take his time.

The reception took place in an ante-room to Hubert Richards's enormous office, similarly high-ceilinged, expansively windowed and glitteringly chandeliered. The size overwhelmed the small number of people present: Cowley's illogical impression upon entering was of a group of people huddled together in a protective vault, the way people clustered in the event of an accident or in fear of some dangerous physical assault. At once a man he didn't know detached himself from the group, striding across to meet him, a professional smile etched into place.

'John Prescott,' the man introduced himself, thrusting out his hand. 'Are we glad to see you! You're the man it's all about!'

The handshake was aggressively firm, professional like the smile. Prescott cupped Cowley's elbow, guiding him almost urgently forward to the waiting group. As he approached Cowley saw the party was practically divided, as if there were two teams. There was a knot of people – one an extremely attractive woman – around Burden, whom he recognized from American television broadcasts. Cowley thought the political cartoonists were remarkably accurate. Another praetorian guard flanked the ambassador: Ralph Baxter and Paul Hughes were in the gathering, among several other people whom Cowley didn't know. There was a range of drinks on the tray a steward offered. Cowley took orange juice.

Prescott adopted the role of host, introducing Cowley to his set of people, but so quickly that Cowley missed some of the names. Burden's greeting was as professional as his assistant's. The attitude was avuncular. He several times referred to Cowley as 'my boy' and said he knew Cowley was going to get 'the goddamned bastard who did this to my little girl'.

'I'm taking part in tomorrow's press conference,' announced the politician, looking briefly towards the ambassador, who nodded in confirmation. 'So we've got a lot to talk about.'

'I've outlined things on a daily basis to the ambassador,' said Cowley. He was increasingly glad he hadn't told Richards about the first murder. As he spoke Cowley looked across to the assembled diplomats. They were all staring back at him, expectantly.

'Know all about that,' said Burden, impatiently. 'I need the *complete* inside track.'

Thank God he'd been in touch with Washington, providing the easy escape, thought Cowley. How easy would it really be? It wasn't his problem: not a lasting one, at least. He felt sorry for the diplomats. Nearly all of them looked like rabbits caught in a poacher's light, tensed for the explosion of the gun. 'I think we should talk later tonight.'

'*Precisely* what I want,' agreed Burden, enthusiastically. 'Good man!'

He'd graduated from being a boy, recognized Cowley. Burden moved away to mingle with the embassy staff, a politician permanently at work. Prescott was attentively at his elbow. A plump, vaguely dishevelled man who had been with the Senator approached, smiled and said: 'James McBride, in case you missed it first time. I handle the media. Guess it's going to be pretty hectic tomorrow.'

'Probably,' Cowley accepted. Apart from arranging to meet Danilov first, he hadn't thought much about it. 'Noon, right?'

'Noon it is,' confirmed the other American.

Would the material promised from Washington arrive in the following day's diplomatic bag? If it did, Cowley decided he would have the confrontation that afternoon or early evening. Where? Here at the embassy? Or at home? The embassy would probably be best: more properly official. He'd not alerted Washington in advance of the encounter – determined to be utterly sure before he made any accusation – and he certainly wasn't going to make any disclosure at a press conference he was reluctant to attend in the first place. Objectively Cowley realized he'd be open to criticism for withholding the very announcement everyone wanted, if he got a confession. But being even more objective, Cowley decided the criticism could only come from Burden in his desire to be centre stage. He was sure the FBI Director would support the in-field decision to wait until all the conclusive evidence was assembled, to avoid any evasion. 'I'm not sure it's going to be very worthwhile.'

'You any idea of the coverage this is getting, back home?' demanded the press spokesman.

'Some,' said Cowley. One of the instructions he'd received from Washington was to urge the Russians to continue separating the murder of the taxi driver and Ann Harris. It was difficult to imagine Burden's reaction if he learned of the link. Which, Cowley supposed, was inevitable, eventually. There was a valid rationale, if the suspicions were confirmed: maybe Burden's fury would be mitigated by the possibility of a trial taking place in the United States. That reflection began another but Cowley halted it, determinedly: he was tiptoeing into legal minefields he wasn't trained to explore and which were none of his concern. His job was to assemble the evidence, make the arrest and let wiser, superior minds take it from there.

'You know what? This time tomorrow you could be a media star! You realize that? You're going to be televised into millions of homes all across America – all across the world, I guess – as the American G-man hunting a Russian maniac. What do you think of that?'

In truth Cowley didn't think very much of it at all. 'The term G-man isn't used inside the Bureau any more: I'm not sure it ever was, particularly. It was . . .' Cowley hesitated, realizing what he was going to say, acknowledging its validity now. '. . . a publicity hype,' he finished.

'So what guidance can you give me?'

'Guidance?'

'The Senator's going to be right up there with you,' explained McBride, patiently. 'I know you're going to brief him later, but I want a steer I can give some of the press: particularly the TV majors like NBC and CBS. That way you'll know what's coming at you. No awkward questions you didn't expect. Everything looking cool and under control. Know what I mean?'

Cowley sighed, looking around for the steward: he didn't want another drink but it would have been a minimal break from this conversation. 'Yes,' he said, evenly. 'I know what you mean.'

'So what's the word?' McBride smiled again, encouragingly.

'The inquiries into Ann Harris's murder are ongoing. It's a new investigation, little more than days old. It is, as you know, a joint investigation with the Russian authorities. That cooperation is proving very satisfactory.'

McBride remained looking at him, the smile uncertain now. Cowley was conscious of movement just behind him, to his right, and turned to see both Baxter and Hughes. He wondered if they had approached in time to hear what he said.

'Go on,' prompted McBride.

'That's it,' said Cowley, shortly. 'Anything else you want, you'll have to get from FBI headquarters in Washington.'

The press spokesman's face became serious. 'Now wait a minute here, buddy. That's a whole bunch of crap and we know it. We try a slip and slide like that and we're all of us going to get roasted. And the Senator doesn't get roasted. Not ever.'

Before Cowley could respond, Baxter said: 'Doesn't sound like you're getting very far.'

The steward reappeared at last, and Cowley replaced his empty glass and took another. 'There's a Bureau rule against discussing murder investigations at cocktail parties. Takes all the fun out of the evening.'

'I suppose it has to be difficult, this early into an inquiry,' said Hughes. He was holding his cigarette in the same hand as his glass: it looked like whisky, from the colour of the contents.

'Sometimes there's an early break,' said Cowley. 'Lots of evidence just lying around, to be picked up.'

'But not this time?' persisted the financial director.

'Bits and pieces,' said Cowley.

'You guys better excuse me,' said McBride, striding off after the glad-handing Senator.

'So you could be here in Moscow for quite a while?' suggested Baxter. 'Have to make sure we look after you. Sign you into the club, put on a dinner or two.'

'Too early to say yet how long I'll be here.' Neither man appeared any longer offended by the previous day's encounter. Across the room Cowley saw McBride in a mouth-to-ear conversation with Burden: almost at once Burden looked back in his direction, frowning.

'So you don't anticipate it being a very productive press conference?' said Hughes.

Cowley decided the way the man was holding both his glass and cigarette was overly artificial. 'Maybe the Russians will have something to say.'

'Wouldn't they have told you, if they had?'

'Maybe. Maybe not,' answered Cowley, honestly. The Senator and his followers were approaching, trailed by the ambassador.

'I would . . .' began Baxter but the Senator talked over him, dismissively. 'I think it's time we talked.' He looked sideways, to the ambassador. 'Your office free?'

'Yes . . . please . . .' volunteered the anxious Richards.

Cowley put his glass on a small side-table as he followed Burden through a linking door into the familiar room: he thought it was even more attractive at night, illuminated by the chandelier. Every one of Burden's party came into the office with them. Burden went directly to the ambassador's desk, settling heavily into the chair. The others ranged themselves in a half-circle in close attendance.

'I gather there's been a misunderstanding between you and Jimmy here?' said Burden, nodding in the direction of the press official.

'I don't think so,' said Cowley. It was pointless their playing verbal ping-pong, batting nuance and ambiguity back and forth between themselves. 'I am very early into an investigation. I am not permitted to discuss any part of that investigation with you. I have been told to suggest your contacting FBI headquarters in Washington for any information. There's really no purpose at all in our having this or any other sort of meeting.' Cowley heard what sounded to be a surprised intake of breath but didn't know from where. Certainly it wasn't from Burden. He'd come forward in the ambassador's chair, wide-eyed beneath a lowered head, dark-faced with annoyance.

'You know who you're talking to, boy?'

Demoted, thought Cowley. He stood regarding the other man, feeling no apprehension. The stupidity didn't deserve an answer.

'I asked you a question, boy.' The anger clipped off the end of the words even more than usual.

'I obviously know the personal circumstances and you have my sympathy,' said Cowley, turning towards the door. 'I say again, I was told to suggest you contact Washington direct, for any information. There are very good communication channels here.'

'Don't you walk out on me!' roared Burden.

Cowley halted, half turning back. 'This is embarrassing. But it's not a situation of my making. I don't want to be part of continuing it. I am not trying to be offensive. Or obstructive. I am simply following specific instructions from Washington.'

Burden appeared to realize that the situation *was* of his creation and to exacerbate it would make him look even more ridiculous. His escape was to redirect the anger. 'That bastard Ross!' he said.

'I would expect the Director to take your calls,' offered Cowley.

'A lot of people are going to take my calls. A lot of people are going to get them, too.' Burden attempted to sound ominous, but that wasn't any more successful than the earlier effort at intimidation.

As he continued towards the door Cowley saw the attractive blonde in Burden's party turn away to prevent the Senator seeing her obvious amusement.

This was going to be the best one. The cleverest. It was going to be balanced on a knife-edge – there was a giggle, at the image – but the confusion would be complete. A blonde. A blonde really would be good. The one that failed off Ulitza Kislovskii with the sudden appearance of the man friend had been blonde. Hadn't failed. Wrong to think that. Been interrupted, before it had started. Couldn't have failed if it hadn't started. Forget it. Hadn't happened. Where was the panic? There should have been panic by now. Newspaper stories. People frightened. Wanted people to be frightened. They would be, after this one. Really the cleverest. Blonde. And buttons. Red buttons. That's what the real things were like, red buttons.

The complete list of psychiatric patients whose case history showed possible similarities with the fixations manifested by the killer of Vladimir Suzlev and Ann Harris comprised twenty-six names when it was submitted to Major Yuri Pavin. With the need to have two officers present at every interview, and the even greater need to get those interviews completed as soon as possible, Pavin requested three extra men, anticipating the objections. Which came at once. There were officially written complaints that such a concentration of manpower would halt two other ongoing investigations, one a fraud case, the other an inquiry into currency speculation. General Lapinsk ruled that both should be suspended. The decision worsened the criticism throughout Petrovka towards Dimitri Danilov and to a lesser extent towards Pavin. The Major considered addressing everyone involved in the questioning in the early morning charge-room assembly, but upon reflection decided against it, believing it would appear as if he were defending himself when he did not consider he had anything to defend himself against. He stressed the importance of the

186

psychiatric questioning when he assigned individual names to the paired groups. The response from every one was sullen indifference. Perhaps, decided the Major, Danilov himself should make the assembly-room address. He was the Colonel in charge, after all: it was his responsibility.

Then he read the overnight report of a two-man team engaged on another aspect of the inquiry, and in his initial excitement Pavin lost all concern about the psychiatric report problems.

Before telling Danilov he would have time to carry out the other inquiry the man had ordered, after seeing Vladimir Suzlev's widow again. It was all coming together!

Chapter Twenty

With a lot to crowd in before the press conference, Danilov got up early, slipping out of bed with practised ease to avoid waking Olga. There was a clean shirt in the drawer, although it wasn't very well pressed, but they hardly ever were. It took a long time going through kitchen cupboards and shelves to find black polish, to cover the neglected tear in his shoe. When he found it, the polish was hard and atrophied, oddly topped with a white powder. It didn't achieve much of a shine but the tear was less visible. While he waited for water to boil for tea, he wetted his hair and at once regretted doing so: it was so short it stuck up, like wheat in a wind. It would dry before the conference and the inevitable photographs. Olga hadn't stirred by the time he left the apartment, the carefully removed windscreen wipers wrapped in paper.

He was ahead of the morning rush hour, reaching Petrovka sooner than he expected, which made him even earlier than he'd planned: the Militia building was in transition between night and day shift. His floor was deserted. In his now brightly lit office Danilov wrote out the morning schedule, beginning with Pavin and running through the other preparations as he waited for the American to arrive to be taken to meet Lapinsk and the Federal Prosecutor, in advance of the actual conference. Finally he sat considering the conference itself. He'd never attended such an event before and didn't know what was expected. The reason for the advanced encounter with the Director and the Prosecutor, he supposed. All he'd have to do was take their lead. Particularly about both murders. Were they going to disclose the connection today? Danilov smiled, suddenly, at his own question. The reservation about the possibility of an embassy involvement still existed. Would an apparent insistence upon making a linking announcement today force the American into some sort of disclosure? It might be worth trying. In which case he'd have to brief Lapinsk and Nikolai Smolin in advance, to ensure their proper response. *Definitely* worth a try, he decided. Danilov was reaching forward, to make an unnecessary reminder note on his pad, when Pavin entered the office: he never completed the note. Pavin, who never moved quickly, positively flustered in, his normally dour face broken by an expansive grin. The expression was so unusual that Danilov saw for the first time that the man had a gold-edged filling on an eye-tooth.

'I've got the restaurant *and* the man,' announced the Major. Across the desk he offered the security agency's reception photograph of Ann Harris with her hand on the arm of Paul Hughes.

Danilov smiled up at his assistant, in what appeared to be matching triumph but which included a lot of relief. 'No doubt?'

'Absolutely none. The restaurant is called the Trenmos: it's a combination of two names, Trenton, in New Jersey, and Moscow. Very American and very popular with the embassy. They ate there a lot: were well known. And the reservation, for that night, was actually in Hughes's name. And there's even more. I took the photograph this morning to Suzlev's taxi firm, when I made the check you ordered. Three other drivers remember Hughes as one of Suzlev's regular customers. He used to practise his Russian, just like the wife said.'

Danilov went back to the photograph before him. 'We've got him! . . . Shit! It was there and I missed it! Look!'

'What?' said Pavin, astonished by the outburst.

'I even *thought* something was odd at the mortuary but I didn't *see* it was,' said Danilov. 'And that was it — *see*! How could I have missed it?'

'What?' repeated Pavin, bewilderment replacing astonishment.

Instead of replying Danilov offered back the photograph. 'Look at him!' he insisted. 'Look at the hand!'

'The finger's twisted!' isolated Pavin, instantly.

'The index finger of the right hand,' agreed Danilov, more calmly. 'It will obviously need to be confirmed forensically, for courtroom evidence. But it's twisted so that it couldn't give a proper impression. Just as none of the lateral pocket loop prints in Ann Harris's apartment have a proper impression of the right hand that held the vodka glass. Or made prints in the bathroom. Hughes's prints and those we found will match! I know they will!' Danilov no longer felt inferior. That was, he conceded to

189

himself, *just* how he had felt from the moment of Cowley's arrival: inferior in scientific facilities and personal ability and in personal training and even – the most uneasy admission of all – in how he looked and dressed, compared to the American. But not any longer: not completely. In appearance maybe, but not on any other level. He'd drawn even, professionally proving himself equal. Now he wouldn't have to stage any phonily rehearsed disclosures at pre-conference encounters. Because now he *knew*. So how *would* he handle it? He wasn't sure, not at that moment.

'That's what the American would have been doing in the evidence room,' Pavin guessed. 'Checking the fingerprint sheets.'

'Most probably,' Danilov accepted. What he'd just learned might carry the investigation on. But, like so much else in the case, it created as many questions as it provided answers. There was far more political implication than before. And what was the Russian jurisdiction? Could he, a Russian investigator, enter the US embassy to question an American diplomat? He was sure he couldn't. Whatever the result of any questioning, could Hughes invoke diplomatic immunity? Probably. Did what they had discovered really incriminate the man in murder? Not necessarily. Or merely extend a suspicion heightened by the telephone transcripts that the Cheka had reluctantly made available and which showed Hughes to be a liar? Maybe nothing more than that.

'Now we've got to take it forward,' said Pavin, prescient as always. 'It's the complication everyone was frightened of. It won't be easy.'

'It's never been easy.'

'You going to tell the American?'

'I haven't decided, not yet.'

'It doesn't look as if he was confiding in us.'

'One of us is going to have to tell the other sometime,' pointed out Danilov. 'Otherwise it becomes ridiculous.' So much *was* ridiculous.

'Do we have enough to make an arrest?'

Danilov examined the question. 'Maybe if Hughes were Russian. Certainly enough to bring a Russian in for questioning: people are always nervous, being interrogated in a police station. Stalin's best legacy to the Russian legal system.'

'Stalin's unintentional legacy,' disputed Pavin, with rare cynicism. 'And Paul Hughes isn't Russian.'

'Then no.'

'What about the press conference?'

'An intrusion now,' said Danilov.

'You're not going to say anything there?'

'Not publicly,' said Danilov, although an idea began to germinate. 'Far too early for that. But Lapinsk must know. The Prosecutor, too.'

'What about postponing the conference?'

Once more Danilov examined the Major's question, acknowledging the point and wondering whether he had been right in thinking, as he was sure he once had, that Pavin would forever remain at his current rank. Danilov said: 'It would be convenient. But wrong. It would convey the impression of a sudden development: build up expectation.'

'I would have thought . . .' Pavin started, but stopped at the intrusion of the internal telephone.

Danilov nodded to the announcement and said to his assistant: 'The American, on time as ever. He's learned the Marlboro trick.' When the escorted Cowley was shown into the room, Danilov was instantly aware of the immaculately pressed suit and the hard-starched collar of the shirt, pin-secured, that he so much envied.

At once Cowley said: 'I think this press conference is going to be difficult. Your people have agreed to Senator Burden taking part. God knows why. Or what the point is. It'll be a circus.'

The Western ease in criticizing politicians, so new in his own country, still surprised Danilov. He was quite uninterested in any press conference now. Feeling his superiority, he said: 'You haven't discussed it, with the Senator?'

Cowley regarded the Russian sourly. 'I have been instructed not to divulge anything of the investigation, to any outside party.'

Danilov's germinating idea flowered, but he decided to give the other man one opportunity. 'How about me?' he said.

'You?'

'In an hour I am going to introduce you to my Militia General — someone I suppose you would call the Moscow police chief. And to the Federal Prosecutor: Attorney General, if you want a comparison. I've no idea how they will want the press conference to be conducted, but I think they'll expect you and I to be in agreement with each other: know precisely where we are in the investigation.'

'I'm sure they will,' said Cowley, smoothly. He didn't like the evasion. Although he did not altogether trust Danilov – he put trust on a different level than this present consideration – he genuinely liked the rumpled Russian with his tight haircut and his permissible pride in his ability to speak English, which he supposed matched his own in the ease he had found with Russian. He didn't feel he had any choice in the deceit. The forensic results that had arrived overnight in the diplomatic bag had provided far better evidence than he'd expected – even though the unnecessary elimination stuff had to be gone through – and he anxiously needed further guidance. Which he'd already asked for, before leaving the embassy that morning. And until he got Washington's reply – although he was sure he could predict what it would be – it was impossible for him to confide anything.

'So you believe we do?' pressed Danilov. 'That we both know where we are?'

Danilov *did* have something! It was poker with strangers whose game he didn't know, all cards face-down, unsure of the value of his own. 'I'd certainly like to think so . . .' A pause. 'Wouldn't you?'

The familiar, evasive response, Danilov recognized. It had been Cowley's choice, not his: the man had been given his chance, chosen the course he wanted to follow. 'Yes,' he said, heavily. 'I would have liked to think that. You've shared everything with me?'

Cowley nodded, wanting to use the directness. 'And you've shared everything with me?'

Danilov nodded agreement back. Confrontations to come, he thought: some sooner rather than later. 'Shall we go?'

It was only when Pavin turned from Stolesnikov Street towards the conspicuous Marxist-Leninist Institute on Pushkinskaya that Danilov appreciated the ironic coincidence of Ann Harris's apartment being in the same thoroughfare. Danilov expected Pavin to park in the Institute's facilities, but at the adjacent Prosecutor's premises the Major sounded sharply on the horn. The signal was instantly answered by the high iron gates swinging open to admit them. Pavin put their car next to General Lapinsk's official, freshly washed Volga.

Their smooth and quite unexpected reception continued inside. A uniformed attendant ushered them to the second floor and into a reception room where Lapinsk and Nikolai Smolin were already waiting. Danilov knew he and the American were fifteen minutes ahead of their appointed time. He went through the introductions, assuring the other two Soviet officials there was no problem in any discussion being conducted in Russian. For several moments after the formal greetings, the four men stood in an uncertain group, no one certain how to proceed. At last, with ill-concealed reluctance, Smolin took nominal charge, which had to be his role for the conference.

'There have been over a hundred journalist applications to attend today,' the Prosecutor said. 'And the television teams all have support staffs. We've arranged simultaneous translation. The television companies have also asked for individual interviews, after the open session . . .' The Prosecutor hesitated, indicating Lapinsk. 'I have all the police reports, up until yesterday. Is there anything else I should know?'

The first of the confrontations, thought Danilov. He looked briefly to Cowley, unsure how the American would react, before saying: 'We know who was in her apartment the night she was killed. And he's lied, not admitting that he was there. His name is Paul Hughes. He's an American economist, her superior at the embassy.'

There was absolute silence in the room, each of the other three men staring fixedly at Danilov. The American's face was impassive.

Smolin said: 'The proof's incontrovertible?'

Danilov recounted the evidence in the order of uncovering it. He itemized the prints of the twisted finger on the glass and elsewhere in the apartment, a deformity from which Hughes visibly suffered, and set out the proof of Hughes and the girl being at the Trenmos on the evening of her death, the table reserved in Hughes's name. And finally disclosed the positive identification by the other taxi drivers of Hughes being a regular client of Vladimir Suzlev. Danilov nodded, to include Cowley,

193

and said: 'There hasn't been a formal accusation. But in a preliminary interview, he lied. He denied being particularly friendly with her – certainly didn't admit being in her company on the night of her death. He also lied about the reason for after-hours telephone calls. He insisted the conversations were all official, connected with their work. They weren't. I have the complete transcript, every word they exchanged. There's no question of their not being lovers: in two he openly refers to pain, to hurting her.'

The attention was still absolute but the expressions were changing. Smolin was looking around the small group, as if for guidance. Lapinsk was frowning, concentrating upon the American at the obvious disclosure of Russian telephone interception and recording. Cowley was almost imperceptibly shaking his head, a gesture of disappointment: Danilov wondered about what. He hoped it was at the American's realization of his mistake in not sharing whatever it was he had independently discovered.

'There's a lot to consider,' said Smolin, stating the unnecessary obvious in the manner of a profound statement.

When Cowley began to speak, his voice wavered, high and low. He coughed, clearing his throat as Lapinsk was also doing, creating a frog-like duet. Stronger-voiced, Cowley said: 'I was asked by Washington, before coming here today, to express again our gratitude at your not publicly suggesting there could be an investigation *within* the embassy into these killings. And to thank you, too, for keeping separate the murders of the woman and Vladimir Suzlev. I think there is a real need for these things to remain unpublicized.'

Lapinsk rattled more coughs. 'This man Hughes. You say he hasn't been formally interrogated? Had this new evidence put to him?'

'No,' said Cowley. How could he have believed he was ahead? All he'd had – having recognized at that hostile embassy meeting the obvious significance of Hughes's twisted finger – was forensic proof returned in the diplomatic bag that morning of a lateral pocket loop print from the glass in the Pushkinskaya apartment matching those on the memo pad and *matryoshka* dolls in Ann Harris's office. Cowley could understand Danilov holding out: he'd been doing the same himself. What he couldn't explain was that having done so – having found the proof by himself – the

Russian had then presented it all to the police chief and the prosecutor not as an individual coup, to gain all the personal credit, but as a joint discovery, the way they were supposed to be working.

'And how is it going to be done?' asked Smolin, quietly, focusing upon the political difficulties.

'I don't know. I will have to take advice from Washington,' Cowley admitted.

'Clearly there can't be any premature disclosure at today's press conference,' said Lapinsk.

'Which leaves us with little to say,' Smolin pointed out.

'And which was the situation until thirty minutes ago, before we were told this,' argued the Militia General.

The Federal Prosecutor looked intently at the FBI agent. 'There is probably a diplomatic argument against any Russian involvement whatsoever in the questioning of this man, Hughes?'

'I would expect so,' Cowley conceded. 'That's the sort of advice I was talking about needing, from Washington.'

Smolin nodded. 'You'd agree with me, wouldn't you, that the murderer of Ann Harris is also the murderer of Vladimir Suzlev?'

'There can be little doubt.'

'A Russian victim, as well as an American one.'

Cowley was as intense as the other man, trying to isolate a manoeuvre he could not at the moment see. 'Yes?'

'I want a bargain,' declared Smolin, sure of his strength. 'I will agree to there still being no disclosure today of the Suzlev murder. I will also agree to there being no reference at the press conference to this man Hughes. And I will further agree there should be no move against Hughes until you get complete guidance how it should be handled from Washington . . .' The Russian Prosecutor hesitated, the concessions presented. 'In return for which I want a positive undertaking that when you interview Paul Hughes we – the Russians – have identical and complete access in that confrontation.'

'There will be objections,' Cowley anticipated, feeling he had to make the point.

'That *has* to be our agreement,' insisted Smolin.

'Or you will announce the Suzlev murder? And that the fellow American with Ann Harris on the night of her killing is to be questioned about both?' Cowley had no counter-arguments, nothing with which to resist the pressure.

'I'm not going to issue ultimatums,' said the Federal Prosecutor, having literally done just that.

'It will have to be a Washington decision,' said Cowley.

Smolin gave a nod of acceptance. 'I think you should also advise them that the government here in Moscow would take the strongest exception to any effort being made unexpectedly to repatriate Hughes to the United States.'

'I think you've made your position exceptionally clear,' said the American. He – and the embassy and even Washington – were hog-tied.

Smolin smiled, a surprisingly youthful expression. 'I'm glad we understand each other so completely! Does Senator Burden know anything of this?'

'No!' said Cowley.

The Prosecutor's smile became one of further understanding, at the quickness of the reply. 'You don't intend to tell him?'

'Senator Burden is highly regarded, held in great esteem in Washington,' said Cowley, seeing a pathway to safety. 'I believe he is in daily communication with my Director, through the embassy.'

Smolin momentarily lowered his head, in contemplation. Looking up he said: 'Would it be wise for me – for one of us – to indicate a possible early conclusion to this investigation?'

'Not at all!' said Danilov, quickly. 'Any suggestion like that would create enormous pressure for us to say more. And not just from the press; from the Senator and his staff.'

As if on cue the attendant who had escorted Danilov and Cowley reappeared to announce the arrival of Burden and his party. Danilov saw that the interpreter from his one visit to the American embassy had been assigned, to assist. The interpreter clearly recognized Danilov but gave no indication. Probably the young man was offended, like all the others. Danilov intercepted a look directed at Cowley by Burden, and thought other people appeared to be offended by each other as well. He stared curiously at Cowley for a reaction but the American detective showed nothing. There was a flurry of introductions. Burden allowed

Danilov a minimal handshake, but said: 'You're the investigator who speaks English, right?'

Danilov guessed it was Baxter, at the embassy, who had issued the warning: he saw the man for the first time at the rear of the group. Also at the rear was an extremely attractive blonde woman, who gave the briefest smile. 'Yes,' said Danilov.

'So tell me, in English, how we're doing on this.'

The interpreter positioned himself to translate simultaneously and Danilov was conscious of Smolin's frown of irritation, at being ignored so soon after learning from Cowley that Burden was briefed at the highest level. For Smolin's benefit he said in Russian: 'I think the Federal Prosecutor should advise you,' and at once repeated it in English, for the American politician. Burden's eyes came open, in quick outrage, but Baxter, forever the professional diplomat, actually stepped forward to intercede, moving the introductions on. Momentarily Danilov thought Burden was going to refuse to move away, but abruptly the man turned to Smolin and Lapinsk. Because of the need to translate everything, Danilov was able to listen and to consider everything that was said and he was impressed – and surprised – by the way Smolin handled the encounter, which he knew to be something completely new for the man. Burden fired questions rapidly, hardly allowing one to be interpreted before posing another, his head slightly sideways to a young, fresh-faced aide who frequently prompted the Senator. They were still engaged in the exchanges when one of the Russian attendants came into the room to announce the press were assembled. Burden insisted at once that the press could wait ('I want to hear more') but Smolin saw the escape from the American pressure, leading them out towards the lecture room.

As they began to move Cowley came alongside Danilov and said: 'We need to talk, directly after this.' His face was tight with what Danilov inferred to be anger.

'Of course.'

'Properly,' said Cowley.

'That's what I've been waiting for us to do,' said Danilov. He hadn't intended the discussion between Cowley and the Prosecutor to turn out as it had – he hadn't anticipated at all how

Smolin would react — but he wasn't dismayed at what had happened. He enjoyed not feeling inferior any more.

A raised dais had been erected at one end of the hall, split laterally by a baize-covered table. The seating put Smolin, Lapinsk, Cowley and Danilov in a line, with the row continuing for Burden to sit between John Prescott and James McBride. The rest of the American party, including Baxter, stood at the side of the dais, but lower, at the level of the hall. The room was packed. The area directly in front of the platform and the table was a snakepit of wires and cables, feeding microphones and TV units already arranged. Among the wires hunched camera-laden photographers: at the follow-my-leader entry on to the stage there was an explosion of flash-guns and television lights flared on, making it difficult to focus upon any of the assembled journalists seated in the main body of the hall. There was a simultaneous translation booth at the far end of the table, and through the glare Danilov could make out many of the journalists holding ear-pieces to their heads. Further along the table Burden and his aides were doing the same.

Smolin had a presentation prepared. Practically at dictation speed he read out a statement of the facts of Ann Harris's murder: name, age, position at the American embassy and circumstances of her body being found, although omitting the bizarre details. Russia was grateful for the offer of American investigatory help and an agent from the FBI was liaising upon scientific matters here in Moscow. The investigation was in its very preliminary stages but as the Federal Prosecutor he had no doubt of its eventual successful conclusion. He also welcomed the presence in Moscow of Senator Walter Burden, uncle of the dead girl, to whom on behalf of the Russian Federation he expressed his deepest sympathy.

Danilov was conscious of the shifts of impatience from the journalists he could see in the first few rows during the Prosecutor's opening. There was the briefest of pauses when Smolin stopped talking, no one appearing sure whether he had finished or not, and then a babble of shouting. For the first time the control of the unpractised Smolin wavered. The Prosecutor sat confused on the dais, looking to Lapinsk for help. But it came from McBride, the media expert. The American stood to take charge, yelled several times 'OK guys, let's calm it down and get started, shall we?' and after a while re-established some sort of order. And then, remaining standing, picked out the questioners demanding attention: sometimes he did so by name. The opening questioning centred upon the progress and content of the investigation, which McBride referred to the Prosecutor or Lapinsk, who in turn signalled either Danilov or Cowley to respond. Cowley most of the time deferred to Danilov, whose discomfort increased, particularly when the third or fourth question demanded his identity, which he gave haltingly. Cowley was called upon immediately afterwards to identify himself. In response to the same question asked several different ways Danilov insisted that inquiries were progressing routinely, but Cowley caused a fresh barrage of demands by saying that there were certain lines of inquiry that were being pursued. At once aware of the mistake, the American withdrew, denying there was any expectation at this early stage of an arrest.

'Is it true there was some defilement of the body?' The question, in a strong American accent deep within the hall from a man whom Danilov could not see, silenced the underlying murmur that had been constant since the conference began.

McBride looked inquiringly along to the two detectives. Danilov shook his head, indicating Smolin. Cowley saw the gesture and nodded towards the Prosecutor as well. Smolin bent sideways, to the Militia General, which took him away from Burden, who had said nothing about the head shearing in any public statement so far, and was leaning out to speak to the Russian. Unaware of the Senator's attempt to attract his attention, Smolin blurted that Ann Harris had been shorn by her murderer.

The outburst from the hall was such that even Danilov, who believed he had adjusted to the strangeness of an international press gathering, was bewildered. McBride lost control of the questioning, so there was a cacophony of shouts that no one could hear. While he was blinking around the room Danilov found himself instinctively pressing the straying hair into place and hoped the nervousness hadn't been caught on film or by one of the photographers. Once more McBride quietened the room, to make the questions intelligible. There was an uproar of demands for the significance of the hair cutting: most included the word 'maniac' to describe the killer. There were as many demands to know what else had been done to the body, to which neither Danilov nor Cowley replied. The progression to sexual assault was inevitable, and Danilov insisted there was no evidence of there having been any. A query about the reason for Burden's presence gave McBride the opportunity to include the politician for the first time, and Danilov was grateful for the obvious shift of camera lights and attention. Spared the glare he concentrated upon the questioning, trying to identify from the voice the man whose question about defilement could obviously refer to the girl's hair.

Burden played to every emotion. He talked of loving his niece ('a sweet, beautiful and brilliant girl') and of his personal determination to see her killer ('this monster') brought to trial. He had come to Moscow personally to meet the investigatory team and to pledge ('this is my personal undertaking') any further American help that might be needed. He avoided but did not rule out the question of further FBI personnel coming to Moscow. With no way of knowing, at this stage, how long the investigation might last, he did not intend remaining in the Russian capital until its conclusion but would return if and when circumstances demanded. Asked what verdict he expected from a successful prosecution, Burden said: 'Those of you who know me well — and it's good to see a few old friends here today — will also know my support of capital punishment. A person who takes a life doesn't deserve to have one.' That reply brought the questioning back to the Federal Prosecutor, who confirmed capital punishment did exist in Russia and added to another query that it was carried out by pistol shot. Burden said at once: 'That sounds just fine to me.'

Danilov found the individual television appearances more difficult than the general conference. There were three, all for American networks, and he insisted upon Cowley being at his side at every one, which meant the FBI agent did most of the talking, although Danilov was pressed to speak in English. He did so feeling like a performing animal. Before each appearance, a make-up person carefully combed his hair into place, for which he was grateful. Burden was also interviewed separately by each of the networks: for two of the appearances the politician had Danilov and Cowley sit with him, as if he were in some way controlling the investigation. Danilov sat throughout with his shirt glued to him by perspiration.

John Prescott hurried towards the two detectives the moment they re-entered the ante-room in which they had earlier assembled and said at once to Cowley: 'The Senator has been in touch with Washington. You'll be getting guidance some time today. I thought you should know.'

Cowley looked curiously at the younger, eager man. 'OK. Let's see what the reply is.'

'It might be a good idea for both of you to be a little more forthcoming in the meantime,' suggested the man, including Danilov in the approach.

Cowley nodded, understanding. 'Like I said, we'll wait.'

Danilov said: 'I think the Senator should get all his information from the Federal Prosecutor: that's how it should properly be done.'

Prescott shook his head, in exaggerated sadness. 'It's a big mistake.'

'Thanks for your concern,' said Cowley, a Washington player recognizing another Washington player.

'We're all staying at the Savoy,' announced Prescott, following the game plan. 'It's got a pretty fantastic dining-room. Why don't you both join us for dinner tonight? The Senator would like that.'

'I've already got a commitment,' Cowley apologized. Which would be easier, dinner with Burden and the sycophants or dinner with Andrews and Pauline? He didn't think it was a good comparison.

'And I've got a prior engagement, too,' Danilov refused. Larissa's shift still made the late afternoons convenient.

The hopeful smile slipped from Prescott's face. 'Sorry you couldn't make it.'

'Maybe another time,' said Cowley insincerely, as the other American walked back to Burden's group, which was gathered in stilted conversation with the two other Russian officials. Cowley turned to Danilov. 'I'd like that talk before I get back to the embassy, to discuss everything with Washington.'

'But not here,' said Danilov. The sweat was drying, cold and uncomfortable, on his back.

'Your office is in the opposite direction.'

'Why don't I buy you lunch?' He guessed he had sufficient roubles – just – and although the service would have been better in the foreign-currency part of The Peking the larger section that accepted Russian money would not be crowded this late. 'How about Chinese?'

It would make a change from Lean Cuisine, thought Cowley. 'I think maybe I deserve it.' What would Pauline make for tonight? In Rome she'd been awarded a diploma for Italian cooking, to add to the Cordon Bleu qualification she'd gained in a two-month residential course in Paris.

It took another fifteen minutes for the two investigators to excuse themselves. The Soviet section of the restaurant was more crowded than Danilov had expected but they got a table. Cowley said he didn't have any particular preferences, so why didn't Danilov order for both of them: he didn't drink, so he wouldn't have any wine.

'You didn't play it straight,' Cowley accused at once, the ordering completed.

'Did you?' challenged Danilov, just as quickly.

'I thought so.'

'I don't,' said Danilov. 'You checked the twisted fingerprint in the evidence room when you came back to Petrovka, right? But didn't tell me what you were doing.' He was still enjoying the feeling of superiority.

'I didn't have the comparison back from Washington, from the stuff in Ann Harris's office, until this morning,' tried Cowley, defensively. 'What was there to tell?'

Danilov had ordered vodka in preference to the sugar-sweet Chinese wine. He sipped, to give himself time, and said: 'How about suspicion? You'd seen Hughes's hand, when you talked to him.'

'You suspected it, too. With better reason. You had the transcript of the telephone conversations but all you gave me was the fact of out-of-hours calls. Why the hell only give me half the thing to hit him with? You were fucking about, waiting for me to move.'

'With good reason!' seized Danilov, still believing himself ahead in the exchange. Slightly relaxing, with an admission, he said: 'And I didn't have the transcripts: I had to get them, additionally.'

'From intelligence monitoring of diplomatic telephones?'

'I got them,' said Danilov, shortly, refusing the confirmation. 'It's our advantage.'

Danilov had ordered the duck and was glad, when it came. There were also stuffed dumplings and sour prawns. Appearing reminded, by the delivery of the food, Cowley said: 'What about them eating together on the night of the murder? He couldn't have jerked me around like he did if I had been able to hit him with that!'

Danilov did not want to disclose completely how desperately close he had been to knowing nothing until the last minutes before the conference. Using the American's opening, he said: 'Waiting. I think you didn't tell me what you had because you wanted to keep the situation with Hughes completely within the embassy, so you could ship him home. Now you can't. Certainly not without creating a major diplomatic uproar because by now his exit, diplomatically protected or not, will have been banned.'

He'd lost, Cowley conceded. He said: 'The duck is good.'

'It's the obvious speciality.' I've won, thought Danilov.

'Maybe we should re-define the working relationship,' suggested Cowley, capitulating.

'I think that would probably be a good idea.'

'I appreciated the inference in front of the prosecutor and your boss that everything was a joint discovery: that it was an even-Steven investigation,' said Cowley.

'That's what I thought it was going to be.'

'Have we made our points, do you think?'

'I believe so.'

'It would be stupid to shake hands or anything like that, wouldn't it?'

'Quite stupid,' agreed Danilov.

'I won't get any playback from Washington, about anything, until tomorrow. I'll call.'

'I'll be waiting.' Danilov decided that everything had worked out well: extremely well. There still had to be Paul Hughes's confession, of course.

The meal cost fifty roubles. Danilov wondered if Lapinsk would let him reclaim it. He doubted it. The system didn't work as he understood it did in the West, with expense accounts.

Larissa was waiting behind the desk but emerged the moment he entered the hotel, to meet him in the foyer. She was smiling, enjoying herself in front of the other receptionists who shared the same rendezvous arrangements, and said: 'Can I show you direct to your room, sir?'

Danilov turned with her towards the elevators, conscious of the smiling attention. 'What's all this about?'

'I'm proud of you,' she said. 'You looked terrific on television. We switched from Russian to CNN, when the satellite came on. CNN were heading their news coverage with it: running the conference live. You looked wonderful. Why have you had your hair cut so short, incidentally? I like it, but then I liked the grey bits, too. Made you look distinguished.'

Danilov was unhappy she had so easily guessed the reason for the new hair-style. Ignoring her question, he said: 'I didn't like the conference.'

The elevator stopped at the sixth floor and he followed her out. Larissa said: 'You looked as if you did.'

'This isn't getting any easier.'

'What's that mean?' Larissa secured the lock but didn't come forward to be kissed as she usually did, remaining at the far side of the room to frown at him curiously.

'Just what I said: that it isn't easy.'

'Just like it wasn't easy the other night at dinner?'

'You made the difficulties there. Olga suspects.'

'So what?'

'So it's difficult.'

'Why don't we stop thinking about you for a moment?' challenged Larissa. 'How do you think it is for me, with a slob like Yevgennie?'

'Horrible,' conceded Danilov at once. He humped his shoulders. 'There isn't anything I can say that would help: just that I feel sorry. I still don't see why you behaved as you did.'

Larissa slowly began to disrobe, actually humming to herself a vague tune to accompany the striptease, which became more and more raunchily explicit with the more clothes she took off.

'I wanted you to feel me when I was wet but you wouldn't. Why wouldn't you?'

'You tried to make it obvious, to Olga and maybe to Yevgennie. You were trying to create a situation, weren't you?' demanded Danilov. He'd set out to show his annoyance but realized he sounded weak and petulant instead.

'Feel me now,' insisted Larissa, completely naked.

'I think it would be an idea to cool things off for a while.'

Larissa pulled back the bed covers and lay provocatively displayed for him, one leg raised, the other stretched out before her on the bed. 'Do you really mean that?'

'Yes.'

'Sure?'

'What's the point of hurting people?'

Larissa frowned. 'Who?' She appeared genuinely perplexed.

'Olga. Yevgennie.'

She laughed. 'All Olga has is a suspicion! And the only way to hurt Yevgennie would be to take his brandy bottle away. And do you really care? Wouldn't you like to sort things out, so that we could be married?'

'It's complicated, you know that,' said Danilov, refusing to answer. He'd never intended the affair to become this serious. Still didn't. So why had he allowed it to happen? Surely he hadn't been trying to prove he was still attractive to a vivacious, beautiful woman, despite the encroaching greyness he'd got rid of in a barber's chair and the stomach bulge he constantly tried to suck in! Of course not! He *had* enjoyed the flattery, though. And Larissa was beautiful and vivacious.

'Why don't you come and fuck me, to help you make up your mind?'

Going towards her, Danilov realized the dinner episode hadn't been for her personal enjoyment, a private joke. Larissa was pushing the situation, *wanting* Olga to find out.

There was a giggle of delight, quickly stifled as the television transmission ended. Worried. How they should be. Looked it, all of them. Frightened. Right they should be frightened. How it was important they should be. Sensational, about the hair. Not a maniac, though. Got that wrong. Cleverer than any of them.

205

Prove it, now the hunt was properly announced. Hunt but never find. Never know where to look. How to look. Going to worry a lot more, all of them. Never get it right. The giggle came again, longer this time. Then the hum.

Chapter Twenty-One

It was inevitable that he would be late for dinner. Within minutes of his personally dispatching the 'Eyes Only' cable to the Director fully setting out the circumstances and suspicion surrounding Paul Hughes – and the complete Russian awareness of it – the direct telephone call came from Leonard Ross, on the secure line.

Andrews, who was still in the FBI offices reading the exchanges and actually took the call from the Director, said: 'Jesus H. Christ!' holding out the receiver, as if it were hot. As Cowley took the telephone, Andrews mouthed that they would hold the meal, for as long as it took.

Ross didn't waste time with pleasantries, dictating his questions so precisely that Cowley was sure the Director had them written out in front of him: Cowley had little doubt the entire conversation was being recorded, for others to hear later. Cowley repeatedly insisted that at that stage all they had was strong circumstantial suspicion, not actual proof, and insisted just as frequently that it had been made quite clear at his meetings that day with Russian officials that Hughes would not be permitted to leave Moscow to be questioned in America.

'What about diplomatic immunity?'

'A Russian's also dead,' Cowley reminded him. 'They'd refuse to recognize immunity. We don't stand a chance of keeping the lid on.'

'The ambassador know this?'

'I waited to talk to you.'

'Burden?'

'No.'

'I'll need to consult at this end.'

'What about the ambassador and Burden?'

'Nothing, until I get a guide here. There's some more stuff coming for you, in the pouch. And the mind doctors think they can create their psychological profile, from what you've sent.'

There was a pause. 'You're quite sure, about the Russians' attitude?'

'Positive.'

'You'll get complete guidance by 8 a.m. tomorrow, your time.'

Cowley was too late to go back to the guest quarters to change. He was about to leave the embassy when he thought about taking something, so he detoured to the commissary. He'd wanted flowers but there weren't any. There were chocolates but they were in practical square or oblong boxes, nothing ornate or fancy, for special occasions. Was this a special occasion? Of course it was. He was seeing his ex-wife who'd remained a friend, although a distant one, both in time and place. It was right, practically expected, that he should take her something. It had to be chocolates. He bought the largest box available. Was it pushing forgiveness and understanding too far, to include Andrews in the gift-giving? Why not? Cowley picked a bottle of French brandy, wishing he had been able to shop better elsewhere, particularly for Pauline. But where? Andrews was his guide for Moscow. And he could hardly have invoked the help of her present husband to buy a present for his ex-wife, no matter how civilized they were all trying to be. Why hadn't he anticipated the situation and brought something from America? The choice would have still been difficult. And *shown* planning, which might not have been a good idea.

Andrews expansively opened the door of the compound apartment, drink already in his free hand. 'You're hardly late at all. Pauline's got everything on hold.'

Cowley was surprised by Andrews's babbled uncertainty: there was even a shake to the man's hands. Cowley handed over the brandy, smiling up at Pauline as she came from a side-door he presumed led to the kitchen. She was wearing a red woollen dress which fitted quite tightly, moulded to her figure. She appeared as slim as ever, although perhaps slightly heavier-busted. When she came further into the light of the entrance hall he saw that her hair, which had always been very black, was streaked with grey at the sides. Perhaps it was difficult to get good tinting in Moscow: he would have thought there would be some facility for wives at the embassy. He thought she looked wonderful and wanted to tell her so. He didn't, of course.

'Hello William,' she said. She'd always used the full name, never Bill. There was a tentative accompanying smile.

So they were all uncertain, Cowley accepted. He'd forgotten the deep-throated Southern accent. He'd mocked her about it, when they'd first met and in the early years, before everything went wrong, calling her Scarlett and telling her she could call him Rhett. Stupid, childish stuff, never admitted to anyone: no point in bringing it to mind now. 'It's good to see you.' Stupid, childish words.

There was a momentary impasse, the three of them crowded into the tiny hallway. Cowley thrust the chocolates towards her and said: 'I wanted to get something different: more original. Sorry.' He was stumbling, tongue-tied. It shouldn't have been like this.

'It was very thoughtful,' Pauline accepted.

'Let's not hang around here!' urged Andrews, propelling them further into the apartment. 'Settle down! Relax!'

The apartment was inferior to the suite he occupied in the newly built compound, the only point of comparison he had. The hallway wasn't really a hallway at all, just an entry box with a clothes closet. The living-room was another box: literally square-sided and more cramped than it deserved to be by the inclusion of American furniture and converter-connected television and stereo equipment. The lid of a drop-down cocktail cabinet literally overhung one of the chairs, displaying the drinks. Cowley stood not knowing where to sit. Pauline stood not appearing to know what to do or say, either. Another impasse.

'Drinks!' bustled Andrews, enthusiastically, depositing the brandy among the regiment of bottles in the cocktail cabinet. 'What are we all going to have to drink? Let's relax! Enjoy ourselves!'

Cowley chose the settee, needing it for his size. 'Maybe a juice.' He was conscious of Pauline's frown.

'Scotch,' she said, still looking at Cowley.

'Forgot that you didn't, not any more,' said Andrews, to the other man. 'Need to get supplies.'

As Andrews disappeared into the kitchen, Pauline said: 'Barry told me but I didn't believe it. Since when?'

'Seems like forever.'

'Which sounds like it's difficult?'

Cowley thought about it. 'Not really. Sometimes. But not often.'

'You're looking good on abstinence.'

'You're looking good, too.' Which was a lie. He was surprised about the greyness. There were the faintest of lines around her eyes, too. He still thought she looked wonderful.

'It's Boeuf-en-Croûte,' Pauline announced. 'Liver pâté and hot goose liver cooked together to start. We can get most things from the commissary if we plan ahead.'

She'd remembered the favourite. Polite consideration, nothing more, he told himself. What more *could* there be? 'I guessed it would be something special.'

'It's not,' she insisted, modestly. 'Just ordinary.'

'How've you been?'

'OK, I guess. Moscow's difficult. Insular. Everyone is on top of everyone else here.'

Andrews burst back in from the kitchen, grape juice in hand. 'Pauline caught you on CNN today!' At the cocktail cabinet the man poured himself a heavy Scotch, adding only one cube of ice. 'Said you looked great. Very authoritative.'

Pauline smiled, more widely this time, showing the teeth she had worried so much about having capped, because of the expense. 'But you didn't look very comfortable at times.'

'I wasn't,' Cowley admitted.

'Not hugger-mugger with Senator Burden, he of all power and influence!' exclaimed Andrews. 'He's the guy who makes careers in Washington.'

'Or breaks them,' Cowley pointed out.

'That sounds interesting?' demanded the resident FBI man.

'I think I'm caught in a power play, back home: between a rock and a hard place.'

'Then get out of it,' Andrews advised. 'This could be your big chance: we've talked about it. Don't fuck it up.'

'I'm trying not to,' said Cowley. He avoided looking too quickly at Pauline: when they'd been married he had never sworn in front of her in company, believing it showed disrespect. When he did look, she seemed unaware of the obscenity.

'Getting personal calls from the Director is pretty impressive stuff,' insisted Andrews.

'It's the politics of the thing,' Cowley dismissed. He looked once more to Pauline, curious if she would be bored by shop talk. She didn't appear to be. But then she'd always been interested in the job.

'Come on, buddy!' urged Andrews. 'You're flying high: you know that. Lucky bastard.'

'We're not into an arrest situation yet,' said Cowley.

'It can't be long.'

'I thought William came for dinner, not interrogation,' intruded Pauline, gently.

Andrews was at the cabinet again, refilling his glass. 'Just talking,' he said. 'Call it envy.'

'I've things to do in the kitchen,' said Pauline. To Cowley she added: 'Meat still rare? And Italian dressing on the salad?'

'The Goddess of the kitchen,' said Andrews, proudly. He put his glass down heavily. 'Shit! I forgot the wine. It'll take me a minute to get some from the commissary. Keep everything on hold!'

'I really don't . . .' began Cowley, but Andrews was already on his feet, hauling his protective coat about him. Cowley saw Andrews had changed his shirt beneath the same suit he had worn that day.

'I need to check the cable traffic anyway: never forget the time difference with the outside world.' The door slammed loudly behind him.

Pauline sat back in her seat. 'It won't take long. Nothing will spoil.'

'Does he often check cable traffic during the evening?'

'You know Barry. Mr Ambition himself.'

'That why he took this post?'

She nodded. 'Necessary career move. He expects to get Washington next time. We should hear soon.'

'I know.'

'If he did get Washington, he would be working under you, wouldn't he?'

'Not unless he was assigned to the internal Russian division, within the United States,' said Cowley. As its head he had the

211

right of veto over staff appointments within his section, he remembered.

'I was very nervous about tonight,' admitted Pauline, suddenly. '*Am* very nervous.'

'I wasn't sure, either. I'm glad I came though. Very glad. It *is* good to see you again.'

Pauline smiled, more easily than before. 'I'm glad, too . . . I mean there's no real reason why we shouldn't have got together, is there . . . ? And it *is* Moscow, which is different from anywhere else . . .' She floundered to a halt. 'Do you think you could get me another drink?'

Cowley took her glass, curious at her difficulty. Surely . . . ? He refused to let the question even form. Another thought intruded. There didn't seem much personal feeling between her and Andrews. No tenderness, no touching. But had there been between him and Pauline, when they'd been together? Pauline wasn't the type of woman who needed that sort of attention: she'd be uncomfortable with it. He said: 'How long have you been drinking Scotch?'

She shrugged. 'I don't know. A couple of years, I guess. But just socially. You really off it completely?'

He returned with her drink, nodding. 'Quite a while now.'

'No relapse?'

'Nope.'

'That's good.'

Cowley was unsure whether the remark was genuine or just politeness. 'I think so.' She'd pleaded so much, so often: tried anger and tears and threatened the divorce there had eventually been. A new feeling came, with the recollection, a positive sorrow at how unhappy he must have made her. She hadn't deserved it: not any of it.

'What about . . . ?' she started, then stopped.

'No,' he said, guessing the incomplete question. Her other unhappiness: humiliation as well as unhappiness, his hand up every available skirt. He'd really given Pauline the whole package.

'No one?' Her surprise was obvious.

'No one.'

'That's sad,' she said, unexpectedly.

Now he was surprised. 'Why?'

212

She shrugged again. 'I don't know. It just is. I always thought you'd get married again. I kept waiting for something on a Christmas card. You're the sort of person who needs to be married.'

'With my track record!' He was intrigued at her assessment. He wondered what was keeping Andrews at the embassy.

Pauline's shoulders rose and fell again. 'Mistakes happen.'

Was that how she'd categorized their marriage, a mistake that could be dismissed with a shrug? He didn't want her to think of it like that. 'You happy?' he said, then at once: 'No! I didn't mean that! I'm sorry. That was out of order; forgive me!'

She nodded, agreeing with his self-correction. 'Who's ever really happy?'

'A lot of people.' He shouldn't push it like this.

'I'm OK. Moscow's not an easy place for anyone.' She stood, abruptly. 'Time I made the salad,' she said, finding an excuse.

'Anything I can do?'

She grinned at him from the kitchen doorway. 'I don't think I can handle all these changes at one time.'

Andrews's return prevented any further conversation. There was a clink of bottles from a plastic sack. 'Jesus, it's cold out there!' He smiled brightly, first at Cowley, then at Pauline's reappearance, and said: 'You guys been all right?'

'You were a long time,' the woman accused.

Andrews held the plastic bag aloft. 'Essential errand.' He set the wine out on the table, three bottles each of red and white. To Cowley he said: 'And there was a message for you. *And* I got ambushed. It was a busy, busy time.'

'What message?' demanded Cowley.

Andrews left the table, for his wife to arrange the place settings and to clear all but two of the bottles on to a side dresser, offering Cowley the cable slip. 'Blood content of the body is estimated to be two pints short, the predictable loss. So I guess she was killed in the street after all. The report is going to be in the overnight pouch, with some other stuff. Our medical people aren't impressed by the standards of Russian autopsies, it would seem.'

'What's this about being ambushed?' asked Pauline, from the table.

Andrews replied still looking at the other man, not his wife. 'Prescott, the Senator's monkey. He was hanging around outside the office. Wanted to know if I was working with you on the murder. I said I wasn't, to get him off my back. He seemed disappointed.'

'What else did he say?'

'Asked if I knew anything at all. I said I didn't. He told me the Senator would be grateful if I could pass anything on: that he'd keep in touch.'

'Everything you know is classified from *everyone*,' said Cowley, repeating the earlier warning. 'That includes Burden and the ambassador.'

'Don't worry,' assured Andrews. He lighted a cigar, slumping into a facing chair. 'I'm glad this happened. Us getting together like this. Just like the old days, right?'

'Close,' agreed Cowley. They'd practically been a threesome in London. He supposed it had been inevitable that Pauline would turn to the other man, when things got as bad as they did between them.

'Right that it should be like this. Adult.'

'Yes.' Cowley guessed the other man had had quite a few drinks before his arrival. Just as quickly he refused the criticism. How many times must Andrews have thought the same about him, at dinner parties in London? Had he sounded like this? Probably worse. Poor Pauline.

'This *is* the social scene in Moscow, eating in people's houses. Pauline and I will introduce you around: there are some great guys at the embassy.'

'It could all be over quite soon,' reminded Cowley. 'I could be on my way back.' What would the orders be from Washington tomorrow? He didn't enjoy working like this, having constantly to delay and get guidance from the other side of the world. He would have liked to have confronted Hughes that afternoon, after getting all the Russian evidence.

'I really don't feel I've done enough, workwise.'

'You've helped a lot,' assured Cowley, meaning it. Andrews had taken a lot of the routine transmission stuff and evidence-logging off his shoulders. What *would* he say, if were asked about having Andrews in his Russian division back in Washington?

'You want me to do anything more, all you've got to do is ask, OK? Really.'

'OK,' Cowley accepted.

The meal was magnificent, as Pauline's meals always were, and the evening became easier as they ate. By the end there were even reminiscences about their time in London together, the husband roles reversed, which Cowley imagined at first would have been difficult but wasn't. Over coffee Andrews asked what it was like at Pennsylvania Avenue, without openly admitting his expectation to be posted there after Moscow, and Cowley talked of the differences from field work. 'A lot of internal politics.'

'But necessary, careerwise?'

Mr Ambitious, thought Cowley, Pauline's expression still in his mind. 'Certainly the place to be seen and to impress.'

'Just give me the chance,' said Andrews, eagerly.

The evening ended with their insistence that he should come again very soon and not stay by himself in the new compound and with other people from the embassy the next time. Cowley insisted in return that he should reciprocate by taking them to a restaurant they liked. At the door Pauline came forward for a parting kiss, which Cowley gave her lightly on the cheek, because it seemed quite natural to do so. He said he'd enjoyed it, which he had. And thought so again, back at the embassy suite.

He wasn't tired so he made himself coffee and sat thinking about the evening. He was intrigued by her response to the question he probably shouldn't have asked, about her being happy. Unthinking answer to unthinking question, he decided. She seemed very quiet, deferring to Andrews's approval a lot of the time. But that could have been his imagination. And was it any of his business? She wasn't his wife any more. Not his responsibility. Not that he'd shown enough – none, which had been the problem – when they had been married. Their first protracted time together since the divorce, Cowley reflected. So how had it been for him? A lot of nostalgia. A lot of regret, too, at what he'd done in the past. Love? Of course. He'd never fallen out of love with her, just destroyed hers for him. *You're the sort of person who needs to be married.* Was he? Cowley felt discomfited by the assertion. He certainly felt lonely, most of the time. Lost even. But easing loneliness wasn't marriage. So what was his definition of marriage? A question he wasn't qualified to answer: didn't want to answer, certainly not tonight. If he wasn't completely happy as he was, at least he wasn't completely unhappy: he had made his private adjustments, marked his own boundaries. To anyone outside, he was a success. Only he felt otherwise: knew just how much he'd failed, a failure for which no professional achievement could compensate. He *had* enjoyed the evening. And would enjoy more with her. With them. And he wanted to take them out, too. Somewhere special. But where? No problem. He'd ask Danilov. Who better than one of the city's foremost detectives?

Would there still be amicable contact with Dimitri Danilov? With anyone in Moscow? Tomorrow there was the challenge to Paul Hughes, who had a tell-tale twisted finger and lateral pocket loops in his prints and who'd lied and whose intercepted conversation they now had with Ann Harris, talking of sex and pain and what they were going to do to each other. All to be exposed tomorrow. The warning he'd given Andrews that night would probably be right. Maybe there wouldn't be the opportunity to meet other people from the embassy or for any more evenings with Andrews and Pauline or pay-back dinners in Moscow restaurants.

Cowley was still feeling no fatigue and didn't expect to sleep, but he did, very deeply, so he was distantly aware of the telephone ringing several times before he came sufficiently awake to lift it.

'There's been another one,' announced Danilov. 'She's lived. I'll be at the embassy for you in ten minutes.'

The shaking wouldn't stop: couldn't stop. Huge, aching shudders. Had to stop it. Get control. Horrible. God, it had been horrible. Terrifying. She'd risen from the dead. Literally. Surged up from the pavement, screaming, snatching out. Sure she was dead; had to have been dead. Felt the knife slide in, although not as smoothly as usual. Felt the life go out of her. And she'd fallen like the others. Lifeless. Lay still while the hair came off. But then surged up, grabbing, as she'd gone on to her back. Screaming. Terrible, terrible screaming. Wouldn't have seen. Couldn't have seen. Impossible to be completely sure, though. No description. Too dark. Too confused. No danger then. Had to stop the shaking. It hurt. Ached. Bitch. Cow. Why hadn't she stayed dead? That's what she should have done, stayed dead. Only got a few buttons. And dropped most of the hair. Wasn't the same, only a few buttons and so little hair. Second failure. Worse this time. She hadn't seen, though: no description. Be able to do it again.

Chapter Twenty-Two

They approached the hospital well before dawn, driving hurriedly through empty, yellow-lit streets: Moscow was utterly deserted and cold, a moonscape with houses. The talk was stilted, just one or two-word exchanges: Danilov knew only that it was a woman in her thirties, that the attack had happened quite near her home on a street named Granovskaya, and that she'd survived. Pavin was already at the bedside.

Cowley brought both their feelings into the open. 'It was our fault. We spent all our time worrying about diplomatic niceties and gave him the chance to do it again! What the hell were we thinking of? It was all so *obvious*. We knew it could happen!'

'She lived,' repeated Danilov.

'Luck. Nothing to do with us.'

Cowley was initially numbed by the hospital. But for the very occasional sight of a uniformed nurse or a white-coated attendant he would not have believed himself in a hospital at all. Rather it was like moving through a tiled but condemned underpass taken over by squatters, maybe in New York's Little Italy or Washington's Anacostia. There was litter underfoot and even beds in the corridors, humped with sleeping, snuffling people like he'd seen in documentaries on American television of homeless derelicts who had moved into public facilities due to be demolished. It took Danilov a long time to find an attendant sufficiently interested to guide them to the emergency section, where there appeared to be more staff: certainly more activity. Here there were no overflow beds in the corridors. Strip lighting gave better illumination than in some of the earlier parts through which they had walked.

Pavin must have seen them approaching, although neither saw him. The burly Major emerged from a minute, single-occupancy side-ward as they reached it. Considerately he spoke Russian slowly, for Cowley's benefit. Her name – Lydia Orlenko – and an address to trace her husband, a metro train driver, had come from her handbag, which had also contained ten single dollar bills. She was a waitress at the Intourist Hotel who normally got home around 1 a.m., although that morning she hadn't. She'd been found by a Militia foot patrolman, who'd heard her screaming. She'd been shorn by the time he reached her: he'd seen no one running away from the scene of the attack, in a narrow passageway between two housing blocks. She'd been hysterical, beyond any comprehensible speech: by the time she'd reached hospital she had relapsed into unconsciousness. Fortunately Pavin had arrived before surgeons began operating: he'd been able to ask the doctors to record some medical evidence as they worked. Her blood was B Positive. The wound matched those of Ann Harris and Vladimir Suzlev, five centimetres across at the point of entry of a knife sharp along one edge, five millimetres thick at the other. The difference from the two murders – an important factor in her surviving – was that this time the thrust had not been clean: the attempt had been between the eighth and ninth rib and from the right, like the others, but it had actually caught the upper rib, deflecting the passage to the heart, which had been missed completely. The intercostal muscle had been penetrated and the right lung punctured by a wound only nine centimetres deep. She was still under the effects of the anaesthetic but she was in good health, only thirty-two years old, and the surgeons were sure she was going to make a full recovery.

'The husband and the patrolman?' demanded Danilov.

Pavin gestured along the corridor. 'In the waiting-room.'

The two men were sitting in silence, facing each other from opposite sides of the room, which was quite empty apart from chairs arranged around all four walls. The uniformed patrolman was smoking, *papirosi*, the butts of the hollow-tubed Russian cigarettes already around his feet. The husband was wearing a loud, brown-checked jerkin that reminded Cowley of blanket material, over oil-stained blue work overalls. Both men looked curiously at the American, instantly recognizing a foreigner.

Cowley let Danilov lead. The patrolman had been walking along Granovskaya when the screaming started. It had taken him a few moments to locate the alley, because it was so small. The woman had been propped up on her left elbow, hysterical, shouting nothing he could understand. He'd thought she'd been wildly drunk until he'd seen the blood. At the same time as seeing the blood he'd realized her hair had been cut off, in clumps, and strewn all around her. She became unconscious before the ambulance arrived. She'd been entirely alone when he reached her and he'd neither seen nor heard anyone running away. He'd obviously entered the alley from Ulitza Granovskaya: at its other end, it emerged into Semasko. He hadn't thought to go on, to check that street for anyone: his concern had been to get help for the wounded woman. He was sorry if he'd done wrong.

Boris Orlenko was a nervous, sharp-moving man who spoke too quickly and stuttered because of it. He said his wife had been a waitress at the Intourist Hotel for five years: mostly she worked in the ground-floor coffee-shop but occasionally she helped out in one of the upstairs restaurants. She always walked home, even when she was on late shift, because they lived so close. He couldn't understand why she had been attacked and wanted to know if they did. Why had her hair been cut off? It didn't make sense. None of it made sense. She was just an ordinary person, with nothing worth stealing. They were both just ordinary people. He had to be at the terminus by six: would he be allowed to get away by then? If not he'd have to telephone somebody: it would cause problems at the depot. He could come back to see his wife when he finished work. That would be all right, wouldn't it?

'Did your wife ever speak of knowing people – anyone – from the American embassy?' asked Cowley, coming into the questioning for the first time.

Orlenko fidgeted, uncomfortably. 'The embassy? No. She knew Americans . . . not knew them, you understand. Served them, at the hotel. That's all. I suppose some could have come from the embassy. She never said.'

'What about regular American customers? Someone who came a lot?'

The Russian shook his head. 'No one. Not that she said.'

'Do you think she would have done? Did she talk about the hotel?'

Orlenko frowned. 'Not a lot. Just sometimes. You're American, aren't you? What's she got to do with the embassy?'

'Nothing,' said Cowley, sighing. He looked to Danilov to take over, but the Russian detective shook his head, with nothing left to ask. To the seated men Danilov said: 'You can both go: we know where you'll be.'

'No possible connection with the embassy this time,' said Cowley in English, as the two filed out.

'We didn't know Suzlev concentrated upon embassy customers until we saw his wife a second time,' Danilov pointed out. 'It's the woman here who's important.'

It was another hour before Lydia Orlenko recovered consciousness and almost a further hour again before they were permitted into the minuscule side-ward. She was lying on her left, the side furthest from the wound, with a pillow behind her to keep her in position. There was an arched frame over the upper part of her body but beneath the bedding, keeping its weight off. Her shorn head was completely covered by the sort of protective mobcap that women wear for hygienic reasons in places where food is prepared. She had her eyes closed and was breathing deeply and Danilov thought she might have gone to sleep again.

'Lydia?' he said, quietly. 'Lydia Markovina Orlenko?' Her eyes flickered open, but heavily, without immediate focus. He was stooped low, close to her: her breath stank appallingly, fouled by the anaesthetic. 'Can you hear me? Understand what I'm saying?'

She grunted, thickly.

'I'm from the Militia: from Petrovka. I have to know what happened.'

She moved, very slightly, and there was an instant wince of pain. 'Hurt.'

'How were you hurt?'

Her eyes cleared, properly registering him at last. 'Don't know.'

There was a chair in the room, but Danilov ignored it, kneeling on the floor beside the bed. Cowley did the same, but with more difficulty, because of his size. There was no room at all for Pavin, who remained just inside the door, able to hear everything for his notes. Danilov said: 'You finished work and left the hotel to walk home, as you usually do. What street were you on, approaching the alley? Granovskaya? Or Semasko?'

'Semasko. From the hotel. Always.'

'By yourself?'

'Yes?'

'No one with you?'

'No.'

'How about behind? Following?'

'Didn't see.'

'Or hear?'

'No.'

'What happened at the passage?'

'Went in. Always do. Dark, but I know it. Hurt me.' Without warning or any movement of her body, to indicate the breakdown, the woman began to weep, a solitary tear path forming along the side of her nose.

She moved to wipe it away, but whimpered with the pain of the movement. Danilov felt for his own handkerchief and realized he didn't have one. Cowley passed his along the bed and the Russian gently wiped the wetness away. He said: 'It'll hurt more if you cry. You're safe now. Tell me what happened then.'

'Someone behind me, very close. Very close and then pressing into me. Hand over my mouth, so I couldn't breath: squeezing my nose. Hurt me. Pulled me backwards. Then awful pain. Something going into me. Felt like burning. Tried to scream but I couldn't. Hand too tight across my mouth. Fell down. Awful pain. Then I can't remember . . .'

She began to cough, whimpering again each time at the jar to her back. Danilov tried to help her to some water from the glass by the bedside, but she couldn't drink properly and some spilled on to the pillow. As close as he was he detected the bruising on her upper lip and under her nose and remembered that Ann Harris and Vladimir Suzlev had both been similarly marked, according to the pathology report.

Tentatively Lydia Orlenko moved her head, keeping it on the pillow but looking down to include Cowley. 'Who are you?'

'Another policeman, helping me,' answered Danilov, speaking for the other man. 'You *can* remember, after falling down. You screamed. A patrolman came.'

'Can't remember *falling* down, after the burning in my back. I was just there. Like waking up. Felt him over me. Standing, looking down. Screamed and tried to hit him, to push him away. Did hit him. Heard him grunt when I hit him. Then he was gone. Screamed more then, to keep him away . . .' There was a fresh outburst of painful coughing. She shook her head against more water and said: 'Stop! I want the pain to stop!'

'You're doing very well,' encouraged Danilov. 'Telling us a lot of important things. You're sure it was a man?'

She hesitated. 'He wore trousers. And a jacket.'

'No topcoat?'

'Quilted jacket.'

'Listen carefully,' ordered Danilov, speaking very precisely. 'You must tell us what he looked like: *everything* you can remember.'

At the door Pavin strained forward, notebook ready.

'Nothing,' said the woman, shortly.

'No, Lydia Markovina. That won't do. You must describe him.'

'Didn't see. Behind me, at first. Then I was on the ground. I could see trousers but not the top of him. I told you, it was very dark in the passage: completely dark.'

Danilov came forward, anxiously. 'OK,' he said, coaxing. 'The trousers. What were they like?'

'Just trousers.'

'Colour?'

'Dark.'

'Blue? Grey? Black?'

'Dark,' she insisted.

'Cloth? Or maybe jeans?'

'Cloth.'

'You must have seen the shoes.'

'Not properly. Not that I can think of. I think they were boots. Rubber.'

'Long? Or short?'

'Short. The sort that come up to the ankle.'

'You could see up to his waist?'

'I suppose.'

'Was he fat? Thin? Medium?'

'Don't know. Medium maybe.'

'When he grabbed you from behind you said he pressed into you. What about then? Did he feel either fat or thin then?'

'Quilted coat,' she reminded. 'There was the fatness of the quilted coat.'

'If you could see to his waist, what about a belt? Was he wearing a belt?' Some belts had distinctive buckles, Danilov thought, hopefully.

'Not that I could see: can remember.'

Danilov sighed. From his side Cowley whispered, in English again: 'She said he was leaning down towards her.'

'When you woke up, on the ground, were you on your face? Or your back?' resumed Danilov.

'Twisted. But more on my face.'

'Then he turned you?'

'Yes.'

'How?'

'Turned me,' she repeated, with a hint of indignation.

'Where did he put his hands? On your shoulders? Around your waist? Did he touch you privately, where he shouldn't have done?'

There was almost a smile but it didn't form. 'Felt a hand on my shoulder. Then on my breast. Squeezed me there.'

Danilov nodded, glancing up to ensure Pavin was making the note, which he was. 'So he *must* have been bent close over you? Why didn't you see his face?'

'I was on *my* face then!' said the woman, close to indignation again. 'I didn't know what was happening. I was very frightened: kept my eyes shut. Didn't *want* to see.'

'There must have been an outline: an impression. How tall was he?' As he asked the question, Danilov stood, gesturing Cowley up beside him. 'As tall as me? Or as tall as him?'

'You. Not as tall or as big as him.'

'What about hair? All right, I know it was dark: you couldn't see. I'm not asking about colour. But could you see a lot of hair? Or not? Could he have been bald?' She wouldn't know yet that she had been cropped, Danilov realized.

'Nothing like hair. I think there was a cap. But not one with a peak. The type of woollen hats people wear to ski.'

'The grunt,' reminded Cowley.

'You said when you hit him that he grunted?'

'Yes.'

'Where did you hit him? What part of the body?'

'The chest, I think. That's how I felt the quilted jacket.'

'And it was a grunt? Not a word?'

224

'No. And I don't think I hurt him. I think he was surprised: almost frightened. A frightened cry.'

He would have certainly been both at the sudden eruption of someone he believed dead, accepted Danilov. 'But you couldn't recognize any meaning in the grunt or cry?'

'No.'

'Did it sound like a Russian voice? Or foreign?'

Her face furrowed, into a frown. 'Don't know. It was just a sound.'

'She felt his hands on her face,' said Cowley.

'Tell me everything about the moment he grabbed you: put his hand over your mouth and nose,' picked up Danilov.

Momentarily forgetting what would happen, Lydia Orlenko shuddered, but was stopped abruptly by the pain. 'I couldn't move, from the fright. It was horrible. Smelled. And felt clammy.'

Pavin was forward again, as they all were.

'What do you mean, clammy?' demanded Danilov.

'How his hand felt, against my face. Clammy.'

'You mean he was sweating?'

'No, not sweating. Cold actually, but clammy too. Horrible.'

'Gloves?' suggested Danilov.

'They didn't feel like gloves: certainly not wool. His hands felt very smooth. And clammy. But something hard . . .' Warned now, she was careful bringing her hand up, this time to just above her chin. 'Something hard there. Hurt me.'

With the spot identified, Danilov saw a bruise additional to those on her nose and upper lip. 'What about the smell?'

'Tobacco. Definitely tobacco. Very strong.'

'On his hands? Or on his breath?'

'Don't know. It seemed to be all around me.'

'What about cologne?' prompted Cowley.

'Was there any perfumed smell? Scent; something like that?' asked Danilov.

She frowned. 'Maybe. I'm not sure. Just tobacco really.'

Danilov was silent for a few moments, trying to think of another pathway. Doing so he found questions he had failed to ask Pavin. He hoped the Major had maintained his customary routine. To Lydia Orlenko he said: 'Didn't you fight at all? Struggle when he grabbed you?'

225

'No. I was stiff; couldn't move. I just wanted to scream but I couldn't. And he was strong. Jerked me backwards, suddenly. If I hadn't been against him I would have fallen earlier, before the burning in my back. What's happened to me? Am I badly hurt ... ?' She blinked, at her own question, and her lip began to shiver. '. . . going to die?'

'You're not going to die,' promised Danilov, urgently. 'You've been stabbed but the doctors have seen to it. You're going to get better.' He guessed her more immediate concern was going to be the missing hair: there was no reason to upset her by telling her at this stage. He bent towards her, on the bed, and said: 'Something else that is very important: and that you must be completely honest about. You won't get into any trouble, about anything, if you're honest.'

Cowley saw the frown deepen on the woman's face and thought Danilov had phrased the question badly, frightening her in advance.

'What?' she said, warily.

'Do you know any Americans? Particularly anyone connected with the embassy here in Moscow. Someone maybe who comes into the hotel regularly: someone you've come to recognize?'

The woman remained silent for several moments: briefly she closed her eyes and Danilov was worried she had drifted off under the lingering affects of the anaesthetic. Suddenly her eyes blinked open. 'Not from the embassy,' she said. 'Not that I know of. American tourists come to the hotel, of course. But I don't get involved in any currency dealing. Honestly. I know that's against the law. Wouldn't do it.'

Danilov frowned at the automatic denial from Russians whose work brought them into contact with foreigners. 'I told you that you wouldn't get into any trouble, about anything. I know about the dollars in your handbag. I don't care if you take dollar tips and convert, on the black market. *Do* you know anyone in particular?'

'No,' she said at once. 'That's what they were, tips.'

Danilov looked inquiringly sideways to Cowley, who said: 'A precise time?'

When Danilov relayed the question, the woman said: 'I left the Intourist at twelve fifteen: I had to log the time on my work sheet, so I know. It takes me thirty minutes to get home. It always does. I was almost there, maybe five minutes away.' She paused, breathing heavily. Then she demanded: 'Where's Boris? Does he know?'

'He came earlier. He's gone to work now. He's coming back.'

'He worries about his job,' said the woman, not seeming distressed at the apparent neglect. 'Not like a Russian at all.'

A doctor arrived at the door behind Pavin as Danilov was standing up from protesting knees. Danilov said: 'We've finished, for the moment.' To the woman he added: 'We might be back, to see if you've thought of anything you've forgotten to tell us now.'

Outside in the corridor, Danilov said at once to Pavin: 'Anything from the passageway itself?'

'Nothing obvious. There's been a complete forensic search and I've ordered the alley closed, in case you wanted to see. I've collected all her clothing for forensic examination, as well. Gone through the items with her husband.'

'I want to see Hughes,' said Cowley, quietly.

Danilov turned to the American. 'Not alone.'

Cowley's hunched concentration was momentary. He looked up, checking his watch, the merest suggestion of a smile on his face. 'It's a quarter of six.'

'Yes?' frowned Danilov.

'Hughes lives *outside* the embassy compound. I have the address. A street named Pecatnikov.'

'Within the murder area marked off on the map,' identified Danilov. He smiled back, understanding the direction in which the other man was leading. 'At Ann Harris's apartment it was a Russian entry. How would we explain your being with me?'

'I can't stop you carrying out your job as you see it in Moscow: certainly not after this further attack. And the time, at this very moment, means it's impossible for me to consult with anyone. I appreciate you informing me of your intention. And at least by being with you I ensure an American presence.'

Danilov finally answered the smile. 'We can drive by Petrovka, to pick up what we might need to confront him with.'

Pavin drove. On the way through streets still not properly awake Danilov added: 'Let's enumerate the points.'

Cowley nodded, splaying a hand to count. 'Let's start with Pecatnikov: proximity within the area of every attack. We know he was in her apartment the night before she died, from the fingerprints on the glass and in the place itself. The same fingerprints are on the joke *matryoshka* dolls in her office at the embassy. And on some souvenir Bolshoi ballet tickets: I was told at the embassy, early on, that Hughes is a ballet freak. There's your positive sighting of them together, at the restaurant. And the telephone conversations and log of the calls. We can't put it to him yet, but I'll bet you a turkey dinner that we can get calligraphic proof that it's his handwriting on those notes about pain. Suzlev's widow talked to us about a regular embassy customer, who always tried to speak Russian. Again at the embassy I was told that Hughes speaks the language pretty well: likes to practise. And this woman says he smelled of tobacco: Hughes smokes strong French cigarettes. A lot of them.' He came to a near-breathless halt. 'Anything left out?'

'Tuesday,' said Danilov. 'Last night was a Tuesday, like all the rest.'

The door of the Pecatnikov apartment was opened quickly and by Hughes, although he was wearing a dressing-gown, the carefully arranged hair disarrayed from getting hurriedly out of bed. He looked at Cowley and Danilov, then at Pavin behind them carrying the evidence bag, and said, flatly: 'You're here.'

'You don't seem surprised,' said Cowley.

'I guessed it would happen.' Hughes backed into the main room, leaving the door open for them to follow. He had his hands cupped protectively before him in such a way that the deformed index finger was clearly visible on his right hand, bent sideways as if it had been broken and wrongly set. From what was obviously the bedroom a woman called: 'Paul? What is it?'

The economist looked to the men around him. Cowley said: 'Your choice.'

'Something's come up with the embassy,' Hughes called back. 'Leave us, would you?'

'So you were expecting us?' said Cowley, not wanting to prompt any more than he had to.

'I didn't kill her,' said the economist. 'You must believe me. I didn't kill her.'

'Which one?' demanded Danilov, entering the interrogation.

The reaction from the day's press conference was phenomenal. It had led the three major American television networks and CNN throughout the previous night – with extensive TV coverage in other Western countries as well as in Russia – and newspapers throughout the world maintained the interest with enormous coverage, sometimes occupying entire pages. The more sensational newspapers of America and England used headlines like 'Moscow Maniac' and 'Red Terror'. Unnamed sources allegedly talked of terrified women walking in groups if they went out at all and others insisted on the formation of protective vigilante squads.

A synopsis of the television reports and of the leading American newspaper accounts was telexed and faxed overnight to Burden by his Washington office, for the Senator to digest as soon as he awoke at the Savoy hotel.

He was stirring when the interrogation of Paul Hughes was beginning, less than a mile away.

Chapter Twenty-Three

Paul Hughes stared fixedly at the Russian, mouth slightly agape, throat lumping in small, swallowing movements. There was a bigger swallow as he closed his mouth, but before he could speak Cowley said: 'She didn't die tonight, Paul. But your taxi driver did: the taxi driver you always asked for, Vladimir Suzlev. So we're looking at two. Now we want you to tell us all about it.'

Now the economist went from one to the other and then turned the movement into a positive head shake of bewilderment. 'What are you saying? I don't know what you're saying!'

'Your speed,' said Cowley, quietly, almost conversational. 'Tell us your way, however you like.'

Danilov's concentration was divided. He was intent upon everything about Hughes but he was also aware of the manner of the FBI man's questioning, admiring it, unaccustomed to the approach. With the sort of evidence they had the Russian way would have been aggressive, demanding a confession: maybe even making an arrest without any preamble, waiting for the breakdown at the police station after hours or even days of confinement. This was very different. There was no accusing hostility in Cowley's attitude. The approach was solicitous, friendly even: yet on the way to the hospital to see Lydia Orlenko it had been the American who had shown the anger and later Cowley who'd evolved the ice-thin manoeuvre for a Russian involvement in this interrogation. Should he adjust, put his questions the same way? Or just modify slightly, remain the unknown threatening figure next to Cowley's kindly consideration?

'About Ann?' queried Hughes, cautiously.

'Sure. About Ann,' encouraged the other American.

Hughes shrugged, looking away from them at last, vaguely towards his feet. He began fingering the edge of his dressing-gown. 'And so it all comes tumbling down. Job. Wife . . .'

Danilov moved to speak but there was the smallest, halting gesture from Cowley, so he stopped.

'. . . my fault,' Hughes went on. 'I know it's my fault: always has been. But at least Ann knew the score. Enjoyed it.'

'What was the score, Paul?' asked Cowley.

The man looked up, smiling hesitatingly. 'Sex. I liked it. She liked it: it was hardly a secret at the embassy that she liked it. Everyone's too close together here in Moscow.'

Danilov saw his opening. ' "I didn't mean to hurt," ' he quoted. ' "Please like it." Your notes: the ones you wrote to her.'

'Not me!' blustered Hughes.

Over his shoulder to Pavin, Danilov said in Russian: 'Log.' The telephone records came immediately into his hand from the efficient assistant. Turning back to the American, quoting again, Danilov said: ' "Just a little. You know it's good for me . . ." He looked up. 'That's you, three weeks ago. She said: "OK, but not much. Don't really hurt. It's not my bag, you know that." You said: "You do it then: whip if you like. Make me sorry." She said: "That might be good . . . I don't mind head . . . like it. Greek too, but Christ you hurt me last night. My tits bled, you bastard." A month ago she said: "You didn't say you were going to do that when you tied me up. How would you like it with a dildo up your ass . . ."'

'Jesus!' Hughes broke in, eyes bulging, mouth open again. 'That's . . .'

'. . . only a small part of what we know,' Cowley told him. 'She might have liked sex but she didn't like pain as you do, did she?'

Hughes remained staring at Danilov. 'You tapped my phone . . . were tapping my phone . . . there'll be a protest . . .'

'Shut up, Paul!' said Cowley, the friendliness dropped like a curtain. 'And let's cut the crap, OK? Just the truth from now on.'

'I didn't kill her!'

'We think you did,' said Danilov. 'We know all the lies you told.'

'I had to, didn't I? Think how I was caught up! My position!'

Danilov was aware of the slight tightening of Cowley's hands, the only hint of anger. Cowley said: 'Tell us about last Tuesday: not *last* night. The one before. And the entire truth this time. No tidying up.'

'I need to smoke. Can I smoke?'

Cowley nodded agreement. 'Take your time.'

The economist did, fumbling for cigarettes from a side-table and then appearing to have difficulty with a lighter, as if he were trying to delay as long as possible the final confession. The pungent smell of the French tobacco permeated the room. Cowley and Danilov looked at each other. Hughes brought the pack back to the chair with him, settling himself, gazing down at the floor again. 'It was usually Tuesday,' he began, haltingly. 'I work out at the embassy gym that night. Angela expects me home late: thinks I have a few drinks afterwards. Last Tuesday we went to the Trenmos, Ann and I. She liked it there . . .' He looked up, briefly, towards Danilov. 'She wasn't very fond of anything Russian. We had a meal: went back to her place like we usually did. Had a drink. Went to bed. Then I left . . .' He looked up again, to both of them. 'That's it.'

'No, it isn't,' said Danilov, just ahead of the other irritated investigator. 'Do it again. From the restaurant. What did you eat? What did you talk about?'

Hughes shrugged. 'Can't remember what we ate.'

'What did you talk about?' repeated Cowley. 'Were you happy, the two of you? Or not?'

'OK,' said Hughes, shrugging again, the evasion blatant.

'Stop it, for Christ's sake!' said Cowley, the friendship curtain still down. 'Or would you rather come with us to a Russian station-house? You're outside embassy jurisdiction: I'm here as a concession. You fancy a Russian prison interrogation, where I wouldn't have access?'

Danilov took the cue, turning to Pavin to return the telephone log and nodding, as if some decision had been made between them.

'No!' pleaded Hughes, at once, too alarmed to argue about diplomatic immunity. 'No, please! I'm sorry. OK, so it wasn't a good evening. It was all coming to an end, we both knew that. The messy part: getting on each other's nerves.'

'So you argued?' demanded Danilov.

'No, not argued!' Hughes retorted. 'Just irritated with each other: things I said annoyed her, things she said annoyed me.'

'But you still went to bed?' said Cowley.

'That's what it was all about.'

'It was uncomfortable at the restaurant,' Cowley goaded. 'What happened back at Pushkinskaya?'

'Had a drink or two, like I said. Usual squabble: she was very house-proud, almost a fetish with her. She wouldn't let me smoke that night, not like she normally did. She was being awkward, on purpose: said concessions were being withdrawn . . .'

'But they weren't, in bed?' broke in Danilov.

'Old times stuff,' dismissed Hughes. He smiled hopefully at both of them.

Neither detective smiled back. Cowley's hands flexed. Danilov said: 'Her breasts were bitten.'

'She liked . . .' Hughes began, but Cowley, too loudly, said: 'Don't! You try it once more and you're downtown on your own and I couldn't give a fuck. I'll *insist* you go downtown.'

Hughes's cigarette had a long hang of ash. He stubbed it out hurriedly, strangely seeming to wither physically. 'She let me. That was all. She let me.' His voice was cracked, jagged. Then he said: 'Jesus, this is awful! Embarrassing!'

Sure he knew how to play the interrogation now, Danilov said: 'Ann Harris's death was awful, too. She was stabbed in the back. All her hair was cut off. What was wrong with her hair? Didn't you like it? Or was it some sex thing, like the buttons and the shoes?'

'What buttons and shoes? I don't understand.'

'When you're ready,' said Cowley, accepting the denial for the moment. 'You were in bed and you bit her.'

'Not like that! You make it sound . . . like it was . . .'

'. . . Deviant? Dangerously violent? Something we shouldn't find unusual involving a girl who was killed and abused the same night with your teethmarks in her breasts?' interrupted Danilov.

'It was what we did!'

'Why Suzlev?' demanded Cowley. 'Why kill him?'

'I didn't kill him.'

'You did,' insisted Danilov.

'Paul?'

The American economist had been slumped, almost unnaturally bowed forward, but he stiffened at his wife's voice. There was a sound like a groan as he half-turned towards the living-room door at which she stood. Unlike her husband she was dressed, in

233

a red skirt and homeknit sweater decorated with matching red swans proceeding across the front, a squat woman on the point of fatness, freshly washed face shining free of make-up, her hair completely grey without any attempt at disguising dye or tinted highlights.

'Paul?' she questioned again. 'What is it? What's going on? What's happened at the embassy?' Towards the end she extended her look beyond her husband, inviting a reply from anyone.

'I asked you to leave us,' said Hughes. His voice was even more broken.

The dumpy woman looked puzzled, but at the same time appeared to realize her husband was under some sort of pressure. She smiled tentatively and said: 'Can I get anything? Coffee?'

'Just leave us. Please,' said Hughes.

She didn't move, at once. Then, with the skeletal words people use in times of personal uncertainty, she said: 'I'll be in the kitchen if you want me.'

Hughes scratched a match back and forth to light another cigarette and both Cowley and Danilov shifted, practically at the same time, angrily aware that the momentum had been broken. Trying too quickly to bring it back, Cowley said: 'Was that how it happened, Paul? A lot of small arguments, early in the evening? Some sex stuff that got out of hand? Then, before you knew what was really happening, she was dead?'

Danilov prevented himself looking curiously at the FBI agent, who'd proposed a sequence they knew hadn't occurred, supposing the man was simply trying to frighten the economist into an admission.

'No!' wailed Hughes. He looked up at them, eyes filmed. 'We went to bed, right? She let me do what I wanted. We actually made love, but it wasn't good, not for either of us. It was late by then: I had to get back. I said I'd see her the following day. I got dressed and left. Came straight back here.'

'How did you come?' asked Danilov.

'Walked. It's very close.'

'Before you left Pushkinskaya there was no more argument?' Cowley pushed the explanation back.

'No.'

234

Both investigators discerned the reluctance. Cowley said: 'What was it?'

There was the familiar shoulder movement. 'She called me a bastard.'

'Why?'

'Wanted me to stay longer, I supposed. It had been very quick. I guess that was it. Wasn't happy.'

'You mean she wasn't satisfied?' insisted Cowley.

'I guess.'

'What about you?'

'Me?'

'Were you satisfied?'

'Yes.' Mixed with the earlier reluctance there was doubt this time.

'You sure you didn't hang around, waiting for her to leave the apartment?' said Danilov. 'Followed her to the alley near Gercena where it was dark enough to kill her with no one seeing?'

'I didn't *know* she was going to leave the apartment!' denied Hughes. 'How could I have done?'

'Maybe she told you. Left with you,' said Cowley.

'That's ridiculous!' said the man. 'Why should she do that?'

'You tell us. Why, after going to bed with you, making love to you, did Ann Harris get up out of bed and walk – inadequately dressed – to where she was found?' said Danilov.

'I don't know!' The denial was another wail.

Danilov thought he heard a sound, a chair scrape, from the kitchen.

'Why did you kill her, Paul?' said Cowley, abrupt but quiet, friendly again. 'Tell me why you killed Ann. And the cab driver. And attacked the woman tonight. Or don't you know? Is that the way it is, Paul? Don't you know? Just something that happens? Talk it through with us, whichever way it comes into your head.'

Hughes's reply was quiet, too, his voice beseeching. 'I didn't kill Ann. I don't know anything about a taxi driver. I don't know anything about any woman, tonight. I don't know, a lot of the time, what either of you are talking about. I lied about Ann. I admit that; all of it. I had to, after she was murdered: knew I could be destroyed if you found out, although I realized it was almost inevitable that you would. Trying to put it off, I guess. Hoping it wouldn't happen.'

'Where were you last night?' persisted Cowley.

'Here,' said Hughes, too hurriedly.

'It was a Tuesday,' reminded Danilov. 'You didn't go to the embassy gym?'

'Early,' said the man, indistinctly, looking down again.

'Your wife's in the kitchen,' said Cowley. 'You want me to call her in to ask what time you got home?'

Hughes appeared to shrivel further. 'I was with someone, after the gym. I got back here late.'

'How late?' pressed Danilov.

'I don't know. Eleven. Twelve. Nearer twelve, I guess.'

'How about after twelve? Nearer one, in fact. After attacking a woman whom you didn't properly kill, in an alley off Granovskaya Street?'

'No!' came the plea, again. 'I was back before twelve.'

'Was your wife awake?' asked Cowley.

'Sort of. She was aware of me coming in.'

'You going to call her from the kitchen? Or shall I?'

'No!' repeated Hughes, pleading more desperately. 'Don't involve her. Please don't involve her!'

Cowley sighed. 'You know what we're talking about! We're talking about a double murder. And an attempted murder. We're questioning you about every one of them. And you're frightened about your wife finding out you had a piece of ass on the side!'

Hughes looked speechless at both investigators for several moments. Then his head began to shake. 'I don't know what to do.'

'I know what you're going to do,' said Cowley, coming forward towards the other American. 'You're going to tell us, to the minute, where you were last night. And the moment I think you're lying, as you've tried to lie like the stupid asshole you are since we got here, I'm going to close all this down and have you taken to a Moscow police station and I'm going to have the Russians issue a press release, saying that you're being questioned in connection with a double murder. You can either tell your wife on your way out or let her see it on CNN. So from the top. What time did you get to the gym?'

'Six,' said Hughes, dully.

'Six exactly? Not earlier? Or later?'

'Definitely six. I had a game arranged, with Andrews . . .' The smile came hopefully. 'He'll remember. Tell you.'

'What time did you leave?'

'Seven. He'll confirm that, too.'

'Then where?'

There was the hesitation. Cowley pulled impatiently back from the intent way he had been sitting, glancing at Danilov and shaking his head in dismissal. 'OK, let's wrap it up down at the station!'

'Pam,' blurted Hughes. 'Pam Donnelly. That's where I was. With Pam Donnelly.'

It took several moments for Cowley to remember the immaculately dressed economic assistant at the embassy on the day he'd first questioned Hughes. He recalled, too, the photographs of the Hughes wife and children, on the man's desk. 'Doing what?'

Hughes began the shrug, but stopped it. 'She made supper, at her place.'

'Yes?'

'You don't need me to tell you.'

'That's precisely what I need.'

'We went to bed. Made love.'

'Think of Ann, while you were doing it?'

'That's a cheap shot!'

'Tell me about it!' sneered Cowley, intentionally goading the man, who instead interpreted the remark literally.

'That's why the situation with Ann was ending,' said the financial controller. 'Because of Pam. It's been going on for a few months.'

'Did Ann know?'

Hughes shook his head. 'I don't think so, not about Pam. Just that it was over between her and me.'

Danilov thought the questioning was slipping sideways. 'This other woman, she'll be able to say what time you left?'

'Yes.'

'Where's her apartment? Inside the compound? Or out?'

'Outside. Vesnina Street.'

'How did you get back?'

'Car.'

Danilov wondered how the American safeguarded his wind-screen wipers. 'It would only have taken five or ten minutes, to get to either Granovskaya or Semasko, by car.' They hadn't asked the patrolman who found Lydia Orlenko if he'd heard a car driving away.

'I don't know where Granovskaya or Semasko are! I came directly home, after leaving Pam!'

'We're going to need to speak to your wife,' said Cowley. 'You're going to *need* us to speak to your wife.'

'I don't want to hurt her.'

'With your preferences, that sounds a pretty odd remark,' said Cowley. 'Don't you think anyway you went past that a long time ago?'

Hughes made another effort to straighten, pulling the dressing-gown around himself. 'I didn't do it, any of it. You'll accept that, eventually. Why wreck her life, telling her things she doesn't need to know? It's only sex. My business. It's not a crime. I haven't committed any crime.'

Cowley stood, realizing for the first time an ache, from sitting as long as he had. Looking down at the other American, he said: 'Courts decide whether crime has been committed or not. And will, in these cases.'

Angela Hughes emerged from the kitchen the moment he knocked, and Cowley wondered how much of their conversation she had already heard from being obviously behind the door. She came apprehensively into the room. Both Danilov and Pavin stood. Pavin offered a chair. 'What is it?' she said. It was difficult to hear her words.

'An embassy confusion,' said Hughes, ahead of anyone else. 'That's all. An embassy confusion.'

The woman looked curiously between Danilov and Cowley. 'You are investigating the murder of Ann: I saw you both on television, at a press conference!'

'That's it!' said Hughes, in panicked desperation. 'Still something to do with Ann.'

'What?' There was the slightest suggestion of strength in her voice.

Cowley saw she had toast crumbs speckling the front of her

swan-procession sweater. As the only possible spokesman, he said: 'Mrs Hughes, we'd like you to help us on a small point. Tuesdays Paul uses the embassy gym. Stays on maybe. What time did he get home last night?'

The curiosity came to her face again. 'What's important about last night? Ann was murdered a week ago.'

'We're just filling in squares, familiarizing ourselves with everyone's regular, normal movements at the embassy,' said Cowley. 'Please, Mrs Hughes. Last night?'

The woman looked very directly at her husband. Her voice hard, she said to him: 'What do you want me to say?'

'The truth,' came in Cowley 'I—*we*—want the absolute truth.'

Still looking at Hughes, she said: 'Around eleven thirty. Maybe just after.'

'You're sure it was before midnight? Not after?'

'It couldn't have been after,' she asserted, definitely, looking back to Cowley at last. 'I woke up, sort of, when he got into bed. And then I heard the church clock strike, in Pecatnikov. It strikes every hour: not the quarters. Just the hour. I know it was midnight, because I counted the chimes. I do that, if I wake up during the night. Don't know why. I just do. I think lots of people do.'

Neither Cowley nor Danilov looked at each other. Hughes became even straighter in his chair, his demeanour beginning to be that of a man expecting an apology. Foolishly he said: 'Well? Satisfied?'

'No,' deflated Cowley, at once.

'Satisfied about what?' demanded the woman.

No one answered her. Indifferent about showing the same consideration as Cowley in front of the economist's wife, Danilov said: 'January 17 was a Tuesday. Where were you on January 17 . . .?' He looked fully at Angela Hughes. 'Do you remember the time your husband got home on January 17?'

'How the hell could anyone remember something so unimportant after five weeks . . . ?' began Hughes, outraged, but his wife cut across him. 'There's no way I could have remembered,' she said. 'I was on home leave in Newark, New Jersey, with our sons, for the last three weeks of January: I wasn't even here, in Moscow, on the 17th.'

There was a brief period of absolute silence, before Cowley said: 'Mr Hughes, I'd appreciate your getting dressed to come to the embassy with us now. We'd like to speak to . . .' He paused. '. . . The rest of the staff in the finance division.'

To Cowley, the woman said: 'What's he done? Why are you talking to him like this?' And then swinging around to confront her husband she said: 'Tell me what you've done!'

'Nothing!' Hughes insisted, with matching forcefulness. 'You heard what he said. They want to speak to my staff: proper – essential in fact – that I am there. It's my responsibility.' He finished actually moving away from the group, sparing himself any further demands from anyone.

'This isn't right!' she protested, turning upon them. 'Not right at all! You're not telling me the truth.'

'Mrs Hughes,' said Cowley, the patient consideration faltering. 'The person to tell you the truth is your husband. But not now. Later.'

Dressed – although carelessly shaved – Hughes's demeanour shifted surprisingly in the car going towards the American embassy, something close to confidence showing in the man. As they connected with the inner ring road, he actually turned smiling to Danilov, whose question it had been back at the apartment, and said: 'Isn't that funny? I'd forgotten all about Angela being back in America on January 17: wouldn't have got the significance, not for a long time.'

'What significance?' asked Cowley.

'*You* tell *me*,' replied Hughes, defiantly. 'Why is January 17 so important? What happened then?'

Danilov was unsettled by the man's changed attitude. Trying to upset it, he said: 'Don't you remember? That's the night Vladimir Suzlev, the taxi driver, was murdered.'

'Aah!' said Hughes, drawing out the expression. More defiant still, he said: 'That makes January 17 *very* important, doesn't it. Crucial, in fact. Good.'

Their arrival at the embassy prevented any continuation of the conversation. By unspoken agreement, Pavin remained with the car in the side road separating the embassy from the museum to Fedor Chaliapin. The entry guard was the marine whom Cowley had encountered on his first day and seen on subsequent visits.

Cowley insisted Dimitri Danilov was coming into the legation upon his authority, and Hughes further bewildered both investigators by saying that he also guaranteed the Russian's admission.

Pamela Donnelly responded immediately to Hughes's summons, hurrying through the door without knocking and smiling broadly until she saw the other two men, belatedly coming to an uncertain halt, the smile fading.

'It's all right,' said Hughes quietly, calming. 'You remember Mr Cowley, from the other day?'

The girl nodded, guardedly. She was as carefully dressed as before, mid-calf brown leather boots a perfect match with the deeper brown velvet skirt, the sweater cream this time, with no motif. She didn't look the sort of girl who would enjoy having her nipples bitten or enduring any other sort of pain for that matter. But who could tell? Cowley said: 'We want you to tell us something. The truth. About January . . . particularly a period about five weeks ago.'

She looked questioningly at Hughes. He said: 'It's all right, darling. Tell them everything. They know about you and me. So it's important you tell them what they want to know.'

Pamela looked back to Cowley. 'What about January, five weeks ago?'

'Do you remember Tuesday, January 17?'

She frowned. 'Not particularly. Should I?'

'We want you to,' came in Danilov. 'Were you and Mr Hughes together that night?'

She looked uncertainly again at Hughes, who nodded. She said: 'Yes.'

'It was five weeks ago,' said Danilov, picking up on Hughes's earlier protest. 'Can you be definite about that specific date?'

'Yes,' she said again, shortly. She was beginning to colour.

'Why so sure?' pressed Cowley.

'I don't like this . . . it's . . . it's unpleasant,' she objected.

'It's important, darling. Very important,' said Hughes, urgently. 'Tell them everything they want to know.'

Refusing to look directly at them, Pamela said: 'Angela was in America. For three weeks. The middle week – the 17th was in the middle week – Paul virtually lived with me all the time . . .'

241

The colour deepened. 'Certainly stayed with me every night. He only went home between times to change.'

'At night?' demanded Cowley.

'Sometimes. We'd go back together, pick up what he wanted, and go on somewhere.'

'He didn't go out alone, on the night of that Tuesday?'

'Not any night. Why?'

'They think I killed Ann,' Hughes announced. His voice was flat but he smiled, inviting astonishment at the absurdity of the suggestion. 'There was another murder before her. On the 17th.'

'What!' The girl was pebble-eyed with astonishment. 'But that's . . . incredible.'

Cowley had thought she was going to say absurd or ridiculous; that's what alibi-providers usually said. 'What about last night?'

'Paul came to my place from the gym. I cooked a meal.' She stopped, refusing to go on.

'What time did he leave?'

'Sometime after eleven. Quarter after, maybe.'

From his desk Hughes said to Danilov, 'Which gives me fifteen minutes to get to Pecatnikov, just like Angela told you.'

'Would you be able to swear in court, on oath, to everything you've told us today?' asked Cowley, resignation in his voice.

'In court?' echoed the girl, alarmed.

'If you were asked?'

She looked at Hughes, briefly, then said: 'Yes. If I had to.'

'So would Angela,' Hughes insisted. 'You heard what she said.' The supercilious assurance was fully restored again: he had his hands cupped across the desk, the right one uppermost, showing the twisted finger that had seemed so important such a short time ago. 'Is there anything else we can help you with? Any of us?'

'Not for the moment,' said Cowley, trying for a way to puncture the pomposity. 'Maybe later. Your wife will probably have questions of her own.'

Cowley escorted Danilov out of the embassy, to the waiting car. There he said: 'I guess I'll have a lot of overnight messages.'

'And I have to brief the Director and the Prosecutor.'

'We'll speak by phone,' said the American.

Barry Andrews was in the FBI office but away from his desk, pacing back and forth in front of the window. When Cowley entered, Andrews said: 'Thank Christ you're here! Where the hell have you been?' He gestured to a pile of messages and diplomatic pouch material. 'They're going ape-shit in Washington, particularly over Hughes. You're to keep the Russians from getting anywhere near him: you've personally got to get him back. Hidden in a box if necessary.'

Cowley scooped up the waiting papers. 'There was another attack last night,' he announced, wearily. 'This time the victim didn't die. And it won't be necessary to ship Hughes home in a box. He's a sado-masochist and Christ knows what else, but he didn't kill Ann Harris. Or anyone else. He's got alibi witnesses all the way.' He hammered his fist against the desk, at once regretting the theatricality. 'We've been wasting our fucking time! For days we've been chasing the wrong leads to the wrong man!'

'But who . . . ?' started Andrews, stopping abruptly at the stupidity of the question.

'I don't know,' said Cowley, depressed by what he saw as defeat. 'Now we don't have a clue; not a single goddamned clue.'

'What about the woman last night? There must be *something*!'

'Nothing that points anywhere positive. Just that her attacker was a man. She fainted or went into shock or something, when she was stabbed. Says she didn't see his face.'

Andrews sat at his desk, lighting the first cigar of the day. 'Hughes's wife provide his alibi?'

'The most convincing part.'

'How'd she take it, knowing her husband was screwing around?'

'It didn't quite come out that way: it will, I guess, when she thinks about it.'

'And who would have thought it, about innocent little Pamela?'

Cowley shook his head, irritably. 'That's all immaterial now.'

'What are you going to do?' asked Andrews.

Cowley looked down at all the messages. 'Read my mail. Then call the Director and tell him I was wrong.'

'That's not going to sound good, after the uproar you caused in Washington with the original warning about Hughes.'

'Tell me about it!' said Cowley, repeating the earlier cynical cliché. He didn't feel cynical. He felt foolish and angry at himself, for making the mistakes. Andrews was right. The admission wasn't going to look at all good in Washington: in fact, it was going to look bloody awful.

Cowley took everything back to his compound suite but did not immediately read it, wanting to try at least to feel physically better. He left coffee filtering while he showered and shaved, his mind blocked by the forthcoming telephone conversation with the Director. The leads towards Hughes *had* been convincing, the obvious path to follow. And he *had* been correct in the peculiar diplomatic circumstances, alerting Washington in advance of any interview. But he didn't need to read the incoming messages from Washington to imagine the panic. Obviously the Director would have discussed everything with the Secretary of State. So Paul Hughes's sexual proclivities were public knowledge in the State Department. Would it affect the man's future career? Almost inevitably. And that destructive information would have come from him. The necessary fall-out of an investigation. He wished the attempted self-reassurance had been more successful. All in the past now, he told himself. So what was the future? He wished to Christ he knew.

Being clean and shaved was the only improvement to the way Cowley felt. He poured coffee and still in a towelling robe settled to the messages, reading every exchange concerning the economist to prepare himself, reflecting beyond possible harm to Hughes's career to the possible damage to his own. Overly pessimistic, he decided, seeking further reassurance. Wrong turns frequently occurred in investigations. This one – again because of the goddamned circumstances – was just more serious, that's all. And entirely his own fault, Cowley decided: his and the Russian's. They'd lost sight of what they were supposed to be doing and got into an infantile competition, each trying to outsmart the other, prove who was the better detective. And both ended up looking jerks. Not Danilov, the American corrected immediately.

The bulk of the remaining documentation was technical. The American post-mortem report was throughout critical of the Russian examination, claiming evidence could have been lost by its glaring carelessness. The American pathologist was only prepared to estimate the thickness and penetration of the stab wound to Ann Harris because of Russian incision clumsiness. Samples of

244

hair that remained after the shearing had been subjected to deoxy-ribonucleic acid analysis, as had her blood, to isolate the molecular structure of her chromosomes and establish her individual genetic pattern. There was a request for available hair from the first victim, for similar analysis. The nasal bruising was obviously consistent with a hand being clamped over the victim's face and then with the victim being pulled backwards, from behind. Chin bruising and inner lower lip contusions not listed in the Russian report were also consistent with this. Cowley underlined that paragraph, remembering the similar bruising earlier that morning upon Lydia Orlenko's face. The two fingernails that had been roughly broken had left jagged splits and edges. The shattering of the nails could have happened either from striking the ground when she fell or by scratching her assailant in a last, frantic fight. No evidence had been found to support the scratching theory, from scrapings beneath the broken nails. But such evidence could have been lost during the first post-mortem, by movement of the body during transportation to America or by the delay in their receiving the body for examination. If the finger damage had been caused either by falling or fighting, the shattered parts should have been recovered by the scene-of-the-crime search. Such parts might also have had attached forensic evidence like blood or skin that could have been matched to the assailant by DNA comparison.

Cowley sighed, pushing the autopsy report aside. Nothing, except justifiable complaints. Or at least nothing that at the moment had any significance. Cowley halted the dismissal. There was *one* item of significance, which was further proof of Paul Hughes's innocence. If Ann Harris had scratched hard enough to break her nails, Hughes's face or hands would have been marked. And they hadn't been, anywhere.

Back at the FBI facility in the embassy, Cowley personally transmitted all the details of the exonerating interview with Paul Hughes to Pennsylvania Avenue. Andrews remained with him throughout, reading each document after its dispatch. At the end the local man shook his head and smiled and said: 'It happens. The damned case has only just begun.'

The connection from the secure booth in the embassy communications room to the FBI headquarters was instantaneous, with no interference whatsoever. At Leonard Ross's insistence, Cowley verbally went through everything that he was sure the Director would by now have in front of him, in the fifth-floor office. There was silence for several moments after Cowley finished talking, the unspoken condemnation more accusing than any direct words. Eventually Ross said: 'A complete mistake?'

'The evidence seemed compelling,' Cowley insisted.

'I'd intended you should escort Hughes back. I want you back here,' declared the Director. 'Get a flight today.'

'I . . .' Cowley started, but was cut off instantly.

'. . . What?' demanded Ross.

'Nothing,' said Cowley. 'I'll make the reservation.'

With such a complete telephone system available literally in front of him, Cowley called Dimitri Danilov from there instead of going back down to the FBI room. Determined, on his part, against continuing the competition he believed to have blurred their professionalism, Cowley announced his return to Washington, but said he wanted to meet Danilov before leaving, to discuss the outstanding requests of American scientists. Danilov had a further reason for a meeting: following the previous night's attack upon Lydia Orlenko – and now there was no longer any reason to conceal a possible connection with the US embassy – the Federal Prosecutor and the Militia Director had decided the delayed public warning should finally be issued.

When Cowley returned downstairs and announced his recall, Andrews frowned and said: 'When will you be back?'

'I don't know.'

'You will be coming back?'

'I don't know about that, either.'

'I said at the very beginning that I didn't envy you this one.'

Cowley thought the man had said something different that night in his apartment, but he wasn't interested in continuing the discussion. All he could think about was how badly he'd fouled up. 'Maybe you're lucky to be publicly out of it.'

'That's what I was thinking,' admitted Andrews.

Burden reviewed the media coverage at a breakfast meeting in his suite: there were copies for everyone of what had been printed.

McBride said, invitingly: 'Pretty damned good, don't you think?'

'So far, so good,' agreed Burden. 'Last night the FBI Director wouldn't take my call. I was told the Secretary of State was unavailable. The ambassador here knows fuck-all. The FBI people here won't cooperate . . . we're being given the run-around.'

'I don't know who else – where else – we can go,' ventured Prescott.

At that moment Beth Humphries came into the room, ashen-faced. Unspeaking she offered the Senator the Russian announcement of the linked murders, running on Reuter's English language service.

'Now we've got it!' declared Burden, looking up. 'I'm going to light a fire under the bastards that will roast them . . .' He looked to McBride. 'Get every reporter and television station you can find here, in two hours.'

'Called back to be disciplined?' queried Pauline, at once.

'He caused the most God-awful flap, raising the alarm about Hughes,' said Andrews.

'Could it affect his career?'

'Easily, at this level of political importance.'

'Poor William.'

'It could well be poor William,' Andrews agreed.

Chapter Twenty-Four

Cowley decided against reopening the Arlington apartment he had closed down before leaving for Moscow. Instead he checked into the J. W. Marriott on 14th and Pennsylvania, within convenient walking distance of the FBI building. He'd slept intermittently during the flight, the rest of the time calculating the practical advantages of coming back to America. It gave an opportunity to interview Judy Billington, the college friend in whom Ann Harris had confided so fully. And possibly John, the brother in New York, with whom she had also shown some openness. Cowley had also evolved some queries of his own to put to the Bureau's scientific division and hoped personally to get down to Quantico to discuss the psychological profile of the unknown killer.

He had outlined the scientific evaluations to Danilov at their meeting two hours before flying out of Sheremet'yevo airport. The Russian investigator had been familiar with deoxyribonucleic acid, or DNA, tests to establish genetic fingerprinting, although he'd had to concede such technology was at the moment inadequate for use in Russian police work. It was Cowley's claim that a psychological and even physical profile of a killer they didn't even know could be created by the Bureau's Behavioural Science Unit that had bemused the Russian. Cowley's insistence that the FBI regarded profile creation as a positive investigatory aid and that the unit had created accurate assessments of thousands of criminals in advance of their arrest had failed to convince the other man. At times he'd openly laughed in disbelief. Cowley wasn't sure of the precise date, but he believed the Bureau had used the practice since the 1950s and would have thought enough scientific papers had been published since that time for the Russians to have at least learned about it, even if they didn't trust it.

The same corn-and-milk-fed secretary came forward to meet him as he entered the FBI Director's suite, but this time Fletcher was forewarned by Cowley's call from the downstairs foyer and didn't have to be summoned. Fletcher's greeting was as supercili-ous as it had been for the briefing, just over a week before. Had it really only been just over a week? By the number of days, certainly. But to Cowley it seemed much longer: ages longer.

There was no smile from Leonard Ross, just the barest nod of greeting. The Director said: 'Not an auspicious start.'

'The circumstantial evidence looked good.'

'You said so on the phone. And I read your report.'

'And there were some operational difficulties,' offered Cowley. 'They're still being obstructive?'

'No,' corrected Cowley. 'There were problems of adjustment: there had to be. It's settled now.' Was it? He'd put it directly to Danilov, during their farewell encounter the previous day, that a lot of the mistakes had arisen through unnecessary personal competition, and the Russian had agreed. But there was no guarantee Danilov would keep his word to cooperate absolutely in the future. Which was not to doubt the man, but whatever instructions Danilov received from his superiors. Any more than he could guarantee to keep *his* word against positive orders from the man in whose office he was now sitting.

'So how come they got to Hughes when I'd strictly ordered it shouldn't happen, under any circumstances?'

A lawyer's aggression towards a flawed witness, gauged Cowley. He recited the explanation he'd evolved with Danilov at the time, intent upon the Director's reaction, which was imposs-ible to guess from the man's unchanging expression. 'Hughes lives *outside*,' Cowley concluded. 'The Russians *let* me accompany them, in the middle of the night, to interview the victim and then straight from the hospital to Hughes's apartment. I had no alternative: no time to consult.'

Ross nodded, a slow, doubtful movement. 'It happened,' he accepted. 'Didn't become the problem it could have done. Or has it?'

'I don't understand,' frowned Cowley. The Director was clearly critical, but it didn't at this stage appear to be a suspension-from-the-case situation.

'You sure — I mean *absolutely* sure — about Hughes's alibi?'

'The wife is particularly strong. Gives the impression of total honesty and her evidence, against the woman who survived, makes the timing utterly impossible. And the girl's account corroborates all the wife says and clears Hughes of the first murder.'

'Wives and mistresses have got together in the past: dozens of times,' argued Ross. 'Women do the damnedest things for men. I've never understood it.'

Cowley shook his head. 'There was no time for them to prepare a story that sticks together like theirs does.'

'The State Department are bringing the kinky bastard back,' Ross disclosed. 'Hughes hasn't finished answering questions, by a long way. The CIA are using words like disaster. Hughes is going to spend more time wired to a polygraph than Frankenstein's monster. There won't be a secret left, about Ann Harris or anything else, when the CIA finally unplug him from the lie detector.' The white-haired man shook his head, a discarding gesture. 'Anything more since your overnight report?'

'The Russians are going to go public on the first murder. And the most recent attack.'

The Director frowned. Then his face cleared, in understanding. 'It would have happened while you were in the air, of course. They already have. Burden's given yet another press conference, in Moscow. He's complained information has been withheld: said he felt the entire investigation was being mishandled. Or that there was concealment, for political purposes. He's talked about raising it from the floor of the Senate. Got his usual headlines, all over this morning's papers. Knowing Burden he'll probably claim it was his presence that forced the Russian announcement and warned the people of Moscow. Christ, that man's a pain in the ass!'

'It would have made it even worse, delaying any longer,' suggested Cowley. 'We were in a no-win position.'

'It's already gotten worse,' said Ross. 'He's already called the President, from the Moscow embassy. Repeated the earlier threat about who has the power up on the Hill. He's flying back for the girl's funeral. Which doubtless he'll turn into another media event.'

Politics and crime never mixed, reflected Cowley: which made it surprising how often the two were stirred together. 'He has to be told everything?'

'I'm damned if I'll have law enforcement conducted to please

250

Senator Walter Burden!' said Ross, vehemently. 'He'll be told what I choose to sanitize and tell him. He and the President are career politicians. I'm not.'

He was definitely not being taken off the case, Cowley realized. There was a relief that went far beyond his professional ability not being seriously questioned: that the Director was accepting errors were unfortunately inevitable this early in any investigation. He *wanted* to go back and start again and not make any more mistakes and be there when they manacled a killer. To prove what to whom? Himself to himself, he supposed: to show he hadn't lost the edge, after three years out of the field. Who else was there, anyway? Absurdly Pauline's name – Pauline herself – came into his mind. Why should he want to impress his ex-wife? Because it mattered to him to do so, pointless though it was now that she was married to another man. To clear his mind Cowley talked of the interviews and meetings he wanted to have, now he was back in America. Ross agreed to everything.

'Other things first,' cautioned Ross.

'What?'

'The reason I brought you back. We're due at Langley in an hour.'

There was always a fluster about a Director's departure from Pennsylvania Avenue, particularly from the main entrance within the inner courtyard, and today Cowley was part of it and was conscious of the attention of everyone in and around the vestibule and from the overlooking windows. Cowley knew just how quickly rumours cooked in the microwave of FBI headquarters and was curious about what was being said about him at that moment. Whatever, he would be labelled someone in ascendancy, because failures didn't get to ride with the Director. The glass screen was raised between them and the driver, enabling unrestricted conversation, but the Director initially kept to small-talk, asking about Moscow and the embassy and the investigation methods of the Moscow police.

As the driver took Memorial Bridge, to get over the river, Ross looked directly across the car and said: 'How's it working out personally, with Andrews?'

'Well,' said Cowley. 'He's helpful in every way he could, within the embassy. We've been together socially. No problems at all.'

'That's good. No resentment at being restricted to the embassy?'

'None.'

'Personnel want to settle the reassignment. We're moving Harvey Proffitt from California. Giving the guy a chance.'

'Andrews talked to me himself about his tour being over.'

'He say what he hopes to do next?'

Cowley didn't think he should rely upon the conversation with Pauline, although he knew she would be right. He shook his head. 'No.'

'Not anything about being attached to the Russian division back here?'

'Nothing.' Cowley waited for the Director to ask if he would have any personal feelings about it. Ross didn't.

Instead he said: 'Personnel have asked to bring him back, for discussions. Would that inconvenience you, at the moment?'

It would mean the complete burden of communications falling upon him, Cowley realized. But discussions were standard procedure in these sorts of career move. To object, as he was entitled to object, could hinder that career: the career of a man who'd cheated him and stolen his wife. Cowley wished the last thoughts hadn't even occurred, especially as he'd already decided that hadn't ever been the case. He said: 'Of course he should come back.'

By the time the admission formalities to the Langley complex were completed, a man was waiting in the main foyer to escort them. There was no identification. Cowley was instantly reminded of Fletcher, back at FBI headquarters. Perhaps there was a cloning farm somewhere in the Mid-West producing featureless and characterless personal assistants for Washington chief executives. They went directly to the seventh floor, in the CIA Director's personal elevator. There were three other men and a female stenographer with Richard Holmes. Cowley supposed the three unnamed men were part of the Agency's Russian section. He would have thought the meeting could have been quite satisfactorily conducted between himself and them, without the presence of both Directors. And probably would have been but for

Moscow telephone calls to the President from the chairman of the Ways and Means Committee. He was aware of witnessing at first hand the Washington self-defence art known as Watching Your Ass.

'I've indicated the concern,' said Ross.

'So?' said Holmes.

Cowley was disconcerted by the cursory tone of the demand: maybe he should start watching his own ass. He definitely wasn't going to respond in front of a recording stenographer to a single-word question like that. 'What, precisely, are you asking me?'

'Is Paul Hughes being set up by Russian intelligence?'

Cowley weighed his answer. 'I have no idea,' he said, finally.

One of the aides sighed, but Cowley didn't detect which one.

'We want the specific details of Hughes's telephone interception,' Holmes insisted.

Again Cowley hesitated, anticipating a later demand and aware he was going to look an inexperienced amateur, even a bungling one, in their eyes. He replied chronologically, trying to avoid the admission, talking of getting Hughes's embassy telephone number as one Ann Harris had called, of Hughes's lying explanation at their initial interview, but of the man's collapse when the verbatim conversation was put to him at the later, early morning confrontation after Lydia Orlenko had been attacked.

'Now let's go back over all that again,' said Holmes, with forced patience. 'Why didn't you challenge Hughes's first explanation with the verbatim record?'

He *was* going to be shown up, Cowley accepted, desperately: there was no possible way he could watch – or save – his ass. 'At the first interview I didn't have a transcript: just the number.'

'I don't understand that,' complained one of the aides.

'That's just how it happened,' said Cowley, miserably. 'We were following a normal investigation routine, trying to check out any known acquaintances of Ann Harris. At the beginning I was provided with Hughes's embassy number, nothing else.'

'By whom?' demanded another aide.

'Danilov, the Russian detective.'

'Who produced the transcript?'

'Danilov.' It was already looking bad and was going to get worse. Not simply bad. Appalling.

'Where is it, in full? I haven't seen it. Just your verbatim note of what was put to Hughes at the second interview,' intruded Ross, beside him.

Exposed by his own Director, thought Cowley: at the moment he felt he could have been exposed by a child of ten. 'I don't have it.'

'You don't *have* it!' echoed both Directors, in unison and shared astonishment. The sighing aide sighed even more deeply.

'Mr Cowley,' said the Agency chief. 'I'm trying very hard to follow what you're saying. But you're not making it easy. We know there's an intercept direct into the offices of the head of the economic section of the US embassy in Moscow. We know the man had sex habits that expose him to blackmail. And we are being told – I *think* – that those intercepts could also throw up intimate facts about the dead relation of one of the most important people in Washington, someone who is going to become even more important. Let's take it slowly, a step at a time, so it'll all become clear to us. You said – your words – that Danilov *produced* the transcript. If he produced it, where the hell is it?'

Cowley waited a long time before speaking, not wanting to be caught out by a misplaced word any more than he already had been. 'I would like to make something clear; something I think is necessary to explain. I am – was – in Moscow investigating the murder of the niece of someone you rightly describe as one of, if not *the*, most important politician in Washington. It's already clear she's the victim of a serial killer who's also killed a Russian and is going to kill again, if he's not caught. At one stage it appeared that killer was Paul Hughes. Can you imagine the fall-out of an American walking the streets of Moscow, killing people, one the niece of Senator Burden? I can't! Of *course* I recognized by even getting the number that there was an intercept. But that was *not* my immediate concern: my immediate concern was getting an admission from the man. Arresting him . . .' Cowley hesitated, aware that if he disclosed the moment he learned of the transcript – when the Militia Director and the Federal Prosecutor demanded a Russian presence at any encounter with Hughes – he would be admitting how he'd misled his own Director. He was soaked in sweat, able to feel the wetness beneath his arms and making its way down his back. Shifting the lie, anxious it would not be the misplaced word he was frightened of uttering, Cowley continued: 'Danilov did not produce the transcript until we were facing Hughes, in his apartment, the second time. And not to *me*. To quote from, to break Hughes down.'

Silence iced the room.

'And you just made notes?' sneered an aide.

'At that time, yes.'

'That explanation could be considered a speech of mitigation,' said Holmes, joining in the sneer.

'It was intended to make clear what I considered perfectly acceptable circumstances,' said Cowley, careless of the taut faces of the men sitting opposite. He'd lost so much there wasn't a lot more he could lose.

'Have you *seen* any part of the transcript?' asked one of the unnamed Russian experts. He spoke breathily, identifying himself as the one who sighed.

'No,' admitted Cowley.

'Didn't you think the transcript important to have?'

'Not at that exact moment!' said Cowley, regretting the indignation sounding like a plea. 'I was doing *my* job, not yours. And at that moment I was trying to get a confession.'

'So you don't have the sequence of the conversation, to know who was calling whom?'

Cowley looked steadily at the CIA Director. 'I did not tell you – neither did I suggest in any report I sent from Moscow – that it was Hughes's embassy telephone that was tapped. *You've* inferred that. I understood from Danilov that the calls to Hughes were *outgoing*, from the girl's apartment . . .' He suddenly decided that he did have cause for indignation. The meeting – perhaps interrogation was a better description – *was* turning events into an unjust accusation of his ineptitude. 'Why is the sequence important? You know, from what I've told you, that there *is* a tap.' Just as Andrews had told him, on the night of his arrival, that there were taps in the new embassy building, he remembered.

'From his office telephone Hughes presumably speaks to a lot of others far more important than his kinky bed partners,' suggested

Holmes. 'The Berlin Wall might be souvenir pieces now and the Cold War supposedly history, but we're not shutting up shop, any more than what was the KGB. Economics — just how fast and how far Russia is going down the financial tube — is the prime target. We want to know how big a damage limitation we might be looking at here.'

'Maybe as extensive as the one the Bureau would have been involved in if Hughes had been the killer,' said Cowley, wanting to score if he could.

There was more face tightening. The sighing man said: 'Can you get the transcript?'

Cowley glanced worriedly at the stenographer, unsure of the commitment. *If* the Russian investigator had intended the promise to abandon the personal competition. And *if* Russian intelligence didn't insist that whatever it provided was excluded from any cooperation. Too many ifs. 'I would hope to be able to.'

'Is Danilov truly Moscow Militia? Or could he be from the Cheka?'

'We're working from Militia headquarters. His is in a used office, occupied a long time.'

'That doesn't mean it's *his* office. Why can't it be a prop?'

'He knows his way around it: is familiar there. He acts like someone accustomed to investigating crime,' insisted Cowley. Imagining another scoring point, he said quickly: 'If Danilov were an intelligence officer, *why* would he blow Hughes, if Hughes were targeted or already suborned? Why, for that matter, would they let him?'

'To bring about exactly what's happened,' said the CIA Director. 'It doesn't matter if Hughes comes through the polygraph tests like George Washington and the apple tree. Or goes on to resist all the other questioning there's going to be. We're not going to be able to believe him. So we and the State Department are going to have to go back through everything the man has ever provided during the time he's been in Moscow and reassess and re-analyse and adjust every decision that might have been made, based upon it. It's called disinformation and it's a bastard.'

In the car returning to Washington, Cowley said: 'I'm sorry. It wasn't very good back there, was it?'

'No,' said Ross, shortly.

'Do those guys look for microphones in the john, before they sit down?'

'For cameras, too,' said Ross. 'It's the way their minds work.' He hesitated, thinking how good it would be to get out of Washington permanently. Pointedly he added: 'I'd like to do better, if there's a next time.'

When Cowley called Quantico from his hotel, a behavioural psychologist named Peter Meadows said the profile was complete with the additional material about the failed attack and that he'd be happy to discuss it. Judy Billington said on the telephone she didn't know how she could help. Cowley said something might come up, as they talked. She said it would have to be after the funeral, naturally. Naturally, Cowley agreed.

They'd decided to wait, because Yezhov's mother was sure he would be home within the hour, which he wasn't. Now they were annoyed. The senior detective, Ivan Truchin, was an ice-hockey fan who had front-row seats for tonight's game and was anxious about being late. His partner, Anatoli Zuyev, had an appointment of gratitude with a garage owner for whom he'd obtained a consignment of tyres, and wanted to get his money that night. The woman roamed the apartment on Bronnaja Boulevard, arms wrapped around herself, not knowing what she was protecting herself against: they'd refused to tell her what Petr had done, but she was sure it would be bad. She was terrified.

It was almost another hour before he came home. Petr Yezhov knew authority at once and withdrew inside himself. They couldn't trap him – lock him up – if he didn't say more than he had to. He confirmed with a nod that he was a labourer at the marshalling yards at Kursk Station. When they asked what he was doing on the night of January 17, his mother hurriedly assured the policemen he had been at home with her: Petr couldn't remember dates and would have looked guilty of whatever it was. He hadn't been home on January 17. She said he'd been with her the night Ann Harris had been killed, too. Which was only partially true. He'd gone out for one of his walks around ten o'clock and she had been asleep before he returned. Yezhov told the Militia men he didn't know anything about any attack, on any women. He was better now: he knew it was wrong to do that

257

any more. He said he didn't know where Gercena or Granovskaya were. It was getting late for both detectives when they made him open the locked door to his room. They were surprised at its neatness, which they ruined with the quick roughness of their search, rifling and discarding through bedside drawers and cupboards and making him open a cardboard suitcase beneath the bed. It contained photographs of railway engines: Yezhov liked railway engines, which was why he enjoyed working at Kursk Station.

In the car, as they left, Truchin said: 'Another waste of time, like all the rest.'

'Thank fuck we finished as quickly as we did,' said Zuyev.

Back in the apartment, his mother made Yezhov sit directly in front of her, reaching out to hold both his hands, as she had when he had been a child – younger than he was now, certainly – and she'd wanted him to admit doing something wrong. 'Have you been bad again? If you've been bad you've got to tell me, Petr Yakovlevich.'

Chapter Twenty-Five

There wasn't a clean shirt. Olga complained the machine was broken again. She didn't know when it might be fixed. Until it was, he should take extra care to keep his cuffs and collar clean. Driving to Petrovka in the unmarked car, Danilov was waved down on the corner of Serova by a felt-booted, uniformed Militia man. There was a smell of stale sweat when the officer leaned through the window: Danilov wondered how often he changed his shirt. The man insisted Danilov had been exceeding the speed limit, for which there was a statutory fine if an on-the-spot summons were issued. He supposed it was difficult, keeping to a speed limit in a nice car like this; it had to have cost a lot and be expensive to run. He smiled in contented anticipation of the bribe when Danilov reached into his jacket. He stayed smiling when Danilov produced the Militia identification, shrugging in resignation as he stepped back, his time briefly wasted. Danilov was curious at the amount the officer made during an average week by such extortion.

Pavin was already in the office when Danilov reached Militia headquarters. That morning's briefing meeting with the Director had been postponed for an hour: Lapinsk had been summoned to the Foreign Ministry. There was nothing from any of the ongoing routine inquiries, but Yevgennie Kosov had called personally, wanting to speak as soon as possible. When Danilov returned the call, Larissa's husband said it was to do with the murders but he didn't want to discuss it over the telephone. Why didn't they meet for lunch: he'd already made a reservation at the hard-currency room at Kropotkinskaya 36. Danilov frowned, both at the prospect and crackle-crackle dialogue: more imported American films on the impressive video, he guessed. He said lunch was a good idea, interested to see what the restaurant would be like: he'd heard about it but never eaten there. He wished he'd had a clean shirt. While he waited for Lapinsk, Danilov made arrangements with the hospital to revisit Lydia Orlenko.

He was kept waiting more than an hour. When he finally entered Lapinsk's top-floor office Danilov knew from the coughing, like a misfiring engine, that the old man had emerged from a bad meeting at the Ministry.

'There's a lot of annoyance at the complaints the Senator has made,' Lapinsk announced. 'There were Interior Ministry people at the meeting today, as well as Foreign. Nikolai Smolin, too.'

'What about the security agency?'

The Director nodded. 'Gugin attended.'

'Are they taking over?' He would have expected Lapinsk to be happier, if that decision had already been reached.

'Not yet. Gugin made it seem there was already a great deal of cooperation: that it was virtually a joint investigation.'

'So they're still trying to avoid it?' Mixed with Danilov's satisfaction was the awareness that he was being left in charge by default, not from any expression of confidence.

'Yes.'

'But that could change?' guessed Danilov.

'We've got to make available to Gugin everything we get from America, through our liaison with the FBI.'

'To prepare them completely if they *are* ordered to take over?'

'That's the obvious surmise.' There was no reluctance in the admission. Lapinsk's face relaxed for the first time at the prospect of being spared a problem from which he was eager to escape.

Danilov supposed it was only a matter of time before he was discarded, as a failed investigator, an embarrassment. And unless he could bring about a quick pre-emptive breakthrough – which he already knew he couldn't, because there wasn't a single avenue left to follow – then the time would be measured simply by how long the former KGB managed to evade the ultimate, inevitable responsibility. Why the hurt resentment, the anger at Lapinsk for the obvious acquiescence? Pride, he supposed. But what place did pride have for Dimitri Ivanovich Danilov? It certainly hadn't had much importance when he'd headed a Militia district. And realistically had been little more than an affectation after the transfer to Petrovka, with his attempt to sever his manipulative ties to the past. What, practically, had it achieved? Had it made him a better detective? Made it easier to solve cases? Impressed and influenced his police colleagues? Certainly not the latter. The reverse. His pride – or rather his facile attempt to achieve it, refusing to compromise, refusing to be introduced by others in the initial friendly welcome to the sort of smiling entrepreneurs necessary at every level of Russian life – had marked him as a suspicious oddity, someone to be avoided until higher-echelon common sense prevailed and he was shunted sideways into the obscurity from which he had emerged. The excuse for which could come from the transfer to the Lubyanka of this investigation. Where would he be shunted? He didn't know of anyone being sent *back* to a district, from Militia headquarters, although he supposed it must have happened. He doubted, if it had happened, that the move had been to a command position, which he had abandoned to come here. There were other, uniformed divisions, of course. Maybe there'd be a place for him there. Not a relegation quite so ignominious as street duty; but perhaps something within the chain where he could benefit from the kickbacks from smirking Militia men ambushing motorists on street corners. Danilov blocked the self-pity, surprised how easily it had come. In needless justification, he said: 'We held back from any public warning to make it easier if the killer had been the American!'

'There hasn't been anything official from Washington,' said Lapinsk. 'How could there be, for that very reason! It's only the press and television reaction to what the Senator said. The Foreign Minister is calling in the American ambassador, for consultation. The media are demanding more information: more press conferences and access to the woman who survived.'

'Are we going to give it? Any of it?'

'I don't want to take part in any more conferences. Neither does Smolin.'

'Does that mean I have to do it?' asked Danilov, directly.

'Not by yourself. That way we'd be accepting full accountability for delaying as we did,' the Militia Director reassured him. 'You'll only do it with the American. And only then after it's made clear to the American ambassador that we no longer see any reason why we shouldn't disclose *why* we held back.'

'That would put Paul Hughes – and the US embassy – under siege,' predicted Danilov.

'Which everyone at this morning's meeting would prefer to us being under siege.'

Danilov recognized that privately the pressure was being neatly shifted back to America, although publicly – having been identified at the first press conference as the joint investigating officer – he would still be connected to the sensation created by the American politician, which really wasn't a sensation at all. Reminded of the press conference, Danilov recalled the query he'd raised with Pavin and still wanted answered. 'Maybe Cowley will bring back some guidance, in addition to whatever the ambassador will say.'

Lapinsk shrugged, almost indifferent, and Danilov guessed the old man already considered the irritation removed from him. He certainly didn't appear greatly interested in the rest of the conversation about the routine inquiries continuing at psychiatric institutions and throughout the Militia districts in the area of the killings and the attack.

Danilov reached the hospital earlier than he expected, ahead of the arranged appointment. Lydia Orlenko was still alone in her closet-sized ward but lying more on her back than before, although still not completely allowing her weight to press down. She was bundled in bandages, made bolster-busted by them. Danilov thought he recognized the stains on the bed linen from his earlier visit. He was glad the American was not with him; bed linen was probably changed every day in American clinics. Danilov perched on the small chair but leaned forward towards her, as he had done before. Lydia smiled in hesitant half-recognition. She still wore the mob-cap, covering her shorn head, and referred to it at once. 'You didn't tell me what had happened to my hair. You should have told me.'

'It will grow again,' assured Danilov.

'That's what they say. I don't know.' Her bottom lip wobbled. 'I liked my hair. Don't want to be ugly. Boris liked my hair.'

'I want to talk more about that night,' said Danilov hurriedly, not wanting her to collapse on him. 'I know there are gaps, when you probably fainted. But tell me about before, when you can remember. *Everything* you can remember before.'

'I was walking from the hotel, like I said. At the time I told you. I didn't know he was behind, not until his arm suddenly

came over my shoulder and his hand closed over my mouth.'
Carefully Lydia raised her hand to the round bruise on her chin.
'. . . I don't think his hand *closed* over my mouth,' she qualified.
'It was more a slap, bringing his hand back *into* my face. That
– and the terrible pain – knocked the wind out of me. But I felt
his strength, as he pulled me backwards. I remember trying to
fight against falling backwards. But I couldn't.'

'Is that when you smelled the tobacco on his breath?'

'It wasn't on his breath,' she contradicted at once.

'But you said . . .' started Danilov, and then stopped, because
she hadn't said: she'd told them of smelling tobacco and he'd
assumed it was on the attacker's breath. 'How, then?' he finished.

'It was an all-over smell, not like it is when it's on a person's
breath: then it's sort of directed, isn't it? Concentrated?'

Danilov nodded, although he was not sure he completely understood. 'And you're still sure about the clammy hands?'

Lydia shivered, but halted quickly. 'That was the worst part,
except for the pain. The way his hands were. Unnatural. That
and the sound . . .'

'What sound?' This second visit might be as useful as the one
to the taxi driver's widow.

Lydia frowned, slightly turning her head the better to look at
him. 'I told you about the sound.'

'You said he grunted, when you lashed out at him. Hit him in
the chest.'

'No,' said the woman, although not positively arguing. 'There
was a hum. Not at first. Like I said, I didn't hear anything at
first. Didn't know he was behind me. But when I came to on the
ground, he was humming.'

'Humming! Like a tune, you mean?'

'No,' insisted Lydia. 'Not an actual tune. Just a sound, in his
throat. The sort of noise people sometimes make without knowing it when they concentrate. That's how the grunt came about,
I suppose. My hitting him just made the hum louder, for a
moment.'

Danilov pressed even closer: her breath still smelled badly.
'Now think, Lydia Markovina! This is extremely important. The
hum, the sound, however you like to think of it. Could you detect
anything about an accent; anything that might have been a word,

even? Was it Russian? Or something else? Think! Think before you answer!'

The frown came again. She considered the question, as he'd demanded. Then she said: 'I can't say. It was just a sound, moaning as much as humming. No words. No accent . . .' She smiled, shyly, and deep in her throat made a sound which Danilov thought more of a groan than how she'd described it. 'Something like that,' she said.

Small things, decided Danilov: small things that might fit into a bigger whole, if ever they got to the man. 'You said, before, that you couldn't make out his features when he leaned over you. Is that so? Nothing has come to you since, about how he looked? Anything about his face?'

'He wasn't big, not like your friend. Nothing about his face. It was always in the dark.'

Danilov straightened, from bending forward, feeling the strain in his back. 'We'll leave it now,' he said. 'We might come back again.'

'The nurse said he was a murderer. That he's a maniac and that he's killed other people.'

'Yes,' said Danilov.

She gave a pained shudder. 'So I'm lucky not to be dead too?'

'But you're not,' said Danilov, not wanting her to become fixated on her escape. 'That's why I want you to go on thinking of anything that might help me catch him.'

'Boris said you took all my clothes.'

'To be examined. There might be evidence.'

'He will *be* caught, won't he?'

'Yes,' assured Danilov. But possibly not by me, he thought.

Danilov decided that during the day it wasn't necessary to take the windscreen wipers off: even at night he felt ridiculous doing it and still sometimes pinched his fingers. There was instant recognition when he named Kosov. A smiling manager escorted him to a room to the right. It was easy to isolate the foreigners – tourists and businessmen and possibly diplomats – but Danilov just as easily picked out the self-favouring Russians proving themselves an élite. Kosov was in the centre of the room, displaying himself more favoured than most by being at a table capable of seating four. Danilov was early and suspected Kosov had arrived even earlier so as to play the considerate, attentive host. Danilov would not have really been surprised if Kosov had worn his uniform, but he hadn't. The blue-striped suit was well cut and clearly Western-made, the coordinated blue shirt crisp and fresh; without positively thinking of the action, Danilov shrugged his cuffs back beneath the sleeves of his jacket. Kosov stood effusively to shake his hand and remained standing while Danilov seated himself. There was a diminishing bottle of vodka already on the table; unasked Kosov poured Danilov a full measure, raising his own glass in a toast. Danilov responded, self-consciously. Kosov demanded they get the ordering over, insisting that the *schi* was the best cabbage soup in Moscow and recommending the smoked sturgeon to follow. Danilov agreed to both. Kosov offered the wine list, saying there was a selection of both Californian and French, as well as Georgian. Danilov refused to choose, saying he didn't mind. Kosov chose a French Beaujolais: 1983 had been a good year, he declared.

Kosov topped up their vodka glasses and said: 'There's quite a fuss, over the Senator?'

'Yes.'

'*Is* there a cover-up? Something we don't know about?'

Had he been trapped into this meeting to pass on gossip with which Kosov could impress his doubtful friends? 'Not at all. There was a line of inquiry that it suited us not to make any announcement about before we did. The Senator likes seeing his own picture on television too much.'

'What line of inquiry?'

'It came to nothing.'

There was the slightest of pauses, at the avoidance. 'It will be awkward if the man really does say something in the American Congress: I heard him threaten it on television.'

'That's the concern of politicians,' said Danilov, wanting to get to the point of their being in the restaurant. 'Mine is to find the man who's doing the killing. Or trying to find him. You said you had something?'

Kosov smiled, refusing to be hurried. 'I have special friends,' he said.

'You told me.'

265

'This could never be evidence, you understand? They won't cooperate like that.'

'Just let me have the guidance.'

'These friends of mine employ a lot of people. Particularly to drive around Moscow, servicing outlets.'

Danilov knew at once the man was talking about black-market deliveries guaranteed by Kosov against interruption by any curious Militia. Which was precisely what he'd once done for a grateful Eduard Agayans. Could the informant even *be* Agayans? It was possible: maybe more than possible. 'Late at night?' he suggested, wanting to show his awareness.

'The best time,' smiled Kosov, enjoying the exchange. 'That request you made, a few days ago, referred to a particular area?'

'Yes?'

'These drivers are talking about someone they see in that area, late at night. Someone who always seems anxious not to be seen. Ducks into doorways or alleys when the lorries or vans get close.'

Danilov held back the sigh. How many people were there likely to be in a city of ten million people unwilling to attract attention at night? 'A man?'

Kosov nodded. 'Always the same route, according to my people. Gorky Street . . .' He hesitated. 'Or Tverskaya, if you want to be a strictly accurate policeman after the street renaming. He's seen a lot on Gercena, which is close to where the American woman was killed, isn't it? On the ring road, linking the two: my people use the ring road a lot. And Granovskaya.'

My people, picked out Danilov. Who was the more beholden to whom, Kosov to the Mafia or the Mafia to Kosov? Danilov was fairly sure he knew the answer. 'What's he look like?'

Kosov shrugged. 'Average height, apparently. At this time of the year he wears a woollen ski hat. And a padded jacket, against the cold.'

The winter wear of practically every one of those ten million Muscovites, reflected Danilov. Yet the description *could* tally with the vague account given of her attacker by Lydia Orlenko. He began his cabbage soup: it was as good as Kosov promised. 'What about facially?'

'Hides away.'

It didn't – *couldn't* – amount to any more than the dozens of suggestions about mysterious or suspicious people reported from the other Militia stations which had already been examined and rejected by his disgruntled street teams. It would be wrong, however, to be dismissive just because the information had been given inflated importance by a man performing as Kosov was; he'd have Pavin brief the street teams about this one, to be checked out like all the rest. 'I'll circulate it,' he said.

'Already done, among my people,' said Kosov, using the phrase again.

'Militia people? Or your special friends?' The Beaujolais was as good as the soup.

The assured grin came back. 'Both,' said Kosov. 'If the drivers see him wandering about, I'm going to be told. If they can, they'll grab him.'

Danilov sat with his wineglass suspended in front of him. 'I don't think I like that!' he protested. 'What right have they got? That's vigilante stuff.'

Kosov's grin became an expression of surprise. 'What the hell do rights matter? You're hunting a maniac: giving public warnings to women to keep off the streets! You worry about rights and niceties, trying to find a man like that? All they'll do is hold him until I get there. Or one of my officers does . . .' There was another shrug. 'If he has got an explanation, then fine. If not, you've got your man.'

Just like in the video movies, thought Danilov. He was deeply uncomfortable, positively reluctant, at the idea of unofficial posses made up of black-market delivery men. But they *did* crisscross the streets of Moscow, covering more ground and seeing more than a lot of Militia or army patrols. And Kosov was correct: he was hunting a maniac. 'That's all they'll do? Hold him until the arrival of the proper Militia?'

Kosov's smile returned, at the obvious concern. 'I told you at the beginning, they don't want to get deeply involved. *Can't* get deeply involved. Isn't this sturgeon magnificent?'

'Very good,' agreed Danilov. He couldn't directly forbid Kosov's arrangement in any case.

'When are we going to make an evening together again?' demanded the other man.

'Soon,' said Danilov, unenthusiastically. 'I'll get Olga to

267

arrange it.' Larissa was on the afternoon shift again. He could go straight from lunch to the Druzhba Hotel. But he wasn't going to, although he guessed Larissa would have been amused by his going to her after lunch with her husband. Certainly she'd be expecting him to contact her.

'Television fixed yet?'

'Not yet.' Danilov's more pressing concern was the washing machine. If they had a replacement for their own they wouldn't be reliant any more upon the communal basement facility, which was rarely a facility at all.

'Don't forget what I said about introductions to people,' urged Kosov. 'You introduced me once: why can't I do the same for you?'

'I won't forget,' said Danilov. What place did professional integrity have, if he could even think, as he had done only minutes earlier, of going to Kosov's wife directly after eating with the man? Very little. Wasn't he posturing and performing, just as much as Kosov? Maybe even worse. At least Kosov was honestly corrupt, if that wasn't too much of a paradox. The man wasn't a cheating hypocrite, which was how Danilov was coming to regard himself.

There was small-talk about the Kosovs' planned foreign holiday, interspersed by the man's repeated efforts, which Danilov avoided, to learn why the public warning about the maniac killer had been delayed. At the end of the meal Kosov paid from a thick bundle of American dollars, which, if the currency legislation were strictly interpreted, it was illegal for him to possess. They parted with Kosov promising news very soon of the mystery wanderer and Danilov telling the man to be careful, although he was not quite sure what he intended the warning to mean.

Danilov did not drive directly back to Militia headquarters. Instead he took a widely sweeping route that took him part of the way along Vernadskaya and past the Druzhba Hotel where he knew Larissa would be working and probably waiting for him. But still with no intention of stopping. He looped on to Leninskii Prospekt, quite close to the offices where the taxi driver's widow worked, to go by the premises from which Eduard Agayans controlled the majority of his activities. Danilov slowed, gazing at the once familiar block, and on impulse went into the slip road to stop completely. The block was smeared with street dirt and looked locked and unused. But that was always how it had appeared when he was cooperating with the black marketeer. Behind that boarded, shuttered front Danilov knew there would be foreign-made television sets that didn't flicker and fade. And laundry machines that spun clothes almost dry, after washing. There would be no question of Agayans forgetting him, any more than he'd forgotten the florid-faced Armenian and the brandy ritual before any meeting. Wasn't it time to stop being the hypocrite? To become like any other Russian, even Russian policemen? Urgently, annoyed at having made the tempting detour, Danilov re-started the engine, hurrying out into the traffic to get back to his office. Not yet: he wasn't ready to give in yet.

At Petrovka he told Pavin of the sighting in Kosov's district, without disclosing the unofficial detention help that had been proposed. He didn't tell his assistant about the possibility of losing the investigation to the Cheka, either. Pavin said he was still checking out the query from the press conference. When Pavin said there was nothing worthwhile from any of the psychiatric institution enquiries, Danilov said: 'Let me see all the discounted reported. I want to go through them personally.'

Pavin nodded. It would probably be a good idea. None of those he'd read himself showed the sort of inquiry that should have been made, the resentment at being assigned the job virtually obvious from every page.

'I've been meaning to ask,' said Danilov. 'How did you manage to replace those stolen windscreen wipers as quickly as you did?'

'Took them off another police car,' said Pavin. 'How else?'

'The only way,' Danilov agreed. Another Moscow realist, like so many others, he recognized; so many others except himself.

'What's going to happen to us?'

Paul Hughes looked impatiently at his wife. 'The question doesn't make sense. What *can* happen to us?'

'Why are you being recalled?'

'I told you. For consultations. That's not surprising, is it? Ann Harris was a member of my staff.'

'I don't see why you've got to go all the way back to America. Why couldn't it be done by letter? Or report?'

'I don't know either,' said the man, looking up from his packing. 'You know the sort of waves someone like Burden can create: it's got to be something to do with that nonsense at his press conferences.'

'Were you sleeping with Ann Harris? Doing things to her I won't let you do to me any more?'

'Stop it, Angela!'

'Were you? I want to know!'

'I'll get to see the children, before I come back. You want me to tell them anything, from you?'

'Nothing I haven't written, every week since we've been here. So you were fucking her? Hurting her? Did she like it? Was she braver than me?'

'I can't see my being away for much more than three or four days. A week at the most. Anything you want me to bring back?'

'How do you know it will be a week? How do you know you will be coming back at all?'

'Don't be stupid! If I were being permanently recalled you would have been included as well. This is what the message said. Just consultations.'

'Did you kill her?'

Hughes turned from the bed on which his half-packed suitcase lay, fully to confront his wife. 'You know damned well I didn't! What the hell's wrong with you?'

'I'm frightened! That's what the hell's wrong with me! And I think I've got good reason.'

'I'm not the phantom maniac! If you don't believe me about Ann Harris, what about the Russian woman? You know for a fact I couldn't have carried out that attack. So I can't be involved with any of it.'

She stood regarding him steadily for a long time. Then she said: 'Perhaps it would be a good idea for me to go back to the States, whatever happens.'

'What's that supposed to mean?'

'You know as well as I do. Maybe better.'

'This is an accompanied post, for married men.'

'I think I'm through doing things for your career.'

'Wait until I get back here. So we can talk about it properly.'

'We stopped doing things properly years ago.'

'Please, Angela!'

'The little-boy-lost plea! That didn't used to come for a long time yet.'

'Wait until I get back.'

'See a lawyer in Washington, as well as seeing the kids. That's what I'm going to do. I don't think I'll have any problem claiming cruelty, do you?'

There were twelve buttons: would have been more if she hadn't come alive the way she had. Six more at least. And some hair. Wanted more buttons. More hair. Why? Just because, that's why. Important there should be at least one more to take buttons and hair from to show up what idiots they all were. No mistakes this time, though. No more bad choices. Or ones that came alive. Two mistakes already, one after the other. Too many. Next time would be perfect. Mustn't get to like it too much. It was difficult, not to like it. Felt powerful. Hugely powerful. Had the power of life and death. But it would mean he was mad, if he liked it too much. That's what they'd say. What they *were* saying. Maniac. In all the papers. Wasn't mad. Not mad at all. The opposite. Clever: cleverer than all the others. So only one more. Maybe two. Definitely no more than two. Didn't really want to stop. So *much* power. Wasn't mad. Wish there was a way they could know. That would be best of all, if there was a way they could know. Show them the power. Wasn't possible, of course. Pity. Just two more. Or maybe three. Definitely no more than three.

Chapter Twenty-Six

There was a tailback from a three-car accident on the 95, which delayed Cowley getting to Quantico. He detested being late for appointments, so there was an illogical annoyance, without a sensible focus. When he finally arrived, to the snap-crack-pop of agents practising on the training academy's target range, the psychologist said it didn't matter: he'd shunted into a car himself the previous week, so he knew what it was like. And the hold-up had given him a final opportunity to read through his assessment.

Despite the reassurance he'd received in Moscow, Cowley said: 'I was worried there wouldn't be enough to create the profile.'

'That's what we're paid for.' Peter Meadows was a small, intense man whose glasses seemed inadequate despite their thick lenses, because he constantly squinted and leaned forward to peer through them. He was in chino jeans and loafers: the roll-neck sweater was wearing thin at the left elbow and there was a definite hole in one sock. In contrast to the man's outward neglect, the office in the Behavioural Science Unit was immaculate, the impression of near-clinical cleanliness heightened by the harsh, hospital-glare brightness of the artificial neon throughout a basement area with no natural light. Nowhere in the office were there any obvious personal or sentimental possessions, like family photographs or qualification certificates. Meadows smiled, brightly, and added: 'But there are difficulties you must keep in mind.'

'Such as?'

'Russia,' said the psychologist, simply. 'Our assessments and profiles are predicated from an American society: certain basic characteristics that we calculate to be common, throughout. If your killer is Russian, some of those assessments might be a little off course.'

'Some?' pressed Cowley. 'But not all?'

'Not all,' agreed the man. 'General things first. I'm tagging him asocial. The most important thing about that classification fits in

272

with where the murders and the failed attack took place, all in fairly close proximity. When you get him, he'll live in the area: asocials attack close to their homes or workplaces because they feel most secure there. Usually asocials don't know their victims: I'm not going to be dogmatic about this, but the victims are probably chosen at random, complete strangers to him. Asocials don't bother to conceal their victims, after the crime, which again fits what you've given me.'

'What about specifics: the shoes, hair and the buttons?'

'One at a time,' insisted Meadows. 'The positioning of the shoes indicates obsessive neatness: the shoes are the most likely items to fall off, in an attack. So they must be restored. Putting them by the head could be taken as a plea for forgiveness, too: there's no hate or dislike in the killing. But your asocial will know he's doing wrong and that he's causing pain. He's saying sorry. But let's not slip past the neatness. He'll wear cross-over jackets: they're smarter than single-breasted suits. He'll wear suits on a Sunday: on a vacation. Always have a sharp crease in his pants. Always have clean shoes. The neatness could extend to personal cleanliness, although that doesn't always follow. If it does, he'll wash his hands a lot. Have clean fingernails.'

'What about the hair?'

Meadows turned down the corners of his mouth, in a doubtful expression. 'A lot of scope here. Could be he's ugly: wants to make the people he kills ugly, too. Maybe he's simply bald – could be medical baldness, from chemotherapy or nervous depilation – and just wants to make them look like he does. Certainly there'd be a connection to the obsessional neatness: so he won't be *completely* bald. There'll be hair that doesn't fit his own idea of how he should look. Then again it could just be a souvenir. I've read that the hair is scattered about but he probably keeps some. Souvenirs are very important to them.'

'So he'd have it, if we make an arrest.'

The bright smile came again. 'That would make it all very easy, wouldn't it?'

'Which leaves the buttons.'

'Nipple fetish,' said the behaviour expert immediately. 'Well documented, readily obvious. Ann Harris had bruised, bitten nipples: the Russian woman talked of her breasts being fondled.'

'We think we know who bit Ann Harris. He was a lover who liked inflicting pain. He has an alibi.'

'Russian?'

'American.'

'Does he fit the profile?'

Cowley tried to put the pieces together. 'Similarities. They wouldn't lead me directly to him. Are you saying it's a sexual motive?'

Meadows came forward for better focus, forcefully shaking his head. 'Not in the way that you and I would think of sexual gratification. There's rarely penis penetration from an asocial attacker. The satisfaction is psychosexual. Where there's a connection again. Asocials use sharp, pointed instruments: a penis substitute. Like the knife in this case. Never a firearm.'

'Would there be a mental history? We're obviously running institution checks.'

Meadows made another doubtful expression. 'It's always worth going through the system: your man could have shown disturbances involving one or all of the manifestations he's now demonstrating. But don't necessarily look for it progressing previously to murder. Killing is the *final* explosion: the ultimate towards which he's been building. If you want to target, go for someone with a mental history that shows a nipple fixation: maybe actual mutilation that brought about his arrest and led to his being institutionalized. There'd be a progression there. When he mutilated the nipples before, he got arrested and locked up. Maybe because he was known to the women he attacked. Providing he evades capture, he's not going to get locked up by killing them, is he? In fact he's *protecting* himself by killing them. Cutting off their buttons is cutting off their nipples, a substitute like the knife is a penis replacement.'

Cowley wondered how Danilov would have reacted to this lecture. Despite the unquestionable eighty per cent statistical accuracy of behavioural profiles, Cowley found it easy to understand the Russian's scepticism. 'We seem to have shifted from generalities to specifics.'

'Unavoidable,' said Meadows, sharply. 'Generalities again. Keep the murder area under surveillance. Asocial killers are often compelled to return to the scene. It's another satisfaction for them, to relive the crime.'

'Let's revert to the sexual aspect, for a moment. Would he be heterosexual? Or could he be homosexual?'

'Invariably heterosexual. I can't recall a reference case where the man has been homosexual.'

'So there would be a wife? Or girlfriend?'

'Possibly. But not necessarily. An asocial is basically a loner: often someone abused in childhood. If there is a wife or girlfriend, he will have abused her breasts. If he's unmarried, he might have employed a hooker, again to abuse her breasts. Probably wouldn't have tried to screw her. I understand Moscow's got a pretty active hooker fraternity. It would make a lot of sense to ask around.'

Cowley had the impression that he was learning and understanding a lot while at the same time discovering nothing of the man he was pursuing. Would Danilov be making any progress on his own in Moscow? Time, hopefully, to get back to specifics.

'So when we find him he'll be neat, his pants pressed, his jacket is cross-over, his shoes clean. He could possibly have a hair problem and be ashamed of it. He'll live in the area we've already marked off. He'll be a loner, although he might have a wife or girlfriend. He might also have used prostitutes, concentrating upon their breasts.'

'Don't tell me!' protested the psychologist.

'What?'

'You know a hundred guys, just like him!'

Cowley smiled. 'It *is* pretty general.'

'I'm only sketching the outline: you've got to colour in the picture,' Meadows insisted. 'But let's try a few more specifics. I've considered both autopsy reports: the Russian one was practically another attack, by the way. Your killer will be five feet eight inches tops, not less than five seven. Ann Harris was five feet five. The act of pulling her backwards, the way your killer attacks, would reduce that height by as much as five inches. So the knife goes in with just the slightest upwards bias. He's right-handed, of course. And he's strong. He's not stabbing, giving himself some momentum to get the knife into the body. He's pushing. That needs strength. And there's strength in the hold over the mouth, leaving the nasal bruising. And that round chin abrasion is important, both on Ann Harris and on the woman who lived. Your man wears a ring, on the pinkie finger of his left hand. I read two things into those factors. He's fit: maybe exercises. Although from the tobacco smell the Russian woman talked about he's not fanatical about his health. And there's a contradiction here to what I've already suggested. He's not *that* obsessionally neat, to wash his hands a lot. If he'd washed his hands, he would have reduced that smell. From the way he clamps his hand over the mouth and nose he's probably had some martial arts or military training.'

'Something worries me about that known physical contact he had with the Russian woman, Lydia Orlenko,' said Cowley. 'I talked to her very soon afterwards: heard her describe it. She was revulsed by the hand. She said it was clammy, but not wet. That it didn't feel like the skin of a hand. Neither was it any sort of glove. So what the hell could it be?'

Meadows frowned, surprised by the question. 'I think it *was* a glove.'

'But I just told you . . .'

'. . . what about a *rubber* glove?' Meadows broke in. 'The sort of thing women wear in a kitchen. Even a surgical glove. Ever felt them, against your skin? Particularly the surgical type? It *is* a clammy sensation. But it's not wet. Try it for yourself. I did, after the forensic guys back in Washington suggested it to me. Feels just like the woman described it.' The man physically shuddered. 'Nasty! And very clammy.'

'If he wore surgical gloves, there could be some medical connection? The entry wound that killed both the man and Ann Harris went cleanly between the eighth and ninth rib. Which would indicate some medical knowledge.'

'And the Russian woman was probably saved because the knife *hit* the rib. I'm a psychologist, not a surgeon. I would have thought in the circumstances – in a darkened alley, suddenly seizing a victim from the rear – it would be practically impossible even for a trained physician to guarantee getting between the two ribs.'

'There's something about the nipple fetish that worries me,' said Cowley, speaking as the doubt came to him. 'What about

Vladimir Suzlev? Why would a man with a nipple complex attack another man? Unless our killer *is* homosexual.'

'Whoa!' cautioned Meadows, raising halting hands. 'I said colour in the picture, not black it out completely! Surely there's a much simpler explanation for the attack on Suzlev: it's even obvious from the evidence you've already got. With Suzlev, *no* buttons were taken. Because your killer realized when he turned him over that he *wasn't* a woman. Even though he wore his hair long enough to be *mistaken* for one, in the near-darkness and in the split second before the knife went in.'

Cowley nodded, taking the other man's interpretation. 'Lydia Orlenko talked about him feeling her breasts. At the time it seemed obviously sexual. But it could have been his assuring himself that she *was* a woman. In the bundled-up way people dress in Moscow at this time of the year, it would be difficult positively to decide anyone's sex, particularly in a dark alley.'

'I'd go with the confirming theory, rather than straight sex. Physical sex isn't ever a factor in these sorts of murders.'

'But he *does* know what he's doing?'

'Oh yes,' said the psychologist, quickly. 'And that it's wrong. Asocial killers are invariably clever. And cunning. The game – challenging the authorities to catch them, keeping one step ahead – matters a lot to them. I've read Senator Burden's complaints, about things being kept secret: a cover-up. Your killer would have been angry about that. He wants to know he's frightening people: causing panic.'

'How about *using* the media?' suggested Cowley, again speaking as the idea occurred. 'Could we evolve some way to challenge him back? Use his own madness to make him disclose himself? I think we could quite easily manipulate the Moscow media, which is what he'll be reading and watching.'

Meadows gave another doubtful expression. 'It's been tried. Worked sometimes, but not often enough. And there's a risk. You start playing mental games at a distance and you're going to get all sorts of nuts coming out of the woodwork. You end up with copy-cat killings. And looking for more than one murderer.' The man shook his head. 'I don't think it's a good idea. Not at this stage, anyway. I know all about political pressure –

that's why I had to get the profile out as quickly as I did – but try everything else first.'

'Anything else I should be looking for?'

Meadows pursed his lips, contemplatively. 'General guidance,' he offered. 'He'll probably have been neglected as a kid. Not properly know what love is. If he *is* married, their sex life won't be good. As I've already said, asocials have trouble with the physical act. Fantasy plays a part, particularly with the violence. He'll probably enjoy violent pornography: absorb himself fantasizing about it and carrying it forward into a definite attack. So look for pornography, when you make an arrest: it'll be a pointer.'

'You've helped a lot,' thanked Cowley. 'I appreciate it.'

'Don't rely upon it!' warned Meadows, again. 'The Behavioural Unit has had its successes, some pretty impressive. But it's *not* a science: it never can be, despite a lot of people claiming that it is. At best it's a psychological art, developed from experience. So it's an aid to detection, not a replacement for it. You'll still have to follow investigative procedure. And keep in mind at all times what I said at the very beginning: the profile might not be any good at all because you're hunting a Russian, not an American.'

'It's still been useful,' said Cowley.

'I'll be interested to see how close we made the fit, when you get him,' said the psychologist.

'*When* we get him,' said Cowley.

The arrival delay was compounded by his spending more time than he'd expected at Quantico and even heavier traffic on the 95 returning to Washington, so he was quite late again getting to Judy Billington. Her apartment was less than a mile from his own shut-up flat, with a better view of the Washington Monument but nearer the airport: as he drove up, Cowley had a constant view of the commuter aircraft hovering for landing permission like predatory birds, waiting to plummet on to their prey.

The girl answered the door in a loose, figure-enveloping sweater, over jeans that in complete contrast were skin-tight. She wore loafers, although unlike the man he'd just left, Judy did not wear any socks, holed or otherwise. Her hair was so black Cowley decided it had to be dyed to deepen its natural colour. She wore it very short. The only make-up was around her eyes, and black again, as if she were trying to create an effect. He started to apologize for his lateness as he entered the apartment. She said it didn't matter; she'd taken the entire day off, after the funeral. Cowley said he hoped it had gone OK. She grimaced at the remark, asking if funerals of murder victims ever went OK. Cowley decided he deserved the put-down.

'You want anything? Coffee? Booze?' There was a glass of white wine alongside a chair in which she had obviously been sitting before he got there.

Cowley declined, choosing his own seat on a couch which ran in front of the window with the panorama over the river. It was an unavoidable fact of murder investigations that a victim's mail was read: that was how he'd located her. He was grateful, for her time.

Judy listened patiently, occasionally sipping her wine, a smile quite close. When he finished, she said: 'Shocked by what you read?'

'No.'

'Hard-assed G-man, eh? You know you're the first FBI agent I've ever met.'

She was trying hard with the repartee. 'We come in all sizes,' he said, quickly regretting his own effort, not knowing why he'd tried.

'That must be convenient.' The look was openly appraising, the smile finally forming. 'I'd guess you're the jumbo version, right?'

Why the hell was he letting this happen? 'You and Ann were pretty close, from the letters?'

'Close enough, I guess.'

'I've only read one side of the correspondence: yours to her. Do you have hers?'

Judy shook her head. 'She was like that at college. Kept every-thing. Theatre tickets. Programmes. Letters. Notes. A fucking magpie. I'm the opposite. Can't stand clutter. Souvenirs bore me.'

Cowley guessed she said fuck to see how he'd react, which he hadn't. He was thinking more about the point she'd made. There was a possible paradox in Ann Harris's hoarding – neat though that hoarding had seemingly been – and her scrupulous cleanli-ness. 'You didn't keep *anything*?'

'Sorry.'

'What about personal contact, while she'd been in Moscow? Any phone conversations? Vacation visits maybe?'

'She came back, about a year ago, on home leave. There was always talk of my going to Moscow but I never got around to it.' She appeared surprised that her glass was empty, rising with it in her hand. 'You sure about not wanting anything? It's Chablis.'

'Positive.' She clearly knew how good her body was: there was an exaggerated hip movement as she went into the kitchen annex. She would probably have been offended if she'd known what little effect it had upon him. He tried to look as if he were enjoying it as she returned, not wanting the performance to have been entirely in vain. 'You see much of her, when she was back?'

'Sure. Three or four times.'

'Think back!' demanded Cowley. 'As much as you can. To the visit and to the letters. I want names ... any name, Christian name or nickname. A lead, to the guys she went with. Anyone.'

Judy toyed with the glass, held before her in both hands. 'No names,' she said at last. 'There was a guy who worked out at the embassy gym ...'

Hughes. How much of that morning's profile could fit the economist? Would the CIA polygraphs prove the alibis a lie, after all?

'... and one of the diplomats, although that was a one-night disaster ...' she giggled. 'Got drunk, couldn't get it up and cried. That's what she told me, anyhow ... Someone she called Mr Droop. There was a musical on Broadway: *Edwin Drood*. She got it from that.' The smile widened. 'There was one identity. The ambassador had the hots. Always used to touch her ass or her arm, supposedly easing his way past her at receptions or when they were in the same place socially: it's the sort of things some guys do. Always included her in official things, too. But he could never bring himself to make the big pass. Ann thought it was funny. She guessed it would have been another hold-it-for-me-while-I-cry number.'

'What about Russians?'

'She couldn't stand Russia!'

'We're not talking about the place: we're talking about men. She didn't hate men.'

280

'No Russian men. And I think she would have told me.'

'What about other embassies?'

There was an immediate nod. 'Her first thing was with an attaché at the French embassy . . .' She looked up, pleased at the recollection. 'And a name! Guy. His name was Guy. She was crazy about him at first: said he was fantastic . . .'

At last! thought Cowley. So it wasn't a fruitless afternoon: he could get the complete identity of an attaché named Guy in minutes. 'You said at first. What happened?'

Judy regarded him curiously. 'He went back to France, of course. Over a year ago. They kept in touch for a while but he was married, like they all are, so it kind of fizzled out.'

Cowley felt almost physically deflated, nearly as deflated as he'd been at the end of the interview with Hughes. Deciding to use what he knew about the economist and the dead girl, hopefully to jog Judy Billington's memory of other things, he said: 'The guy who liked to hurt her, in bed: you wrote to each other about it. Did she ever talk or write about feeling threatened by him? Or anybody? Ever imagine she might have been picked out?'

'Stalked, you mean?' For the first time the woman became properly serious.

'She *was*, by somebody.' At Quantico the psychologist had told him victims were invariably strangers to their killers. So why was he pursuing this point?

It took Judy longer this time to answer. She did so shaking her head. 'Never that she thought she was being picked out. She didn't mind the pain bit, not altogether. Just sometimes. Said they were all a bunch of kinky bastards.'

'You're absolutely sure she wasn't ever involved with a Russian?'

'If she was, she didn't say a word about it.'

At least Quantico hadn't been wasted, although so much of what he'd been told seemed to be information that would be useful *after* an arrest, not directly guiding him towards making one. About which the psychologist had warned him, he remembered: normal investigation methods had to come first. 'You've been very patient.'

She frowned. 'Have I helped?'

'Sure,' he lied.

The provocative smile came back. 'You look better in the flesh than you did on television, from Moscow. You looked very pissed off there.'

'It was a media event. There wasn't any point.'

'Can you believe what that asshole Burden did today? He posed for the photographers at the cemetery. And answered questions for reporters. Practically shoved Ann's parents out of the way. She told me once how he dominated her mother and father, but I never believed it was as gross as that.'

'I would have thought by now he would have run out of complaints about the way the investigation is going.' Cowley paused. Cynically he added: 'But then maybe I wouldn't.'

'The *Washington Post* said you'd been sent specially to Moscow.'

'Yes.'

'Other times you're based here?'

Cowley just stopped short of saying his regular apartment was practically within walking distance. 'Yes.'

'When you get back — when it's all over — why not call me sometime?'

'Sure,' agreed Cowley, with no intention of doing so.

He watched Burden's cemetery media event on Live at Five, back at the hotel. The Senator said he intended to give the FBI the courtesy of a reply to his belief in a cover-up, before initiating a public debate in the Senate. A beautiful, innocent girl shouldn't be used like a shuttlecock in some God-knows-what international diplomatic mess: it was too bad if Russia had something to hide.

Cowley sat shaking his head in disgust. It was all performance, he thought: Burden at the interment, Judy Billington after the same ceremony. Who was bothering to grieve for Ann Harris? He guessed her parents were: somebody had to.

The FBI Director saw Burden's telecast, too, on the set in the Secretary of State's office to which he had been summoned yet again.

'It's a direct Presidential order now,' insisted Henry Hartz. 'It's got to be the whole truth, from now on.'

'OK,' said Ross. 'He'll get the truth.'

Paul Hughes was intercepted at immigration at Dulles airport.

282

There were four men: the one who did the talking and produced the correct identification genuinely was from the State Department.

'I didn't expect this sort of treatment!' said Hughes, settling comfortably into the back of the waiting limousine.

'You probably don't expect a lot of the treatment you're going to get,' said one of the CIA men. It wasn't a chance remark: it was important for Hughes to start to sweat right away.

Petr Yezhov didn't walk all the time. There were certain places where there were seats, dark places where he knew people couldn't look at him, where he sat and rested. He stopped that night near the Chekhov House, on Ulitza Sadovaya Kudrinskaya, on a bench beneath a sparse collection of trees, wanting to get things clear in his mind, which was always difficult. His mother didn't believe him. He didn't care unduly about that: she never properly trusted him. He was worried about the men, though. They were official: people who had to be obeyed. People who had to be obeyed could lock him up again. He was very frightened of that happening.

Chapter Twenty-Seven

Leonard Ross was determined everything should work on his terms, although no one was ever to know it. Which was why he personally telephoned Senator Burden's office, politely requested the meeting through John Prescott and assured the personal assistant there would not be the slightest inconvenience in Ross's going to the Dirksen Building. The front entrance was cankered with photographers, reporters and television cameramen when the FBI Director, accompanied only by Fletcher, got there: when their arrival was realized, other journalists hurried to join the main group from side doors through which a less public entry might have been attempted. Ross shouldered his way through the question-yelling throng, insisting he had nothing to say prior to the meeting and nor would he have afterwards; any statement would come from the Senator. The Director and his aide were not finally free from the crush until passing through the door into Burden's suite. Prescott was waiting in the ante-room: Ross guessed the young man's superior smile reflected the attitude further inside. It did.

Burden did not rise from behind his football-pitch-sized desk. Beth Humphries was immediately alongside, although at a separate table: in front of her was a tape recorder, in addition to an already open notebook. James McBride, the media organizer, was on the couch that ran the length of one wall. He did stand. In contrast to Burden's high-backed, padded-armed chair, the seat already placed directly in front of the desk was steel-framed, standard office issue. Ross went unquestioningly to it, smiling back to Prescott. 'We'll need another one.' The seat produced for Fletcher was steel-framed, as well. Ross decided everything was going far better than he could have hoped.

Burden cleared his throat, relaxed back in the enveloping chair, a man contentedly sure of himself. He said: 'I hope at last all this nonsense will end.'

'I hope that too,' said Ross, a man impatient of the charade of

Washington. He saw the woman start the recording machine as he spoke. She also began making written notes. Looking back to the Senator, Ross said: 'I do not think that any member of your staff should be present, during our discussion . . .' He nodded sideways to Fletcher, who by now also had a tape recorder working. '. . . if you agree to that, my assistant will withdraw also.'

'I don't agree!' said Burden at once, addressing posterity rather than the FBI Director. 'I want a full record of this.'

'You're sure about that?'

'Don't patronize me, Mr Director!'

'I don't feel I am the one being patronizing, Senator. I sought to give you a chance.'

'*You* sought to give *me* a chance!'

With the legal pedantry of his background, Ross spoke directly towards the woman and her machine. 'Let the record show that the Senator was offered the opportunity of a discreetly private conversation.'

'What the hell are you talking about?' It was too soon for any real change, but there was just the slightest tightening of the earlier, completely relaxed demeanour.

The FBI Director refused the answer. Instead, jerking his head beyond the window, he said: 'There is a mob of media people out there.'

'We don't control the press,' said Burden, glibly.

Again towards the recording machines, the Director said: 'Let the record show that there was no advanced FBI liaison with any member or outlet of the media. Nor will there be, after this meeting, from either myself or my personal assistant, Nigel Fletcher. We are the only FBI personnel present at this meeting.'

The complacency began to crack. Burden came forward in his chair and said: 'I just asked you what the hell that sort of remark was all about!'

'Making provable records,' said Ross, simply. 'That's why you have a stenographer taking notes, as well as making a complete verbal recording, isn't it?'

'There have been times in the past when I have told . . .' The politician halted, to correct himself. '. . . *asked* you to be careful, Mr Director.'

'Which is what I am being, Senator: what we're both being.

So I'll repeat my earlier suggestion. I think it would be advisable for us to talk alone, neither with staff present.'

Burden's attitude now was the alertness of a jungle animal – a creature of the political jungle – sniffing the wind to detect an intruder into his territory. In a quiet voice – jungle animals don't make sounds that might alarm – Burden said: 'You tell me what you're talking about, sir!'

Once more Ross gestured beyond the window. 'I'm talking about media circuses and self-promotion and possible impediment of a criminal investigation. And of matters of a personal nature.'

It was possible to see Burden's face colour, to reach puce: so long and so rare had it been for anyone publicly to confront the man with such disregard that for several moments Burden had difficulty making the words form. 'I'll destroy you, Ross! You hear me! You're destroyed! Dead!'

The FBI Director sat as easily as he could in his steel-framed chair, not feeling the need to reply. Beth kept her head lowered over her notebook. There was the creak of leather, from where McBride had resumed his seat. There was no sound from behind, to identify Prescott. Burden was leaning positively forward over the football expanse, waiting for a reaction. Still Ross refused to give one. He was actually thinking of the theatre of a courtroom, reflecting how much better he had enjoyed it, even before his elevation to the bench. It was possible to resign the FBI Directorship, he supposed. But not yet: not too soon after this episode. It had always been important to win, when he was an advocate. The attitude hadn't changed.

Forced finally to continue, Burden hissed the words. 'I demand to know the truth, about what happened to my niece. The *whole* truth. In front of witnesses. Now!'

Ross prolonged the response, groping through his briefcase for the papers he wanted and then sorting them. Satisfied at last, reading from Cowley's verbatim recollection of the intercepted telephone conversations, he quoted: ' "I don't mind head. Like it. Greek too. But Christ you hurt me last night. Made my tits bleed, you bastard . . ." '

'. . . What in the name of God?' exploded Burden, starting from his chair.

When Ross looked briefly up, he saw Beth's face was close to being as red as the politician's. 'You demanded to know,' Ross said, selecting a second transcript and starting to quote again. ' "You didn't say you were going to do that, when you tied me up. How would you like it with a dildo up your ass . . ." '

'Stop it!' roared Burden.

'I'd like to,' said Ross, calmly. Exaggerating, he went on: 'Those are your niece's words, Senator. There's a lot more. Positively recorded. There are a lot of letters, talking like that, too . . .' Ross hesitated, looking again at Beth: all Burden's staff would have a very low level of security clearance. So Hughes couldn't be named. Ross resumed: 'She was sexually involved with a member of the American embassy, who we think was either being targeted or has already been suborned by Russian intelligence. At this moment, somewhere here in Washington, he's strapped to a lie detector: before the interrogation is over he's going to tell us everything we want to know. Which will unavoidably include every detail of the sado-masochistic affair he enjoyed with your niece. And which she clearly enjoyed, to a point. At first, we thought he'd killed her. It doesn't seem now that he did . . .'

Ross paused, for breath. Exaggerating again, he said: 'That was why there was the news blackout: to get him back here, into American jurisdiction. Which also protected the reputation of your niece. And let's talk more about her. This man wasn't her first lover, according to what we know. We don't see any point in that becoming public knowledge. It won't, not from the FBI or from any other source. We don't yet know if she was involved with a Russian. She may well have been . . .' Ross had to pause again, his voice becoming strained. 'What cover-up existed was for the benefit of America. And your niece. Any further protests from you will seriously impede the questioning of a member of the American embassy who has been compromised. It will also, inevitably, lead to the disclosure of your niece's involvement. I think to involve your niece in any of this is unnecessary. Misleading, too, because her connection would obviously mean yours, as well . . .'

'Me!' the politician managed at last. 'It's me they're trying to embarrass!'

How easy the man's arrogance was to manipulate, thought Ross. He said: 'And they would succeed, wouldn't they, with any public disclosure?' He half twisted, including the media organizer in the discussion. 'The line seems pretty direct to me. An embassy official compromised by Russian intelligence, involved in an aberrant sexual relationship with a woman known to be extremely close to an uncle who is a potential Presidential candidate. Would you like to face a press conference upon all the implications of that, Senator? Perhaps discuss your niece's sexual inclinations, at the same time?'

The collapse wasn't like the gradual deflation of a balloon, more of an abrupt pop. Burden buried his head in his hands, so that his voice was muffled. 'Oh my God!' he said. 'What am I going to do?'

'That's a matter for you, as it always has been,' said Ross, briskly. 'I have told the press outside – whom I understand you *don't* control – that there will be no statement from the Bureau. Only from you. If you decide to talk further, we would appreciate one of your people advising us. We would consider ourselves no longer restricted, in putting our case as well . . .' He allowed the pause, nodding sideways to Fletcher. 'I understand the President wishes to know the outcome of this meeting. I shall let him have a complete transcript. Is there anything further I can help you with, Senator?'

Burden's colour had swung through the complete spectrum. When he looked up from his cupped hands, he was finally ashen, eyes stretched in genuine horror. He appeared initially unable to reply to Ross's question, merely shaking his head, as a boxer shakes his head to clear a flurried attack. When he finally spoke, it wasn't a reply at all. He said: 'Do you imagine a long career here in Washington, Mr Director?'

'No,' said Ross. 'I've come to dislike the place.'

They had to crest their way through the renewed wave of journalists as they left. This time Ross didn't even bother verbally to refuse a statement, shouldering his way through towards the car. In the limousine returning down the hill, Fletcher said: 'That was absolutely awful, wasn't it?'

'I thought it went very well,' answered Ross.

Cowley broke his direct return to Moscow to stop in New York to meet John Harris. For the first time there was some obvious

288

grief, but not as much as Cowley had expected. The meeting produced even less than that with Judy Billington. Reminded of the girl as the taxi pulled into Kennedy airport, he tore up the piece of paper listing her telephone number and discarded it in the waste bin on his way to the check-in desk.

At the moment Cowley's plane lifted off, five thousand miles away in the direction in which it was heading Dimitri Danilov stretched up from his complete study of the haphazardly made and carelessly recorded interviews with psychiatric patients, past and present, whose history showed any of the tendencies for which they were looking. He should have been angry at the inefficiency, he supposed: it would have even been possible to censure the officers, because their names were on the reports. But he was too tired. And there was no point – and certainly no benefit – in getting angry at the deficiencies of the Moscow Militia.

He'd isolated four cases he immediately considered to be the most obvious for re-examination.

One involved a man named Petr Yakovlevich Yezhov.

Chapter Twenty-Eight

Again Barry Andrews was waiting at Sheremet'yevo airport for Cowley's arrival. This time there was no uncertain hesitancy between them. As Andrews took the embassy car out on to the rutted highway, he said: 'How did it go?'

'Could have been better,' said Cowley. Any different answer would have been a lie obvious to the other man.

'You didn't get hauled off the case. So what happened?'

Cowley recounted the concern about Hughes and what was going to happen to the diplomat, considering it the only positive development, although contributing nothing towards finding their killer. He sanitized the critical interview at the CIA complex, not wanting to admit the complaints to the other man. Throughout the account Andrews drove gazing directly ahead, just occasionally shaking his head. When Cowley stopped, the local FBI man said: 'Jesus! The guy's been a jerk and you've got to despise him, I guess, but I still can't stop feeling sorry for the poor bastard. Can you imagine what he's going to go through?'

'It'll be hell,' agreed Cowley. He was surprised at Andrews's sympathy. It wasn't an attitude the other man had shown in cases in the past. He wondered whom Andrews was going to find for his racquet ball games in the embassy gym. He'd have to find someone: Andrews was as dedicated to physical fitness as he was to every other activity. In London, it had been jogging.

As if aware of Cowley's reflection, Andrews said: 'He thought everything was OK. We had a drink together in the club, the night before he flew out. He said to go on keeping Tuesdays free for when he got back.' There was disbelief in Andrews's voice. 'Who's going to tell Angela?'

The lights of the city began to form, far away to their right. Cowley said: 'Not our problem. Personnel, I guess.'

Andrews looked quickly across the car. 'It could be my problem, couldn't it? We're talking phone taps somehow getting into the embassy. I could be criticized there.'

290

'How could you have prevented it?' asked Cowley. 'The embassy is electronically swept. The failure's technical, not yours.'

'Hughes was told he was being withdrawn for consultation,' said Andrews, unconvinced. 'That's what I've been told.' He came off Tverskaya, on to the ring road towards the embassy.

'And that's what you're going for,' assured Cowley. 'I spoke with the Director, about your relocation.'

Andrews stopped the car outside the new compound but didn't move to get out. 'You talked with the Director, about *me*?'

'Not the way it sounded,' qualified Cowley. 'He wants you to go back, for talks, but wondered if it might be awkward with all that is going on here. I said no.'

Andrews smiled, briefly. 'That was good of you.'

'You didn't think I'd hold you back, did you?'

'You could have done. And for proper professional reasons, nothing else,' said Andrews, leading the way into the living quarters. 'I appreciate it, Bill. Really.'

The guest suite smelled stale and musty but it was too cold to open any windows. 'Any contact from Danilov?'

'I told him you were coming back tonight. He's expecting you tomorrow.' Andrews paused. 'Anything else from Washington?'

'The interview with the girlfriend, Judy Billington, didn't produce anything. Neither did her brother. But I got the psychological profile.'

'What's our maniac serial killer look like?' Andrews went familiarly to the drinks cabinet. He poured himself a Scotch without asking if Cowley wanted anything.

'Like about a million other guys. Neat. Tidy. Knows he's doing wrong. Maybe making a challenge out of it. But there's a big question mark. If we assume – as we've got to assume now – that our man is Russian then none of it could be any sort of guide.' Cowley smiled, in resignation. 'So we get the usual caveat: routine investigation first, profile as an aid, nothing more.'

'I've done the course, heard the Quantico lectures,' said Andrews. 'Wouldn't it be the damnedest thing if Hughes turned out on the polygraph to be the killer after all?'

'Wouldn't it, though?' agreed Cowley. And be a further setback for him, having cleared the man. Pointedly he moved his case

291

further into the small apartment, towards the bedroom. Andrews remained propped against the drinks cabinet, missing the hint.

'What about the profile? Fit Hughes?'

Cowley tried to assemble a mental comparison. 'Could do,' he conceded. He wished it didn't.

Abruptly Andrews changed the subject. 'Pauline says hello.'

'She's OK?'

'Fine,' assured the other man. 'We've got an invitation for you, for a get-together at the club. I put you down for it, to come with Pauline and me. Now I'll be back home.'

Cowley shrugged. 'Can't be helped.'

'Hey!' said Andrews, the idea suddenly coming to him. 'It needn't make any difference to you and her. Why don't you go together?'

Cowley frowned. 'I'm not sure that would be a good idea.'

'Why not? We're all friends, aren't we? Proper friends. So it would be silly not to go. You'd both miss something that might be fun, for no good reason.'

'I don't know.' How would it be, to be by himself with Pauline?

'Why don't I talk to Pauline about it? See how she feels?'

'If you like.' There was no good reason why he shouldn't take her, Cowley supposed. He knew already that he'd enjoy it. And there wasn't any difficulty between himself and Andrews. It was the man's suggestion that he should take her. It would even be creating a difficult situation that didn't exist to refuse.

Andrews finished his drink, pushing himself away from the cabinet at last. He smiled and said: 'Let's face it, old buddy, now everything's gone cold you could be here a long time. It might be an idea to get around a bit more among people at the embassy.'

Ryurik Bocharov was a profoundly ugly man, just slightly too tall medically to be described as a dwarf, his domed head completely bald, his efforts to express himself jumbled and confused, so that few could understand. There was a history of violence to women, usually towards prostitutes who refused his custom. After rendering them unconscious he cut off their hair: he always told psychiatrists he wanted to make them as ugly as he was. He never, however, collected buttons. Neither did he show any interest in their shoes. Since his last release from custodial care, he had worked as a porter in an open market near Kujbyseva Ploschard. He was a bachelor, living in utter squalor among a group of other derelicts in one of the occasionally used outbuildings attached to the GUM warehouse, on the side bordering Sapúnova Prospekt.

It took Danilov twenty-four hours even to locate the man, and very quickly he wished he hadn't, because from the very beginning he doubted that Bocharov knew anything about the crime and the engulfing smell was far worse than Novikov's dissecting room, without the minimal benefit of any disinfectant. Bocharov showed the head-turning, frozen-lipped reticence Danilov recognized from institutionalized people, denying everything but able to account for nothing. The man's innocence was obvious, however, within minutes: he was left-handed.

Danilov returned distractedly angry to Kirovskaya, the whole day unnecessarily wasted. Each psychiatric team had been specifically instructed that the killer was right-handed. So there was no excuse for the team that had checked the man to have missed the one fact that made it impossible for Bocharov to have been the killer. Unless Bocharov hadn't been interviewed at all. Which was what Danilov suspected.

Olga was surprised to see him so early in the evening and said so.

Still distracted, Danilov said: 'An inquiry ended earlier than I expected.' It would, in fact, have been an ideal opportunity to visit Larissa: he should contact her tomorrow.

'I haven't prepared any food. I didn't expect you.'

Danilov poured himself a Stolichnaya, neat. He didn't ask about ice, not trusting the small freezer compartment of the refrigerator. He'd forgotten to put any ice-cube trays on the outside balcony, where they would have frozen naturally. 'I'm not hungry. Is the washing machine fixed?'

'It goes, but slowly. Nothing looks clean.'

'But you've managed to wash something?'

'Not yet. There didn't seem any point if it was going to come out dirty.'

Danilov extended his glass. 'Do you want something?'

'To talk. I'm glad you're home. I want to talk.'

Danilov carried his drink to his lumpy chair, unsure how the packing in the seat and back had become so ridged. The television squatted before him, in baleful mockery: like Bocharov had stood before him, that afternoon, Danilov thought. It was fortunate Cowley hadn't been with him, to have realized the inefficiency. He wondered what the American would bring back from Washington. Trying to anticipate what Olga was going to say, he loosened a few notches on his integrity and said: 'I suppose we have to think about a new television. And a washing machine.'

'What's wrong with us?' Olga demanded.

Danilov's surprise was genuine. 'What?'

'You've got someone else, haven't you? Having an affair.'

'Don't be ridiculous.'

'Don't *you* be ridiculous. For all your interest I might as well not exist. When was the last time we made love? You can't think that far back, can you?'

Danilov hadn't been able to remember that night coming back from the uncomfortable evening with the Kosovs, either. Trying a practised retreat, he said: 'Maybe I've been neglecting you. I'm sorry. But you know the sort of case I'm involved in. The pressures. That's all it is.'

'You didn't give a damn long before this case. Is it Larissa? I think it could be Larissa.'

'Of course it's not Larissa. There's no one. I told you that.' Illogically — or maybe not illogically at all — he wondered if this was how guilty people felt under interrogation in some dank interview room. Feeling the need to say more, he added: 'Larissa Kosov is a friend. Of us both. I am not her lover.' He was immediately unsure if he should have gone on.

'I don't believe you.'

Danilov extended his hands, the gesture spoiled because he was holding the vodka glass in one of them. 'I can't say any more than I have. That you're imagining everything.' Wanting to move, to do something to deflect the attack, Danilov got up and walked towards the kitchen annex to top up a glass that didn't need refilling. The alcohol burned when he drank it, still in the kitchen.

'If you want a divorce you can have it. We'll have to go through the counselling procedure, but that only takes a month or two. Then it'll all be over.' The declaration had obviously been rehearsed: towards the end Olga's voice had begun to waver, denying the bravery.

294

'I don't want to divorce. Please stop this! It's all nonsense!' Didn't he want a divorce? He didn't know: hadn't thought about it. He didn't think he wanted to marry Larissa.

'I know Larissa is prettier than me. Looks after herself better. Probably better in bed. Is she, Dimitri Ivanovich? Is she better than me in bed?'

Yes, thought Danilov: a hundred times better. He said: 'I won't talk like this. About our friend like this: *our* friend. *I am not having an affair!*'

'I don't want to go on like we are now. You've created a situation. You've got to make a choice.'

Danilov wished he knew what he wanted to do. 'You're wrong. So there's nothing to talk about.' The denials were beginning to sound empty even to himself.

Olga shook her head, a sad gesture. 'Make up your mind, Dimitri Ivanovich. Soon.'

Both feigned sleep quickly that night, but neither did, each knowing the other was pretending. Danilov knew Olga expected him to make love to her. It was better not to try at all than to make the effort knowing that he would fail.

Chapter Twenty-Nine

Cowley gave in his eagerness to receive, initially holding back
only about Paul Hughes. For the evidence collection he was so
anxious to get to along the corridor he handed over the critical
American autopsy report as well as the Quantico psychological
profile'— which Danilov received quizzically — and dismissed the
meetings with Judy Billington and John Harris as fruitless. In
return Danilov, relieved, said hair samples *had* been retained from
Vladimir Suzlev, so the FBI request could be met. Lydia Orlenko,
who'd given more details about the attack, was naturally upset
about her hair but would probably agree to losing a little more:
Pavin could get it. At that moment the Major was interviewing
a psychiatric patient whose case history recorded a shoe fetish:
he'd personally interviewed one whom he'd eliminated because
the man had been left-handed.

Reminded about fetishes, Cowley said: 'The psychologist who
prepared the profile says buttons indicate a nipple complex.'

'Which Hughes appears to have,' Danilov pointed out. Could
Pavin locate a larger chair to make the American more comfortable? There would be little point in bothering if the Cheka took
over, because Cowley wouldn't be coming here any more. Would
the man be allowed at Dzerzhinsky Square? It was an additional
complication that didn't seem to have occurred to anyone.

Cowley hesitated, uncertain how much he should disclose.

'Hughes has been withdrawn. He won't be coming back.'

Danilov nodded, slowly. 'Withdrawn to be questioned further?'

The obvious anticipation of a trained detective or of a planted
intelligence officer, wondered Cowley, remembering the doubt
about Danilov at the CIA meeting. He could be wrong — he'd
been too often wrong already on this case — but he found it
difficult to think of the Russian as anything but a policeman.
'He'll be questioned further.'

'Will we be told the result?' asked Danilov.

Cowley guessed the other man was still suspicious, despite their cooperation agreement just before his return to Washington. 'I would expect to hear, if anything relevant emerges.'

The recall was obvious, Danilov supposed. And at once concentrated the thought. And *would* have been obvious to Gugin from the beginning, just as it would have been obvious when the man had made the telephone transcripts available that the Americans would instantly recognize the source and act upon it. So Gugin had planned – *wanted* – it to happen. One realization led logically to another, bringing a burn of anger: he'd played the performing monkey to the intelligence agency's organ-grinder. The anger deepened at the thought that it should have occurred to him earlier. 'And you'll tell me, if you hear?'

He had to make a decision, thought Cowley: they *would* go round in circles, chasing their own tails and getting nowhere, unless they started operating as a team rather than competitors. He said: 'At our last meeting I gave you an undertaking. I mean to stick to it.'

Danilov smiled at the reassurance, which he hadn't sought. 'I intend to do the same. After what's already occurred, I don't think either of us can afford to do anything else.'

Cowley was unsure whether he should continue the honesty by openly making the request. He'd gone a long way to creating the initial difficulty by covertly making the fingerprint comparison, he reflected. 'I would like my own copy of the telephone transcript.'

Danilov didn't respond for several moments. Gugin would have probably expected this demand, too. So to agree would mean his continuing to be the organ-grinder's monkey. To refuse would endanger the fragile working relationship still not provably established with the American. Practicality was more important than pride, he decided, easily: being manipulated by Gugin was a side issue, little more than an irritating distraction. He tapped the documentation that Cowley had delivered and said: 'Why don't I read this, while you're getting whatever you want?'

The sequence was as Cowley had described at Langley, the conversations seeming to be *from* Ann Harris *to* Paul Hughes. But without the actual tapes, it would always be impossible to establish the precise order. Not his concern any more, thought Cowley. He'd obtained what he'd been told to get. And it supported his account: now it was for the CIA to establish whatever they wanted from their own interrogation of Paul Hughes.

Pavin was re-emerging to get the required hair sample from Lydia Orlenko when Cowley returned to Danilov's office. The American stood back to allow the Major to leave. Beyond him, from his jumbled desk, Danilov nodded after his departing assistant and said: 'Another blank. The man he went to interview had been re-admitted to hospital by the date of Ann Harris's murder.' The fact that the re-admission had not been recorded on the first report was yet again clear proof that the original street team had not bothered to visit this man, either. Danilov added: 'Pavin tried to see another one on the list but there was no one at the flat.'

'There was a Tuesday during the time I was away,' reminded Cowley.

'There was nothing,' said Danilov. 'So now it looks as if the day has no significance, either.'

The second interview Pavin had attempted had been at the Bronnaja Boulevard apartment of Petr Yezhov. He had not been at home, but his mother was. She'd seen the obviously official car stop in the forecourt below and tensed for the knock, which came within minutes. She'd hunched in a chair, motionless against any betraying sound – even breathing lightly – until the knocking stopped and she heard the footsteps retreat. She was sure Petr was lying, denying he'd done anything wrong: was absolutely convinced of it.

In the old days they'd operated a schedule convenient to them both, Danilov always getting there around six in the evening on his way home, a time when Eduard Agayans had fixed the arrivals and departures of the lorries he wanted unhindered the following day. Danilov observed it that night, wanting to be sure the Armenian would be at the Leninskii block. He'd already formulated an excuse for the visit and on his way evolved another even more childlike rubric. If Agayans was there, he was meant to have a meeting: if the office was empty, he wasn't meant to re-establish contact with the man and wouldn't try again.

Agayans was there.

But there was a long delay in the door being opened. Danilov waited, patiently, knowing he would be under self-preserving scrutiny from various vantage points. Agayans eventually unbolted the door himself, gazing through the narrow gap he allowed with frowning, almost disbelieving curiosity. The smile came with the final recognition, but the former back-slapping, hugging exuberance wasn't there. Instead the Armenian nodded, in some private reassurance to himself, and said: 'Hello, old friend. Welcome back. I hope I'm glad to see you.'

The door was briefly opened wide enough for Danilov to enter, just as quickly closed and bolted again. Danilov was at once aware of the change. Previously the offices, glassed squares around the vast warehouse expanse, had been a beehive of activity, the warehouse floor swarming with people loading and unloading regiments of lorries. Now more than half the offices appeared deserted − Danilov could only count a total of six people in all of them − and there were only two lorries down below. Neither was being worked upon. The place had an abandoned, slowly dying air.

Unspeaking, Danilov followed the wiry, black-haired man to his personal den: after the slightest hesitation, Agayans took the brandy bottle from a desk drawer, half filled two tumblers and offered one across the desk. Danilov accepted, waiting for the familiar toast. Tonight there wasn't one.

The invented reason for Danilov's visit had been to inquire about mystery wanderers Agayans's drivers might have seen on their nightly journeys around Moscow, but Danilov abandoned the pretence at once. Instead he said, simply: 'What's happened, Eduard?'

'There have been a lot of changes,' said the black marketeer.

'I don't need to be told that. Why? How?'

'I know you are not involved,' said the Armenian, obscurely. 'You didn't know: *don't* know.'

'Tell me!' said Danilov, impatiently.

'I don't have Militia friends any more. My lorries get stopped. The contents stolen. My customers have to look elsewhere. I am being squeezed dry.'

'But I introduced you . . . made sure . . .'

'Introduced me,' agreed Agayans. 'You couldn't make sure. For a time it was as it always had been. Then the hijacking started: the stealing of entire consignments by the organized syndicates.

I protested to Kosov, of course: asked for the protection that was understood always between us. He told me not to worry: that he would see to it. His visits became less frequent. He didn't seem to want anything. The lorry interception got worse. I asked him again but Kosov said there was nothing he could do. Now he doesn't come at all.'

'Which syndicate?' asked Danilov, already guessing the answer.

'The Dolgoprudnaya. They're very organized. A brigade. Six months ago they not only stole my lorries, they broke the arms of both drivers and both mates. People are frightened to work for me now.' Agayans leaned across the desk, adding more brandy to Danilov's glass. 'I need help, Dimitri Ivanovich. I want things to be like they were before. I wanted to come to you, but I didn't want to inconvenience you at your new place.'

Danilov nodded his thanks for the discretion. 'What about others like yourself?'

'The same,' confirmed Agayans.

A mess in which he did not want to become involved, decided Danilov, at once. He'd come, finally, intending merely to re-establish contact and benefit in a way he believed would still retain his integrity, offering to buy at a price the man would fix what he'd known Agayans would have for sale: barely illegal, according to Russian standards. This was an entirely new dimension: territory upon which he couldn't intrude. Kosov controlled the Militia district now. He had no power here any longer: no excuse for interceding. So what was he going to do? What reason could he even give for his presence there, that evening? Where was his escape? Lamely, regretting the words as he uttered them and swerving as he spoke, Danilov said: 'I'm sorry. I wish . . . I had no way of knowing . . .'

Agayans appeared to miss the mid-sentence change of direction. 'So I am glad to see you. I know you'll help.'

Danilov guessed the other man would spot an obvious lie with the quickness of the entrepreneur he was. Slowly Danilov said: 'You know I am not in this district any more. My influence is limited: hardly any at all. I can speak to Kosov: *will* speak to him. But there can't be any promises.' It was the best he could do: all that he could do.

Agayans regarded him sombrely across the desk. 'I see.'

'Kosov is a friend,' exaggerated Danilov, hopefully. 'He will listen.'

'He's owned by the Dolgoprudnaya,' stated Agayans, simply. 'He'll listen to them first.'

'Let me speak with him.'

The Armenian lifted and dropped his shoulders, in resigned defeat. 'You didn't know about my troubles, before this evening. So why did you come again, Dimitri Ivanovich?'

Danilov shook his head, positively. 'It doesn't matter, not any more.' Objectively he doubted that a new washing machine and access again to clothes she couldn't buy in the shops would have helped his problems with Olga anyway. He was going to have to resolve the situation with his wife and Larissa soon. He wished he knew how.

Russian intelligence control every airport, so Colonel Kir Gugin knew within an hour about Angela Hughes's departure for Washington forty-eight hours after her husband's recall, aware even that it was Ralph Baxter who accompanied the solemn-faced woman to Sheremet'yevo. The following day, the exit of Pamela Donnelly, the other woman with whom Hughes had been involved, was recorded with equal efficiency.

Gugin decided the entire operation had gone perfectly. The Americans would be in turmoil. Should he leave it there? Or sow more seeds? There was no urgency.

Barry Andrews arrived outside the FBI building half an hour before the scheduled appointment, so he killed time in the nearest coffee-shop, which ironically was at the Marriott Hotel in which Cowley had stayed, a few days earlier. A proper hotel, he recognized, angrily: not like the shit-hole into which he'd been booked across the river, at Pentagon City. Wrong to show the annoyance, though: have to calm down before the interview. It didn't matter where he was staying: only there for a couple of days.

It was still early when Andrews presented himself in the reception area of the Bureau headquarters. The clerk said Personnel were expecting him.

Chapter Thirty

Nadia Revin enjoyed what she did and did it well. But entirely on her own terms, only accepting clients whom she approved in advance, after meeting or at least seeing them. She did not actually consider herself a whore. Whores didn't choose. She did. It elevated her from the level of the streets. She had never ever taken a person physically ugly or misshapen. Or fat: fatness was ugly. And most certainly never a drunk. They always had to be Western, of course, preferably American because of the payment in dollars. Englishmen often carried dollars, too, which made them acceptable. French she found mean. And Italians too effusive: during lovemaking several had actually tried to kiss her, which she'd found repugnant.

Nadia was beautiful and knew it, although not conceitedly: how she looked and how she dressed, always in black-market Western clothes, was all part of a profession in which she was an expert and about which she had an ambition she was determined to achieve. She kept her hair blonde and extremely long, well past her shoulders, because men seemed to like it that way and it allowed her to wear several different styles, all of which she knew went well with the deep blackness of her eyes and her high Slavic cheek-bones. She was not big-busted and glad of it, because she thought of big breasts, which usually sagged, as she thought of fatness, although she knew some clients with tit obsessions were disappointed. As someone offended by fatness, Nadia was fastidious about her own weight, consulting scales daily, using her dollars on the uncontrolled open market to buy the vegetables and the fruit her one-meal-a-day diet dictated. Of course she never touched alcohol. Drugs, of every sort and so easily available on the streets of Moscow, were even more unthinkable: heavy, normal smokers were on her list of rejected bed partners. She was long-legged, and that appeared to heighten her almost to six feet, although she was no more than five foot nine inches tall. The impression was largely conveyed by the way she held herself, extremely upright, chin and head high, flat stomach held taut. From Western films and magazines, she knew it was a model's stance: she'd practised for several months, until it was now quite natural and automatic.

She liked sex and knew all its variations. But while always ensuring every client was completely satisfied, she was as careful in its practice as she was about everything else. The dollars ensured Western-manufactured, black-market condoms which were far more sensitive than the thicker Russian product, and Nadia always insisted the men wore them, to protect herself from any sexual infections but particularly against AIDS. For the same reason she refused to engage in oral sex, although she never objected to a client performing cunnilingus upon her: she actually liked it. Occasionally men who described her figure as boyish wanted anal sex, which she allowed but again insisted upon a condom. She would not participate in group sex, even in a gathering as small as herself with two men, because she was aware of the physical dangers of the profession: she believed she could resist one man if a situation became ugly but not two. Neither had she ever participated in pornographic photographs, still or movie.

Nadia's preference – indeed the basis of her ambition – was a career as a selective call-girl. She rarely lingered in the foyers of the Western-currency hotels, like other whores: that would have identified her with them and she wasn't one of them. Instead she waited in the tasteful apartment on Uspenskii Prospekt, near the Hermitage Gardens, waiting for telephone calls from well rewarded receptionists at the Savoy and the Metropole and the Intourist and the Moskva. She only actually went to the places after receiving the telephone message and even then, initially only to meet her prospective client, before deciding whether to accept him.

If she *did* accept it, the encounter continued properly, as such things should. Nadia would never allow a fumbling, groping meeting: the back-against-the-wall couplings were for the street girls, not for her. It either had to be in the clients' hotel rooms or at Uspenskii Prospekt, for which she always had her small BMW available, which had been expensive to buy and was a headache to protect from theft but was a sign of class: whores in Moscow did not possess cars. But she considered even that – your room or my apartment? – to be rushed. Nadia knew elegant, sophisticated call-girls didn't rush. Lonely men enjoyed more than just sex: lonely men far from home wanted *complete* companionship. Nadia liked discreet, unhurried drinks – reciprocal trade for the cooperative hotels, after all – and then equally unhurried dinners in the hard-currency restaurants where the pace of service showed Western understanding, not Russian apathy. She was socially fluent in English and French. She knew the failings of *glasnost* and *perestroika* and could talk intelligently about them, just as she could talk intelligently about important political events in the West. And about Western films and Western books, because she read as well as spoke English and avidly studied the *Wall Street Journal*s and the *Herald Tribune*s she bought from the various hotel outlets: sometimes, from contented clients, she even got the books she'd seen reviewed and described as bestsellers. They looked good on the bookshelves at Uspenskii Prospekt to those men who came home.

She already had four regular clients who made contact whenever they were on business in Moscow, three American, one French. Two of the Americans now brought presents when they came. One lived in New York – he'd shown her photographs of the apartment in Manhattan and the weekend house in Westchester – and had said it would be terrific if she lived there instead of here, where he could only visit three times a year.

Which was what Nadia intended to do – fulfilling her ambition by going to America – although not under his patronage. She'd had no need for male protection in Moscow and definitely intended retaining her independence in Manhattan. Her apartment would be high, with a view across the river, although she wasn't sure which one because she hadn't worked out the difference yet. She'd establish the same system as here, through receptionists and concierges and doormen: she didn't imagine it would be difficult. She'd increase her list of regular clients, men who respected her, felt proud to have her beside them in restaurants. During the day, she'd shop at Bergdorf Goodman and Saks and Bloomingdale's, which she knew were smartly sophisticated from what she'd read.

Nadia had already made her visa application. The man from

New York was due in another six weeks: at the moment she was undecided whether to ask him to sponsor her, which she understood would speed up her getting into America. She didn't want the permanent, wrongly understood burden of him in America and guessed he would be nervous of the permanent, wrongly understood burden of her, imagining she wanted more than just an entry facility. It was something she had six weeks to think about, although she was already a long way towards deciding to ask the man. She had no family and therefore no ties to Moscow. Neither did she have the attitude about Russia that so many others did, as if they were tied to the country by some invisible umbilical cord.

She felt the excited anticipation of someone embarking on a new career. Which was, she supposed, exactly what she would be doing. Very soon now.

On this occasion there was no coffee served by broad-hipped ladies with iron-grey hair, and Ralph Baxter was already attentively with the ambassador, so Cowley guessed it was going to be a meeting of complaint, if not censure.

It was and it began at once. Hubert Richards said: 'I was to be told of everything involving this embassy. You blatantly withheld from me this disgraceful business of Hughes and Miss Harris. And of Miss Donnelly, who has also been withdrawn. Mrs Hughes, too, of course. *And* you brought a member of the Moscow Militia into the embassy without my permission, which should have been sought. The first proper information I received of any of this came *from* the State Department, to me here. Which is preposterous!'

The ambassador had the hots echoed in Cowley's head, from his interview with Judy Billington. Could Ralph Baxter be the other, unnamed diplomat who'd cried when he got too drunk to make love to the dead girl? Cowley supposed he could be censured for bringing Danilov on to the premises, but not for much else. He didn't consider there was anything for which he had to make a grovelling apology. 'The situation was governed by circumstances. The way it happened was unavoidable.'

'Bringing a Russian detective into this embassy was avoidable,' Baxter insisted, joining in the attack. 'There was sufficient time

305

to have fully briefed the ambassador *before* you returned to Washington. It would have then been quite possible to keep up the correct order of things, with us providing rather than receiving the information. It was *all* avoidable.'

In tandem, Richards announced: 'I am protesting to the Bureau. Both direct and through the State Department. Your behaviour was arrogant and disrespectful.'

Momentarily Cowley couldn't remember who else had been described as arrogant, and then recalled it had been Danilov, that first day: it seemed a favourite accusation at the embassy. How seriously would any complaint be taken against him? Everyone in Washington already knew the sequence of events: even that he'd brought a Russian investigator into the embassy. So the repeated news wouldn't come as any startling revelation. 'I don't accept that I was either arrogant or disrespectful. But on the subject of information exchange, I consider I was not fully advised – which I could have been – about the sort of woman Ann Harris was. Now it's no longer relevant: at the time I sought help, it might well have been.' The two other Americans exchanged looks, and once more Cowley wondered if Baxter had been the disastrous one-night stand mocked by Judy Billington.

'I want to know – now and *fully* – of anything else that might affect this embassy,' Richards insisted.

'You will have been warned of the security breach on telephone communication, into the embassy?' questioned Cowley.

Baxter nodded: 'We have already been advised that electronics experts are flying in to conduct a survey throughout the embassy. The entire staff are anyway under permanent instructions to be guarded in what they say on an open phone line.'

Advice that neither Ann Harris nor Paul Hughes had followed, thought Cowley. 'There's obvious concern that Hughes might have been isolated by Russian intelligence, as a blackmail target. The woman, too.'

Richards nodded again, as if he already knew that, as well. 'Nothing else?'

'Nothing,' assured Cowley. He hoped neither man considered this the beginning of a complete information exchange between them. He certainly didn't regard it as such.

'The list of articles taken from Miss Harris's flat refers to correspondence,' said Baxter. 'Does it contain anything that might cause any further possible embarrassment to this embassy?'

Cowley looked steadily at the man. 'Like what?' he said, question for question.

Baxter shrugged. 'I don't know. Anything.'

You wanted information, thought Cowley: so squirm, you bastards. 'I have reason to believe, from the letters and inquiries I made among her friends back in America, that Ann Harris had been involved in sexual liaisons with other men, in addition to Paul Hughes.'

Both men regarded him impassively. It was Baxter who spoke. 'Who?'

'I don't have names,' said Cowley. Pointedly he added: 'Not at the moment. I'm sure I'll find out, by the end of the inquiry.' There, he thought: sweat.

Paul Hughes went through four days of unremitting polygraph interrogation by a rotating team of CIA technicians before the machine gave a blip, indicating an inconsistency. The questioning at that stage did not involve the KGB and blackmail: they were still building up a full historical profile, taking Hughes's movements back to the time when his wife was on home leave and Vladimir Suslev had been killed. Asked specifically if he had been with Pamela Donnelly on January 17, Hughes said he had. And the polygraph needle jumped.

Pamela Donnelly was interviewed the same day, in the more formal and intimidating surroundings of the FBI headquarters in Washington. Pressed repeatedly, the girl said she was sure she and Hughes had been together throughout Angela Hughes's absence. After three hours she admitted there had been two nights when she and Hughes had been apart. She couldn't remember if one of those nights had been January 17: in tears she finally conceded it could have been.

'Hughes could be triggering the machine because he knows the significance of January 17,' one technician pointed out, during a break.

'Or he could be a murderer,' said his more cynical partner.

'The machine doesn't react when he's directly asked if he killed them.'

307

'A polygraph isn't infallible. You know that.'

In his fifth-floor office, Leonard Ross decided against alerting Cowley in Moscow to the apparent inconsistency. There had been too many false starts. He decided, with his legal training, that he needed more and better evidence.

Chapter Thirty-One

Cowley's evening with Pauline at the embassy club was less difficult than he thought it might have been. Richards did not attend but Baxter did, and although not openly affable, the man played host like the trained diplomat he was, constantly introducing Cowley to embassy staff, always close at hand to move him on from group to group. There was steak and ribs and salad with the choice of five dressings. Cans of American beer floated in bins of gradually melting ice, alongside a selection of hard liquor and rows of Californian wine. A juke-box claimed to contain the latest American top ten: the attempts at dancing were awkward and quickly abandoned, despite the efforts of the sing-along marine detachment with their once-a-fortnight permitted excuse to get close to secretaries and female researchers and archive staff. One of the marines won the raffle: the prize was a child-sized white bear that growled when it was bent forward. The marines kept doing it. From what he believed he had learned of Ann Harris, Cowley found it easy to understand why the dead woman boycotted the majority of such occasions.

A lot of people had obvious difficulty restraining themselves from asking about the murders or Paul Hughes or both. Some – usually on their way to drunkenness – were not restrained. Cowley blocked every attempt at prolonged talk about either, repeating that he was forbidden to discuss any ongoing investigation or anything about the financial director. He lied that he did not know the reason for the man's recall. All he allowed was that they were hunting a maniac and that it was a difficult case. He agreed with everyone that Ann Harris had been a wonderful girl. Several times, when the conversation appeared to be getting too persistent, Baxter intervened to suggest that there were other people he had to meet. Cowley didn't encounter anyone, during the social exchanges, who actually said they liked Moscow. Always stated during any conversation about Moscow in particular and Russia in general was the precise length of time — occasionally detailed in days — their tour still had to run.

He thought Pauline looked very good: beautiful, he'd decided, when he'd collected her from the apartment. Her hair appeared less flecked with grey, making him suspect a home tint, and the tiny lines around her eyes weren't there any more. She wore dark blue, with a white blouse edged in a matching colour, which he thought suited her better than red. There was no difficulty, either, in their being together, because except for their arrival they rarely were: Pauline made the initial introductions, before Baxter took over, and then she mingled with her friends, only occasionally joining up with him. He noticed she drank Scotch again. He took root beer. They sat at the same benched table to eat, with about eight other people: Cowley just managed half his T-bone. Pauline only bothered with salad and didn't eat all of that.

Cowley caught her yawning a couple of times around ten o'clock and she agreed to leave the moment he suggested it. It needed another fifteen minutes for Cowley to make his farewells. A lot of people said they'd see him around: Cowley thought they probably would.

She took his arm quite naturally as they circled the embassy block to get to the old, attached compound where she lived: he couldn't remember their walking like that when they had been married. He liked it. Pauline said: 'Pretty grim, eh?'

'People were very nice to me. I enjoyed it.'

'Another revelation about the new William Cowley,' said Pauline, lightly. 'Now the diplomat! It wasn't too bad, I suppose. I think I enjoyed it too.'

They got to the entrance to the compound. Cowley stood back, for her to enter. She held the door open behind her, so he followed. Inside the apartment she said: 'It's not booze, so I guess it's coffee. Pour me a small Scotch, will you?'

Cowley did so, thinking it was all very relaxed and easy: two people who had grown used to each other over a very long time quite comfortable in each other's presence, not needing to give any sort of performance to impress or please. Happily married people. He wished it were still so.

He encountered her at the door of the minuscule kitchen, on his way to get ice. Without any exchange of words they swapped drinks, for her to get her own. He chose an easy chair. She sat on a couch, directly opposite, on the far side of the room. Too far away, he thought. And immediately corrected himself. He shouldn't make any stupid move, to spoil everything. She wasn't his wife any more.

'Much pressure about Ann and Paul?'

'Quite a bit,' he said. 'I got very good at dodging.'

'Me too. People think I'll know all about it.'

'Do you?'

She nodded. 'Barry's told me some. It was pretty common knowledge that Ann moved about a bit, but I didn't know she was quite like she was.' She stopped, then quickly added: 'I didn't say anything to anyone, of course. Barry briefed me not to: it was like listening to you, all over again.'

Cowley nodded, knowing she wasn't lying. Pauline had always been absolutely honest: his deceit when they were married had always been in complete contrast. 'It's thrown up a bad security situation at the embassy.'

'Barry's worried it might reflect upon him: you know what he's like, about anything affecting his career.'

'You looking forward to going back home?'

'I guess.'

Cowley frowned. 'You don't sound sure.'

She shrugged. 'Course I'm sure.' Pauline looked briefly into her glass. 'He's going to ask to stay in the Russian division. That means you have to agree, doesn't it?'

Cowley smiled, although sadly. 'We've already talked about it, he and I. Of course I won't do anything to block him.'

'Some people in your position would, given the opportunity.'

'I could be pissed off with that sort of remark.'

Pauline coloured, slightly. Hurriedly she said: 'I didn't mean . . . I'm sorry . . . that was rude . . .'

'Hey!' said Cowley, surprised at her distress. 'I only said I *could* be. I'm not.'

'I'm glad you and Barry are getting on OK,' she said.

'Just me and Barry?'

'Don't.'

'What did you mean the other night, about being happy?'

'Nothing.'

311

'*Are* you happy?'

'Enough. Maybe . . .'

'Maybe what?'

'I was always sad we couldn't have kids, you and me. Barry refused, always. Some crap about not wanting to bring children into a bad world. I wish he hadn't.'

Cowley got the impression Pauline was staring into her glass to avoid him seeing her emotion. Illogically — cruelly, if it mattered so much to her — he was glad that Andrews and Pauline hadn't had children. It . . . He stopped the thought developing, annoyed at himself.

'I'm sorry, beginning this conversation. I didn't mean to upset you.'

'It's OK.' Pauline took a deep breath and said: 'Did you and Barry sort out the problems of the world the other night? You took long enough.'

'I guess,' said Cowley, accepting the change of subject.

'We've bought a house in Washington. About two years back. At Bethesda. It's out on rental at the moment.'

Back on safe ground, thought Cowley. 'If Barry's application goes through it's not automatic he will get Washington,' warned Cowley. 'There's a bigger counter-intelligence detachment in New York and San Francisco.'

'If Barry *did* get Washington, we'd all be in the same city.'

'Yes.'

'I think I'd like that.'

'Me too,' said Cowley. She was guiding the conversation now, not him.

'As friends. Not for any silly reason.'

'Sure.' He decided not to press what she meant about silly reasons. He'd enjoyed himself — *was* enjoying himself — but imagined the evening would have been more uncertain if Andrews had been with them.

'This isn't difficult, is it?' she demanded, presently. 'Us being together like this, by ourselves?'

'Not difficult at all.' Not true, he thought: always a liar.

Pauline smiled, holding out her glass. Guessing his thoughts as he poured more whisky she said: 'Don't worry. Our roles haven't been reversed.'

312

'I wasn't thinking that,' he said. Another untruth.

'I just feel like it tonight. This will be the last.'

Cowley returned with her drink. 'Have you heard from Barry while he's been in Washington?'

She shook her head. 'Just a message today through the embassy that he's on his way back. Before he left he said he hoped to get some indication if he's going to get your division: even talked about checking out the house in Bethesda, to make sure we could take it over when we got back.' She smiled, shrugging. 'You know Barry: always sure things are going to go the way he wants.'

Had that been the way the man had thought when they were all friends together in London, planning to move in on Pauline? As realistically objective as he could ever try to be – disregarding all the times he conceded the abject failings that had destroyed his marriage – Cowley knew he would never ever be able completely to forgive or exonerate Andrews for what had happened. It wasn't going to be easy – not for him, at least – if they were all in the same town together. 'I'm not sure he'll get a steer that quickly. He may.'

Pauline completed her drink, held the glass up for examination and declared: 'Finished!'

Cowley had only drunk half his coffee. What remained was cold. 'I should be going.'

'Barry says the case is stymied: that there's nothing to work on, now that Paul's been eliminated,' she said.

'There's a few ongoing, routine things. Nothing positive.'

'Barry says it could affect you badly at the Bureau if you don't get an arrest.' Still that disturbing honesty.

'It could.'

'He'll kill again, won't he?'

'Inevitably, unless we get him first.'

Pauline shuddered. 'Sometimes I'm scared.'

From looking after him for so long, nearly thirty years in a few months time, Valentina Yezhov knew how he would agree to be touched and how he wouldn't. He didn't mind his hands being held, the way she'd held them when he was a child, comforting and reassuring him by her presence. She sat directly before him, both of his hands in hers, their knees touching, and said: 'A man

313

came back. Another one. People want to talk to you. I can't help you if I don't know what you've done.'

'Nothing,' insisted Petr Yezhov. 'Nothing wrong.'

'So why do they keep coming? There must be something you're not telling me.'

'Isn't.'

'Look at me, Petr!' his mother insisted. 'I want you to look me fully in the eyes and tell me there's nothing.'

Yezhov's eyes flickered towards hers but couldn't hold.

'Look at me!' she commanded, loudly. 'Look honestly at me!'

This time the look lasted slightly longer before his eyes wavered and dropped. 'Didn't do anything. Don't want them here. Tell them to go away.'

'You don't want to go into one of those places again, do you Petr?'

'No!' said the man, making himself look at her fully at last because of the importance, needing to convince her. 'Won't. Ever.'

'You will, if you've done something you haven't told me about. You'll be locked up for longer this time: much longer.'

'No!' whimpered the man, clutching at his mother's hands until they began to hurt. 'Won't. Haven't done anything.'

The media demands, fuelled by Senator Burden's initial complaints, increased rather than diminished because of what the press regarded as official and suspicious silence. There was open opinion and comment column criticism of an inept and clumsy Moscow statement, released through the Tass news agency, that there were lines of inquiry that at the moment could not be made public, but which it was hoped would lead to a positive development. Newspaper, magazine and television suspicion was greatest in Washington where, in a dramatic reversal, Senator Burden's office announced there would be no further press conferences or public statements about the murder of Ann Harris. Senator Burden had been given private reassurances that everything possible was being done to bring the murderer to justice: any further discussion would be counter-productive.

Chapter Thirty-Two

Barry Andrews ignored the pilot's usual advice about keeping the safety-belt fastened while seated, slipping the buckle aside and smiling up at the china-doll stewardess. With something to celebrate – he was *sure* he had something to celebrate – he ordered champagne. He'd still wanted a more positive indication. There had been no reluctance by the Personnel panel disclosing his promotion to G-13 grade. Or any way to misunderstand their obvious approval of his past record. Outstanding, the chairman of the board had said: which he'd already known it to be but which was still good to hear. Cowley was the problem, he decided: the inability – because of the Moscow business – to get the necessary acceptance from the Russian division director. Which was, Andrews accepted, the one uncertainty he couldn't anticipate or do anything to affect.

He took the wine, watching the bubbles rise. So what would Cowley do? Stay strictly professional, judge the appointment on its unquestioned merits and approve it? Or take the heaven-sent opportunity to settle a still tender score and reject it? Andrews's mind stayed with the second possibility, examining it completely. He'd exposed himself badly if there was a rejection. It would be recorded on his unblemished file, without any explanatory note, for every other department head to see if he had to apply elsewhere. Leaving the obvious inference that he had some failing not shown up by the record which made him unacceptable. Not badly exposed, he tried to reassure himself. There was no secret in Pennsylvania Avenue, about the break-up and his remarriage to Pauline. So any rejection by Cowley wouldn't need an explanation. Everyone would understand immediately why it was and if anything the criticism would be directed towards Cowley himself, for allowing personal feelings to affect professional decisions.

There'd never been open anger, not even in London when Pauline had demanded the divorce and they'd confronted him, purple-faced from the previous day's booze, sweating and befuddled by that day's intake, and announced their intention to marry. Instead Cowley had cried, like a child about to lose a toy, his nose running to make his face even wetter. Nor anger later, either, when the man was sober and they were going through the formalities. And certainly, since the Moscow episode had begun, he hadn't detected any deep-rooted feeling against him. There'd been the spat about returning the stuff from Ann's office, but that had been professional irritation, which Andrews could understand: it was the personal stuff he *couldn't* understand. Andrews decided, abruptly, that Cowley was a wimp. Always had been. Just didn't drown it in a booze bottle any more, that's all. He was glad the cloying togetherness of Moscow was ending: he'd done his best – Christ, hadn't he done his best – but it hadn't been easy. Cowley the wimp hadn't suspected, of course: hadn't suspected a thing.

Andrews gestured for his empty glass to be refilled. Cowley wouldn't block him, he decided confidently. He'd think of doing so, obviously: wouldn't be human if he didn't. But in the final analysis he'd be the complete professional he'd always been – even during the drunken period – and make his decision on the merits of the proven record and the recommendation of Personnel.

But what if Cowley didn't do that? What if Cowley was a bastard and allowed himself the pleasure of a refusal?

He *wanted* the Russian division: was determined to get it. What about appealing the decision, if Cowley turned him down? There was a job discrimination tribunal, but there was a catch–22 in using it. Even if you won, you got yourself labelled a troublemaker throughout the Bureau. Which could be a worse, unofficial, stigma than an unexplained official rejection on your file. In this case, though, it would stigmatize Cowley equally badly, for letting personal feelings influence a Bureau decision.

Premature concern, he told himself: nothing could block him, get in his way, not now. Which was why he'd ordered the letting agency to serve notice on the tenants in Bethesda. Get Pauline in there as soon as possible, sorting things out, getting the place right in the way she knew he liked to live. But there was Moscow to pack up. She'd have to do that first. Maybe they'd stay for a while in an hotel, although not the shit-hole in Pentagon City, while she got things ready. He'd go through it all with her, when he got back. Didn't want her to get anything wrong. She did get things wrong, sometimes. It was annoying when she got things wrong. Stupid.

He'd give a farewell party, Andrews decided. Invite everybody to the social club, not just from their own embassy but from others as well, the Brits and the one or two people he'd got to know among the French. Andrews smiled, caught by a thought. It was ironic — even amusing — that one of the guests would be William Cowley, to be left behind in Moscow hunting a killer he was no nearer finding now than when he'd arrived.

His mind back on the man whose decision could settle his future, Andrews concluded that as soon as he got back — tomorrow, definitely — he'd tell Cowley of his official application and directly say he hoped the man would support and accept it. No reason why he shouldn't. Absurd not to say something, in fact: might even offend the man, antagonize him unnecessarily, for him to learn about it from some official memorandum in the diplomatic bag from Washington. It was a positive benefit, not the delaying nuisance he'd first thought it to be, having Cowley *in* Moscow where they could talk about it openly, face to face.

The request to re-fasten seat-belts came with the announcement of the Amsterdam stop-over. Transit passengers could briefly disembark if they wished. Andrews decided to stay aboard: even try to get some sleep if he could. He wanted to be as fresh as possible when he arrived in Moscow. He had a lot to do.

Dimitri Danilov was becoming depressingly convinced that he had missed something among the evidence they had assembled, maybe some unconnected, minuscule piece of information or fact that was either obstructing them or, alternatively, pointing them in the wrong direction, just as they'd already once gone in the wrong direction, although at that moment Danilov would have welcomed any direction to follow, wrong or otherwise.

He accepted, the depression worsening, that the orders he was issuing now were little more than clutching at straws, activity for activity's sake, with little hope of producing anything positive. At last Pavin had discovered the identity of the press conference questioner, which opened a narrow pathway to continue along.

317

Pavin was also instructed to locate the one remaining psychiatric patient whose apartment on Bronnaja Boulevard had always been empty, once to an approach from Danilov himself.

The daily meetings with Lapinsk became scenes of constant argument but without any definite point, the older man clearly passing on ill-tempered pressure from above, irritably anxious for the whole insoluble business to be taken from the Militia.

And Danilov, justifiably but unsoundly, passed the criticism on down. He took over the morning duty conference on the day after Cowley's return – the day of Lapinsk's strongest rebuke – to lecture the ineffective street teams on their failures, itemizing particularly by name the officers who had conducted the provably flawed psychiatric inquiries, declaring and meaning it that he intended attaching his complaints to their work files. Such a challenge would have been unheard of at a Militia district or precinct level. It was positively unprecedented at the echelon of Petrovka, where everyone regarded themselves as above question or censure. The response was predictable and immediate, by the same afternoon. The resistance and sneers towards Danilov went beyond the headquarters building, reaching out into the districts because the Petrovka officers methodically manned telephones to spread stories claiming Danilov's panicked incompetence and impending demotion. Pavin, confident of their relationship, post-poned his visit to Bronnaja Boulevard to tell Danilov he shouldn't have staged the confrontation and most definitely shouldn't have threatened recorded discontent: professionally it would achieve nothing apart from creating an unbridgable gulf between himself and all junior officers. Equal-ranking officers would shun him, regarding him as a disruptive, incomprehensible threat to the established system. Senior officers, even General Lapinsk, would dismiss him as a fool. Danilov recognized every assessment to be true. And he wished he even felt better having made his stand. He didn't.

On several occasions since the encounter at Leninskii Prospekt he'd considered speaking to Kosov about Eduard Agayans, but hadn't. He wanted the intervention to be forceful but appear at the same time a casual, oh-by-the-way approach, not a positive protest. He was reluctant to put himself in a subservient position with the other man, asking as a petitioning intermediary for

Agayans to be allowed to operate as before. He wanted to speak from the level of an equal whose views should be respected and acted upon when he insisted the black marketeer *should* be allowed to resume business. And Danilov accepted that he was not equal: that he had no bargaining power. He decided to wait for the right opportunity, whenever and whatever that might be.

He supposed there would never be a right opportunity with Larissa: perhaps there never had been.

He actually welcomed her obvious reluctance to see him that evening, imagining it might make the encounter he intended easier, until he entered the selected hotel room behind her and realized that it was all part of the familiar play-acting, the aggrieved demi-mondaine demanding to be wooed.

'You never bring me presents!' she pouted at once. 'The other girls I work with get presents. I don't.'

Something else that was true in a day of various truths, conceded Danilov. 'I'm sorry.'

'Do you think your prick's bigger than anybody else's: that it's enough, by itself?'

It had seemed sufficient until now, reflected Danilov. 'I had a difficult situation with Olga the other night.'

'So?' said Larissa, carelessly.

'She accused me of having an affair with you. By name.'

'So?' said the woman, again. 'What did you say?'

'Denied it, of course. Said it was nonsense like I did before when she started talking about you.'

'So why are we talking about it now?' He wasn't behaving as he should, standing there. There should have been more apologies: promises of a gift. She put her hand up, playing with the buttons of the blouse she would soon slowly start to take off.

'I think it's time we started to ease off.'

Larissa stopped fingering the blouse opening. 'What?'

'Maybe call a halt to the whole thing.'

'Call a . . . what the hell are you saying?'

'I think it's time we stopped, Larissa.'

'Stopped! Just like that!' She snapped her fingers.

'Yes.'

For the first time her manner wavered. 'Don't say that. As if it didn't matter. As if it was just a fuck: that it didn't mean

319

anything. It wasn't like that for you, was it? Tell me it wasn't like that.'

'Of course it wasn't!' he said, trying to imbue the feeling into his voice. Falling back on cliché, he said: 'But it isn't as easy as that. There are other people.'

'Who?' she demanded. 'Olga? Yevgennie? That's all. They don't matter. I can divorce Yevgennie: *want* to divorce Yevgennie. You can divorce Olga. We can be *married*! That's what you want, isn't it? What you've always wanted.'

No, thought Danilov. He'd never wanted that. He wasn't sure what remained between himself and Olga, but he'd never really contemplated anything permanent with Larissa. So why had he begun and pursued the affair? Reassurance, he supposed, unable to think of another word and deciding it was the right one in any case: he'd wanted the reassurance that he could still impress a beautiful woman if he tried. Which was pitiful: pitiful and selfish and cruel and despicable. Obscene even. He was ashamed of himself. 'I don't want it.' He had to force himself to say the words. When she flinched, as if she had been physically slapped, he said: 'Not now. Not yet. I have to think . . . to decide.'

'When? How long?' She was pleading now, the confident arrogance all gone.

'I don't know . . . that's why I think we should ease off . . . give ourselves time . . .'

Larissa straightened, regaining control. 'You're a bastard. A complete and utter bastard.'

'Yes,' agreed Danilov, knowing it was true. A day of truths, he thought again.

Chapter Thirty-Three

The book cover was red, with black lettering, and Nadia Revin knew it would stand out, look impressive, among the others on the Uspenskii bookshelves. He'd said it was being made into a film, so she determined to read it before putting it away, trying to visualize from the Hollywood actors and actresses whose names and faces she knew who she imagined would take the parts. It was a game Nadia played a lot in the afternoons and early evenings, waiting for the telephone to ring.

She was glad it had rung that night. It had been the sort of evening Nadia genuinely enjoyed, the way it was going to be all the time when she got to America. He had been an urbanely courteous, considerate, dollar-carrying Englishman who had told her to call him Charles and tried from the moment of the first greeting to please her, before himself. It hadn't been difficult. Nadia considered the Metropole the best and most luxurious in Moscow since its refurbishment: certainly it was the most expensive. The food had been superb and he'd known a lot about wine, showing her how to sniff what he called a nose and swirling the sample taste around the glass for rivulets, which he called legs, to form. She'd listened attentively, considering it to be the sort of thing she needed to know, an addition to everything else she tried to learn to make her more sophisticated.

Like reading the English-language newspapers so assiduously. When he'd started to talk about the book fair she'd been immediately able to pick up the conversation from the recent, memorized reviews, one of which had turned out to be for the novel that now lay beside her on the passenger seat of the BMW and which he'd said his firm had published. It had been a fulsome review and he'd been clearly and obviously impressed, as she already was by then, with him.

They'd stayed at the hotel, with no suggestion of her apartment, and that had been right, too, because he'd had a suite which merged perfectly into the relaxed indulgence of the evening. Not that he'd wanted to indulge himself with anything unusual or special, apart from asking her to undress very slowly while he watched, which she did not consider unusual at all. In bed he had remained considerate, wanted her to achieve her orgasm as well as himself, the foreplay leisurely and gentle until she urged him to be faster, harder. And she had achieved it, although it meant briefly losing control, which she didn't ever like to do. She guessed her doing so had made it better for him.

He'd given her $20 more than she'd stipulated, saying it was for a present other than the book, and asked, politely, if he could see her the following night. Nadia had agreed, of course. They'd talked of eating somewhere else – she'd suggested the Atrium or the Stoleshniki Café – and she'd thought they'd probably come back to Uspenskii afterwards. She might even suggest it: certainly prepare some champagne in the refrigerator.

They'd also talked about his having her telephone number, so he could contact her during subsequent visits. She'd readily given it to him, because it was business and regular clients were good business, but Nadia doubted she would be in Moscow for Charles's next trip. The warning card, their established way of early contact, had arrived that morning from the regular client from New York, saying he was arriving three weeks earlier than expected, and Nadia had definitely decided to ask him to sponsor her American entry. She was sure she could phrase it in a way that wouldn't alarm him into thinking she expected any more than help with her admission. No hassle, she thought, remembering the word. He wouldn't be frightened. Hadn't he said, a lot of times, how wonderful it would be if she were set up in Manhattan? Nadia's mind ran on, building plan upon plan. The new man, Charles, had spoken of visiting New York several times a year. He could see her there, just as easily – maybe more so – as in Moscow. It was all going to work so well, she knew: so very, very well.

Nadia took the car around by the dark gardens, black trees starkly naked against the brief snatch of skyline. There were no people on the bordering roads, not this late. She turned into Uspenskii but went by her apartment, turning left to go beside the block to get to the back. A car as precious as the BMW had to be protected, so it couldn't be openly parked in the street. The shed on the rear allotments had originally been built for gardening equipment but made a quite satisfactory garage: the cost of renting it was an additional but necessary expense.

She left the engine running while she released the lock, by the illumination of the headlights. The fit was tight, but she was well practised at manoeuvring the vehicle inside. There was instant, thick blackness when she turned off the lights. She picked up the book beside her by feel.

Even relaxed, as she was now, Nadia was more alert to everything around her than any of the other women had been. Prostitutes – even those who called themselves by other titles and didn't work the streets – developed permanent antennae to potential physical danger. She sensed the presence and began to turn before the hand came over her face and the arm locked around her body, so the attack was not completely from behind. She didn't freeze with terror like the others, either, but instantly tried to struggle, although the grip was strong, almost numbing, so it was impossible properly to fight against. She kept struggling, frenzied when the knife started to go in, snatching backwards for his crotch, the instinctive defence. Her arm and hand twitched and stopped, before it reached him.

There was a lot of hair, more than he'd ever had. A lot of buttons, too. He hummed as he took his souvenirs. Got it right this time. No more mistakes. Perfect.

Because the shed was up a track, off even a paved alley, it was not until the following morning, when it was quite light, that the body of Nadia Revin was discovered, defiled and ugly, like all the others.

Danilov collected Cowley from the embassy compound, as before, and as before there was little conversation on the way to Uspenskii. Viktor Novikov was still conducting his scene-of-the-crime examination when they arrived and became nervous under the blank stare of the critical American. At Cowley's request, the forensic team collected to be shipped back to Washington duplicate samples of everything they considered relevant. The mournful-faced Pavin, who had arrived ahead of them to supervise the evidence assembly, said there was nothing of any immediate significance, not even footprints on the soft, sometimes muddy allotment ground underfoot: at the time that Nadia Revin had been stabbed, the ground would have been frozen hard. One curious discovery had been an English-language book beneath the body. Her handbag had contained make-up, most of it Western-made, book matches from the Metropole Hotel, $150 in cash, a packet of Western contraceptives from which two condoms were missing, and a dildo. There was also an address book, listing the owner's name as Nadia Revin and an apartment in the block beneath which they were standing. A possible key to that apartment was on the same ring holding the ignition and other keys to the BMW.

It fitted, when the three of them got to the seventh floor, in advance of the forensic teams which had been left with instructions to follow. Pavin trailed the two senior detectives throughout their examination, evidence sachets ready.

Despite Nadia Revin's hopes and pretensions, the apartment was a whore's home. The main room had heavy, red-flocked wallpaper. There was no bright, overhead light but the Tiffany shades over the sidelights were red-glassed, too. There was too much overstuffed furniture crowded in, making the place seem smaller than it was. The prints on the wall were art nouveau, chiffon wisped over female nakedness, but no other decorations, certainly not any personal photographs. There was another address book in a bureau: a number of pages listed only given names against hotels and their numbers. The cupboard beneath held an extensive range of liquor.

The intimate red colouring was continued in the bedroom, where a great effort had been made to heighten the mood of opulent sensuousness. The bed had a pole-supported canopy, into which was set a large mirror to reflect the activity below. There was a selection of bound books of pornography as well as some loose, isolated prints held in folders, in a bedside cupboard. None featured Nadia Revin. There was a comprehensive selection showing cunnilingus and fellatio, some groups homosexual, but none portraying bondage or masochistic deviancy. In a drawer above the cupboard were two dildos, several packets of Western contraceptives, oil, and contraceptive and lubricating creams. The wall prints here were of erotic Greek and Roman brothel bas-reliefs, huge-penised men and suppliant, eager women.

There were two clothes closets, one given over entirely to diaphanous silk or gauzed négligés and night-wear: in a pull-out drawer within the closet was a range of sexual underwear, pants without crotches, bras without tips, for nipples to protrude, and lacy garter belts and suspender belts.

It was behind the drawer, which he fully withdrew to take it free of the closet, that Danilov found the hide-away place, a hollowed rectangular space concealed behind a sliding panel that looked at first like the rigid back to the closet. Inside was Nadia Revin's birth certificate, passport, $22,000 in cash and a manila envelope containing documents. Danilov briefly flicked through the papers before offering them to Cowley.

'She wanted to go to America,' said the Russian, simply.

'And Ralph Baxter signed the acknowledging letter to her visa application,' said Cowley, reading more thoroughly.

Chapter Thirty-Four

Everything fitted – the shorn hair, the positioning of the shoes, the severed buttons – yet once more there was no way for them to go forward from the already established pattern. The routine began again, a roundabout making another circle, ending where it began.

Novikov's early and more careful autopsy report gave the same measurements for the weapon, with the exception of the entry wound. The cut here, by what would have been the sharp edge of the knife, was wider than on any of the other victims, nearly six millimetres. The likeliest explanation was that the woman had tried to turn towards her attacker, driving the knife against her own body to cause herself a greater injury. All her perfectly manicured nails were intact, with no evidence of her having fought. There was no vaginal deposit indicating recent sexual intercourse, despite her profession, but this was consistent with the condoms found in her handbag. Novikov insisted that, following the second American post-mortem on Ann Harris and the Quantico assessment that the buttons indicated a nipple fetish, he had closely examined Nadia Revin's breasts for injury or abrasions. There had been none.

The English publisher, Charles McCleary, was traced by noon of that first day. The reservation at the Metropole was in the name of the company which had published the book found beneath the body. McCleary, a bachelor, admitted at once and quite openly being Nadia's client the previous evening: they had arranged to meet that night, too. He'd paid her $100, with a $20 tip, and given her the book. It had been a pleasant evening. She had shown no indication of being worried or frightened. She had not talked of a quick-tempered minder or a ponce, or of any outside pressure. Four members of the hotel staff, including the night receptionist and the night security guard, confirmed that McCleary had not left the hotel, either with or without Nadia Revin.

The single names listed against hotel telephone numbers proved to be those of receptionists, counter staff and concierges who had acted as Nadia's touts. On the off-chance of finding a connection, however tenuous, Danilov had Vladimir Suzlev's taxi company checked again to see if Nadia Revin had been a regular customer or whether any of their drivers also acted as customer spotters. The company denied all knowledge of the woman and showed unconvincing indignation at the suggestion that their drivers would ponce for a prostitute.

At the Militia commander's invitation Cowley went with Danilov to a delayed morning conference with General Lapinsk, at Ulitza Petrovka. The American expected the demand to be made for Danilov to accompany him for a meeting with Ralph Baxter, in return for the concession apparently being advanced to him, but it wasn't suggested. Danilov recited the preliminary findings to the muted background of Lapinsk's coughing, and when the investigator finished Lapinsk said: 'So it's another random killing, like the others? No obvious, logical way to go?'

'That's how it looks,' agreed Danilov, unhappily.

'We're going to have to make a statement,' said the General.

He spoke looking at the American, and Danilov realized that Cowley had been invited to the meeting to share the responsibility for any decisions reached there. For several moments Cowley did not respond, surprised at being questioned so directly. Then he said: 'I think the more sensational reaction to the earlier killings was increased by delaying the first announcements. For which, as I know you are already aware, we in America were grateful.' There was a lot of purpose in his being allowed into this discussion: Cowley wished he could work out all of what it was. Yet again plenty to discuss with Washington: he was glad Andrews had returned, to ship back all the duplicated material collected from Uspenskii Prospekt. Senator Burden was not going to welcome his niece now being linked to the killing of a Russian hooker.

'I would expect you to participate in any press conference,' warned the old man, openly, still speaking directly to Cowley. 'Do you need to get authority from Washington?'

Cowley wasn't sure. 'I'll ask.'

'And I think it would be proper for the statement to be issued jointly, both here and in Washington,' Lapinsk continued, tightening the pressure.

Danilov wondered if all this had been Lapinsk's idea, on the spur of the moment, or demands prepared well in advance of another possible killing with the Federal Prosecutor or possibly even beyond Nikolai Smolin, involving some even higher official in the Foreign or Interior Ministry. He was surprised at the blatant anxiety to extend the liability.

So was Cowley. 'A Washington statement about the murder of a Russian national in Russia?'

'It is a joint investigation,' Lapinsk insisted. The cough rattled.

Cowley was unsure whether to remind the General that the FBI's supposed presence was in a support role of scientific liaison. He quickly decided not to: in his eagerness to duck behind every and any barricade, Lapinsk had conceded precisely what the Bureau had wanted to achieve. Which might be an advantage later. 'I will advise Washington. They will obviously want to know exactly what your statement will be.'

Lapinsk nodded. 'It would also be best if the statements were issued simultaneously, at an agreed time.'

Definitely *not* Lapinsk's sole idea, decided Danilov: these staged insistences betrayed a great deal of advance planning and thought.

'I will advise about that, too,' promised Cowley.

As they descended the stairs, back to the level of his own office, Danilov said: 'I suppose I should apologize. I didn't know it was going to be like that.'

Cowley smiled across at the other man. 'No need for apologies. It was just like being at home.' Watching Your Ass Time, Russian style, he thought.

Ralph Baxter leaned attentively over his embassy desk while Cowley outlined the barest details of another murder identical to that of Ann Harris. And then, obediently, stared down at the mortuary block photographs of the shorn Nadia Revin. Forever a man of quick movements, he jerked his head up, frowning incomprehensibly. 'Why are you showing me these?' The moustache twitched.

'Don't you know her?'

The bespectacled diplomat went back to the photographs. 'Of course not. Why should I? You said she was a prostitute?'

'Yes.'

'Then what on earth are you talking about?' Baxter's voice rose in his outrage.

Cowley offered a photocopy of the embassy letter signed by the other man that had been in Nadia Revin's closet hiding-place, saying nothing.

Baxter began to read just as attentively, but then stopped, checked the signature with growing dismissiveness and laughed across the table. 'It's a long-term visa application!'

'I know.'

Baxter remained smiling as he depressed an intercom button, identified a reference number and sat back, waiting. Almost at once a secretary entered whom Cowley recognized from the social club gathering, although they had not spoken. The woman recognized him, too, smiling and nodding. Baxter took what she carried and without reading it offered the top document back across the desk to Cowley, together with the notification that had been retrieved from Nadia Revin's apartment. Both were identical, apart from Baxter's signature. 'You any idea how many visa applications we get here, every day? The line's around the block, all the time. It's a *pro forma* letter, for Christ's sake! We send out dozens of them, asking for more information when the request is for long-term entry permission, which this clearly was, although I haven't bothered to check: don't need to. As the senior consular official, I have to sign . . .' He renewed the offer, with the rest of what the secretary had brought. 'That'll be her file. If it helps, you're welcome to keep it as long as you like.' The grin widened. 'I bet it doesn't list her profession as hooker.'

It didn't. Nadia Revin had described herself as a student of Moscow University, from which she attached a testimonial, wishing to visit America to study for a thesis on East-West cultural differences: she was probably an expert already, reflected Cowley. The section of the form upon which sponsors had to be listed was blank: it was that omission which Baxter's letter had asked to be supplied. The necessary photographs showed a strikingly attractive girl, blonde hair cascading beyond her shoulders. There had been a lot strewn around at the scene at Uspenskii Prospekt, he remembered.

'So you never met her?'

'Of course not! I must sign twenty of them every day of my life, without even reading the names and certainly not an already printed letter. It's a production line. I'm sorry!'

Another totally acceptable, totally understandable, totally end-blocked inquiry, decided Cowley: it *had* been an obviously official letter, so he supposed he shouldn't have expected anything more. 'I can keep the file?'

'Help yourself,' agreed Baxter. 'You really are clutching at anything here, aren't you?'

'Yes,' Cowley admitted. Why did everyone have an answer?

'So it's another dead end?' said Andrews, fifteen minutes later in the Bureau office.

Cowley shrugged. 'It obviously had to be checked.'

'You're forgetting the Quantico lectures,' Andrews pointed out. 'Nothing comes from the background of their victims.' With Cowley so preoccupied it probably wasn't an opportune time to raise his personal situation. But there didn't seem a lot that the other man could practically do, at that moment. To reassure Cowley that the routine had been cleared, Andrews added: 'All the forensic has been packed and pouched. And I've checked all your outward messages. There's nothing back yet.' He paused. 'Pauline said it was a good night at the club.'

'I enjoyed it.'

'So did she.' There was no point in pussyfooting around. 'I've applied to be attached to your division, when I leave here.'

'She told me you were going to.'

Andrews made himself look directly at the other man. 'It needs your approval.'

'I know,' said Cowley unhelpfully, awkwardly, looking back just as directly.

'I wanted to tell you myself, like this,' said Andrews. 'Not for you to get a message from Washington, without my saying anything.' Come on! Say something, for Christ's sake!

'This is best,' Cowley agreed, still unhelpfully and knowing it. Why was he doing it, he asked himself. It was like bullying.

'I hope it'll be OK,' said Andrews, with obvious difficulty. 'With you, I mean.' He hated – *loathed* – having to plead.

'You really think I'd block you?' It was time to stop being ridiculous.

Andrews shrugged. 'There could be reasons.'

'I told Pauline I wouldn't.' Wrong, he thought at once; he shouldn't have given the impression they'd discussed Andrews behind his back. Quickly he said: 'My approval will go in the diplomatic bag tonight.'

There had been a tension between them, since her outburst, but Olga hadn't made any fresh accusations and Danilov hadn't referred to it, either. Nor had they talked about the planned reciprocal evening with Larissa and Yevgennie Kosov. Danilov didn't expect Larissa to accept now if an evening was suggested, but supposed that if a dinner party didn't take place Olga would regard it as confirmation of her suspicion. He decided to go on saying and doing nothing: Dimitri Danilov, expert at burying his head in the sand, he thought.

With the new murder there was a genuine excuse for Danilov's late return to Kirovskaya. As usual, Olga was in bed, her back turned away from his side of the bed. He didn't think she was asleep but moved around with elaborate care. He wasn't sure but he thought the night-dress was new: certainly it looked fresh. Perhaps the washing machine was fixed. Hopefully he checked the drawer. There were at least six clean shirts, crisp and neatly ironed. He'd have to remember to thank her, in the morning.

Danilov got carefully into bed but lay unsleeping in the darkness, re-examining everything for the hundredth – or was it the thousandth? – time, seeking anything he might have forgotten to do or check that might unlock a door. And finding nothing.

He was still alertly awake when the telephone shrilled.

'We've got him!' announced the thick, slightly slurred voice of Yevgennie Kosov. 'His name's Petr Yakovlevich Yezhov.'

Danilov recognized it.

Chapter Thirty-Five

There was no real justification in his going that night, but Danilov
had always been uncomfortable with the thought of a vigilante
posse: at that moment, as a result of such a posse, a man was in
some sort of police custody for no other reason than taking a
late-night walk in a Moscow street. There was certainly no cause
to rouse Pavin. Or contact Cowley. It was routine, something he
could do himself, and with an additional reason for going alone.
Kosov, predictably inflating the situation, had said he was at the
Militia post: there would be the opportunity, without it in any
way appearing contrived, to talk about Eduard Agayans. Danilov
pinched his finger again, re-attaching the windscreen wipers outside the flat: it was bitterly cold, well below zero, which seemed
to make the bruise hurt more than it should have done. He'd
forgotten his hat. He'd done that the night Ann Harris had been
killed, he remembered.

It was the first time in two years that he had crossed the
threshold of his old Militia station. So late he had expected to
find it sleeping, with just a minimal nightstaff on duty, but there
were two men inside the glass-hatched ground-floor office and a
third at an extensive, light-blinking switchboard which was an
innovation since his command. Danilov didn't recognize any of
them. Lights blazed throughout the building and Danilov thought,
jealously, that clearly there was no difficulty in getting replacement bulbs here, and he was sure he heard sounds behind two
day-room doors. It was impressive.

Danilov had expected to be directed upstairs, to his old office,
but instead Kosov descended to him and Danilov belatedly
realized that the other man, naturally, intended sitting in if not
taking part in an interview being conducted on his own premises:
the cells and the interrogation rooms were on the ground floor.
Kosov wore his complete uniform, even his hat. There were effusive foyer greetings, continuing the display. To the uninterested
counter officers Danilov was identified as a former commander:

needing something to say, having involved the men, Kosov said that if they were needed they would be with what he called the prisoner.

On their way to the rear of the building, Kosov said: 'Bastard tried to escape. Ran like hell. Luckily there were four of my people: two lorries. When they caught him two held him while the others called us. Knew it would work.'

'Where?'

'Ulitza Mickiewicz. Ducked into an alley, when he saw the trucks, but they saw him too. So one went around and blocked off the other end, in Spiridonievskii. He ran, like I said. But he wasn't expecting them to do that, so he didn't have much of a start. He didn't fight, though, once they got him.'

Fortunately, thought Danilov. 'What's he said?'

'Nothing. Cried a bit. Makes a whining, humming sound in his throat.'

'Hummed?' demanded Danilov, instantly alert.

'Like a whine really. Like an animal. I think he's mad.'

Kosov didn't know the psychiatric history, Danilov remembered. 'Where did you get the name?'

'From his workbook. He's a labourer in a marshalling yard. You wouldn't think so. He's very clean.'

They could hear Petr Yezhov before they reached the cell. The sound was neither a hum nor a whine: to Danilov it sounded like the whimpered, repetitive bark of a puppy chained too long in one place. It changed when Kosov opened the cell door, into a longer, more positive whimper, definitely of fear. The man had been hunched sideways on the bunk, boots on the blanket, his arms clutched around knees drawn tightly up to his chest, rocking back and forth. As they entered he briefly uncoiled himself, scrabbling further into the corner where the bunk abutted the wall, then bunched up again.

Danilov decided the man was trying to make himself smaller. There was a bruise under his left eye, and the side of his right hand, nearest to where Danilov stood, was badly grazed, although the bleeding appeared to have stopped. But it was not that which caught Danilov's attention. He was oddly bald, an alopecia sufferer, isolated patches of hair clinging to his head. He looked just like the victims, after they had been shorn. 'Petr Yakovlevich?'

Don't look at them, say anything. Two men. A uniform. Angry uniform.

'Petr Yakovlevich, what were you doing, on Ulitza Mickiewicz?'

Had to get out: stop being locked up. 'Yes.' The voice was high-pitched, girlish.

'Why?' Nothing sensible could possibly emerge from this.

'Yes.' The voice was lower.

'Why do you walk at night?'

'Walk.'

'Why do you walk?' This was cruel. But so had the killing of Vladimir Suzlev and Ann Harris and Nadia Revin been cruel. And the attempt upon Lydia Orlenko.

A trick. Wouldn't be tricked. Say nothing.

'Do you look for women when you walk?'

Didn't do it, not any more. 'No.' Shouldn't have spoken.

'You did once, didn't you? You hurt women. Bit them.' Danilov was conscious of Kosov's startled attention beside him. He prayed the man wouldn't intervene, with some needless comment. Kosov didn't.

Needed *maht*: his mother would know what to say. More than he did: he didn't understand. 'Got well now.'

'*Are* you well, Petr Yakovlevich?'

Yezhov began to rock again, a gentle back and forth movement. The whining sound started.

Lydia Orlenko had talked of her attacker humming, as he bent over her, Danilov recalled. This could be mistaken for someone humming. Danilov's mind ran on, to the American psychological profile he'd disdained – still doubted – as modern witchcraft. There was the strange, disfiguring baldness. Although he was dishevelled and crumpled, the disarray of his clothes was obviously recent, the result of whatever had happened during and after his pursuit and the way he had rolled himself up, inside this cramped cell. There was still a discernible crease in his trousers, the shoes were polished, scarcely scuffed, and his shirt crisper than any Olga had finally put into his drawer, that night. And the jacket was double-breasted: Danilov was sure there had been something in the profile about double-breasted jackets being important. 'Have you hurt people again? Looked for women as you walked at night? Attacked them? You must tell me. It will be better if you tell me.'

Too many words: too many to understand. Where was *maht*? She would understand. *Maht* understood everything. Go on making a noise, in his throat. He couldn't hear the words — too many words — if he made the noise in his throat.

'Tell me, Petr Yakovlevich!'

Both angry now. Wouldn't unlock him, if they were angry. That's how you got locked up, by making them angry. 'Didn't do it. Didn't hurt anyone.'

Danilov wished he could sit down: make the encounter easier for all of them. 'Did you cut off their hair? And the buttons. Why did you do that? Tell me!'

'Want to,' said Yezhov, trying to convey that he wanted to be out of the cramped cell, made even smaller by these two men.

Danilov released a small sigh, of satisfaction. 'That's it!' he encouraged. 'You want to. Why do you want to?'

'Can't be locked up. Inside,' answered the man, honestly.

'Mad,' insisted Kosov, intruding at last. 'I said he was mad. But it's him, isn't it? The one you want?'

Uniforms were always angry. Men who locked you up. 'Better. I'm better. They said. Mother knows.' There. Said a lot. Have to unlock him now because he'd said a lot.

Danilov saw for the first time the blood smear on the wall, over the bunk, guessing that Yezhov had grazed his hand hitting at it. The man *was* mad: retarded and confused, certainly. And with a history of sexual attacks upon women. And had said, minutes before, that he'd wanted to cut off their hair and buttons. Whose hair or buttons? Had he meant the woman — and Suzlev by mistake — or hadn't he meant that at all? 'Tell me how you did it. How you hurt them.'

The doctors knew. Everyone knew. Why did this man want to know again. 'Bit them. Wanted to taste. Not now. Better.'

'You stabbed them, didn't you? From behind? With a knife?'

'Didn't.'

'And then cut off their hair? And the buttons? Why did you put the shoes where you did?'

'Don't know . . .' Yezhov intended the denial to be that he didn't know what the man was saying, what he was talking

335

about, but it was too many words, so he stopped. He hadn't done anything wrong: he was sure he hadn't. But his mother thought he had: kept holding his hands and saying that she had to know, just like this man, although he wasn't holding his hands. What was it, that he'd done? He couldn't remember. He'd tell them, if he could remember. Then they'd let him go. Walk again. He wanted to walk, not feel things tight around him. Didn't like things tight around him. The first time, when he'd been locked up, they'd put him in a funny jacket, with sleeves that didn't end and were tied behind him, so that he couldn't move at all, the tightest thing he'd ever known all wrapped around him. Screamed to get out: screamed and cried and thrown himself around the cell just like this but he couldn't get out of it. Didn't ever want to be put in a funny jacket like that again. In a cell just like this one. He made a great effort to at last look towards the men, towards the one who wasn't wearing a uniform and whose voice was kinder. 'No jacket. Please, no jacket.'

I'm hunting a maniac, thought Danilov: someone deranged, mentally unstable. And he was facing someone deranged and mentally unstable. There could be no question that the man had to be held, for more investigation. *Mother knows.* The home had to be scientifically examined. Danilov's mind stopped, at the word. It was routine for a detained person's belongings to be taken away. It might have been an idea to have examined it all before attempting this befuddled interview. 'Are you going to tell me about it? What you did to these women?'

'No.' How could he tell what he couldn't remember? 'Want to go now.'

Kosov sniggered and said, without sympathy: 'This is pathetic!'

Danilov thought so too, but differently from Kosov. He said to Yezhov: 'You can't go. You've got to stay here.'

'NO!'

The outburst was so abrupt and unexpected that both Militia Colonels were completely startled. Yezhov broke like a spring from his coiled position, swiping out wildly at both of them as he tried to get to the door. The blow caught Danilov directly in the stomach, driving the wind from him: he staggered back, retching, against the unseen wall behind. Another blow missed Kosov. The indulgently fat uniformed man was grossly out of

336

condition but solid-bodied. Yezhov had no support and little momentum as he came up off the bed. Kosov simply stepped forward, blocking the man. But Yezhov didn't fall back. Instead he entwined his arms around Kosov's neck, using the other man to pull himself up. In turn Kosov locked his arms around Yezhov and together the two pirouetted in a tight, violent embrace. Danilov pushed himself away from the wall, breath groaning into him, groping to dislodge Yezhov's arms from the other policeman. He couldn't, at first: the mindless grip was rigid, impossible to shift. Danilov had to use two hands and all his strength to prise first the fingers, then the arm loose. Partially freed, Kosov twisted to get further away from the other man, then drove his knee up full into Yezhov's groin.

Breath and pain screeched from Yezhov. He jack-knifed, and as he doubled up Kosov kneed him in the side of the head, sending him reeling back on to the bunk. His head hit the wall as he collapsed.

Kosov went forward, fist raised, but Danilov said: 'No more! You've controlled him! No more!'

Panting, Danilov still having difficulty in breathing properly, both men backed into the corridor. Kosov crashed the door furiously behind them, automatically looking back in through the sliding peep-hole. 'Can you imagine the strength of that bastard? He's like a fucking gorilla!'

'He was very strong,' Danilov agreed. Lydia Orlenko had made a point of her attacker's strength. And the American medical opinion was that the killer had to be extremely strong, to drive the knife into his victims as he had done.

'But we've got him!' Kosov insisted, leading the way back towards the front of the building.

'I want to see what he had on him,' said Danilov.

'All waiting,' said Kosov, efficiently.

Everything was already in a plastic evidence bag, a list attached. Danilov picked out the contents for himself, itemizing them against the list, and creating a pile on the table in the day-room from which he had earlier imagined hearing a noise. There was a comb, with several teeth missing. Two keys, on a ring. Three unidentified white pills, in a paper twist. And fifteen roubles.

Danilov halted at the workbook from which Yezhov's name had been obtained.

Left in the bag was a knife, in a homemade, roughly stitched leather sheath. And two buttons, one white, one brown, large and ornate, the sort used on women's clothes. Danilov withdrew the knife. The blade was single-edged, the honed edge extremely sharp. Without actually measuring it, Danilov judged the blade to be about twenty-six centimetres long, possibly five centimetres across at its widest part, near the hilt, and five millimetres thick at its back. He guessed it would have perfectly fitted the wounds of each victim.

He looked back up at Kosov. 'I need a telephone.'

Cowley and Pavin joined him at the Militia station in less than an hour, arriving separately, the American first. The prepared explanation, initially for Cowley's benefit but intended to be the official version, was that Yezhov had been detained after being routinely questioned in the street by a Militia patrol officer curious at the man walking so late at night. Several times Kosov offered unnecessary details, which Danilov wished he hadn't. He realized Kosov regarded himself as part of the investigatory team, intending to come with them to the Bronnaja apartment. Cowley snorted a laugh, shaking his head, and said it was difficult to believe the whole thing could be sorted out like this, almost by accident. Pavin immediately recognized the name, as quickly as Danilov had earlier, and said he'd been to Bronnaja twice the previous day without getting a reply on either occasion. The neighbours, recognizing him as officialdom, had denied knowing anything about the family, apart from confirming that the apartment was occupied by a mother and her son.

They trailed back to the rear of the police station and individually regarded Yezhov through the spy-hole, not trying to enter. The man was bunched on the bunk once more, arms hugging his legs tightly to his chest. He was rocking back and forth and making the whimpered, barking sound again. There was blood on his hair-patched head, where he'd hit the wall upon being knocked back from his attack. His face was puffed from crying.

As they went back to the front of the building, Kosov jerked

338

his head towards the American and said: 'Tell him it was good, solid police work.'

'I understand what you're saying,' Cowley advised. 'It seems like you've done a good job.'

'Got him, when no one else could!' declared Kosov, proudly.

As Danilov expected, Kosov strode from the building with them, towards the car. Maybe, Danilov reflected, a uniform would be a useful encouragement to the mother.

Pavin drove, knowing the way. Cowley wondered what they were going to do if there was still no reply at the apartment. Danilov held up the keys that had been in Yezhov's possession and said it wouldn't matter now. Danilov didn't bother to reply when Cowley asked about a search warrant. Like the American, he was surprised by what could be the abrupt simplicity of it all. Unable to follow normal and practical police methods, because the killings were motiveless, this was always how the investigation *had* to be resolved, by chance. It was what he and Cowley had always expected. Yet, so soon, he found it hard to accept. Illogically he felt cheated, denied the opportunity to prove himself as a professional criminal investigator. And there was, additionally, another, different personal feeling. If Yezhov was the killer, it hadn't been solved quite by chance. It had been solved by Kosov, using crooks: law-breakers, at least. Which wasn't how it should have happened. What sort of reflection was that, he demanded of himself at once. A pompous one, he conceded. There was actually jealousy there, too. The need was to arrest a maniac, wandering, murdering. If Kosov was responsible for that, *however* he was responsible, then Kosov deserved the recognition and the credit: the convenient means justified the successful end. No one else was going to be murdered.

It was still not properly dawn when they got to Bronnaja, but Valentina Yezhov saw the car draw up below her apartment: she'd spent a lot of the night there, sleepless, anxious for the first movement that might have been Petr returning from wherever he'd been. Since the initial visit of the Militia and their subsequent, evaded, calls she had never slept until Petr was safely home. Four men, she saw, staring down with her hands to her mouth, nibbling at her knuckles: one in uniform, someone important. Petr had done it again – *something* again – and it was going to be like before, stared at and shunned, unsigned letters left in her box telling her to get out because everyone else in the block didn't want a sex monster living there. It wouldn't do any good, not to answer the door: they'd keep coming back, like they were doing now. She still wouldn't answer, though: she wouldn't know what to do or say, if she had to face them.

The bell sounded, stridently.

Valentina didn't move.

It sounded again, longer.

She didn't move. They'd go away. What else could they do, if there was no one there?

The lock turned. She cried out, more in disappointment at their catching her out than fear of their actually confronting her.

The door had opened at Danilov's first attempt with the keys the detained man had been carrying. The interior of the apartment was in deep darkness, but her crying out identified Valentina. She blinked, unable to see in the first few seconds of brightness, when Kosov found the light switch. She was sitting on a flat, backless couch which clearly made up into a bed during a normal night. She had her hands nervously around her knees, so very much like her son back in the police cell.

It was Kosov who moved further into the room ahead of any of them. He began, too loudly: 'OK, let's not . . .' before Danilov intervened.

'I'll question!' he said, even louder, overriding the uniformed man. Danilov turned, including the American. '*We'll* question,' he qualified.

Kosov's reaction was astonishment, at being corrected. He opened his mouth, to protest, appeared to realize it would be wrong and then shrugged. A wall ornament appeared suddenly to interest him.

'We have Petr Yakovlevich in custody,' Danilov announced.

Valentina made a great effort to compose herself, straightening in front of the four men. The man who was speaking now seemed kinder than the one in uniform, who was walking about the apartment, picking up and putting things down, as if he had the right. Which she supposed he did: he was in uniform. 'Why's he in jail?'

'He might have done something wrong,' said Cowley.

Foreign voice, foreign dress, Valentina identified. The awareness, from the television and the newspapers, came at once, hol-
lowing her out. 'No!' she insisted, loud herself now. 'He didn't
do that! No!'

'Didn't do what?' Danilov picked up. Beside him, Pavin was
recording everything, writing surprisingly quickly for such a ponderous man.

'What you're saying.'

'We're not saying anything,' said Cowley.

'He's better.'

'Why aren't you in bed? It's still night.'

'Waiting for Petr.'

'He's a grown man. Why do you wait up for Petr when he's a
grown man?' demanded Danilov.

'You know!' She pulled a baggy cardigan tighter around her.

'Tell me.'

'He's not a grown man. Not properly grown. Not in his head.'

Neither Danilov nor Cowley looked at each other, but Kosov
came away from a small table at which he'd been standing and
said: 'There!'

'You know he's done something wrong, don't you?' urged
Danilov.

Reluctantly Valentina nodded.

'How do you know?' asked Cowley.

'You've been coming, for days.' She was looking down at the
floor now, voice sometimes difficult to hear.

'Did he tell you what he'd done?'

She shook her head.

'Did you ask him?' pressed the American.

'Yes.'

'What did he say?'

'Wouldn't tell me. Said he hadn't done anything.'

'Has be brought anything home?' said Danilov.

'Is he locked up?' demanded the woman. 'In a cell or something?'

'Yes,' said Danilov, allowing her initially to evade the question.

'He won't like that. He hates being locked up, from the other
times.'

'The other times when he attacked women?' said Cowley.

341

'Yes.'

'Is that what he's done now?' intruded Kosov, wanting to be part of what was happening.

'I don't know.'

'Has he brought anything home?' Danilov repeated.

'I don't understand.'

'Things he wanted to keep, specially.' Danilov wanted evidence to come without suggestion from them.

Cowley recognized the approach for some professional integrity, but not much: this interrogation, after what he considered technically to be forcible entry, contravened every American judicial rule and guideline on the statute book governing witness interviewing and possible evidence gathering. A defence lawyer five minutes out of law school with the worst degree in the world could have had it ruled inadmissible in any court in the United States.

'I still don't understand, not properly. But no.'

'Why does Petr carry a knife?' persisted Danilov.

'He doesn't!' the woman denied, emphatically.

'He was carrying a knife, in a sheath I guess he made himself, when he was arrested tonight.'

Valentina shook her head again, but slower, sadder, this time. 'I don't know about a knife.'

'What about buttons?' asked Cowley.

'Buttons?' The woman stared up at them, in obvious bewilderment.

'The sort of buttons on women's clothes,' elaborated Danilov. 'Did Petre collect them?'

'Of course not!'

'You'd know?'

'Of course I'd know!'

'You clean his room? Look after his things?'

'Yes.' She was faint-voiced, obviously lying.

'Do you look after his room?' Danilov persisted.

'His clothes. He won't let me into his room,' the woman admitted. 'But the other officers went in, when they came. They saw it all.'

It was in the report he'd considered utterly inadequate, Danilov remembered. 'We want to see it again. Now.'

Valentina nodded, dumbly, with no thought of protest. She pulled the shapeless cardigan about her again when she stood up. As she crossed the room to a bedroom door Danilov saw the backs of her slippers were trodden down, like Olga's, so that she had to scuff to keep them on. At the door she looked back helplessly at them and said: 'I haven't got the key. It's locked and I haven't got the key.'

'I have,' said Danilov, walking forward with the second of the two keys on Yezhov's ring. It worked.

The bedroom was immaculate, as it had been for the first police examination. As they entered, Cowley commented quietly to Danilov, in English: 'Everything fits the profile.'

'I know,' agreed Danilov, also in English.

Valentina Yezhov hung back as the four men entered her son's sealed room. Striving for some professional propriety, Cowley said: 'You must come in as well. See everything that we do: be aware of anything we take.'

Obediently the woman came forward, but still only just put herself inside the door.

They all searched, Kosov roughly until Danilov stopped him and warned they didn't want anything hidden by the dismissive way the man was throwing things aside. Pavin, the evidence collector, was the one who really led. And it was Pavin who found the secret place – nothing more than a floorboard, sawn through to create a lid over the natural space beneath. Inside were three pornographic magazines, very old and worn, all masochistic, all showing chained and tethered naked women in various poses of apparent suffering. In a lot of the pictures, their breasts were the object of attack.

Beneath the magazines were two cotton purses. They contained, in total, ten buttons of the sort used on women's clothing.

To Pavin, Danilov said: 'Parcel up all his clothes, for forensic.' To the woman he said: 'I want you to come with us. You've got to help us talk to him.'

Valentina looked beyond Danilov, to where Pavin was at the wardrobe. 'Don't crease his clothes. He doesn't like his clothes being creased. I have to keep everything pressed.'

Cowley recognized the sort of irrational remark people made

under intense, breaking-point pressure. It was also probably very significant.

Chapter Thirty-Six

Refused the lead at Bronnaja, Kosov bustled for control back at his own Militia post, but again Danilov opposed him, accepting the obvious offence although trying to minimize the disagreement as much as possible before the others, his sole concern now to get the investigation properly and professionally concluded. He contradicted Kosov's announcement that they would resume at once the questioning of Yezhov in his cell, insisting instead that any further interviews had to be in a much larger interrogation room in which the man might feel less constrained and in which Valentina could wait until they were ready. There were other things that had to be set in motion first. Pavin had to contact the Serbsky Institute, to summon the doctor who had been Yezhov's most recent psychiatrist: the man was to bring with him Yezhov's complete case history. Danilov himself awoke Leonid Lapinsk, refusing to go along completely with the older man's instant excitement but agreeing that the circumstantial evidence looked overwhelmingly convincing.

They had taken over the day-room in which Danilov had earlier examined Yezhov's possessions, to which were now added the clothes, buttons and magazines taken from the apartment. While Danilov telephoned his superior, Cowley sifted carefully through what had been assembled, with a pen tip, not his fingers.

When Danilov replaced the receiver, the American said: 'The circumstantial evidence against Paul Hughes looked pretty convincing, too.'

'Not like this,' argued Danilov.

'I guess you're right,' Cowley agreed. He was still standing by the table that held the exhibits. 'In Washington the Bureau have specialists on button identification. Have done, for years: buttons are the first things that come off, in violent situations. There's a pyrolysis test. One using a gas chromatographic mass spectrometer. Another involving something called a Foyier Transformer infra-red spectrometer.'

345

Danilov nodded, unoffended at the inherent criticism of Russian scientific methods: certainly with the pathologist Viktor Novikov there had been more than sufficient reason for criticism. 'And DNA?' he prompted, expectantly.

Cowley nodded in return, then indicated the clothes. 'We've got comparison checks from each victim. Suzlev only from his hair, but from all the rest – Ann Harris, Lydia Orlenko and Nadia Revin – all the trace sources like blood and bodily fluids we could possibly want. If there's a speck – something so small it can only be seen under a microscope – on any of this stuff, our people in Washington can find it and match it. Match it so that it's incontestable in any court.'

Danilov stared at the piled possessions, noticing that since he had been there earlier Yezhov's topcoat, which must have been somewhere else in the building, had been added. It was grey, with an attached hood, and heavily padded: the sort of coat Lydia Orlenko had described. There was what looked to be a smear of blood on the left collar; he recalled the bruising beneath Yezhov's eye and wondered what sort of scuffle or fight there had been when he had been seized that night on Spiridonievskii. 'There would appear to be enough to divide between our two forensic laboratories.'

'I understood your people didn't use the deoxyribonucleic acid test in criminal investigations yet?' Cowley challenged, gently.

'There would have to be a division,' said Danilov, adamantly.

'We could be specific about that division,' suggested the American. 'The topcoat, for instance. Lydia Orlenko said her attacker wore a padded topcoat.'

'I think you should have the topcoat,' Danilov conceded. 'And all the buttons. The rest we'll separate equally.'

Like competing children allocating prizes to themselves, thought Cowley, unable to rid himself of the impression of illegal amateurism. Despite which, in the circumstances – always the awkward, conflicting circumstances! – he decided it was the best compromise he could expect. 'That sounds fine.'

Danilov had tea brought in from the canteen and saw that some was taken to Valentina Yezhov, too. When Pavin returned from another office, from which he had spoken to the Serbsky Institute, Danilov itemized how the exhibits were to be split. It

346

was a further half an hour before Kosov, who'd removed himself from a situation of challenge by disappearing into his own upper-floor office, reappeared to announce the psychiatrist's arrival. It gave Kosov the excuse to be involved again: Danilov didn't object.

The Serbsky doctor was a small, fussy man named Aleksandr Iosifovich Tarasov and he was clearly ill-at-ease in surroundings in which he was unfamiliar – probably a psychological failing of his own. He kept patting himself, as if needing the reassurance of a medical uniform instead of the stained and falling-off-his-shoulders suit he was now wearing.

He had treated Petr Yakovlevich Yezhov for an undefined para-noia, although certainly there were elements of persecution. He did not consider the breast fetish, indicated by the crimes for which Yezhov had been detained, to be part of that persecution, however. Yezhov's faculties were impaired – it was difficult to estimate, but he wouldn't put the man's mental age above thirteen, probably less – and the breast fixation could be associated with rejection as a young child by a disappointed mother. Tarasov seemed doubtful of the American opinion that the buttons could be associated with a nipple obsession, although he was aware of such discussion and even theses in international psychiatric journals. He had personally recommended Yezhov's release, believing the man's mental stability adequate for him to live outside a restricted community: being restricted had always caused him great, sometimes self-harming, distress. It was always possible that Yezhov had regressed since his release. It was even more possible, from the man's case history, that the violence already manifested could worsen even to the point of murder. He was, of course, quite willing to sit in on any interrogation: he understood that was why he had been summoned. It was a good idea for the mother to be present: she'd always been a strong, if debatable, influence.

They assembled in the same large room as Valentina Yezhov, who hunched uncertainly at the table, hands clasped around her empty cup, suspecting the worst but still not fully informed as to why she had been brought to the station or why her son was being held there. The crying had worsened, river marks of tears down her face, her eyes red. She recognized Tarasov and instantly invested the psychiatrist, someone whom she knew, with superior

347

authority and demanded to know where her son was and what
– *exactly* – he had done. She repeated the same word, *exactly*,
several times, like a courtroom lawyer.

'He's been bad again,' announced Tarasov. 'Like before.
Worse.'

'No!' It wasn't an outburst, like her son's cell-room reaction.
It was the sad, unquestioning acceptance of some horror that had
always lurked close at hand.

Danilov was unhappy at the number of people there were
crowded into the room. It was necessary for Cowley to be there,
maintaining everything on an equal basis. And for Pavin's presence, to record every exchange. It had been his idea to include
the mother and the psychiatrist. Which left Kosov as the only
intruder. The number had to stay as it was. To Valentina, he
said: 'I want to talk to Petr Yakovlevich. You must tell him it
has to be the truth.'

'Why?' She was hollowed out. She didn't know – couldn't
think – where she could go from Bronnaja Boulevard but knew
she'd have to move on *somewhere*. She'd be a pariah now, someone who'd spawned a monster.

'I want him to tell me.'

Danilov was at the table, facing the woman. Tarasov was
beside him. Everyone else, by unspoken agreement, withdrew to
the edges of the room. Cowley shifted where he stood, against
the wall, disconcerted by this preliminary scene, as he had been
disconcerted by a lot of other things since this day had begun,
when it hadn't been day at all but the middle of the night.

Valentina gave a listless shrug of acceptance, They were authority, official: she'd learned always to defer to authority. It was
safer: you didn't get into trouble if you deferred to authority.

A sound, a bitten-back sob, burst from her when Petr Yakovlevich was brought into the room. His hands were manacled in front
of him. There was a towering Militia man on either side and
another behind, holding a metal chain looped to the manacles in
front: if Yezhov had tried to lash out, as he had in the cell, the
following guard could have flipped him off his feet simply by
yanking on the lead chain. The bruise on Yezhov's cheek was
deepening, purple and brown now. Blood, from the head graze
when he had been kneed back by Kosov, blackly matted his

348

clumped hair. His face was twitching, nerves alive beneath his skin. His eyes rolled, in terror.

Danilov half turned, furious, seeking and failing to find Kosov. Bastard! he thought. Bullying, posturing bastard.

Jesus, thought Cowley, against the wall.

'Take the chains off!' said Danilov.

'No.' It was Kosov's voice.

'Take the chains off!'

The impasse was silent. The chained man focused on his mother. He didn't smile. His eyes still rolled. Flat voice, with no meaning, he said to her: 'No.'

The officer at the rear, the one holding the restraining chain, had been attached to the station when Danilov had controlled it, although he couldn't remember the man's name. Danilov rose from the table, going to them: he held out his hand towards the one he recognized and said: 'Give me the key.' It came from another man, the one to the right. Danilov unfastened the manacles himself and held Yezhov's arm, taking him to sit next to his mother. As he resumed his own seat, Kosov said: 'Your decision.'

Valentina hesitated, then reached out for Yezhov's hand: it was the one on which the blood had dried, from the graze. Danilov saw for the first time that there was a heavy, silver-metalled ring on the man's little finger and remembered the chin bruising – and the suggested American cause – on every victim.

'Tell him he has to answer me truthfully,' ordered Danilov.

Valentina did. 'Everything you're asked,' she insisted. They'd be kind, if she did what they told her.

Yezhov nodded.

'You go walking, at night?' Danilov began.

Slowly, frightened, Yezhov came around to face Danilov. 'Yes.'

'Where? Ulitza Gercena?'

'I think so.'

'Ulitza Stolesnikov?'

'Don't know.' Yezhov smiled hopefully sideways, towards his mother. She smiled back.

'Granovskaya?'

'I think so.' Yezhov smiled more proudly, like a child doing well in a test.

'Uspenskii Prospekt?'

'Don't know Uspenskii Prospekt.'

'What do you do, when you walk?'

'Just walk.'

'Why do you have a knife?'

'Knife?'

'You had a knife tonight.'

'Like it.'

'Why?'

'Safe.'

'When you . . .' began Danilov but stopped, at the movement beside him as the psychiatrist came into the interrogation.

'Remember me, Petr Yakovlevich?'

'Yes.'

'You made me a promise, in the hospital? The same promise, a lot of times? About girls. It was a promise about girls.'

'Don't remember.'

'Have you forgotten what you promised me in hospital? What you said you wouldn't do any more?'

'Haven't hurt anybody.'

'Do you know people have been hurt?'

* 'No.'

'Have you looked for women, for girls, when you've been out at night?' asked Danilov, re-entering the questioning.

'Not allowed.'

'Did you hurt anyone with the knife, Petr Yakovlevich?' asked the psychiatrist.

'No.'

'Why were you carrying buttons?' asked Danilov. 'And why did you hide buttons in your room?'

'Wanted to.'

'Do you think of buttons as something else?' persisted Tarasov, conscious of the American assessment of their significance.

'No.'

'What are they then?'

'Buttons.' Yezhov suddenly frowned, as if he were recognizing the psychiatrist for the first time. 'No jacket. I don't want to wear the jacket.'

Danilov detected the sound of shuffling behind him, from the people grouped along the wall. He sighed to himself. 'You stuck your knife into people, didn't you? Into women, when you were walking?'

There was the faintest sound, a gasping intake of breath, from Valentina but it was loud enough to distract her son, who looked towards her. He smiled, forever hopeful of her approval.

'I want him to answer,' Danilov insisted, annoyed at the deflection.

'Did you stab those women?' said Valentina, using both hands now to hold her son's. 'Look at me! Did you hurt them, with that knife?'

'Don't remember.'

'Did you cut their hair off?' came in Danilov.

'Don't remember.'

'And take buttons from their clothes?'

'Don't remember.'

Careless of Yezhov hearing him, the psychiatrist said to Danilov: 'There is no purpose in this. He probably genuinely doesn't remember, even if he did do it.'

'That's what I want to know, if he *did*!' said Danilov.

'You're not going to learn it this way, with a confession,' Tarasov insisted.

'Could we?' pressed Danilov. 'Not here, perhaps, where he's obviously bewildered. Clearly frightened. But somewhere else: the Serbsky, perhaps, where he'd feel more relaxed?'

Tarasov laughed, in open derision. 'He was never relaxed and cooperative at the Institute.'

'How then?'

'When he decides to tell you. *If* he's got anything to tell you. Maybe never,' said the psychiatrist, with defeated honesty.

'Home now,' announced Yezhov, brightly, not appearing to be frightened any more. 'We'll go home now.'

'No!' said Valentina, her fear surfacing. 'I don't want . . . I couldn't . . .'

'He can't stay here,' said Danilov, talking to the psychiatrist. He was worried, too late, that it had been a mistake to unchain a man as strong as Yezhov who might fight against being returned to a hospital where he had developed a phobia against confinement.

The worry was unfounded.

Tarasov briefly left the room, to summon an ambulance, and brought a medical bag with him when he returned. Valentina encouraged her son to swallow the sedating pill, which took effect before the vehicle arrived. To make certain, Tarasov administered an injection when he was quite sure Yezhov was too subdued to object. The man had to be carried out on a stretcher.

Danilov stopped the psychiatrist at the door. 'I want a blood sample, as soon as possible. And some hair, from what he's got left.'

Tarasov nodded, and walked on.

Cowley wondered how many invasion of privacy statutes existed in America forbidding samples being taken from suspects rendered unconscious. He halted Valentina Yezhov at the door and said: 'I want to know something important. Does Petr Yakovlevich smoke?'

The woman frowned back at him. 'Never! He hates smoking.'

Cowley stood back for her to leave, looking across the less crowded room to the Russian. 'Well?'

'Lydia Orlenko was in shock. We know that.'

'There's not enough. It's all circumstantial, like it was with Hughes.'

'I know.'

The FBI questioning of Angela Hughes was gently sympathetic – even to the extent of appointing a woman agent to conduct the interview – and very early it was disclosed that there was now doubt about her husband's alibi for the day the Russian taxi driver was killed.

'In Moscow you told an agent that your husband came home before midnight on the night when the Russian woman was attacked? That you heard a clock strike?'

'Yes.'

'Are you positive about that?'

'I think so,' said Angela. The intentional doubt in her voice covered any hint of vindictiveness.

'You *think*. I asked if you were *positive*, Mrs Hughes.'

'I thought so, at the time. Now I really can't be sure.'

By the time the transcript reached the FBI Director he had

352

received the alert from Moscow of the arrest of Petr Yakovlevich Yezhov. The Director decided to let both inquiries continue independently: he couldn't decide what else to do.

Chapter Thirty-Seven

In Moscow the days following Yezhov's detention were crowded: more familiar routine, then the wind-down procedure of preparing reports of all the available evidence that in this case would never be presented to any court.

And throughout it all Danilov felt a depressing anticlimax.

He refused to accept it was because of the never-to-be-disclosed true circumstances of Petr Yezhov's initial capture: that would have been ridiculous. He'd dismissed any professional distaste at how it had been achieved on the night of the arrest. And even to contemplate the idea of jealousy of Kosov was unthinkable: he actually intended trying to get Kosov's part in the affair publicly acknowledged. So why? The best explanation Danilov could evolve was in what the American had said: that there could probably never be a trial, despite the preparations he was now having made, and therefore never a legally conclusive ending. Which was scarcely an explanation at all.

Trying to be objective, he recognized he should feel the complete opposite to the way he did and be thoroughly satisfied. Despite Kosov's involvement, the case would be marked on his file as successfully investigated. And most importantly, without any security agency takeover, which made it much more than a personal triumph, elevating it into a success for the Militia as a whole, particularly as uniformed officers could be included as well. The false starts and wrong directions weren't recorded anywhere, were certainly not publicly known, and in the official euphoria of the moment would be instantly forgotten by those who did know, like General Lapinsk and the Federal Prosecutor. He was being stupid, Danilov told himself: behaving like someone wallowing in a mid-life crisis or the male menopause. And he knew he wasn't suffering either.

He deputed Pavin to organize the evidence assembly, futile though the operation possibly was, and stood down the disgruntled squads who had so bungled the routine inquiries. He also talked through with Pavin the threat officially to note on their personnel sheets the criticism against the most inefficient, particularly the two who had failed with the first interview and search at Yezhov's apartment. Pavin acknowledged that regulations existed for such complaints to be appended, but pragmatically pointed out that no one would be censured or transferred from Petrovka; that wasn't the way the system worked. All he would be doing, therefore, would be increasing the considerable ill-feeling he had already generated, without any practical benefit. And he had to go on working at Petrovka, didn't he? Danilov decided not to bother.

He maintained daily contact with the Serbsky Institute and the psychiatrist, hoping for some improvement in Yezhov's condition for further and better interviews to be possible. Tarasov insisted just as regularly that anything approaching a reasonable, comprehensible conversation with the man would be impossible for a long time, possibly forever. Yezhov had realized where he was the moment he'd recovered from the sedation that got him back into the clinic, erupting into a cell-wrecking frenzy, and for his own safety was having to remain almost continuously sedated. Tarasov feared the regression into persecuted paranoia was permanent. Yezhov's mother visited every day: he didn't appear to recognize her, even when they briefly relaxed the sedation. Danilov said he'd keep trying. Tarasov said he could do what he liked, but he was wasting his time.

The daily conferences with Lapinsk continued as well, although after that first triumphant day there wasn't a great deal for them to discuss. The anticipated media hysteria had burst with the Tass announcement of Nadia Revin's murder and continued with the second statement, within thirty-six hours, of a suspect's detention. Lapinsk was glad they had delayed the press conference. Now they had the success of a joint investigation between the United States of America and Russia, the first of its kind, to talk about. Both he and the Federal Prosecutor had reversed their previous reluctance to participate.

It was during the discussion about the press conference that Danilov suggested Kosov should be included. The General was clearly surprised at the idea of sharing the credit. Finding no discomfort in perpetuating the prepared account, Danilov pointed

355

out that it *had* been Kosov's officers who had apprehended Petr Yezhov, although the criminal investigation branch had already isolated the man as a potential suspect: it was right that the participation of a uniformed division should be acknowledged. Lapinsk, prepared to concede anything in his relief that the matter was practically over, said he didn't have any objection. He added that he thought Danilov was extremely generous.

Danilov drove personally and alone to the Militia station, taking the chance of Kosov being there by not telephoning in advance. Kosov was there. He kept Danilov waiting over thirty minutes, which Danilov did patiently, and finally had him make his own way up to the third-floor office, which again Danilov did without offence.

Kosov was in his shirt-sleeves, collar unbuttoned. There was a glass on his desk, generously filled with what could have been either cognac or whisky. He drank pointedly from it as Danilov entered, but didn't offer anything to Danilov.

'You wanted to see me?'

The hostility would have been a useful barrier to use, to avoid the still postponed evening with Kosov and Larissa, Danilov reflected. He located his own chair, just inside the door, and brought it further into the room. 'We're still waiting for positive forensic evidence but circumstantially it looks as if he's the right man.'

'I didn't doubt that he was.'

'No one seems to be doubting it. There's going to be another press conference.' The office was unrecognizable as the room he had once occupied. There was thick, wall-to-wall carpeting, colour-coordinated with the curtains. The desk was of a heavy, dark wood with a leather inlaid top. A matching, glass-fronted bureau occupied most of one side of the room and the chair in which Kosov sat was dark wood, too, although the upholstery was button-backed red leather. It all reminded Danilov of Gugin's office, at the Lubyanka. There was a photograph of Larissa on Kosov's desk. She looked very beautiful.

'I heard.' Kosov sipped from his drink.

'I hardly think it would be fair for all that you did to go unrecorded,' flattered Danilov. 'I've spoken to the General. He agrees you should appear at the conference.'

Kosov's demeanour softened almost visibly: he actually began to smile before remembering his anger at the way the other man had treated him at his own Militia station and quickly clearing the expression. 'Appearing with whom?'

'Myself and the American. The General. Smolin, the Federal Prosecutor. I don't know if there's going to be anyone else. I suppose there could be someone from one of the Ministries.'

Kosov was finding it difficult not to smile. 'It will be a big affair then?'

'Certainly as big as the first one. International, of course. All the American media. World media, in fact. I hope you'll be able to make it. You – your station here – deserve the recognition. It's entirely a matter for you, of course.'

'There *should* be recognition, of what my officers did,' said Kosov, appearing to believe the tidied-up version himself.

'That's what I feel.'

'I could probably get there.'

'General Lapinsk will be very pleased.'

Kosov held up his glass. 'It's whisky. From Scotland. Would you like some?'

'Please,' Danilov accepted, although he didn't particularly like whisky.

The liquor was in the bottom of the bureau, where the glass finished and cupboards began. There was an expansive array of bottles. Kosov carried the whisky back to his desk and poured from there. 'What, exactly, would I have to do?'

'Appear, with the rest of us. Explain how the arrest came about. Say how you and your officers had been on the look-out, after my request for assistance.'

Kosov nodded. 'That's all true,' he said, easily.

'It's agreed then?'

'Absolutely.'

Danilov gestured around the office. 'Quite a few changes.'

'Just made it more comfortable. Personal touches.'

'I met an old friend the other day.'

'Old friend?'

'Someone I introduced you to, before I left. Eduard Agayans.'

Kosov frowned, and Danilov believed that briefly the other man genuinely had difficulty in recalling the name. Then the frown cleared and Kosov said: 'I didn't keep in touch, after a while.'

'He's encountering difficulties, with his business.'

'That's unfortunate.'

'He says some organized syndicates are crowding him out: not letting him operate although there's business enough for everyone.'

'I would have thought your division would have known all about organized syndicates,' said Kosov. He got up from behind his desk and waddled forward, topping Danilov's glass.

'We do,' declared Danilov. The other man could not have volunteered a better opening.

Kosov resumed his seat, serious-faced. 'You mean there's an official investigation being started?'

'Not yet.'

'Not yet?'

Danilov shrugged. 'It's a question of degree, I suppose. If a problem becomes too flagrant, something has to be done about it. Things are very public in Russia now, because of the freedoms. There's public debate, in newspapers and magazines, about a lot of things that never used to be openly discussed. You've seen that for yourself, surely?'

Kosov nodded, remaining serious. 'How comprehensive would any investigation be?'

'I would imagine that if one is initiated it will be fairly extensive,' Danilov suggested. 'I get the feeling quite a lot of attention is being concentrated on it: there's already open talk within the Serious Crime Squads. Some reluctance, I think. Some people have special friends they don't want upset.'

'Has any particular syndicate been named?'

'Not that I've heard.'

'Was Agayans a particular friend of yours?'

'We had an understanding. I liked him.'

'It's unfortunate, when one's friends get inconvenienced.'

'I couldn't agree more.'

'It was some of my friends who got Yezhov.'

'I know. I'll always be grateful.'

'I would appreciate knowing a name – or names – if you hear anything.'

'Of course. I'd like to ensure things aren't made difficult for Agayans, of course. It seems he's suffered enough.'

'Maybe I could speak to some of my friends: see if they know anything about Agayans's problems.'

'I'm sure he'd appreciate that.'

'And you will let me know, about any names?'

'I guarantee it.'

'I suppose I should wear my uniform for the press conference?'

'Absolutely.'

'I'm looking forward to it.'

'I was sure you would.'

Cowley's feeling was not of anticlimax, but there seemed an emptiness about the days, a hiatus between the satisfaction of making an arrest and the finality of a positive conclusion. With time to analyse all that had happened, he realistically accepted that in an American court the circumstantial evidence would almost certainly be dismissed as insufficient to bring charges against Petr Yezhov, irrespective of any ruling about the man's mental condition. And from Danilov he knew the psychiatrist's opinion that the mental condition almost definitely precluded any clinching confession. Which put the proof of guilt, however the case was going to be closed, entirely upon forensic findings either from here or from Washington: he'd expected the American results sooner, although he knew from the daily discussion with Pennsylvania Avenue that what had gone back was being examined virtually fibre by fibre. At least he'd been promised preliminary guidance before the press conference he had been authorized to attend.

There was an uncertain day when it was suggested and then denied that Senator Burden would return to Moscow for the conference, which Cowley had thought to be preposterous when he first heard it. Instead the politician's office issued a statement congratulating all the investigating agencies upon a successful conclusion: the Senator had never doubted the efficiency or professionalism with which the inquiry was being conducted. He probably would go to Moscow for any trial. Burden appeared on television and implied that the reason for his abrupt and inexplicable silence, after his initial easy availability to the press, was because he knew the investigation was at a critical juncture. He hadn't wanted to do or say anything that might have impeded the arrest. He wasn't asked by any interviewer how that could have possibly occurred.

Harvey Proffitt, Andrews's San Francisco replacement, arrived for the hand-over period. He was a young, eager bachelor on his first foreign posting who regarded everything with open-eyed enthusiasm. The media coverage back home of the serial killings had been fantastic: when he eventually returned it was going to be difficult for Cowley to walk down the street without being recognized. He wished he'd been posted earlier, to help in any way he could. Moscow was a hell of an opportunity. He was going to take every bit of it. Andrews's weary cynicism didn't depress him.

Two personal letters from the Director, both marked confidential, arrived for Cowley in the diplomatic pouch. One was a letter of congratulation and commendation, which Cowley hoped was not premature. The other asked if he would like personally to decide the location of Andrews's return posting. Cowley replied that he knew there were slots to be filled in Washington, New York and San Francisco: he was sure Andrews would be satisfactory in any of them, but there would not be a housing problem if he were assigned to Washington.

All of them – Cowley, Andrews, Pauline and Proffitt – went to another social evening at the embassy and Cowley hosted the long-promised return meal at a restaurant Pauline chose, the Glazur, on Smolensky Boulevard. Cowley considered inviting Danilov and his wife, but remembered the difficulty there had been at the beginning between the Russian detective and Andrews and concluded that it might put a strain on the evening. He decided to make it a separate invitation before he returned to America and probably to the Glazur again: the eggplant stuffed with caviare was magnificent.

During what had become a regular coffee session in the Bureau quarters – close to being crowded with the addition of the new FBI agent – Andrews said: 'Looks like I'm going to miss the final act.' He was flying back ahead of Pauline, who was staying behind to supervise the packing of their apartment. Washington was confirmed.

'It won't be much of an act,' Cowley pointed out. 'Nothing will ever reach a court.'

'How much longer do you think you'll be here?'

Cowley shrugged. 'Difficult to say. Shouldn't be too long.'

'I can't imagine it arising – you know as well as I do that she's a pretty competent girl – but if Pauline has any problems can I tell her to call you? Packing up. Stuff like that?'

'Of course you can.'

'It's good that everything's as it was before between us.'

'Yes,' agreed Cowley. He wished the other man would stop saying things like that. He was actually considering it a strain, being constantly with the other man.

The following day, as promised, there was a cable from Washington. Hair samples found in the pockets of Yezhov's topcoat, one pocket of the jacket and in one pair of trousers made positive DNA matches with the hair of Ann Harris, Vladimir Suzlev, Lydia Orlenko and Nadia Revin. There was also positive comparison with buttons recovered from Yezhov's apartment and samples taken from the clothes of Ann Harris, Lydia Orlenko and Nadia Revin. When Cowley spoke to Danilov, the Russian said the Russian forensic team had reported that although there was no blood deposit, the knife *could* have been the murder weapon in every case. They were not prepared, however, to say the knife was *definitely* the weapon.

That night, on the eve of his departure, Barry Andrews threw his farewell party at the embassy club. He got drunk. There were speeches and the ambassador made a presentation. Cowley initially thought it was clumsy that the embassy staff chose a set of *matryoshka* dolls identical to those in Ann Harris's office upon which Paul Hughes's fingerprints had been found, but then realized they wouldn't have known the significance. Cowley danced twice with Pauline. When he invited her a third time, she declined.

He got up early the next morning, reversing their roles to drive Andrews to Sheremet'yevo. Pauline came as well.

'Look after her for me,' said Andrews, at the gate.

'I will.'

'By the time you get back to Washington, I'll probably have your job!' said Andrews, laughing at his own joke.

The polygraph had been discarded days ago, replaced by a much more aggressive interrogation team, a mix of CIA and FBI questioners.

'Pamela doesn't think you were with her on January 17.'

'I was!'

'Why did the polygraph register your uncertainty?'

'I don't know!'

'Your wife says she isn't sure that you got home before twelve, when the Russian woman was attacked.'

'I was!'

'Why would she say she isn't sure?'

'Maybe she's trying to get back at me!'

'You did go over to the Russians, didn't you?'

'No!'

'We've got independent confirmation from a Russian source.'

'Liars!'

'Tell us about it. The killings and the rest of it. We could do a deal if you told us everything.'

'There's nothing to tell!'

'We're going to break you, Paul. Find it all out in the end.'

'I didn't do it! Any of it!'

'Let's start again, from the beginning.'

Chapter Thirty-Eight

They assembled as before in the ante-room of the main conference chamber of the Federal Prosecutor's building, but on this occasion the mood was quite different, incongruously light-hearted. The immaculately uniformed Yevgennie Kosov was clearly nervous but concealing it well, politely deferential to both General Lapinsk and Nikolai Smolin. There had been several clean shirts for Danilov to choose from that morning and Olga had pressed the trousers of his suit without being asked. When he thanked her she said she was going to Larissa's flat, to watch the conference on their large-screen television. She seemed to expect Danilov to say something but he didn't. The American ambassador and Ralph Baxter accompanied Cowley but made it clear they did not intend taking part in the conference, but were there to observe. Cowley remarked to Danilov that the forensic findings settled everything: Danilov admitted, but only within the other investigator's hearing, that he was relieved. Until the Washington confirmation he'd considered the proof too circumstantial, by itself. He still had the feeling of anticlimax.

The room had been set up as it had been for the first conference, with a long row of tables on a raised dais at one end of the room, and translator facilities for the journalists. Danilov guessed the hall was more crowded now than it had been the first time. There was a lot of noise and it was hot under the camera lights. As he sat down Danilov saw the man who had asked the question about Ann Harris's hair shearing and realized he had forgotten to complete the inquiry he'd had Pavin begin. It didn't matter any more.

The orchestrating skills of Senator Burden's media organizer were badly missed: for the first time Danilov was aware of the shallowness of Smolin's voice, which frequently failed to carry, despite the microphones. Several times there were shouted requests, both in Russian and in English, for the man to repeat himself and to speak more loudly.

The Federal Prosecutor tried. He insisted there was no doubt of the guilt of the man they had in custody. With unhesitating distortion, Smolin said forensic tests both in Washington and here in Moscow had positively identified samples recovered from the man's clothing as having come from the bodies of the victims. They had also recovered the murder weapon, a single-edged knife the man had been carrying in a home-made sheath at the time of his arrest. Like a conjuror reaching his favourite trick, Smolin abruptly produced the knife from inside his jacket and held it aloft: there was a renewed explosion of camera lights and repeated requests for Smolin to show it in various ways to various camera positions. Cowley frowned sideways to Danilov, who shrugged: he'd thought the knife was still in the forensic laboratory. That was where it should have been.

Once more there was a moment of surprised silence when Smolin finished talking, but this time it was more understandable because the Federal Prosecutor had provided no identification of their suspect. Demands for a name echoed, both in Russian and English, from several parts of the hall. Smolin said that at this time no decision had been reached about publicly identifying the man. There was a long history of mental illness. There had been two earlier instances of attacks upon women, for both of which he had served periods of detention in psychiatric clinics. He was in such a clinic now. The psychiatrist treating him there had assessed the man incapable of understanding what he was accused of: at the moment and in the foreseeable future it would be impossible to bring him before a court. The absence of any formal charge and subsequent criminal conviction on the overwhelming evidence was regrettable but in the circumstances unavoidable. And because of those circumstances, it would be wrong to divulge a name. Under repeated pressure Smolin conceded that the man was twenty-nine years old, worked as a labourer – although he refused to say where – and was unmarried. He lived at home with his mother.

Trying to keep the chronology in sequence, the Federal Prosecutor introduced Kosov, who performed better than Danilov had expected from the ante-room apprehension. Kosov said the seizure had resulted from sound, practical police work, undertaken from the moment of his Militia station receiving the request to be on the look-out for suspicious characters or behaviour within the area in which all the murders had taken place. The man had tried to hide and then run when he had been challenged by a foot patrol. There had been a brief struggle but the man had not positively tried to resist arrest, although he was extremely – if not unnaturally – strong as he could personally attest. The remark created precisely the questioning reaction Kosov intended and he allowed the cell fight to be drawn out of him.

Danilov despised the boastfulness, but was scarcely successful in minimizing it when the questioning switched to him after Kosov named him as the other person involved in the fracas. Danilov was forced to admit it had taken two of them to subdue the unnamed Yezhov: Danilov guessed – correctly as it later transpired – how that would be appear in print when an American reporter suggested that Yezhov possessed the strength of two men.

The conference shifted, with questions answered alternately by Danilov and Cowley. They disclosed the finding of some buttons in Yezhov's possession and then more hidden beneath the floor-boards of his bedroom. Danilov slightly redressed the prosecutor's earlier exaggeration by deferring to Cowley to explain the pyrolysis and gas chromatographic techniques for matching the buttons and confirming by deoxyribonucleic acid analysis that the hair samples came from the murder victims. To a question from the man who had talked of Ann Harris's defilement at the first conference and whom Danilov knew to be a *New York Times* reporter named Erickson, Cowley agreed that DNA tests were legally and scientifically regarded as infallible.

After the general conference, both Danilov and Cowley gave separate interviews to the three major American television networks and following that took part in a shared interview with British, French and German networks. The British interviewer asked if there had been any friction in their working relationship. Both Cowley and Danilov said there had not, at any time.

Later, in the ante-room, Nikolai Smolin declared the morning to have been a complete success. Having heard the British TV exchange, the Federal Prosecutor added that the whole affair had established that joint investigations were possible, which should be kept in mind in the future. The American ambassador promised to convey the feeling to Washington. He understood there was a personal letter of thanks on its way from the Secretary of State for the complete cooperation of the host nation. Senator Burden was also writing, but had asked in advance for his gratitude to be expressed.

Kosov carefully chose a moment when Danilov was briefly apart from anyone else in the room. 'It *did* go well, didn't it?'

'I thought so.'

'I found it easier than I thought I would.'

'You were very impressive,' praised Danilov, waiting.

Kosov quickly ensured they were still by themselves. 'You heard any syndicate names yet?'

'No.'

'You won't forget to tell me, if you do?'

'Of course not.'

'Have you spoken to Agayans?'

'No.'

'I think he might feel less pressured.'

'That's good,' said Danilov. He'd make another visit to Leninskii Prospekt soon. But not to seek an outright gift. He'd insist on paying Agayans's price for whatever he wanted. He guessed Agayans would want dollars, though, not roubles.

Danilov rode back to Petrovka beside the chauffeur-driven General. Lapinsk said: 'It's a very successful conclusion to my command.'

'I'm pleased it's worked out as it has.'

'I've only got another fifteen months to go.'

'Let's hope it's quiet.'

'Before you arrived this morning I was talking with Smolin about my successor.'

Danilov looked across the car, beginning to concentrate on the conversation. 'Who is it to be?'

Lapinsk smiled. 'A final decision hasn't been made. But you've impressed a great many people, Dimitri Ivanovich. I personally don't have any doubt who it will be. So, in advance, congratulations.'

Danilov said: 'I'm very pleased,' and wished he were more so.

Danilov had been in his office for an hour when the convenient direct-dial telephone sounded. Larissa said: 'You looked very good on television. Better even than last time.' She sounded subdued.

'I thought Yevgennie was good.'

She ignored the remark. 'I didn't know you actually fought the murderer.'

Convicted without the formality of a trial, thought Danilov: he was glad Yezhov's name had been withheld. 'It was really quite different from how it sounded.'

'Olga watched with me. She seemed surprised you hadn't told her.'

'She said she was coming.'

'She asked me, outright.'

The unease stirred through Danilov. 'What did you say?'

'I wanted to tell her it was true. And that I loved you. But I didn't. I said she was being silly.'

'Did she believe you?'

'I don't know. I miss you.'

Danilov supposed he was missing Larissa. 'It's best this way.'

'I don't think so.'

Danilov didn't respond.

'Are you still there?'

'Yes.'

'I've called several times before.'

'I've been out of the office a lot.'

'I'm sorry. For how I behaved before.'

'It doesn't matter.'

'If I hadn't been like that, Olga wouldn't have suspected.'

Danilov supposed she was right. 'It's too late now.'

'I don't want it to be too late. To end.'

'We both decided it had to.'

'I didn't decide. You did. Come to see me at the hotel. Just to talk.'

'There's no . . . it wouldn't achieve anything.'

'I promise not to be like I was before.'

'No.' He shouldn't give in: as much as he wanted to, he shouldn't give in.

'And I won't go on about your leaving Olga and my leaving

Yevgennie. I won't make demands. We can just be together, whenever you want.'

He didn't want her to talk like this; to prostrate herself. This wasn't Larissa. 'There's a lot to do. Tidying up.'

'I said whenever.'

'Maybe I can telephone? We could talk on the telephone.'

'I meant what I said. About loving you. I really do.'

Danilov refused to respond as he knew she wanted. 'I'll telephone,' he repeated.

'It won't become difficult, not again.'

It would if he let it, Danilov decided, replacing the telephone. He thought he knew now what was giving him the unsettled, anticlimactic feeling. The telephone jarred into the office again, breaking any further reflection.

Cowley said: 'All the forensic stuff has come in overnight.'

'We may as well assemble it today,' suggested Danilov. He might even be in time to present it to the Federal Prosecutor, although there was hardly any hurry.

'That's what I was thinking,' Cowley agreed. He couldn't imagine his having to stay in Moscow more than another few days: there was nothing more to do. He wondered if Pauline would accept an invitation for them to have dinner together before he left.

Chapter Thirty-Nine

All Petr Yezhov's clothing tested in America was returned with the detailed forensic report, which meant Cowley had to transport two suitcase-sized containers to Petrovka, where all the evidence had been collected and logged. Two taxis raced each other to get to him outside the embassy in response to the Marlboro signal, imagining a trip to the airport. At Petrovka, Pavin helped him carry it up to the exhibit room, for the separate findings to be compared and finally assembled, as they would be for any presentation in court. All three of them were relaxed, the hard grind over.

'We've got to make a proper submission to the Federal Prosecutor,' Danilov disclosed, repeating that morning's instructions from his briefing with Lapinsk. 'They're going to take the formalities as far as they properly can.' He smiled. 'The world has to see true Russian justice in action,' he added, providing his own judgment. 'We will never lose the Stalin guilt.'

'We'd have probably done the same, in the circumstances,' Cowley accepted, going along with the cynicism. 'Everyone likes to capitalize on a success.'

'There may be an open statement before a judge. The problem is publicly naming Yezhov: the Prosecutor's reluctant to do that.'

'I think he's right,' said Cowley. He wouldn't have to wait around, for either a formal submission or a later court statement: if his presence was thought necessary for either he could fly back. He wondered if Pauline would still be in Moscow.

They considered the Russian findings first, Danilov reading through it aloud, Cowley following on his own copy. The clothes division had left for Russian scientific analysis a jacket, two pairs of trousers, a pair of work dungarees, three shirts, two sets of underwear, a pair of workboots, a very worn pair of training plimsolls and the knife.

From the clothing a number of hairs had been recovered. They had been visually and microscopically compared with hair samples taken from all the victims and in only one instance, a single blonde hair discovered on the jacket, was there any possible similarity. It was with the blonde hair of Nadia Revin. The opinion refused to call it a definite match. There had been minute blood samples recovered from the underwear, both B Rhesus Positive, which was Yezhov's grouping. No samples taken from the workboots had matched with any dirt, mud or dust at any of the murder scenes: although the ground would have been frozen at the actual time of the killing, particular attention had been paid to the soil around Nadia Revin's garage. The knife was single-edged, twenty-seven centimetres long, five centimetres wide at its broadest and five millimetres thick at its unhoned edge. It was a very common type of work or kitchen knife. The width and thickness could be presented as being consistent with the entry wounds: none of the killing thrusts had been identical in depth, but the narrowing of the wound as it progressed through the bodies could again be consistent with the leading, pointed part of the blade. The knife had held no blood traces. There were deposits of citric acid, obviously left from the cutting of fruit. The home-made sheath had been opened, for the inside to be examined. There had been four haem deposits on the inside of the leather. All had proven to be animal blood. There were more traces of citric acid, a minute amount of whey, analysed to be from goats' cheese, and minute particles of nail and skin debris – probably the result of nail paring – again from Yezhov.

Danilov came up from the file. 'And the knife itself.'

' "Consistent with," ' Cowley qualified. 'That's not conclusive. Would you go to court with that?'

'The decision of the Federal Prosecutor,' Danilov recalled, partially side-stepping. 'On balance I think we probably would.' Avoiding no further, he said: 'But I'm glad you've got more.'

They reversed the comparison procedure, Cowley dictating to Danilov's checking: everything from Washington had been duplicated in Russian as well as English. Cowley admired the consideration.

Subjected to American examination had been the quilted topcoat Yezhov had been wearing when he was seized, together with a jacket, a jerkin, two pairs of trousers, three shirts, a set of underwear and one pair of shoes. And the buttons recovered from Yezhov and later from his bedroom cache.

The blood smear on the quilted coat had been B Rhesus Positive and proved, under DNA analysis, to be that of Yezhov himself. From the left-hand pocket of the coat had been recovered four separate hairs, two deeply embedded in the lining. One was positively identified under the DNA test as having come from Vladimir Suzlev. The other three, under the same test, were definitely from Ann Harris. From the right-hand pocket six separate strands were lifted, three also deeply implanted in the lining. One remained unidentified. One was from Lydia Orlenko. Four were provably traceable to Nadia Revin. Three more hairs from Ann Harris were found in the left-hand pocket of one of the pairs of trousers. A single hair from Lydia Orlenko had been embedded inside the left-arm sleeve cuff of the jerkin.

The pyrolysis test on buttons required them to be heated to 770 degrees Centigrade. This converted the material into gas, to be run through a chromatograph mass spectrometer. It had therefore been necessary to destroy four of the samples under scientific test conditions. One of the buttons had beyond doubt formed part of a set of six green coloured fastenings, three of which had remained on the shirt, close to and below where her belt would have covered them, listed as being that worn by Ann Harris on the night of her murder. Five buttons were analysed by a Foyier Transformer infra-red spectrometer: two unquestionably came from the same shirt, actually completing the hacked-off green set. In the holes of two others, one blue, one brown, remained strands of the cotton that had secured identical buttons to the outer coat that Lydia Orlenko had worn when she was attacked, and to the fashionable driving jacket in which Nadia Revin had kept warm on her way home from the Metropole Hotel. Both buttons again proved positive, under pyrolysis.

Cowley paused, briefly looking up from his recitation of the scientific facts. 'There was no comparison possible with three manufactured from a nylon base or one of polyester. Neither from the three . . .' Cowley faltered, frowning up to meet the puzzlement of both Danilov and Pavin. '. . . Neither from the three made from bone, which is not a substance reacting to the stated tests,' he forced himself to finish, unevenly.

There were several moments of complete silence in the room. Then Pavin insisted, defensively: 'The log isn't wrong.'

'We compiled it together,' Cowley agreed.

'Let's do it again,' Danilov insisted.

They did. With the same result.

'It doesn't make sense,' complained Pavin, the man of absolute accuracy.

'There's one way it could,' Danilov suggested.

'It's unthinkable!' blurted Cowley.

'Find another explanation.'

There was a further silence, then: 'I can't.'

The Moscow offices of the *New York Times* are on Ulitza Sadovo Samotechanya, about a mile from the American embassy, so it was convenient for them both to stop en route to taking Cowley to the US compound. The visit only took minutes. Afterwards, they agreed to meet again that evening: by then they would both have guidance. Danilov was quite open about going back to the Lubyanka.

With so much to transmit to Washington – and certainly verbally to discuss as well, on a secure line – Cowley set out at once for the FBI office. But almost at once he paused, changing his mind to make the simple detour. Pauline opened the door, smiling curiously.

'Barry asked me if I'd make sure there were no problems, remember?' Cowley said.

The agreement to a meeting had been instant, as before, but Danilov entered the suite of Kir Gugin more confidently on this second occasion.

Danilov said at once: 'I know how you used me. Congratulations. It worked very well.'

Gugin shook his head. 'You confuse me.'

Danilov was impatient with the charade. 'I want you to use me again. There was more, wasn't there? You hadn't finished.'

The Colonel, whose intended disruption had itself been disrupted by the seizure of Petr Yezhov and who had been seeking a way to recover, smiled cautiously. 'Why don't we talk about it?'

372

'Why don't you just give me what I want?'

The effect would be what he wanted, Gugin reflected: the other man deserved the resentful independence, having realized the earlier manipulation. 'Why not?' he agreed.

Chapter Forty

In one of those bureaucratic decisions defying logic, unless it had to do with saving money, Barry Andrews had again been booked into the temporary, scarcely basic hotel across the river in Pentagon City. The commute to and from FBI headquarters was almost an hour if he hit rush-hour traffic, like he was doing this morning. All in all, Andrews was annoyed, thoroughly pissed off at the thoughtlessness. He didn't deserve it; didn't his record describe him as outstanding? He bet Cowley had never been dumped out in the boondocks, although Christ knows he'd deserved to be, so many times. Andrews felt the anger building and tried to stop it getting worse. Foolish to lose his temper. He'd given himself plenty of time, so it didn't matter that he was stuck in traffic. He'd still be early: early enough maybe to grab some breakfast because he refused to eat anything in that Pentagon City dog's nest. Give him time to settle down. That was the thing to do. Settle down. Stay calm: calm and cool. Today was *the* day. Reward time, after the Moscow imprisonment. Today he was going to get the final assignment of duties, within the Russian division. And ahead of Cowley's return. Showed what little clout the guy had, in his own section, decisions being made without him.

The traffic block shifted and Andrews was able to start moving slowly across the 14th Street bridge. He'd certainly been treated pretty good since he'd gotten back, apart from the hotel. He guessed everyone getting a headquarters posting probably received the welcoming letter from the Director, but he'd liked the gesture: deserved it, too. And all the guys in the division had been friendly, beers after work the first night, always someone suggesting lunch, offers of help from everyone if he needed it. Had him marked out, Andrews guessed. Someone on the ascendancy: asshole creeping. He didn't care. It was good.

He'd respond, of course: invent some problems so no one would think he was too smart, not needing help from anyone.

Which he didn't. Still wise to settle in, though: settle in and see which way the wheels turned. Even the shitty hotel wouldn't be an irritant much longer. He'd kept on top of the letting agency and been promised he could get back into Bethesda by the week-end. Perfect timing for Pauline's arrival. Have to go through it with her again, how he wanted it all to be. She hadn't been properly concentrating in Moscow. The distraction of Cowley, he decided: everyone distracted by William John Cowley, reformed alcoholic, reformed everything, Mr Good Guy. If the man with the beard and the trick with feeding five thousand hadn't got there first, Cowley could have invented a whole new religion.

The traffic was smoother when he left the bridge and Andrews settled more comfortably back in his seat: he'd been unaware of being tensed forward like that. It was going to be interesting, when Pauline got back: watching, listening, picking up the hints that would be there to what they'd done behind his back in Moscow. That was going to be the best part, in the very begin-ning. The first game. Cultivating the revived friendship, putting them together all the time and all the time each of them knowing – because they *always* had to know – that he had her. Who'd won. She was a bitch, he decided suddenly. Didn't deserve him. No matter.

Andrews left the vehicle in the car-park on 12th Street to walk the last few hundred yards, admiring the squat red building as he approached. Had it really been personally designed by Hoover with machine-gun emplacements at the corners, to put down any communist-inspired insurrection? Quirky thing to find out: make a good cocktail-party story, if it were true. He was anticipating a lot of parties.

Entering the darker foyer from the outside brightness of a spring morning, Andrews didn't immediately see the personal assistant who'd hand-delivered the Director's letter. He was almost at the entry security turnstile, activating pass in his hand, when the normally bland-faced Fletcher approached, smiling this time.

'Assignment day,' Fletcher announced. 'I'm to take you.'

Andrews smiled in return, falling into step with the man. 'Any news from Moscow?'

'Being wrapped up,' the man promised.

On their way up through the floors and more monitoring turn-stiles, Andrews said he was glad to be back in America ('although Moscow was a marvellous workplace: don't get me wrong') and that the traffic here was a mess but the weather wonderful and that he might get himself a small boat, either on the Potomac or up on Chesapeake.

'Sounds good,' agreed Fletcher, standing back at the entrance to an anonymous, unmarked room for Andrews to enter.

Which he did. To stop dead, frozen, uncomprehending.

It was a large room but quite bare, just closed metal cupboards along one side and a table dividing it, although not quite in the middle.

William Cowley was sitting at the table. With Dimitri Danilov beside him.

Andrews was utterly astonished, momentarily beyond speech or thought. 'Bill . . . ! What in the name of . . . ?'

'Waiting for you, Barry. Come on in.'

Waiting for him? Why the hell were they waiting for him? He abruptly became conscious of other things in the room. There was a side-table, with a male stenographer and recording appar-atus, red operating lights already on. And other men. He hadn't seen them when he'd walked in but he became aware of them now. Five, all lined along the back. 'I don't understand . . . I mean what . . .'

'We know you did it, Barry. All of them. I want you to tell me about it. Everything. You'll do that now that we know, won't you?' Cowley hoped it wouldn't be a long interrogation. Mead-ows, the psychiatrist at Quantico, had guessed it wouldn't be, but then admitted he wasn't sure.

'Bill! I don't know what the hell you're talking about! Help me here! What's happening?'

So it wasn't going to be easy. Hit him hard, Meadows had advised. 'You miscounted. Miscalculated, too, but you might have gotten away with it if you hadn't miscounted. And forgotten colours. It's always the silly little things, isn't it?'

What was the motherfucker on about? Didn't Cowley know he had to be careful: that he was going to take over the divisional directorship very soon, replacing him here like he'd replaced him

376

everywhere else, even in bed? 'Help me understand, Bill! For Christ's sake!'

'You know. We know. We just want you to tell us about it.'

'Bill!' exclaimed Andrews. Too loud: shouldn't have sounded so loud, like he had something to be frightened about. Didn't have anything to be frightened about.

'Buttons,' declared Danilov, entering the interrogation: the agreed arrangement, against what might happen later, was that the tape would show shared questioning. 'When Yezhov was seized, he had two buttons on him. And there were ten, at the apartment. Making twelve. They were all sent back here, because of America's superior technology. Sent by you. But we got fifteen back: fifteen of which nine all came from the women killed or attacked.'

What did they think they were talking about, trying to trick him? Little people, trying to trick *him*! 'Listen! This isn't right! I just shipped back what you gave me, Bill. You know that. You gave me the buttons in the plastic exhibit bags and I simply pouched them. That's how it was: the job I was ordered to do, by the Director. I'm damned if I'm going to get stuck with some problem I don't even understand, apart from something to do with mistaken arithmetic.'

'This is a pretty big problem and we didn't get our arithmetic wrong,' said Cowley, keeping his voice as low as he'd been instructed at Quantico, although it wasn't easy for him. 'I counted. Dimitri counted. Pavin counted. All of us. Separately. And each of those counts before I handed them over to you. You got it wrong, Barry. Finally fucked it up. Blew it.'

Friends could use his Christian name. Not enemies. Not people he hated: *the* person he hated most of all. Hadn't fucked anything up.

'And not just counted,' Danilov came in. 'We recorded the individual colours, as well. Three red, three green, two blue, one brown, and three fashioned out of bone. No black. Yet two black buttons arrived here: and one of them conveniently, for the conviction of Petr Yezhov, from Nadia Revin's skirt.' He'd been nervous to begin with: nervous at being in America for the first time – alone, vulnerable, not knowing how to behave – and earlier at meeting the FBI Director and then taking part in this interrogation, on show in front of so many Americans, in front of everybody, because it was all being recorded to be listened to and discussed later, back in Moscow. But it was better now it had started. He didn't think there was going to be a confession, though: would have wagered there wouldn't be, if he hadn't wanted the money for other things.

He'd let them talk, Andrews decided. Hear the idiots out.

'You fooled me,' Cowley admitted, sacrificing any later discomfort from the tape play-back to achieve the collapse he wanted. 'I missed it all, until you got the count wrong. Then I went back over everything. It was all disjointed, of course. Like things are. Let me throw something at you. How about your attack upon Lydia Orlenko, when thank God she didn't die?'

'This is ridiculous.' Enough! They should talk, not him.

'How about your remark?' suggested Cowley, relentlessly, allowing himself at last to hate this man who'd stolen his wife. ' "What about the woman last night? There must be *something*!" '

Andrews shook his head, wearily. 'This isn't making any sense. It's quite ridiculous.'

'Now it isn't,' insisted Cowley. 'It didn't make sense, not then. Remember? It was when I came back from interviewing Hughes, about the attack upon Lydia Orlenko. But you didn't *know*, then, who the victim had been. So how did you know it was a *woman*? The first attack was on a man. So it could have been another man. Unless you *knew* it had been a woman.'

Weak shot. Another trick. Perry Mason shit. Andrews gave a heavy sigh. 'I really don't know what we're doing here. Talking about.'

'Let's try another quote,' suggested Cowley. ' "And who would have thought it, about innocent little Pamela?" What about that?'

Andrews expanded another tired sigh. 'Why don't *you* tell me? What about it?'

'I hadn't even talked about Pamela Donnelly's alibi then. So how did you know Pamela was involved, unless you'd tracked Hughes? Discovered he'd switched, from Ann to Pam Donnelly. Which you had, hadn't you? You were stalking everybody, weren't you? Planning your perfect serial murders: murders you'd learned all about from the FBI training lectures . . . ?'

378

'. . . This is pitiful . . .'

'I know how it was,' Cowley pressed on. 'I know Ann had dumped you, for Hughes. So I think you set it all up. Killing Vladimir Suzlev, knowing he was often Hughes's driver, which you could prove. And then killing Ann, taking the hair and everything else to fix all the evidence – like you fixed it in the end – to overwhelm any possible defence Hughes might have. You planned it perfectly, didn't you? You set out to destroy a rival – a better lover than you – and the mistress who despised you. And intended to solve both the killing of Suzlev and Ann Harris to come back here in glory. Must have knocked you sideways when I got assigned, instead of you.'

Still weak. Still deniable. Cowley was fucking himself: digging a deeper and deeper hole, which would bury him. All this shit would be laughed at, in court. Ruin the motherfucker. *Mr Cowley, is it not a fact that my client married your ex-wife, after your marital break-up? Is it not a fact that these entire accusations are motivated by jealousy, an insane desire for revenge? Answer, Mr Cowley! I want an answer! Will the court please order Mr Cowley to answer!* Andrews looked towards the stenographer and the red-lighted machine and said: 'I am very glad this is all being recorded. It needs to be.'

Danilov had been out of the exchange too long: it had had to be this way – the way they had rehearsed on the plane coming from Moscow and again in discussions with the Director and the FBI legal experts – but he was anxious to involve himself in the recording again. Seeing his chance, the Russian said: 'We're sure it needs to be recorded, too.' A pause. Then: 'Mr Droop.'

Not that! Jesus, not that! He'd hated Ann for laughing at him when he couldn't make love to her, sneering at him as Mr Droop. He'd loathed worst of all being called that, pleaded with her not to say it, which had made her say it all the more.

Cowley had to strive for control at the expressionless, blank reaction. It was becoming almost impossible not to scream at this man: shout at him, go across the table and beat the shit and a confession from the son-of-a-bitch. Mockery, the Quantico psychiatrist had recommended: just as he'd recommended they wait for Andrews to arrive expecting to learn of his appointment and get hit like this, instead. Staying, hard as it was, with the guidance, Cowley said: 'That was what she called you, wasn't it Barry? Laughed at you, because you couldn't get it up? Not like Hughes could get it up for her, kinky though he might have been. Mr Droop! Shit, Barry, that's funny! Really funny!'

'NO!' Fuck . . . fuck! fuck! fuck! Why had he said anything? Reacted? Should have ignored it.

'Yes, Barry.'

Had to recover: end this nonsense. He looked back to the empty-faced men between him and the door, then back to Cowley. 'I refuse to go on with this! Get someone here in authority!'

'Mr Droop.' Cowley forced himself to laugh again. 'Imagine being called Mr Droop!'

'Don't call me that! Won't have it!' Fool! He shouldn't have spoken. Ann's fault. All her fault. Whore: dirty, wonderful whore.

It was Danilov who gestured sideways, to the stenographer and all his apparatus. The man seemed to be waiting, primed, his hand going to one of the smaller pieces of equipment. The telephone intercepts that Gugin had provided, along with so much else, echoed into the room, as recordings always seem to echo.

'Hi, Mr Droop! Thought I'd see how you're doing. A week or two since we spoke. Feel better now, Mr Droop?'

'Don't call me that! I told you not to call me that!'

His voice! Incontrovertibly his voice. The scientific bastards here in this building could prove voiceprints, as well as fingerprints and DNA genetics and Christ knows what else! Why were they doing this to him? Wasn't fair.

'Paul hurt me again last night, Mr Droop. Not just my tits, either. He's got this dildo now. Uses it. That turn you on, Mr Droop? You like to play a little, with the dildo? Think it might help? Something needs to help, doesn't it, Mr Droop?'

'Bitch!'

Argue inadmissibility. Illegally recorded and not even here in America: in Moscow, the asshole of the world.

'That's not what you said last time, Barry. Liked me talking dirty last time. Telling you. Got the pecker moving then, didn't we?'

Why had she been so evil? So wonderful and beautiful and exciting. And evil.

'*Don't Ann. Please don't.*'

'*I think it's fun Barry. Except you can't make it. That's not fun.*'

'*It won't happen again, Ann. I promise it won't happen again. Please!*'

'*Promise not to be Mr Droop ever again! Promise me!*'

'*I promise! I really promise!*'

It was Danilov who gestured for the recording to be stopped. There was a moment of complete silence. Oddly, Danilov imagined an attitude of embarrassment throughout the room. Which wasn't odd, he decided. It was absurd. How could they be embarrassed, trapping a monster?

'Fake,' said Andrews, the beginning of desperation. 'Fake. Deniable.'

'We've got a witness,' said Cowley, sweating, wondering how long he could go on prodding like this. 'Remember I told you about interviewing the best friend, Judy Billington . . .' He stopped, as the Quantico psychiatrist had ordered he should. 'That must have worried you. Not being sure if there was anything in the letters you couldn't get to in the apartment . . . just like there turned out to be a recording, as there was for Hughes . . . Didn't that worry you . . . ?'

Ignore it, don't answer.

'You remember me telling you about Judy Billington, don't you?'

Wanted him to speak. Trap himself. Say nothing.

'Ann *did* tell her something, on the home leave. Told her about someone at the embassy: someone she called Mr Droop who tried to be a lover but couldn't make it. I didn't know who that was at the time. But I do now.'

It took every bit of control that Andrews could find but he did find it. Circumstantial but inadmissible: he was sure of it. They were in America now, land of the free and protected. Not an asshole society like Russia, where everything could be bent to fit. There had to be a formal charge and there had to be formal, legally acceptable evidence, and they didn't have it. He was cleverer than them all: always had been. Firm-voiced, unafraid, he said: 'I told you I wanted someone here of authority. Someone to end all this . . .' He turned to the men behind him. 'There'll be a civil action, against each of you. As well as criminal proceedings. Enjoy today. It'll be the last for any of you, here at headquarters. Anywhere. I don't know how you got caught up in this, but I feel sorry for you. Pity you.'

'We've taken a formal statement from Judy Billington. She will give evidence about Mr Droop, if she's called.'

'So will Fred Erickson,' said Danilov. 'You know Fred Erickson, the *New York Times* man, don't you? He regards you as a good contact. Particularly after your prompting him before the Moscow press conference about Ann Harris being defiled in some way, meaning her hair I guess. Which no one publicly knew about then. But guaranteed a sensation.'

'Can't understand why you did that,' resumed Cowley. 'Unless, of course, you wanted to build it all up into a case we were never going to be able to solve. Make us look stupid. Or was it to make *me* look stupid? That's what the psychiatrist, Dr Meadows, thinks. He thinks you hate me: that stealing Pauline away was part of hating me. And that when I got assigned, taking the case and the glory away from you, you tried to kill Lydia Orlenko and then *did* kill Nadia Revin to create a serial killing I couldn't solve. And I wouldn't have been able to, Barry, if you'd left it there. But you couldn't, could you? You'd planned the perfect murders and the perfect solution and you wanted to show how you meant Hughes to be convicted, didn't you? You got confused there. You know what you did? You caught yourself! How about that, Barry! Perfect murders, perfect solutions.'

No! Dear God no! Don't give the bastards the satisfaction of responding. Would have liked to, though. Careful. Mustn't lose control. That's what they wanted. For him to lose control. Blurt something out. Wouldn't though. Knew all the tricks. Like he knew all about serial killings from what they'd taught him in Quantico.

'We'll have your sorority ring, from your left hand,' said Danilov. 'It'll match the bruise measurements on those you killed, won't it?'

Cowley was holding back by his fingertips the furious disgust he felt for the other man. He forced himself to think of the drill, the inviolable rule: always stay objective, never let personal feelings intrude. But how could he stop personal feelings intruding? 'I went to see Pauline, after you left. I wasn't sure, when I got there, what I was even going to say, although I guessed then how you'd fixed the evidence against Yezhov, planting all the stuff you'd collected in the clothing I gave you to send back here. But we didn't have much then. Just the miscount that could have only been you. Pauline was packing: surrounded by boxes and stuff. I was trying to think of anything odd – anything that didn't fit – and I remembered something she'd said, the night I took her to the embassy club while you were back here for the relocation interview. We were talking about the first night; the dinner party. You know what she said then? She said: "Did you sort out the problems of the world? You seemed to talk long enough." It didn't register at the time, but when I went back, looking for things, I asked her what she'd meant. And she told me that within fifteen minutes of my leaving your apartment after that dinner you went out, too. Told her you had something you'd forgotten that couldn't wait until morning to talk to me about. And you didn't get back for two hours. She's absolutely definite, about that. But you didn't catch up with me. You went to Granovskaya and attacked Lydia Orlenko, didn't you? We've timed it out. It all fits quite easily into a two-hour time frame.'

Bitch! Didn't matter. Her word against his, no corroboration. Still in the clear. Still cleverer than them.

' "It was pretty common knowledge that Ann moved about a bit but I didn't know she was quite like she was," ' quoted Cowley. 'How's that strike you?'

Andrews shook his head, in patronizing dismissal. 'This will have to end sometime, I suppose?'

'That was something else Pauline said, after the embassy party. Again I missed it, then. But not now. How come, if Pauline knew Ann screwed around – that it was pretty common knowledge – that *you* didn't tell me? You didn't want me to start looking in your direction, did you? Steered me away, all the time.'

An even weaker shot. Stay disdainful.

Cowley shook his head, both in revulsion and in uncertainty that he'd properly followed the guidance Dr Meadows had suggested. 'I know you're sick. Doubly sick, because we've discussed it with psychiatrists and had it explained to us how, mad as you are, you faked another madness to fit all the profiles of a serial

383

killer and *became* one, by intent . . . Remember telling me you'd heard all the Quantico lectures? I know you have. We've checked all your course attendances, when you learned how to do it . . .'

Bastard was out of control now: wallowing. Nothing to worry about.

'But you even took your sickness lower, didn't you Barry? Beyond belief. No one at Quantico has ever heard of something quite as obscene. I don't suppose obscene is a big enough word, but I can't think of another. Don't *want* to think of another.' The psychiatrist had instructed him constantly to show contempt, judging Andrews's motivation to be personal, between the two of them, but there wasn't much left and Andrews hadn't broken. It wasn't necessary, with all they had, but Cowley *needed* the man to break. He didn't give a fuck about illness, mental or physical. It was personal with him now. Like he supposed it always had been.

What was Cowley talking about? It couldn't be that! Not that!

Cowley forced himself on. 'When I went to Pauline she was packing, like I said. I poked about, making out to help: didn't want to alarm her, thinking you were under suspicion, not then . . .' How the hell could he show more contempt – goad further – than he'd done already? Lying, he said: 'She liked me being there. Told me it was like the old times you kept on about, only better without you there. She felt good about it.' Andrews was flushing, shifting his feet, angry! Cowley said: 'You really think she wouldn't have noticed? Someone like Pauline! Christ that was dumb! That was really dumb! What was it you called her? Goddess of the kitchen?'

Andrews looked warily across the table. No! It wasn't possible! No one was to know!

'She couldn't understand it, of course. Held it up to me and said she knew everything in her kitchen and that the knife definitely wasn't hers. Didn't even fit any of the sets she had.'

'But it *did* fit a set.' Danilov picked it up on rehearsed cue. 'Perfectly. The set I recovered from Ann Harris's apartment on Ulitza Pushkinskaya. It's even printed with the maker's name, Kuikut, on the blade. And it's on the knife rack we took for evidence, too.'

'And the handle has your fingerprints all over it. You should

384

have kept your rubber gloves on: the rubber kitchen gloves Pauline could never understand disappearing like they did. Had to spend a lot of time, I guess, getting the tobacco smell all over them from that cigar habit you specially acquired to connect with Hughes's smoking. With the knife maybe you should have better remembered the Quantico lectures about serial killers needing souvenirs. And stopped yourself. But you couldn't by then, could you? You'd *become* the serial killer you wanted to be.'

Andrews smiled. 'Cleverer than you. Always cleverer than you.' He'd wanted them to know. Now they would. Perfect.

He began to hum.

Neither felt like celebrating – Cowley least of all – but the American decided he had to make as big an effort as possible for the few days Danilov remained in Washington, and they both ended up trying, each for the other.

They ate at the Occidental, close to the FBI headquarters, and at two separate restaurants in Georgetown, a district Danilov preferred to any others they visited. Cowley imposed upon the Secret Service and got the Russian ahead of the normal tour of the White House and waited in a queue he didn't want to be part of to get to the top of the Washington Monument. There was another special visit to the Congress buildings and the usual tourist route to the Lincoln and Vietnam monuments. One night they saw a Shakespeare production at the Kennedy Center. Cowley considered asking Pauline to join them, but quickly abandoned the idea. On the last day they returned to Georgetown, to eat and for Danilov to shop: Cowley planned to drive direct to Dulles airport, when they'd finished.

'It all worked out in the end,' Danilov suggested. They were in a French café just beyond Wisconsin Avenue, at Danilov's request. He ordered soft-shelled crabs, which he'd eaten at most meals.

'We put Yezhov into psychiatric clinic. Sent him irreversibly mad,' Cowley insisted. He'd ordered the crabs, too, although he wasn't hungry. He had more tidying up to do, after putting Danilov on the plane. He was uncertain how it was going to go.

'Andrews's victim, as much as any of the others.'

'We contributed.'

'There hasn't been an investigation in the history of crime where mistakes weren't made.'

'I wish we hadn't made this one.'

'What's happened to Hughes?'

'They've had to stop: worried about *his* mental health. He's denied everything. They're still unsure about entrapment but the inconsistencies about the murder alibis have to be accepted simply as that now, inconsistencies. Maybe the wife was trying to get even: that's what he said. Difficult to believe she'd go that far, but who knows what a woman would do, in her situation . . . ?' He hesitated, sure of friendship with Danilov now. 'You think the KGB, or whatever it's called, had him?'

Danilov made a doubtful head movement. 'He'd have been useful, kept in the position he was. So they would have protected him, if they'd had him already. I don't know, but I'd guess they decided to sacrifice a potential, to cause as much disruption as possible. At which they did pretty well.'

'I'm curious,' announced Cowley. 'About you.'

'Me?'

'There's been a suggestion that *you're* KGB.'

Danilov laughed, hugely. 'Not me. The tapes were, obviously. But I'm not.'

'I don't suppose you'd tell me, if you were,' said Cowley, mildly.

'I suppose not. But I'm not.'

Cowley nodded, satisfied. 'The ambassador is being withdrawn, because of the other recordings. And Baxter. Ann Harris was a very busy girl. It's all pretty devastating.'

'The Cheka will regard it as a good operation,' guessed Danilov. He supposed during his visit to the FBI headquarters he would have been covertly photographed: there would have been fingerprints, too. 'Why didn't you tell me that your ex-wife married Andrews?'

Cowley pushed aside the barely touched meal. He shrugged. 'It didn't seem important. To affect anything.'

'It became the most important fact there was.'

'Hindsight,' shrugged Cowley. 'You sure you got everything you want?'

'Quite sure,' said Danilov. He'd had a far better haircut than he could ever have got in Moscow: at the moment there wasn't any grey showing at all. He'd bought three of the shirts he liked, the ones with the pin that went behind the tie, and perfume for Olga. He'd returned to the perfumery after the first purchase to get a second bottle for Larissa. The grateful Agayans had exceeded himself, changing roubles for dollars, the reverse of how it normally worked. Danilov was still determined against accepting the television or the washing machine or the dresses Olga wanted. He finished eating and said: 'All ready to go!'

'I'd like to know what happens to Yezhov.'

'You will,' promised Danilov. He paused, recalling the distant promise about secrets on a wind-swept murder scene. 'There are still some things belonging to Ann Harris to be returned to the family.'

'Yes?' said Cowley, curiously.

'The letters were listed as correspondence on the evidence list: not itemized. I don't think there's any need to send back all those talking about sex, do you?'

'None at all,' agreed Cowley. 'Always difficult to remain entirely detached, isn't it?'

'Always.'

Chapter Forty-One

There appeared to be as many packing cases lying around the Bethesda house as there had been on his previous visit. And Pauline moved around the room as if she couldn't see where she was going, actually collided with one of the larger containers in the hallway when she went to get coffee.

'The diagnosis is that he's absolutely insane,' said Cowley. 'Beyond treatment, although of course they'll try. They've got to.'

Pauline nodded, but absent-mindedly, as if she wasn't interested.

He wanted to move across to the couch where she was sitting: to hold her, comfort her. He stayed where he was, on the single chair. 'You're the official next-of-kin. There'll be some legal documents to sign. Committal authority. And a hearing, before a judge in chambers. I'll take you, if you'd like.'

She nodded again, listlessly. 'But no trial?'

'He's incapable of facing one. There wouldn't be any point.'

Pauline stirred, forcing herself to concentrate. 'What about the point of clearing that poor bastard in Moscow?'

Her voice was strident: cracked. Cowley supposed she deserved some near-hysteria. 'It's better this way. Yezhov's being cared for. He's not suffering.'

'Better for whom? For the Bureau! And Burden! For the great American public, who'll never learn an FBI man was a mass murderer!'

'And for you,' tried Cowley. 'You any idea of the clamour there'd be around you, if it was all made public?'

'Bullshit!' rejected Pauline, viciously. 'No one's given a fuck about me, making this decision! It's all political!'

'It's better,' repeated Cowley. Why was he being called upon to defend it?

'Expedient,' she corrected.

'OK, expedient.'

'Jesus! Doesn't it make you sick to your stomach?'

'Often.' Cowley watched her look helplessly around the disorganized living-room. He said: 'Barry will officially be listed on permanent sick leave. His salary will continue. Pension, too. There's nothing for you to worry about there.'

'Stop it, William! You're talking like they must talk.'

'I live here, you know. Across the river, at Arlington.'

She'd retreated inside herself, merely nodding.

'I'd like to help.'

'How?'

'I don't know,' admitted Cowley. 'I just want you to know I'm around. Will be around, if you . . . I'm here. OK?'

'Did he mean it to happen?' she demanded, going off on a tangent. 'Did he want me to prepare food with a knife he'd killed people with?' Horrified revulsion shuddered through her.

It was exactly what the psychiatrist had guessed and Andrews had confessed to, under the analysis that was still going on. That he'd wanted Pauline to use it making meals for the three of them, when Cowley had got back from Moscow and they'd invited him over for dinner. Dr Meadows had referred to it as vampire thinking. Cowley said: 'No one will ever know that. I can't conceive it.'

She shuddered again. 'I can't believe we shared the same bed: that he touched me, although he didn't, not very much.'

Stop! thought Cowley. Please stop.

'Would he have killed me?'

Cowley spread his hands towards her, in apparent helplessness. 'I don't know! No one can know. Ever.' Which wasn't true. That was exactly what Andrews had admitted planning, in his final babbled, mad confession. Cowley had heard the tape. *Kill the bitch. And Cowley: kill them both. They fuck, you know? I know they fuck, behind my back.* That and so much more. Hysterical ramblings of intending to kill Ann in her apartment that night, until she had surprisingly emerged, almost confronting him as he was entering from the spot where he'd watched Hughes emerge. Of intending to replace the knife he'd taken after one of his love visits the day after the murder and of finding Danilov had already sealed the apartment. About him, most of all. Of the hatred, from the time they were in London together: violent, insane jealousy,

389

blaming him for every setback, real or imagined, ever since he'd been in the Bureau.

'But he would have killed again?'

Cowley hesitated. 'They think so.' He would have been one of the record-breakers, the psychiatrists at Quantico had predicted: killed and killed and killed again.

'With the knife he wanted me to use in the kitchen!'

'Talking like this doesn't make any sense.'

She snorted a laugh. 'Isn't that it? Isn't it all mad?'

'I don't want you to forget what I said.'

She frowned, confused. 'What about?'

'Me being here in Washington.'

'You and me, you mean?'

The near-hysteria was close again. 'No! Just that I'm around, if you need somebody.'

'No, William!'

Cowley didn't respond immediately. 'If you ever change your mind.'

'I won't.'

'I can say it was a gift from someone here at the hotel,' said Larissa.

Danilov hadn't considered how she'd explain the gift to her husband. The excuse had come very easily: did she accept presents from other people, here at the hotel? He'd been clever enough to buy separate bottles though, Giorgio for Larissa, Dior for Olga. 'I had to guess. I'm glad you like it.'

'I'd hoped you'd come, finally.'

'Just as a friend,' insisted Danilov, hurriedly. She was sitting demurely on the edge of the bed, he more than a metre away on the only chair. She hadn't come forward to kiss him or moved to start taking off her clothes, as she'd always done before.

'Just as a friend,' she agreed, equally quickly.

'Good.' For whose benefit was this performance?

'I love you very much. But from now on, it's all got to be how you decide.'

That was the problem, Danilov recognized. And she knew it. He supposed Larissa thought she'd won. He wasn't sure whether she had or not.